to Ally Rose,
Thank you so much
for snagging this
Copy! You rock!!

Two Kinds of Us

Sarah Sutton

SARAH SUTTON

Golden Crown Publishing, LLC

AF271134

TWO KINDS OF US

For information, contact:

http://www.sarah-sutton.com

Cover Design © Designed with Grace

Image © DepositPhotos – Hay Dmitriy

1 0 9 8 7 6 5 4 3 2 1

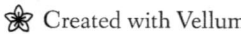 Created with Vellum

To my readers,
You're all massive rock stars

One

The idea of hypnosis sounded like a load of bull until Harrison Russo opened his mouth.

His low and lulling voice never failed to make me shiver, especially the low notes. Every inch of me would freeze, taken to a realm where nothing existed but him.

Yeah, sounded weird. A little like a stalker-y fan-girl. But holy crap, his voice was freaking beautiful.

Of course, his looks definitely added to the appeal. With the reddish-brown auburn hair that glowed in the light, light freckles across his nose, and the world's brightest smile, Harry was drop-dead gorgeous.

I wasn't the only one who thought so. Tonight everyone flocked to Crushed Beanz, the best café in Hallow and home base for his band. Untapped Potential always drew a crowd, but tonight was next level. With each weekend gig, their fan base grew larger and larger, and eventually they would outgrow the café.

If they ever went on tour, I'd *so* be a groupie.

Untapped Potential had three members: Natasha, the

guitarist; Vincent, the drummer; Harry, the singer. Vincent worked the drumsticks expertly as the song went on, creating a beat that no one could keep from tapping their foot to. Natasha leaned into her microphone as she strummed her guitar, voice soft and harmonizing with Harry's.

And Harry's voice, well. We've already established how I felt about it.

"I just need one more shot at forever
Locked and loaded, give me a sign
Everyone says I should've known better
I swear I won't waste my chance this time."

I didn't know any of the members too well, but I probably knew Vincent the best. Mostly because his new girlfriend, Addy Arden, and I had met earlier this past month. She sat across from me now, bobbing her head to the music, a slight smile on her lips as she watched her boyfriend. They'd been in a relationship for only a few weeks, and they were so cute together.

I still remembered the way Addy looked at him at one of the gigs—her whole "just friends" mantra might've worked if she hadn't been undressing him with her eyes.

She'd be a groupie too.

"Thank you all for coming out tonight," Harry said into the microphone once their song ended, and he rested his hand on the neck of his guitar. His words came out sounded tired, raspy after singing. "We're Untapped Potential, and we'll see you next weekend."

"Don't forget to follow us on social media," Natasha cut in, like she did after every show. She'd pulled her dark curls out of her face into two low buns, which had begun to unravel during the set. "We're almost to one thousand likes, so go check us out."

Vincent twirled his drumstick, seemingly content to let them do the talking.

"Have a great night, everyone," Harry called to the crowd once more.

And then the scratchy sound coming through the speakers clicked off. The night was over.

Addy angled her body back toward me, planting her elbows on the tabletop. "It's funny to think that I ever spent my weekend nights any other way," she said, her voice light and dreamy.

"You'll never be able to go back," I teased her, collecting my coat. "Not that it's a bad thing when you're dating the drummer."

She gave me a small smile, leaning her head in her hand and peering at the remaining people. "Isn't it crazy that more and more fans are staying after?"

The crowd had thinned, but there were still a considerable amount of people lingering, capturing the attention of each band member. I tried not to be obvious about it, but my gaze lingered on Harry. His back was to me, giving me the perfect view of the pretty girl he spoke with.

What would it be like if I went up to him? Just tapped him on the shoulder and said... Yeah, I got nothing.

"I should get going," I told Addy, pushing up from the booth. "Tell Vincent they did great tonight for me."

"You could tell the band yourself," she suggested with a knowing grin, reaching up and pinching the material of her watercolor necktie.

I'd been coming to Crushed Beanz to listen to the band play for a few months now, and not once had I ever spoken to a member before the last few weeks. And even then, I only talked to Vincent because I met Addy.

Talking to Harry, the guy who left me speechless just by singing a simple note? I could never work up enough nerve.

Despite that, I winked at Addy. "Next time."

I'm sure it was obvious I didn't mean it.

As soon as Untapped Potential finished their sets, my mood would always plummet. The band didn't play on Sundays, so another weekend of music and happiness had passed, which meant another week of school and responsibilities stared down at me like a gun barrel pointed at my forehead. Dramatic? Maybe. But it was overwhelming how much I wanted to rewind the tape to yesterday afternoon. Just live my life in a perpetual weekend.

No such luck.

"Okay, Jon, give me one for the road," I said as I pushed my way to the coffee counter. "But I want—"

"Decaf," Jonathan finished for me, looking up from sweeping behind the counter. His dark hair was cropped short and curly, his full lips pulled into a familiar smile. "Yeah, you ask for the same thing every weekend, Stella."

I grinned back, slipping onto a barstool while I waited.

"I love this routine we have going. We're on the same wavelength."

"You know, I do this only for you. The counter officially closed thirty minutes ago."

Leaning my elbows onto the counter, I batted my eyes at him. "You love me, just say it."

When I first met Jonathan, we'd instantly clicked. It'd been my first time stumbling into Crushed Beanz back in November, the same time I saw Untapped Potential play. I'd been so enthralled by the music that Jonathan made me something random to drink. And to this day, he made me the same thing every night.

Although I saw him for only a few hours twice a week, Jonathan knew more about me than most people—he knew what secret I kept.

"Thanks for the coffee," I told him with a sigh, staring down at the teal to-go cup, the color so bright and cheery and *not* matching my insides. "See you next week?"

"I'll be here," he said with a nod, giving me a sympathetic expression. He no doubt could easily read my mood. "Chin up, Stella."

As I buttoned up my coat, I turned, glancing out over the lounge one last time. I wasn't sure what I hoped for. Some movie moment where I'd look back and lock eyes with some mega-hot guy? Maybe he'd make his way through the people, wanting to strike up a conversation before the night was over.

Maybe I'd look up and I'd lock eyes with Harry Russo.

Except where he stood, his back was to me, oblivious that I even existed.

I'd parked in a pretty dark corner of the lot, my SUV a spot of black against the snow. My headlights flashed as I pressed the unlock button, my boots slipping over a random patch of ice. Thank goodness January was almost over; warmer temperatures were on the horizon.

Curfew on weekends was eleven-thirty, but since Untapped Potential finished around ten o'clock, I just decided to head home.

Instead of climbing behind the steering wheel, I opened the backseat door and slid in.

Once the darkness fully enveloped me, the process began.

I started by slipping my hands underneath my hair and lifting, loosening the clasps that fastened the wig to my real hairline. It was such a relief once it came off, only because of how *hot* the hair made me. Sweat had accumulated underneath it, the icy air cooling it against my skin. For now, I slipped the black wig into a silk bag.

Next, I grabbed makeup remover wipes from my purse and went to work on rubbing all the heavy eyeliner off. Mom and Dad would kill me if they ever saw me with so much makeup on.

The clothes had to go next, and I stripped as quickly as possible, pulling the tattered turtleneck off and shoving it into my bag. I had a pink sweater tucked inside, and I latched onto it.

It was a Hannah Montana moment in the SUV.

Really, it was a Stella moment.

Stella was a black dress with tears and holes and threads, bare and exposed. A pair of black sneakers. Large earrings and sometimes fake nose ring, even temporary tattoos if I wanted to go all out. Stella was a beautiful, luxurious, sleek, straight black wig.

As soon as that wig came off, I stopped being Stella, the carefree and confident young lady who loved Untapped Potential and dancing on a Saturday night. Instead, I transformed back into Destelle, the girl who lived her life under her parents' watchful eyes.

And I use "lived" as a very loose term.

This bag only ever traveled from the car to a box underneath my bed. If my parents ever found its contents, it'd be game over. Any chance of freedom would be immediately shot down. My future would forever be under their lock and key.

Sella got to be her own person, do what she wanted whenever she wanted. Everything Destelle wasn't allowed to.

I envied her.

Because when I pulled into the three-car garage, when I walked into the mudroom, it felt as if I had a tie around my neck, one that I'd pinched too tight.

After ten, the house always became near silent, but I knew when I rounded the corner and entered the family room, I'd find them.

Sure enough.

Mom and Dad both sat on the sleek couch, like they always did. Mom, with a book in her lap, wore her house robe; Dad, still dressed in his day clothes, thumbed through a packet of papers. When I walked in, they both looked up like robots moving in unison.

"Destelle," Mom greeted, her expression remaining neutral. "Welcome home."

"We've been waiting for you," Dad said, taking his turn in the script we had written and long since memorized. "How was Margot's?"

It changed every so often. Sometimes I "went to Margot's." Other times I'd tell them I was "visiting a different friend from school." One thing stayed consistent: I never told them the truth.

Lying to them used to be so hard, so fear-inducing, and anything else, I'd never take the risk. When it came to Stella and Crushed Beanz, it almost started feeling like second nature.

With my purse slung over my shoulder, I offered them a polite smile. It didn't have teeth. "Thanks for waiting up for me. I had a nice evening."

That was Dad's cue to push to his feet, groaning a little like he'd been sitting down too long. Dad was the epitome of clean-cut. He kept his hair artfully styled, as always, and rarely let his facial hair grow, but if he did, he kept it buzzed to the bare minimum, with a clean line at his cheekbones.

Appearances were everything in the Brighton household.

As Dad walked up to me, he held his hand out, his gold wedding ring shining. He didn't even have to say anything, our ritual so ingrained that our movements were mechanical.

I dug my cell phone out of my purse and placed it and my car keys onto his palm. They'd never told me why they collected my phone and keys at night, but I had an inkling of an idea: they wanted control. And I gave it to them without a fight because the idea of pushing back made anxiety swell within me.

"Thank you," Dad said, jingling my keys a little. He studied me for a moment, causing my heart to trip over a beat. As a juvenile court judge, I'm sure he gave a lot of teens that probing stare, and I had no idea how anyone else could stand it. "What's this?" he asked, reaching out. His fingertip brushed my temple. "It looks like...marker?"

My hand flew up to my face, knocking his away. "Uh, yeah, I—well, I got some on me while Margot and I were doing homework."

"You're supposed to get the ink on the paper, Destelle." Dad's expression was neutral, but his voice sounded wary. He didn't believe me.

"Destelle," Mom said, drawing my attention to her. I braced myself, preparing for them to jump on the lie, but they didn't. "I left the Shang-Wu Scholarship packet on your desk. That deadline is February fifteenth, so make sure you mail it in before then, okay?"

Normally, I'd have been grateful for any subject change, but not this one. Not college stuff. Two weeks until the deadline. My face ached, but the pain barely registered. Destelle was a master at fake smiles. "Thank you for reminding me, Mom. I'll see you both in the morning."

This time, as I headed toward the staircase, neither of them stopped me. On my way to my bedroom, I passed the twins' rooms, Nellie's door shut, Jamie's door open, both probably sound asleep by now. Mom and Dad would've tucked them in an hour ago, no doubt giving them a kiss goodnight on their foreheads.

Neither of them knew the life they had ahead of them, one of scholarships and fundraisers and fake smiles and rules.

Just like it was my life now. Scholarships, fundraisers, fake smiles, and rules to live and obey every moment in time. Except for two nights a week. It felt like I truly lived the life I wanted on the weekends.

My bedroom was pristine, not a piece of clutter or dirty laundry. The gold-colored duvet was folded neatly over the bedding, the pillows perfectly creased. Throughout the white-walled room there were framed art pieces and abstract photos, tastefully placed and professionally mini-malistic.

It looked like a hotel suite rather than a teenage girl's bedroom. If I were to look around this room for one thing completely *me*, I'd come up empty.

Until I lifted up the bed skirt and pulled out a large shoebox. It was the home for all the things I wanted, like printouts of online colleges, as if one day I'd get to attend them.

Online college—it sounded like a dream. I'd taken a college course last semester online and absolutely loved it. From then on, the little seed had taken root. If I did online schooling at least for the basic courses I'd need, I could be wherever I wanted. I didn't have to be stuck in a fancy school or trapped at home.

I could be free, and the idea of freedom was almost as hypnotizing as Harry's voice.

The shoebox was also the home for the silk bag and black sweater. It was a safer place for Stella than the car, where Mom or Dad could easily stumble upon it. No one would think to look in a simple shoebox. So, shoving the online brochures aside, I eased the wig underneath the papers, saying goodbye to that persona for another week.

A noise came from out in the hallway, and when I looked up, I realized I'd left my door open. Jamie's room was directly across the hall, swamped in darkness. He was probably asleep, but it didn't stop me from shoving the shoebox underneath my bed, hurrying over to my door and easing it shut.

My family didn't know about the shoebox or about Stella, and they never could. Being someone else was freeing, inspiring, even if it was for only a few nights a month.

It was really *Stella* who got to live the life I truly wanted on the weekends, and to make sure it stayed that way, my family could never find out.

*M*y alter ego had been born from chance. My best friend, Margot, and I had been out shopping when she went into a wig store to look for clip-in hair extensions. She convinced me to try on a wig for fun, and I transformed into someone else. Crazy how much a new hairstyle made me feel like a different person. Someone exciting. The wig held so much freedom, so much opportunity. The parts of myself that I'd been repressing all my life finally were allowed to flutter free like a butterfly breaking out of its constraining cocoon.

From then on, the idea of Stella fascinated me. Every weekend I'd pretend to be someone else, the person I *wanted* to be. I pretended Destelle didn't exist. Only Stella did.

Except on certain weekends like this one when my parents forced me to attend country club dinners and fundraisers. Stella wasn't allowed to those.

At the beginning of every month, *someone* from the circle of importance hosted a party at the Alderton

Country Club in Addison. Mr. Preston hosted the fundraiser for February, aimed at raising money for endangered sea life.

I never managed to escape the necessity of attending a country club gathering. Image was everything and, according to my parents, we needed to be a united front.

But the twins got to play out in the hallway with all their friends, and I was trapped in the main hall, forced to let people talk my ear off.

I held a stupid fake smile in place all night, mingling with the masses, the muscles in my face having long since gone stiff. Was I even smiling anymore or had it become a kind of pained grimace? Judging by the delight in Mrs. Holland's eyes, whatever expression I wore must've looked convincing enough.

"Oh, dear, you can't go to Castleton—private colleges have far better education," she kept saying, fluttering her hands around as she spoke. One might've guessed it was a quirk, but I knew why she really flapped them. The movement caused the diamond bracelet on her wrist to catch in the light, sparkles shooting everywhere. "Surely you want to make your parents proud, don't you, Destelle?"

Was my smile twitching? It felt like it. "Of course," I told her, becoming still under her stare. "Castleton's at the very bottom of my list, now that I think of it. Father's pushing me to Mullhound College, but Mother wants me to attend her alma mater to follow her career path. Father's not sure I'd make a good lawyer."

Ha. Honestly, he and I were on the same page. Me, a lawyer? What a joke.

But then again, he wanted me to become a brain surgeon, so I wasn't sure which parent was crazier.

Mrs. Holland flung her hand again, gesturing at nothing. "Oh, Mullhound! Such a beautiful campus, you know. Judge Brighton has got good taste—though I'm not surprised. One look at your father and you can tell he's got his wits about him." In a gossiping whisper, Mrs. Holland said, "Mr. Preston attended Mullhound, you know. And look at him now. Owns the biggest recording studio in the state. This is the second fundraiser he's thrown this year, and it's barely February."

"Please, Mrs. Holland. Mr. Preston is always looking for a reason to throw a party," I replied, the words balancing on the tightrope of politeness and teasing. "Not that many of us mind much."

Her smile broadened as she glanced down at her cocktail dress. "It certainly gives us girls an excuse to feel beautiful, hmm?"

Beautiful? Not exactly how I felt in this dress Mom forced on me, with the high neckline and tight fabric. It hugged my hips, but not purposefully provocative—more like in a way that hinted whoever had purchased the stupid thing bought it a size or two too small.

Beautiful. More like a packaged piece of sausage.

"Mrs. Holland," a low voice greeted, and I turned to find Margot saddling up beside me. She wore a white-and-black pinstriped suit, and she'd matched it with a vibrant red handkerchief. She'd recently bleached her hair to make it appear silver, cropped into a pixie cut. "Long time, no see."

I almost laughed at how fast the blood drained from Mrs. Holland's face.

"Margot," she returned, but her voice wasn't nearly as strong and confident as it had been as she spoke to me. "Well, I should make my rounds. Have a good evening, you two."

"What was that about?" I asked with a frown, watching Mrs. Holland's retreating figure.

"She knows I know she's having an affair," Margot said casually. "I caught her making out with someone in one of the coat closets last event."

Immediately, I grimaced, that mental image *so* not appealing. "Why do you always find old people making out with each other? Last time it was Mr. Messner and Ms. Jennings. At least they were both single."

Margot smirked, her red lips stretching. "No clue, but I love having all the blackmail material."

Even though we'd only been friends for the past year, I looked up to Margot. She had a mind of her own. She was the kind of girl I always wanted to be. Confident. She didn't let these stuffy people get to her. She wore what she wanted, did what she wanted, and didn't care if anyone looked twice.

Margot was the one who taught me what it felt like to branch out. Taught me what life might've looked like if you didn't conform. I'd never told her, but Margot was partly the reason Stella came to be.

"Nice suit," I told her, to which she popped her hip to give me a better view. "Is that designed by Malstoni? I thought he wasn't taking custom orders until next winter."

Margot reached out and adjusted her jacket, twirling the cufflinks around in a show-off fashion. "He made an exception." Her heavily lined eyes glanced down my frame, probably noting each roll that the dress accentuated. "Perhaps he can make one for you as well."

"Don't even get me started." I rolled my eyes, trying not to let the full extent of my frustration show on my face. Every time I moved, the tight material strained over the skin at my sides, highlighting every dimple and bump. "This thing is going straight into the trash."

"You've been making your rounds," she went on, folding her arms underneath her chest. "I take it our princess is turning into a pumpkin soon?"

Margot knew that whenever my social butterfly side came out at these things, more often than not it meant I was plotting my escape. She knew weekend nights were typically dedicated to Untapped Potential.

"Not tonight," I said with a sigh, glancing at my watch. It was a little after eight. "Mom and Dad made me ride with them." Crushed in the back seat between twin one and twin two.

"Ah, no giving Harry Hopants the hungry eyes then, huh?"

With a gasp, I smacked her arm. "I do *not* give him hungry eyes. I give him...normal-people eyes. For sure. And don't call him that; it's weird."

"You know, I can't really imagine you with a singer."

"Hey, *I* don't even imagine myself with him. I just like the way his voice sounds."

"And the way his face looks."

I mean, she wasn't wrong.

"Destelle." I recognized Mom's voice immediately, and found her stepping up to me, her pink coat-check tab in her grip. Instinctively, I braced myself, afraid she might've caught any of that conversation. "I need you to run out to my car. I think I left my checkbook in the glove box. The keys are in my coat pocket."

Right. Checkbooks at a fundraiser were almost as important as the champagne flutes. I took the coat tab with my practiced expression. "I'll be right back."

Mom's eyes flitted over Margot, and though they weren't as fearful as Mrs. Holland's gaze had been, it wasn't a warm stare.

"Malstoni?" Mom asked her.

"Of course," Margot replied, almost toneless. "I love Gilfman as much as the next woman, but Malstoni has a special place in my heart."

That made the briskness seep from Mom's gaze, at least a little. Talk designer brands with Mom and she backed down. "I'll be right here, Destelle."

There it was: a dismissal so clear that I almost felt my cheeks pink. Without another word, I turned on my heel and headed out of the dance hall, hearing my best friend's footfalls behind me.

"Funny that she can't get it herself," Margot huffed, keeping pace with me.

"Why else have kids?"

"Touché."

When we got out into the hallway, we stumbled upon the children who'd been forced to attend tonight too. No one really paid attention to them, least of all their parents. They let the kids play unsupervised in the hall, out of sight, out of mind.

There were three kids in the Brighton family: Destelle and the twins, Eleanor and James. Eleanor and James, though, were allowed to use nicknames, whereas I didn't get that privilege. Destelle was my great-grandma's name, and thus forbidden to be tampered with. Eleanor got to be "Nellie" and James got to be "Jamie" and Destelle was stuck being "Destelle."

It wasn't fair.

Maybe that was why when I chose a name for my alter ego, I chose *Stella*.

I spotted Nellie immediately. Nellie always stood out because, even though she was ten, she had the height of a thirteen-year-old. Twin two, Jamie, who still waited on his growth spurt, stood a few inches shorter, but was missing.

"Destelle," Nellie said once she saw me, smiling excitedly. "Where are you going?"

"To grab something for Mom," I said, but glanced around. She and the other kids were playing some sort of card game. "Where's Jamie?"

Nellie's expression faltered a bit, looking sad for a moment before clearing into a blank mask. At ten, she already mastered that. "He's sitting by the bathrooms."

Margot didn't even have to ask. Instead, she merely held her hand out. "Give me your tab, and I'll grab your coat and the keys."

I passed them over before heading down the direction where the bathrooms were, my heels clacking like little gunshots off the shiny marble floor. The golden lights created an almost ethereal glow in the hallway, the fixtures shimmering as if inset with crystals. Elaborate, oozing money. I, however, thought they shined too brightly.

It wasn't hard to find Jamie. A small alcove near the bathrooms led to a storage room, and he always sat there, tucked out of sight. He stretched his legs in front of him as he leaned against the wall, holding a book. His dress pants were a little short on him, and he had undone the top button of his dress shirt, discarding his necktie by his hip.

"James."

He didn't startle at the sound of my voice. "Destelle."

"You shouldn't be down here by yourself."

Jamie looked up, his dark eyes already looking bored with the conversation. "Are you going to say I should spend time with my friends?" He wiggled the book. "Because I am."

"You know Mom wants you to be with people, not off alone."

He frowned at that. "They were playing a card game where they needed pairs. I'm number five. Was I supposed to just sit and watch?"

I crouched in front of him, folding my arms over my knees. "I know you hate these things, Jamie—"

"You hate them too," he cut me off, looking as if he'd made some grand point.

And he wasn't wrong. I also knew that fighting it wasn't worth the trouble. My gaze fell to his book, the way his fingers curved protectively over it. "How did you even get that past Mom and Dad?"

"I snuck it under my coat."

Oh, Jamie. It made me think about the Stella wig, tucked safely away in a box.

Before pushing to my feet, I grabbed Jamie's tie, fitting it back over his head. He didn't fight me on it, but he did scowl. "At least take it back to the other kids," I told him, standing up. "You can read your book while they play cards."

"Why can't I stay here and do that?"

"Because you don't want to," Margot answered for me, and I turned to find her sauntering closer, my pink Claire-Haute coat slung over her arm. "Once you're branded as an outcast, you can't take it back."

Her expression was even, but I still felt a stab of sympathy toward her. "Maybe I want to be an outcast," Jamie muttered, but he closed his book.

"You think that now," Margot said. "But trust me, okay?"

Margot and I hadn't always been friends. There weren't many kids our age who attended the fundraisers, and though we'd both been coming to these since middle school, I hadn't really spoken to her until last year. Mom would never let me. Her parents didn't always attend the country club events anymore, but always forced Margot to go.

Her taste in fashion branded her as an outcast quickly. "What kind of woman wears a *suit* to a *party?*" I'd hear people murmur, judgment dripping from their posh tones. Somewhere along the way, Mom sided with them, and didn't want us being friends at first.

I never really understood why—what, was she afraid Margot's fashion sense would rub off on me? Was she afraid the wild, free-thinker Margot Massey would teach me to think for myself?

Honestly, I wished.

Though Margot never appeared bothered by it, sometimes it would slip through how much the indifferent treatment affected her.

Jamie relented and pushed to his feet. He walked ahead of us, and when we got to the primary area, Nellie's eyes lit up. "Jamie, perfect timing! Will you be my partner this next round?"

"No, I want Jamie," a boy with messy hair complained, frowning. "You can't have your twin as your partner. That's cheating."

"How so?" Nellie demanded, all while Jamie looked back and forth between them, almost as if surprised.

"Thanks," I said to Margot as I pulled my coat on, then buttoned it up. "And hey, you're not an outcast."

Margot shrugged, her shoulder pad twitching with the movement. "Around here, I am. And that's okay—I'd be much more terrified if I fit in."

I thought of how easily Mrs. Holland chatted with me, how quickly she believed my smile.

After a second, Margot withdrew her own car keys from her pocket, offering them to me. "Take my keys. I'll grab your mom's checkbook."

She had an eight-ball looped around her key ring and a chain that said #*1* DAUGHTER. "Where am I going?"

"I'm breaking you out. Your very own fairy godmother. You should be honored."

An image of Margot with wings came to mind, and I snorted. "I appreciate the sentiment, but my parents—"

"You've been making your rounds all night. When I give your mom her checks, I'll tell her you went to the bathroom. She won't even notice you're gone."

That had always been the plan for if I wanted to sneak out for an Untapped Potential gig. In case Mom or Dad ever asked anyone where I was, no doubt they'd answer, "Oh, I just spoke with her," and the conversation would saddle off into some different topic, like the college seed I'd been planting into people's heads. It worked every time.

Except—"Uh, they'll notice when they load into the car and I'm not with them."

Margot raised an eyebrow at me, her tone obvious. "You're riding with me."

"Yeah, *okay*. And how are *you* getting home? You know, since I have your magical carriage and all. Won't your parents wonder where your car went?"

Her expression turned mischievous. "Nah, they probably won't notice. And, come on, what's the point of having blackmail material if you never call it in?"

Slowly, I took the car keys from her fingers, turning them over in my hand. "Can you find a ride without giving Mrs. Holland a heart attack?"

"You're too nice for your own good," Margot said, but even though her expression was flat, her voice was gentle. "I'll find a ride."

I prompted her, "Without..."

"Without asking Mrs. Holland. Buzzkill." Now Margot's voice matched her expression. "You ruin my fun torturing the elderly, you know that?"

"Mrs. Holland is hardly elderly." I chuckled under my breath, taking a step back to where the VIP parking was. The Masseys always go to park close since Margot's dad was the mayor of Addison, whereas Margot had to go to the general parking to find Mom's checkbook. "I'll stop by your house around eleven-thirty. You can take me home from there?"

With a nod, she winked at me. "Don't have too much fun tonight."

As we walked in opposite directions, I looked down at the foreign car keys in my hand, the key chains knocking together. I slid the pad of my thumb over #*1* D*AUGHTER*, wondering where Margot's parents might've picked it up. They had seen it and thought of her. If my parents saw a #*1* *Daughter* keychain, would they think of me? Would they think of Nellie? Would they even think twice?

Pressing the key fob, I heard Margot's car unlock with a beep, offering the promise of an escape.

Without thinking twice, I took it.

I stopped at the house to wriggle out of the sausage dress and grab my Stella bag, so it was after ten-thirty when I got into the club. Untapped Potential would've finished playing by the time I got to Crushed Beanz, so the next best thing? Going to Downtown.

Bayview had a nightclub called Downtown, and on nights when I wasn't quite ready to go home after watching Untapped Potential play, I headed to Downtown. It had live music and sometimes a DJ, giving me never-ending opportunities to dance until I dropped.

The eighteen-plus kind of place *should've* turned away my seventeen-year-old self at the door, except apparently the girls at my private school made fantastic fake IDs.

Bayview wasn't really a popular place among my peers, so I never worried about spotting anyone I knew.

My mascara still felt a little sticky from how quickly I'd swiped it on in the car, like tiny clumps of glue sticking my lashes together. Even though I might've layered on the makeup—foundation, contour, concealer, eyeshadow—I felt *pretty*. I felt fierce and strong and confident, like I could do or say anything.

Confidence came easily when I wasn't Destelle.

The bass thumped loudly as the band played the next song, a cover of a popular one that I immediately recognized. My body picked up on the tempo, swaying to the beat as I made my way through the dancing people. I smiled at the heat that emanated from everyone, the smell of cologne and perfume and sweat mixing in the air. With the pulsing lights and earth-quaking beat, I was at home.

Gently, I coasted my fingers through my wig. *Stella* was at home.

When I danced, I felt more relaxed, as if each sway of my hips and step of my feet unleashed all the pent-up tension that had accumulated in my body over the course of the week.

When I first started out living my double life, the prospect of dancing in public sounded insane. Destelle, who did *nothing* like that, would never have considered it. Stella, though, thrived on the freedom of it. This kind of music had full control of the way my body moved, and as soon as I started dancing, people always came closer to join me. I smiled at a girl with neon purple eyeshadow who began bobbing her head with me. Another girl at her side moved a little off-beat, but she seemed to be having a good time.

Nights like this were perfect. I had a little less than an hour to dance before I had to be home for curfew, and I'd be drinking in every freaking second.

As I spun in a circle, my gaze snagged on a familiar figure, eyes recognizing him quicker than my brain processed. Way quicker. I stared at him almost as if I'd forgotten his name.

At a rapid speed, my eyes took in every inch of him. He leaned against the wall, hands tucked into his pockets. His eyes were on the stage, nodding along to the beat as the pulsing lights danced across his features. His white shirt fit loosely, and black suspenders hugged over his shoulders, more an accessory than anything else. A black tattoo lined his throat, the loosely outlined shape of a hand.

Harry Russo, lead singer of Untapped Potential.

three

 y body stopped moving on its own, and the people I'd been dancing with moved on to find another partner. No one wanted to dance with the staring weirdo.

Because I *was* staring.

Like a weirdo.

It was jarring to see Harry there. Their gig must've ended early, or he just high-tailed it to Downtown once it was finished. Either way, he *was* here, and I couldn't stop gawking.

Destelle would've started panicking at the sight of him. She would've stolen glances all night, hoping he'd spot her at some point and draw toward her on his own accord, like in some stupid romance movie. She would've ended up disappointed. Stella—cool, confident, collected Stella— would've sauntered up to Harry and struck up a conversation, not a care in the world.

Even though I had the wig on now, I *really* didn't feel like Stella. That was why I never went up to him after a gig, because even though I had the appearance of Stella then, there was something about him that made me feel transparent.

But you are Stella, I told myself fiercely, looking down at my ripped leggings, at my combat boots, feet rooted in the middle of the dance floor. My wig was fitted perfectly in place, the clasps secured to my hair. I looked the part. Now I had to play the part.

I took in a deep breath, and like a wave rolling over me, Stella broke through. All nerves of talking to a boy fell to the wayside, and I grounded myself more solidly in my alter persona. I combed my fingers through my hair, the strands soft against my skin, careful not to jerk the clasps free. In time with the beat of the song playing over the speakers, I stepped forward.

And completely bypassed Harry Russo, who hadn't looked up, completely absorbed in the music.

Instead, I walked to the bar, slapping two bucks on the counter for a bottled water. The music still pulsed, but my heartbeat had quieted, conviction slipping in to replace the jitters.

One of the reasons I liked Stella: Say I screwed up and made a fool of myself. Say it was totally awkward and completely mortifying. It wasn't *me*, Destelle. Stella came with no risks.

After twisting off the cap, I took a long refreshing drink of the icy water, a relief from the heat of the club.

And then moved once more.

Harry still leaned against the wall near a trash can, and I turned the bottle cap over between my fingers as I got closer, watching the crowd weave in and out between us. A girl with pink hair obscured him for a moment, and then a guy with a mohawk moved in my way next. I waited until my path cleared, until no one stood between him and me.

Margot would've called me devious.

Honestly, it kind of felt as if I were a super-spy on a stakeout.

Crap, that sounded creepy.

When I was six feet away, the bottle cap slipped from my fingertips.

It bounced away from me, knocking noiselessly against the ground. I lost it for a moment, the opaque lid blending in with the shadows, and then finally found where it came to rest. The momentum was better than I thought it'd be.

Fingers were already curling around it, and when I traced the arm up to find a face, Harry gazed back at me.

Gosh, even from here I could see their color. So freaking blue. Like the waters in the Caribbean or something. For a moment, it left me a bit dazzled, Destelle's personality breaking through.

With an inward smile, I thought, *Hook, line, sinker.*

"Not sure how sanitary that is now," I called over the music to him, stepping closer into his bubble of space. I kept my gaze laser-focused on the cap in his hand, shrugging on a shawl of nonchalance. "After rolling around on the floor, I mean. But thanks."

"Yeah, probably shouldn't put it back on your drink," Harry agreed, and I looked to find his full lips curved into a half smile. His fingers brushed against my palm as he dropped the cap into it, and I curled my hand, pressing the plastic into my skin. "I recognize you."

I jolted. "Uh, you do?"

"You come into Crushed Beanz," he said. "You listen to us play."

I hadn't planned on him recognizing me. Great. Did he think I was some creepy fangirl? Then again, I *had* devised a plan to get his attention. Though, maybe *he* was the creepy one for recognizing me. We'd never spoken before, and yet he recognized my face? Maybe *he* was the creepy super-spy.

Either way, it was super flattering. He noticed me.

But at his words, one memory bubbled up in my mind. That night, I'd sat with Addy in our booth rather than dancing in the crowd. I'd sung the song along with the band, and when Harry had glanced over, I swear it was like we were singing together.

I think that was when my true fascination began, the urge to know him beyond the Crushed Beanz stage and Untapped Potential social media page blossoming like a flower.

"Or maybe I show up for the amazing coffee," I suggested in an innocent tone. "It's just a coincidence that it happens to be every night that you play."

"You weren't there tonight."

My insides broke out into a full-on happy dance. *He knew I didn't show!* "More interesting plans, I'm afraid." The words might've sounded formal, but there was no missing the amusement in my tone, playing off the atmosphere between us.

Harry gazed deeply at me, his blue eyes nearly glowing in the dark. "Hopefully next weekend you don't have any more interesting plans."

Smooth. Between his half smile and lingering gaze, my body hummed with all the attention. Flirting was fun only if someone flirted right back, and Harry never missed a beat.

I could've hugged Margot for convincing me to ditch the fundraiser.

"I'm Stella," I told him before pressing the water bottle against my mouth, tipping my head to take a long drink. Fingers crossed that the curve of my neck screamed *look at me, look at me!*

"Harry."

I fought the urge to say *I know.* "I've never seen you here before."

He nodded at the stage. "I'm friends with the lead guitarist. Wanted to come support him." When his eyes found mine again, there was a bit of a charge to them. The music in the background built up to the chorus, the swell of notes almost energetic. "You here with anyone?"

I turned the cap over in my fingers once more, water bottle in my other hand. "Are *you*?"

His words were a clear invitation. "I'm all alone tonight."

"Are you a dancer?"

It almost looked as if Harry debated his response in his head, and I was struck then with the thought: What if he said no? Talk about awkward. Would I ever be able to show my face—er, Stella's face—at Crushed Beanz again?

He looked past me toward the crowd, then met my eyes once more. After a second of hesitation, the decision he came to prompted him to push off from the wall, rising to his full height. "I guess we can find out, yeah?"

Absolutely.

Quickly, I put the cap back on my water bottle, and with my heart stuttering in my chest, I reached out and grabbed his free hand. His skin was warm against mine, and it might've been my imagination, but a little spark tingled at my fingertips. "I guess we can."

After tossing my empty bottle into the trash can beside him—aim perfect, by the way—I pulled him deeper onto the dance floor.

My heart pumped in tandem with the strobe lights, every molecule in my body vibrating with the beat of the song overhead. Once we got onto the dance floor, surrounded by bodies moving and jumping to the beat, he tugged on my hand, pulling me back against his chest.

His really, really firm chest.

And it turned out that he was a really, really good dancer.

I'd never danced with a boy like this before, wonderfully close and dangerously unhinged. We played off the rhythm to the songs, dancing and swaying to a beat I could feel in my chest. Sure, Eastview Academy had homecomings and proms, and I slow-danced to music with any boy who'd asked. But never anything like this.

Nothing like Harry's hands braced on my hips, each finger a soft imprint through the fabric of my skirt. The lights flashed and bounced, catching in his beautiful blue eyes. Energy mixed in my veins, leaving me unable to stand still. So I danced.

Or should I say, *we* danced. In a way that would've horrified my parents.

Except I wasn't thinking about them. I wasn't thinking about anything other than the beat of the music and the sensation of Harry's body on mine, in a way that felt both intimate and not. In a way that felt heated but normal at the same time. Dancing with him came naturally, like it was some second-instinct buried in my brain though I'd never done anything like this before.

Either way, my body hummed, completely *alive*.

I almost felt like I was dreaming. Like a princess dancing with Prince Charming. They *so* hadn't danced like this in the movie.

His hands lingered at my waist as mine moved up to lace around the back of his neck, moving in tandem with the beat.

I never understood how two people could have chemistry, but now I got it. Even though we'd only spoken once, literally a few minutes ago, there was something magnetic about the moment—near-intoxicating. I'd never felt anything like it, and I was desperate for more, chasing something new to me.

Harry turned me in a circle, my hair lifting off my shoulders with the movement. Sweat gathered underneath the wig cap, enough that it made me feel a bit overheated. It could've also been because Harry's skin was hot when he pulled me back into him, as if he had a fever.

The song slowed as the band worked a new beat in,

enough to mess with my rhythm, and I pulled my hands from Harry's neck. As much as I didn't want to let go, I knew I'd need fresh air soon. Overheating in wigs was easy, and I definitely wasn't going to risk passing out.

"I'm going to step outside," I told him, raising my voice loud over the music. "I need some air."

Harry leaned his head toward mine, so close that we shared the same breath. It momentarily turned my thoughts to mush, the curve of his mouth an inch away from mine. *Hi, hello, I'd like you closer please.* "I'll come with you."

"I'll just be a second," I said, extracting myself from his arms. Though I fought to keep my smile at bay, it broke free when I saw his expression as he looked at me: awe mixed with a little bit of desire.

Hook, line, and sinker.

"I'll be right here," he said, holding onto my hand until I stepped far enough that it dropped.

With a devious smirk, I disappeared into the crowd, the phrase *leave them wanting more* turning around and around in my mind like a mischievous merry-go-round.

I thought about pinching myself, but decided not to risk it.

The icy night air greeted me as I stumbled outside, giving the bouncer a nod before rounding the side of the club. I welcomed the brisk breeze, lifting the wig as high as I could without pulling on my hair. Taking the wig off completely was a tantalizing thought, but I didn't want to arrange the clips again.

So instead, I pressed my hands against my cheeks, hoping to cool off quickly. Dancing with Harry still left me a little disoriented, but in the best way possible. Adrenaline swam through my veins, and I couldn't stop thinking about what might happen when the dancing stopped for the night.

I hoped for this: I'd go back inside, we'd dance a little more, and then we'd exchange numbers. I'd wonder who would text first, probably obsess about it all night, wondering whether he'd text at all. But he would—his first message would be something sweet and flirty, something that'd make me grin ear to ear. Our flirty conversation would morph into something deeper, a bit more meaningful, and then he'd ask me out.

Y'know, fingers crossed.

But I knew one thing for certain: As soon as I left Downtown, I'd no longer be Stella. The girl who danced with Harry would be shoved back into a black bag, not to reappear until next weekend. All the confidence that came with the wig would disappear, as if it never existed to begin with.

I pulled my cell out from my waistband to look at the time and found several missed calls from Mom and a text message from Margot, a dooming chime as the metaphorical clock struck midnight.

Margot: **I told your parents I'd drop you off before curfew, but they keep calling me. Call me back ASAP.**

I pinched myself then—a quick twist on my arm—but her message still stared back at me. With a sigh, I pressed the call back button and listened to the ring.

"Hey," Margot greeted upon answering. "Are you on your way back?"

"Not yet."

"Your mom's already called the house *twice*, Destelle. She wants me to bring you home early tonight. I wouldn't be surprised if they try to track your cell phone. Then what?"

My eyes pinched shut. Of course she was right. Mom, or even Dad, would make the drive to Margot's, knowing I didn't have a car. If I wasn't at Margot's, the whole jig was up.

"Destelle," Margot enunciated, her normally level tone hinting emotion. "Are you listening to me?"

"I have to do something real quick." Something like go inside and make sure Harry Russo got my number. "I'll call you when I'm on the road."

Margot began to protest, but I hung up before she could get another word out, knowing time was of the essence. I couldn't just ditch Harry without saying goodbye, not after a dance like *that*. I at least had to give him my number and then keep my fingers crossed that he'd call me. Maybe *I* should ask for *his* number, be the one in control.

The bouncer let me back in without a second glance, and even though it'd be nearly impossible to find where Harry and I had been dancing in the giant crowd, I started wading through it, keeping my eyes peeled.

But when I saw him, I stopped in my tracks.

Harry stood with the two girls who'd danced with me earlier, and the girl with the purple eyeshadow had one hand on his arm, leaning in close. He dipped his head toward her, a wide, flirtatious smile lining his lips. Even from here, I could see him watching her mouth.

Five minutes. A five minute time out for air, and the spell had been broken. If I walked up to him now, what would happen? Would he turn away from the girls or turn away from me?

I sighed, disappointment hitting me like a tidal wave, wiping away any trace of lingering heat. Playing hard to get did me *so* dirty.

In the end, I turned away from him, reality creeping in and cracking the Stella façade.

Pulling my cell out once more, I sent Margot a text. **Be there in ten.**

"Destelle, can you come into the kitchen, please?"

I stiffened at the sound of my mother's voice, the professionalism of it not settling right for a Sunday afternoon. I sat on the couch, my legs tucked underneath me. Nellie sat to my left, thumbing through her multicolored flash cards. The one in her grip now was *Flamboyant*. Lately, she memorized how to spell random words almost obsessively, wanting to expand her vocabulary. Now, she puffed out her pudgy cheeks in concentration.

Jamie sat on the other couch, his novel open in his lap. He flipped through the pages almost abnormally fast, as if desperate to find out what happened next.

I had a book in my hands too, some self-help novel Mom gave me, though I wasn't really reading it. My parents had decreed that Sunday afternoons were for nourishing the mind. We weren't allowed in our bedrooms until after dinner. The horror.

"Mom is talking to you," Nellie told me helpfully. She wasn't looking at me, her head bent over her cards, dark hair falling into her eyes. I'd always been envious of her hair; she inherited Mom's fine, straight locks while I got the wild curls from Dad. "It's probably about your college stuff. You should go before she yells."

"Spell 'mind your own business.'"

Nellie arched an eyebrow at me, something she just learned how to do and did it often. She thought it made her look more grown up. "M-I-N-D—"

"Forget it," I cut her off with a snort, folding over the page I'd been skimming and shoving to my feet. Jamie didn't even look up from his book, fully engrossed in whatever was happening between the pages.

The few steps from the living room to the kitchen gave me enough time to conjure the perfect expression. Curious, respectful, casual. Eyebrows slightly raised, eyes alert, mouth relaxed.

Mom sat at the breakfast bar, papers spread out around her, and at first glance I assumed she'd brought her work home with her. She did that sometimes, and Dad did more often than not. Days with all the paperwork were good days—they'd be distracted and wouldn't be as strict with the house rules.

Except as I got closer, I realized the papers weren't anything work related. One paper caught my eye first. *Shang-Wu Scholarship Packet.*

Crap.

"I found this in your room when I laid out your clothes for the day," she said to me without turning. Even though my socked feet hadn't made a sound on the floor, she knew I stood behind her. It was almost scary. "Unfinished. Actually, you haven't even started it."

"You said I had until the fifteenth."

Mom turned then, holding another packet in her hand. "It's the seventh, Destelle. And what about the Keesler Scholarship? You haven't started that one either. Destelle, you do realize you need to write *essays* for these, right? The Keesler one requires an essay of three pages."

Scholarships, essays, paperwork. All of it made my brain feel ten times larger than what my skull could contain. "Oh, I didn't realize."

"You didn't?" Mom demanded, peering at me closer. "I would've thought you'd be on top of this."

Being under her scrutinizing eye, I suddenly became panicked.

"It slipped my mind," I insisted, glad that my hands were behind my back so she couldn't see them shaking. "With midterms and homework and volunteering, a lot has been slipping my mind. I'm really sorry, Mom."

Mom's eyes bounced all over my face, watching for a tell. She looked between my eyes, studied my mouth, my posture. She cataloged everything, gauging whether I was being sincere.

"I know you're doing a lot," she said at last, her voice softer by a fraction. "You're doing so much and maintaining your grades, which makes your father and me proud. It's hard to think about college now when there's already so much to worry about."

That caused my ears to perk up, my thoughts traveling to the shoebox underneath my bed. "It *is* hard."

"I can't even imagine you going away to college. I can't imagine how life will be without you at the house." She turned back to the paperwork then, drawing her perfectly manicured nail along the staple in the corner. "Especially if you were to get into Mullhound or Hartford. Oh, you'd be so far away."

Don't do it, I told myself sternly, trying to drag my traitorous thoughts back on track. *Don't bring it up. Don't say anything. Just nod and smile and say what she wants to hear.*

"I could always apply to an online college," I blurted instead, hoping my tone sounded more mildly interested rather than obviously desperate. "There's one that I have a brochure for and—"

"Online college," she said with a startled laugh, one that made any anticipation curl up and die. Withered away, disappearing in the wind. "You're meant for bigger things than that. Law school, for one—oh, you'd just excel."

I stood there, thankful she wasn't directly looking at me. I couldn't feel my expression, so I was sure it wouldn't be a good one.

"Online college," she repeated, this time more scornfully. Mom rolled her eyes at the thought, tucking her dark hair over her shoulder. "Why don't you sit down now and work on these? I think I have one more in my office. I'll go see." She pushed up from the barstool, allowing me to take her place.

Mom left me alone in the kitchen, a buzzing sound filling my ears. Sitting down at the breakfast bar forfeited everything that I really wanted. I would be surrendering to the plethora of college applications and scholarships and the idea of freaking law school. A shackle dedicating me to one future, one that I wasn't allowed to plan for myself.

When I turned eighteen, theoretically I could walk away from all this, turn my back on my parents, and decide on a new path, but doubt rushed in. I didn't know life outside of this. How would I even support myself if I left on my own? How would I live life all alone? And if I left, would my parents ever speak to me again? I didn't want to disappoint them, to live with their judgment. Despite how much I hated their control, the idea of their resenting me made my throat close up.

So, with that in mind, I sat down at the counter, seizing a pen.

I was tied to this life with a rope near impossible to cut. Even though Stella gave me the briefest taste of freedom, there was no true escape.

ntapped Potential had a pretty active social media page, one I followed almost on a religious level. A new post would upload to their page at least once a day, sometimes a song lyric, sometimes an old pic of one of their gigs. And with each post, their viewership grew.

I always wondered who managed the page. Vincent, tall and broody, wouldn't be posting so frequently. So that left Natasha or Harry. Monday morning, when I checked their page before the first bell rang, I hoped it was Harry.

Untapped Potential Status Update:
Trying out a new song this week—lyrics are coming together. "Life is like a strobe light, bright and blinding. Come find me on the dance floor." Swing by Crushed Beanz over in Hallow Friday night to hear it for the first time.

I read the post over and over, wanting it to mean something more, wanting it to have any connection at all to this past Saturday night.

"So, you dirty-danced with Harry Hotpants, huh?" Margot asked, peering up from the sketchbook in front of her. She carried her book everywhere, always designing new fashion pieces in it. Her goal after high school was attending an institute for fashion, and she'd been working on bulking up her portfolio for years. "Did you kiss him?"

"No!" I hissed, whirling around to make sure no one overheard. "Besides, we weren't...*dirty dancing*. We were only dancing." Very, very closely.

"Right." It was clear from her tone she didn't believe me, looking back down to her book. The fashion-style art was starting to take shape as she drew her pencil along the hips of a figure, illustrating a loose sketch of a dress. "I still can't believe you ditched him on the dance floor."

I bit down on my lower lip, picturing Harry at Downtown, his tousled hair and his half smile. That flirty banter still flickered like a flash of heat to my veins, summer sun on frozen snow. I replayed it over and over in my mind, if only to relive how I felt hearing it for the first time. "I only left for five minutes, and when I came back, he found someone new to flirt with."

Margot raised an eyebrow. "That just means you needed to flirt back *harder*."

I had no confidence in myself now, no trace of Stella in sight. "It probably wouldn't have worked out," I said finally, deflating with the flood of thoughts. "Can you imagine how awkward it'd be if I had to explain the whole Stella thing to him?"

Margot shook her head as the bell rang. "It's weird that you talk about Stella as if you aren't her, dude."

"We're different." I couldn't explain just how a wig changed my perspective on things so easily. Heck, it barely made sense to me. "It would be messy."

"You're only saying that because you're chicken." Margot's voice was firm, but not mean. Her pencil still worked steadily.

I opened my mouth to argue, but a distinct voice beat me to it. "Miss Brighton, Miss Massey," Professor Bordeaux called at the front of the class, and both of our eyes snapped up. His cheeks were pink with frustration. "Would it be all right if I started today's lesson?"

Margot swept her hand in front of her. "The floor's all yours."

Professor Bordeaux didn't get that her words were sarcastic; he simply turned around and started pointing at the board.

Even though I tried, my mind wasn't focusing on anything he said.

Not for the first time, I wished I could be Stella around the clock. Stella never had to worry about parents or scholarships. Why couldn't my life be like hers all the time? Because even though Harry danced with her, he wouldn't have danced with me. Guys like Harry would have a type, wouldn't they? And if he was attracted to Stella, in all her tattered and dark-apparel glory, he wouldn't like Destelle, who wore varying shades of pink and $300 jackets. If Harry knew Stella wasn't really *me*, would he run for the hills?

With a soft sigh, I rested my head on my hand, and despite reading the tease of those new lyrics, I felt more weighed down than I had earlier this morning.

The week passed slowly, each day a sluggish sort of torture. Wake up. Go to school. Do whatever volunteer job Mom scheduled for my day. Homework. Sleep. Repeat.

This week, she had me shovel the snow from Mr. Teeter's driveway, vacuum Ms. Lesher's house, and even babysit my siblings. It took forever for Friday to roll back around, and when it finally did, I was so ready for it.

Mostly because I couldn't wait to hear that new Untapped Potential song. I already had the lyrics they'd shared memorized. *Life is like a strobe light, bright and blinding. Come find me on the dance floor.*

Would it be fast-paced enough to make me rock my head with the beat? Or would it be acoustic, a lulling sound that made my chest ache? Despite the fact that things didn't work out between Harry and me, I needed to find out.

I arrived early, but even with a ten-minute buffer, cars had filled every space in the Crushed Beanz parking lot. I had to park out on the employee side. At an Olympic pace, I changed into Stella, then quickly reached into the driver's side door for my wallet. With a pat to my coat pocket, double-checking I had my keys, I pressed the automatic lock on the side of the door.

New Untapped Potential song? I was *so* ready for you.

And it seemed like everyone in Fenton County was as

well. The packed parking lot had been no joke; people filled Crushed Beanz to the brim.

"Big crowd," I said to Jonathan as I got in line for a cup of coffee. He was working on making a coffee for a boy in front of me, who glanced back at the stage frequently as if he were afraid of missing the band. "I don't think I've seen so many people here before."

"It's a lot," Jonathan agreed as he worked, meeting my eyes briefly. "Almost need to hire a bouncer to keep track of numbers."

"You'd have to start charging for entry for that." I looked over my shoulder too, eyeing the crowd. Spotting the booth that Addy and I usually sat in was impossible, but I hoped she claimed it. For tonight's show, I wanted a front-row seat.

At my words, Jonathan turned around, eyes trying to convey a hidden meaning. "Quite the hot topic tonight."

When Jonathan handed the coffee to the guy ahead of me, I stepped closer, lowering my voice. "What's that mean?"

"Means that Untapped Potential has been arguing in the back about that since they got here. One says they should charge entry, the other says no."

I felt my eyebrows shoot up, apprehension sneaking in. "Who's arguing about it?" *Please don't say Harry.* Nothing was more unattractive than someone arguing over money. I'd seen enough of it to last a lifetime.

Jonathan opened his mouth to answer when the kitchen door swung open, revealing the band in their full glory.

"Why are you two so stubborn?" Natasha demanded in her low voice, disdain dripping from her words. She'd left her dark hair loose today, her tight curls loose and beautiful. She stopped before she came out from behind the counter, not moving another inch. "We *should* charge admission—we're the most popular band in Fenton County!"

Harry looked over his shoulder and glared at her, completely unaware I sat only a few feet from him. "Tash, not out here."

Aw, cute. He had a nickname for her. I hated it.

"We didn't finish our conversation!"

His frown deepened. "I already told you. Mr. Castello is kind enough to let us perform—"

"We're boosting *his* business," she said while gesturing at Vincent. "His dad lets us perform here, yeah, but we should be allowed to charge admission."

Vincent's eyes narrowed in response to her words, and if I'd been Natasha, I would've flinched. "My dad pays the band each gig. You know that."

Natasha scoffed, folding her arms over her near-sheer top. "Yeah, twenty-five bucks a gig. Which comes out to *barely any cash at all* when you divide it between us."

Harry lowered his voice, and if anyone had been farther away than me, they wouldn't have heard. "We're not in this for the money, Tash. You knew when you signed up that we weren't here for the money. If you are, you should probably find another band."

Inexplicably, Vincent rolled his eyes, his expression snapping from frustrated to annoyed in an instant, like a flip of a switch. He even walked away before Natasha had a chance to respond.

Jonathan stepped in front of my vision as he filled my usual drink order, and I caught his eye for a quick instant. Through that look alone, I knew exactly what he wanted to say. *Don't eavesdrop.*

As if I could stop.

Natasha stepped forward, completely into Harry's bubble of personal space. She reached out and trailed her red-painted fingernails along Harry's arm delicately, almost like a lover. They looked like a couple. A cute couple. Their complexions complemented each other well, his light to her dark. And she was the perfect height for him too.

Jealousy dug into my skin as I watched them, especially as Natasha dropped her voice. "We should look for other places to play, broaden our horizons. You want out of this town as much as I do—it won't happen if we're playing for free."

Harry didn't push her away. If anything, his expression *softened.* "I just—I don't think we're there yet, Tash."

Natasha hooked her fingers in Harry's belt loops. "You're afraid of branching out."

"I'm not," he said simply, glibly, not giving it too much thought.

With that, he drew away from her, turning toward the stage. He hadn't noticed me, hadn't even glanced my way. But as he moved into the crowd, they clapped and cheered, excited for the show to begin.

"Sorry for the delay," Harry called to the audience, turning on the charismatic charm. "So, in case you didn't know, we're Untapped Potential. We promised a new song tonight, yeah? Should we open with it?"

In response, the crowd cheered loud. Loud enough to make my eardrums vibrate.

"All right. This is a new song we're calling 'Dance Floor.'"

Vincent started the song with a rapid beat of hitting the snare drum, hi-hat, and cymbals, the sounds mixing for a clean intro. After his second run-through of the beat, Natasha joined in on her guitar, the strum a perfect zing like all the songs they played with a practiced precision.

As much as I wanted to go sit with Addy, all the wind had been sucked out of my sails. Natasha's hands on him. In his belt loops. He hadn't even looked my way, didn't notice me. Like a fly on the wall.

It made last Saturday feel so much less significant.

Jonathan patted me on the shoulder, as if picking up on my downward spiral. Jonathan might know if Harry and Natasha were dating. Addy might've known if Harry and Natasha were dating. I could've asked.

But just like I'd surrendered a piece of myself to sit down in front of those college applications with Mom, I'd be surrendering a piece of Stella by asking such pitiful questions.

Harry's voice was liquid silk against my ears, a song sung straight to my soul, filling a bit of the hole that festered in my chest.

"Life is like a strobe light, bright and blinding
One light, two lights, three, and four

Won't you feel the beat with me?
Find me on the dance floor."

Each lyric transported me back to last Saturday, and I could almost *feel* Harry's fingers on my hips, skin on skin. In my head, *I* had my hands on his chest. *I* looped my fingers through his belt loops. We couldn't fake chemistry like that, right?

"A song stuck in my head I can't ignore
I'll be right here waiting
Leaving me wanting more
Come find me on the dance floor."

As they sang, a thought danced like a little devil through my head. They would outgrow Crushed Beanz sooner or later. They'd expand, find a record company to sign them for an album. Or two. CDs, T-shirts, tours—all of that hung in their future. I just knew it.

Would I be in a place to follow them, watch their success as it rolled in? I wanted to be. Or would I be stuck in a college dorm somewhere, tied down to a life I didn't want?

I listened to the rest of the gig from the counter, softly singing along to the songs that I'd long since memorized, sipping my coffee. Not even the caffeine helped amp me up, and as the night came to a close, I seriously lacked my usual energy.

"Thank you all for coming tonight," Harry said into the mic, signaling their end.

"Be sure you're following us on social media," Natasha chimed in.

Harry glanced at her with a smile. "In fact, head over to our page now and let us know—what's your favorite song of ours?"

I heard a few people call out their answers, which elicited a beautiful, deep laugh that rumbled through the microphone, the sound a shot of espresso to my chest.

"Go leave that comment—and tag any friends you think would like it too."

"Goodnight, everyone!" Natasha called, and a beat later, I heard the microphones click off.

I didn't waste any time threading my arms through my coat sleeves, turning around in the barstool chair to eye Jonathan. I wanted to get on the road before everyone else rushed out. "Thanks for the coffee, Jon."

"No refill?" he asked, totally picking up on my low energy. Not that it was too surprising. I was a battery running on empty.

"Not tonight." I simply gave him a small smile as I buttoned my jacket, a Fenta Vitalo trench coat, giving him a final farewell before blending in with the crowd.

Glancing around one last time, I hoped I could spot Harry. Vincent stood by the booth with Addy, giving her a smile. I'd seen him smile before, that lip ring tugging on one corner, but only rarely, and only directed at Addy.

As for Harry and Natasha, I didn't spot either of them.

five

*I*t'd begun snowing as I made my way outside, and I folded my arms over my chest, ducking my head low against the breeze. I loved snow when it first fell back in December, but since it was almost the middle of February, I was *so* over it. Beyond over having to drive in it too.

Jeez, Stella was a negative nelly tonight.

As I made my way around the back side of Crushed Beanz toward the employee parking lot, I thought of my favorite Untapped Potential song to comment on their social media page. I really, really liked that new song, but my mind couldn't help but wander back to that one line. *Find me on the dance floor.*

Harry on a dance floor, his hand coasting down my body, over my hips...

My dark SUV came into sight, a fine coating of snow stacking on top of it. With a little sigh, I reached into my pocket for my car keys, ready to press the unlock button.

But my fingers curled around something round, something *definitely* not key-like. When I pulled it out, it was just lip balm.

I checked my other pocket, but my car keys weren't in that one either.

No. Oh, no, no, no. No way.

This could not be happening.

I rushed toward the car to wrap my hand around the handle, giving it a good tug.

Locked.

I tried the rear doors.

Locked.

Before I had a chance to hope that maybe I left the keys inside Crushed Beanz, I saw them. Through the tinted glass, I could make out my car keys sitting on the bench seat, in plain sight. Mocking. They must've slipped out of my pocket while I changed clothes.

This could not be happening.

Absolutely no flipping way could I call my parents. It wasn't past my curfew, but I was firmly *Stella*. Black wig, heavy makeup, ripped and frayed clothes. They would eat me alive. Heck, they'd probably try to perform an exorcism.

They'd take Stella away for good if they ever knew about her. They'd probably forbid me from seeing Margot too.

Except what were my options besides calling them? If I called any sort of locksmith to open the car, they'd call my parents. Margot wouldn't be able to help me—she was good, but not *that* good. That left...

A piece of a broken parking block caught my eye in

front of my car, bigger than the size of my hand. I stared at it for a long moment. Like the keys, it mocked me too.

Did I really have any other choice?

As I picked up the cold, stupid, heavy thing, my mind began racing for excuses. *I came out to find it shattered,* I could say, but then they would promptly ask me where I was. They wouldn't quite believe it got broken at Margot's house, a house safely tucked inside a gated community.

I accidentally smacked the seat belt into it. Except I wasn't sure you could even break a window with a seat belt. Plus, if they found out it was even remotely my fault, I'd be grounded until they shipped me off to college.

Margot might know someone who could fix a broken window. The girls at Eastview might, too—they were resourceful. Street-smart. That's how I got my fake ID. I just had to hide the damage for a night. I could say I left my windows rolled down because...well, I'd have to think of a reason why. How hard could it be?

I stood back from the car, lifting the cement piece. Drawing in an icy breath, I squeezed my eyes shut, and then I—

"Whoa, what are you doing?"

The sound of someone's voice so close to me made me yelp in surprise, whirling around, cement still poised to throw.

"Don't shoot," he quickly got out, and then winced.

Harry stood a few feet from me, a light-wash jean jacket over his shoulders, wind threading its fingers through his auburn hair. His eyes were wide, his eyebrows raised.

Both hands were level with his shoulders, and looped around a finger in one hand hung his car keys.

For a second, I just stood staring at him, watching as his eyes darted from me to the rock in my hand to the SUV.

"It's my car," I told him, my voice even.

"That's good," he replied, but I couldn't tell if he fully believed me. His expression was unreadable. "Why, exactly, are you about to shatter your window?"

"My keys." The confusion didn't clear from his gaze. "They're inside." And then I added, with a gesture at the car, "It's locked."

Good grief, Stella, where's that flirty attitude from last weekend? Apparently it'd gotten locked in the car along with my keys.

Harry eyed the cement piece. "Seems a bit extreme. Why not call someone to bring a spare set?"

"Can't." *Get a grip, Destelle.*

After another second of silence, the tension left from his mouth. "One sec," he said after a moment, taking a backward step. He pointed a finger at the cement in my hand. "You should put that down."

"*Not* through the car window," I said for clarification, my voice finally gaining some of its life back.

It caused Harry to smile. "Definitely not."

I tossed the cement block back where I'd picked it up from, watching as a few chunks broke off. Harry disappeared only for a moment, and when he came back, he had a long paper-thin metal object in his hand. "Is that a slim jim?" I asked in disbelief, staring at where the bottom curved. "Like, to break into cars?" I'd seen enough action movies to recognize it, but I almost couldn't believe they existed in real life.

"It is," he said, twirling it in his grip. "I had one in my trunk."

"Should I be concerned why you have one?"

"When I'm not singing in cafés, I'm breaking into cars." He winked at me, stepping to the driver's side door of my SUV. Before doing whatever he needed to do with it—because I seriously had no idea how a slim jim worked—he looked over his shoulder at me, face almost redder. Apparently he had a hard time being properly flirty too. "That was definitely a joke. I got locked out of my car once and bought one to get back in."

"That makes me feel better."

He slipped the slim jim into the door, maneuvering the metal expertly. As I watched him, two feelings bubbled up inside me. Apprehension—it was *really* weird that he knew how to do this so easily.

And attraction—watching him break into my car was weirdly hot. Especially since I'd been moments away from shattering the window like a caveman.

My knight with a shining slim jim. My parents would be proud.

A soft *pop* filled the air, and Harry carefully extracted the metal. With a grand gesture, he opened the driver's side door. "That looked way too easy," I decided, narrowing my eyes at him.

"It's more complicated than it looks." Harry pressed the *unlock* button, and all the locks in the car popped. "It helps that you have an older car model. If it had automatic locks, those are so much harder to get into."

I raised an eyebrow at him.

"I had to do some internet research to learn how to do it," he told me with a laugh, one just as beautiful and rumbly as it'd been a few moments ago over the microphone. I really wanted him to do it again. "This better be your car, or else you made me an accomplice to auto burglary."

"Technically, it was all you." My lips finally curved into a smile, probably because the threat of getting in trouble had evaporated. After opening the back seat door, I snatched my keys with relief. "I seriously owe you one."

Harry leaned against the open car door, his eyes tracing mine. Even in the night's darkness, they were so vibrant. And even though the collar of his jean jacket turned up against his neck, I could see the tattoo at his throat, the inky lines like shadows against his skin. "Maybe in exchange for breaking into your car, you can tell me why you ditched me last Saturday?"

He cares! I had to squash down the Destelle level of excitement, trying to play it off. "More interesting plans came up."

"Ouch." But he smiled. "No interesting plans tonight though, huh?"

"Not tonight." Even though I started to shiver from the cold, no way was I getting in the car. Not yet. "And besides, I'm not in the habit of fighting for a guy's attention. When I came back, you looked well occupied."

Understanding flitted across his features. "Those girls

did ask me to dance," he admitted, "but I told them I was waiting for a dark-haired beauty to come back and sweep me off my feet."

I nearly chuckled, ready to fire back a flirty response, but a different dark-haired beauty popped into my mind's eye. "You mean your girlfriend?"

He raised an eyebrow. "My girlfriend?"

"I'm just saying, when she finds out you go to night-clubs to dance with random girls, she'll be pissed."

Amusement swallowed his features whole then. "I don't have a girlfriend. You think I'd dance with you like that last weekend if I did?"

"One can never be too sure," I said as a gust of wind slipped through the parking lot, tugging at my hair. The wig strained against the clips in my real hair, making me wince. "You and the guitarist seemed pretty close."

Harry drew his boot through the gravel on the ground, shaking his head. "Not that kind of close. Not anymore."

Not anymore. So they had been before, but not now. I wasn't sure what to think about that.

I gripped the edge of my car door tightly as I eyed him, trying to think of the next thing to say. "The new song was really good," I said. "It was edgier than what you've written before—the beat was harder, and your voice matched it well."

Light flickered in his eyes, like my words surprised him. Then again, I'm sure a lot of people were generic with their compliments. *Great song* or *I absolutely loved it.* A slow smile curved at his mouth. "I don't think it's that hard to guess the inspiration, hmm?"

Come find me on the dance floor.

"I'm not really looking to date right now," he went on, drawing a fingertip along the glass in a way that gave me a shiver, wondering what that delicate touch would feel like on my skin. "At least, that's what I told myself before last Saturday."

I lifted a teasing brow. "I must be one hell of a dancer."

"You have no idea."

Yeah, shivers. All down my spine. Everywhere.

"Since I rescued your poor window from being shattered," Harry continued in that same low and dreamy tone, "does that mean I get your number?"

I'll admit, there were a few times when I imagined Harry Russo asking for my cell number. Maybe we'd accidentally bump into each other after a show, or Addy would play matchmaker and introduce us, or Harry would jump from the stage because he was so swept up with my beauty.

Okay, that last one was a little wild, but actually living this moment—*Does that mean I get your number?*—was better than any imagined scenario. "I—I think that sounds fair."

Without another word, Harry pulled a thick black marker out from his pocket, offering it out to me.

"I can just plug it into your phone," I said with a startled laugh, but grabbed the marker anyway.

"I left it back inside," he told me, tugging up the sleeve of his jacket to offer his bare forearm to me. A few freckles dotted there too, so light that they almost disappeared into his skin. "Besides, what better way to make sure the marker works?"

I had to take a step closer to him, moving into his personal space. His eyes were tender as they watched me. Almost in a way that made me shiver, and not from the wintery breeze. I took ahold of his arm, holding my breath as I drew the marker across his warm skin.

"There," I murmured, pulling back to analyze the seven numbers. "But don't call me tonight."

When I looked up at him, we were only mere inches apart. I should've stepped back, but I wanted to stay trapped in his bubble, sharing personal space. "Not tonight?"

"Tomorrow," I insisted for two reasons. Once I got home, Mom and Dad would take my cell away. They definitely didn't need to be lurking in on *that* conversation. And as for the second reason, I wanted him to think about me tonight. I wanted to dance in his head like I'd danced with him last weekend, and much like he'd been dancing in my mind since. "Thank you for rescuing my window, Harry."

"No problem, Stella," he murmured, and I swear, my heart skipped a beat. If he could say my name five more times, that'd be great.

I got into the car before I voiced any embarrassing thoughts, trembling from the adrenaline that flickered through me. A bone-shaking thrill that made it hard to sit still, hard to wipe away the smile that felt permanently etched onto my lips. Chemistry.

Even though I usually changed out of Stella after Crushed Beanz, I'd have to drive somewhere else to change since Harry stood outside the door, hands in his pockets.

He still had his jacket sleeve pushed up, my phone number visible on his arm.

I knew one thing for certain as I backed out of my parking space and headed out of the employee lot: I wouldn't be able to shut my brain off until he finally called me tomorrow.

*H*onestly, not much was worse than brunches at Le Petit Bateau. Mom and the other ladies from her social circle all gathered around a table, eating expensive shrimp and drinking their weight in martinis and glasses of wine. And of course I was forced to witness all of it, except I only drank water.

The only person who made it the slightest bit bearable was Ms. Nancy, who sat across from me. Older than the hills and crotchety.

Her name was actually Nancy, but Mom always told me to add the "Ms." to be polite. She was invited to these brunches only because everyone hoped to get a slice of her will. Or at least that's what I assumed since they weren't inviting her for her personality, which was at total odds with their prim and proper attitude.

I, however, absolutely loved Nancy. She reminded me of an elderly version of Margot.

Right now, she sipped her second glass of red wine, clearly not paying attention to the conversation.

"Oh, Alice, I mean it—you should really look into building that addition when the ground thaws. Wait too long and you'll be too old to enjoy it. Like me!"

Mom tipped her head to the side. "We're holding off for now. David's not sure if we want to stay in Addison long-term, you know. He's been thinking about Biscayne Park. They have better neighborhoods and their private schools are top of the line."

"How are you enjoying school, Destelle?" Mrs. Conan asked me, pointing a very long finger in my direction. It wavered in the air, like she wasn't sure where exactly I sat. "I hear Eastview is a very fine school."

"Oh, the education I receive is far more important than my enjoyment, and it's a good education. I definitely get that at Eastview."

My tone came out plasticky and robotic, but I didn't miss Mom's polite smile. Mrs. Conan was the managing partner at Mom's firm, AKA her boss—before every time the ladies gathered, I got the usual "be on your best behavior, Destelle" speech. As the ladies murmured with approval, I'd say I did okay.

Nancy caught my gaze and rolled her eyes; my BS didn't fool her.

"I can't wait until I start high school in the fall," said Grace, the girl beside me. She was Mrs. Conan's daughter, and though she didn't frequent the banquets too often, she never missed a brunch day. And she always insisted on sitting right next to me. "I'm so bummed you'll be graduating, Destelle. How cool would it have been if we could've been in high school together?"

"It would've been so fun," I returned, though I wasn't sure I believed the sentiment.

Trapped between my thigh and the cloth of the chair, my cell phone vibrated, and I quickly shifted before it made too loud of a noise. My heart jumped into my throat at the possibility of *who* could be texting me.

Hiding it from Mom's view, I risked a glance at the screen.

And the excitement dropped.

Margot: **How's Brunch with the Bee-yotches? Anyone brag about their latest car yet?**

I flipped my hair over my shoulder, trying to look as nonchalant as possible as Ms. Jennings ran her finger along her martini glass.

"Yvette, did you see my new convertible? All the men at Alderton always brag about engines and such, but I finally realize how fun cars are."

Holding in a snort, I tried texting with one hand.

Me: **Whoa, that was freaky. Ms. Jennings just did. You have ESP?**

Margot: **More like PTSD. I know how those brunches are.**

Without warning, a sharp pain pricked at my lower thigh, and I looked over to find Mom settling back in her seat, giving me a look as stern as she dared with the brunch ladies present.

Did she *pinch me?*

I slid my cell back under my leg, my cheeks heating before I shoved down the bubbling emotion.

"So, Destelle," Grace whispered, as if she wanted to have a conversation just between us even though we sat at a table full of gossips. "Meet any cute boys lately?"

Boys. I avoided the subject at all costs, especially at these brunches. "N-Not really."

"She hesitated!" Ms. Jennings said gleefully, leaning her elbows onto the table. "Tell us, dear. Give us all the details."

All the eyes suddenly on me made it nearly impossible to open my mouth. I didn't want this attention. Mom had to be staring at me, but I couldn't bear to look at her. She'd be able to tell if I was lying and I absolutely couldn't tell them about Harry.

"All right, who got the garlic-roasted shrimp?" a low voice called from behind me, and suddenly a mouthwatering scent of seafood and vegetables washed over the table. I slumped in my chair with a barely contained sigh of relief, watching as everyone's attention went from me to the food. Bullet dodged.

Mom raised her hand. "I did."

An arm expertly slid Mom's plate in front of her, careful not to knock into her martini glass. Something black was smudged along it, but before I could get a closer look, it shifted away. "And the grilled salmon?"

"Oh, me," Mrs. Holland said, glancing around the table. "Salmon is one of the best fishes for you, you know. One of the healthiest."

Nancy raised a plucked eyebrow at that, causing all of her wrinkles to crease. "What's the unhealthiest?"

"Well, anything fried, of course."

Nancy winked at me as I reached for my water. "I'm glad I got the fried codfish, then."

The server walked around the wide table and set Mrs. Holland's first plate in front of her, reaching for her side of steamed vegetables from his tray.

No way.

I jerked so sharply that the edge of my water caught on the table, spilling it everywhere.

Grace shoved her chair back with a shriek, as if the water was really acid about to touch her skin. Mom sprung right into action, collecting her cloth napkin and pressing it to the tabletop, trying to soak up as much water as possible.

I, for one, sat in shock, unable to comprehend the moment. I mean, it *seemed* obvious, but my mind couldn't wrap around the idea that this scene could be real.

For the longest disorienting moment, I thought I simply imagined him. His beautiful face and body were definitely not in the middle of this restaurant, and that tattoo on his neck was *not* there.

Harry Russo held the tray of food on the other side of the table, six feet from me, and I definitely didn't look like Stella.

"Oh, are you okay, dear?" Mrs. Holland asked, voice sounding more amused than sympathetic. "Accidents happen all the time."

"You would know," Ms. Jennings murmured as she sipped her martini, gaze on Harry. "We should call you butterfingers."

Harry was looking at me—I *felt* it—but there was no

way I was glancing up. "I can bring over some extra napkins in a sec."

My face was flaming, so hot that I knew my skin had to be scarlet, and I tipped my head so my hair covered my profile. *Be cool, be cool, be cool.* I couldn't even bring myself to respond.

"We've cleaned up most of it," Mom told him, voice clipped. I knew she was probably holding herself back from reprimanding me. She dropped her soaked napkin on the edge of the table. "I think we'll be all right."

Harry had his red hair pulled back out of his face, though a strand had escaped from the tie, and he had it tucked behind his ear. His white collared shirt fit him snugly, black apron tied neatly over his waist.

And at any second, he would look up and see me.

"Who got the shrimp scampi with the extra butter?" Harry asked the ladies, glancing around the table. Before our eyes could connect, I dropped my gaze, my pulse a thunderous beat in my chest.

He won't recognize you, I told myself, but even my thoughts were a bit disjointed. *You look* drastically *different. Different hair, less makeup. There's a reason you contour your face so dramatically when you're Stella. He won't recognize you.*

Harry set Mrs. Conan's shrimp scampi in front of her, switching out his empty tray for another one full of food. I spotted my Greek salad on it, knowing that any moment he would ask whose salad it was, and I'd have to say—

"That salad is Destelle's," Mom told him, laying a hand

lightly on my shoulder. "It's the fat-free dressing, right? No croutons?"

Kill me, I pleaded to the universe, refusing to look up. *Kill me right now.*

"Yep, Greek salad, fat-free dressing, no croutons." Harry rounded the table once again. As he leaned in close, gently setting the salad in front of me, I held my breath again. Even so, his scent still permeated. So warm, like cinnamon and spice. He set Grace's food down beside her next, glancing at the last dish on his tray. "And, last but not least, the fried codfish."

Nancy eyed him openly as he placed her plate in front of her. When he pulled back, she laid her hand on Harry's arm. It suddenly became a battle of who had the more intense, inappropriate gaze while they looked at Harry— Ms. Jennings or Ms. Nancy. "Can I have another wine, sweetie?"

Harry gave her a killer smile. "I'll let your server know."

"You can't swap out for her?" she carried on in the same low voice. "You're easier on the eyes."

Ha. No kidding. But I had to vehemently disagree with Nancy on the fact that he should replace our server. That was like a really, really bad idea.

"Unfortunately, my shift's almost over. But you ladies enjoy your meal."

Before he walked away, Harry smiled around the table at us, and it might've been my panicked line of thinking, but I thought his eyes lingered on me.

"Why wasn't he on the menu?" Nancy demanded, not

even being discreet about staring at his backside as he walked away. "Did you see that tattoo?"

"That boy is too young for you, Ms. Nancy," Mrs. Conan murmured in a conspiratorial tone.

"And he looks like *trouble*," Mom interjected, folding her napkin across her lap, judgment dripping from her voice. "Ms. Nancy, I don't think you need more wine."

"I have to agree with Ms. Nancy—he was *cute*." Grace tapped her chin. "And a little familiar."

Nancy rolled her eyes at all of us and grasped her silverware. "Looked like he had his eye on Destelle there, anyway."

I could feel all the ladies turn to look at me—Mom's stare especially—but I forced myself to stir the nonfat dressing into my salad, careful not to let any spill over the sides.

I still couldn't wrap my head around the fact that Harry worked at Le Petit Bateau. I'd never noticed him on our previous brunch days. Had he been working here long?

Although I wasn't supposed to know Harry, I tried to crane my head as discreetly as possible, attempting to spot him. He had said his shift was almost over—had he left? That'd probably be a good thing. He didn't know Destelle, and the least amount of interaction with him as Destelle was best. Especially when I had my mother at my elbow.

My phone vibrated once more underneath my leg, and I itched to pull it out. Mom would no doubt catch me, probably pinch me again. But I couldn't help myself.

Margot: **Maybe someday something actually interesting**

might happen at those things. You might die of boredom otherwise.

You have no idea, I longed to text back, but I set into eating my salad, my mind still reeling.

"Thank you for being on your best behavior," Mom said on the car ride home, both of her hands clutching the steering wheel. She drove the speed limit, eyes never leaving the road. Always responsible. "I know those lunches can be...trying."

More like mind-melting. "I enjoyed the company."

"Oh, I almost forgot. I signed you up for a half hour time slot at the senior facility downtown on Thursday, at five-thirty. I know that's cutting it close to when we eat dinner, but that was the last time slot they needed filled for the week. They need someone to chat with the patients for a little while. If you're a little late getting home, that's okay."

I focused on my breathing, slow and steady, in and out. "Thank you for always being on the lookout for opportunities," I told her quietly.

"I mailed the scholarship packets out," she informed me, breaking for a slow-moving car. "Except the one for the Alderton Foundation—you missed a question on it, one about what your college plans are. I left it on your desk. We should come to a decision for when the acceptance letters come in. I know all the choices can be daunting, so we should weigh the pros and cons seriously."

I stared out the windshield, the snow-covered land-scape passing us by.

"The big-name colleges are still on our list," Mom went on. "Mullhound is on there as well, as is Hartford. What was the other one we were thinking of again? Castleton University?"

A word that Mom used triggered in my mind. *Our.* On *our* list. As if she had just as much say in the choice of where I attended college as I did.

"Destelle," Mom said, her voice gaining strength. "Are you listening to me?"

"I'm listening," I replied automatically. "I was also thinking about Ashton."

Once it was out of my mouth, I couldn't take the words back.

"Ashton," she echoed, confusion furrowing her brow. "I can't recall that one. Where is it located?"

I curled my hands into fists, wishing my nails were longer so they'd bite into the skin. "It's an online school."

They were fighting words, and I knew that. Especially since we *just* talked about this. But hearing her talk about my future as an adult like she had complete control of it made me want to scream. In Mom's mind, I might as well have told her I wanted to join the circus. She wanted me, her firstborn, to go to a fancy college. One where tuition was a fortune.

And I knew exactly why she wanted that for me. It wasn't because she wanted me to have a nice education.

She only wanted to brag about it to all her friends. "Oh, Destelle got three scholarships" or "Destelle went to Mullhound" or "Destelle got into law school." My name got thrown into the mix, but it was never about me.

"We discussed this, Destelle. Online school isn't good enough for you," Mom decided at last, and her level voice surprised me.

"I could get the same degree as I would at some expensive university. Or at least take my basic courses there. If you would look at the school's website—"

"Your head all in the clouds. Well guess what, Destelle?" She let her agitation show, her chest rising and falling faster. "Reality is coming. And if you keep clinging to these notions of staying home, accepting the bare minimum, not doing anything with your life, reality is going to *hurt.*"

Sometimes when Mom said things like that, it felt like we were strangers. We'd lived in the same house for nearly eighteen years, yet she knew nothing about me. "Notions of staying home"? If she knew me, she'd know that I dreamed of getting as far away from Fenton County as possible, to live in the world outside from what I knew.

Online college courses wouldn't be the perfect lifestyle if I wanted to stay home—they'd be perfect for when I wanted to leave. With online courses, I wouldn't be tied down to one place. I wanted to travel, to see what the world had to offer, to be *free.* I didn't have to worry about keeping Stella under wraps, didn't have to worry about my parents breathing down my neck. I could live whatever life I wanted.

Mom cleared her throat expectantly.

She pulled into our driveway and the fire in me went

out, leaving nothing but devastation. "I understand, Mother."

My cell phone rang as Mom shut the car off, the garage door closing behind us. I looked at the caller ID, and the unfamiliar number had the sadness shaking off in a heartbeat, overwhelmed by a swarm of nervous butterflies.

"Who's calling you?" Mom demanded to know, just as she demanded control of every other thing in my life.

"Margot," I answered immediately, a lie falling so expertly from my lips that it surprised me. "She texted me at brunch, and I told her I'd call her back."

Her interest lost, Mom climbed out of the car. "I'll see you inside," she said, and shut the car door behind her.

The call reached the fourth ring when Mom went into the house, leaving me alone. Hurriedly, I pressed the accept button, raising the phone. "Hello?"

"It's tomorrow," a familiar low voice murmured directly into my ear. "And not like I was dying to call you or anything, but that was the longest night of my life."

I looked down at my tights, at the way my pink skirt folded over my legs. I could feel my curls brushing along my neck. It felt wrong to be talking to him as Destelle, but I tried to channel Stella as best I could. "Seems a little dramatic."

"I was hoping for *romantic*," he returned, a chuckle drifting through the phone. "But the real question is, when can I see you again?"

If he only knew that he'd seen me less than an hour ago.

I pressed my feet into the all-weather floor mat of Mom's car, the heat from the interior ebbing away as cold crept in. Even so, I didn't want to move. "I'm such a busy girl," I mused, tipping my head against the seat. *Ooh, that was good. Very Stella.* "So many things to do, so little time."

"Too busy for a mediocre band that plays on weekend nights?"

"You are not mediocre," I objected at once. "I...I just don't know if I can make it to the gig tonight." With that tiff with Mom, I wasn't sure she'd be charitable enough to let me "go to Margot's."

"Well, what about tomorrow?"

I stuck my free hand in my coat pocket, running my fingers along the soft lining. "Did you forget you don't play on Sundays?"

"You ever heard of Dial and Dine?"

I had. Dial and Dine was a food delivery service in the Fenton County area. Margot and I frequently ordered from them whenever we had our sleepovers, placing our order from our cell phones and getting the food within the hour.

"I'm delivering food tomorrow night. I pick up shifts a few nights a week. Since it's Valentine's Day tomorrow, there's typically a bonus in payment since it's a holiday."

I'd always wondered what it'd be like, delivering food and getting paid for it. Margot said she'd hate a job like that —she wouldn't be able to stop herself from stealing fries.

When I didn't respond, Harry added, "You should come with me."

"Come...come with you?" I stammered, sure I'd heard him wrong.

"I know it's not as fun as getting coffee or anything," he hurried to say, and for the first time since we'd started talking, I could hear nervousness leak into his voice. "It'd probably be pretty boring to sit there, actually, but—"

"I thought you weren't looking to date right now," I said playfully, throwing his words back at him. "And now you're asking me out for Valentine's Day? I'm getting mixed signals here."

I could hear Harry's smile in his voice. "This is a classic case of a guy eating his words."

Yes, eat them, I'm totally okay with that.

"When were you going to deliver food?" I already tried to sort out everything in my head. I had an early curfew on school nights, but I could always say I needed to run to the library or something. Needed to work on a last-minute homework assignment with Margot. Whatever the excuse needed to be, I'd figure it out. "What time?"

"Probably around six? That's usually when the dinner rush picks up."

Six o'clock on Valentine's Day. My heart skipped a beat. I rolled the information around in my mind. Curfew was nine on school nights. Plenty of time. "Can I drive?"

His voice sounded curious. "You?"

"I just met you," I pointed out, folding one arm across my chest. My fingers were getting a little numb. "And even though you're cute, I'm overly cautious."

"You think I'm cute?"

I wanted to see his expression so badly, see the teasing amusement dancing like fire in his eyes. Flirting was easier to do over the phone, but I wanted to see every little expression that came with his words. Desperately. "Maybe a little."

"Well, then." His words were lowered and rough as if he were speaking barely above a whisper. "How can I say no?"

Every inch of my insides buzzed, jumping for joy.

"You've heard of Le Petit Bateau, right? In Addison?"

I nearly snorted. "Yeah, I've heard of it."

"We could meet there around six tomorrow."

Sounds perfect, my dreamy thoughts mused, but I put together a cool and casual, "Works for me."

Just then, the door to the house opened once more, and Mom stuck her head out. "Destelle," she all but snapped, face creased. "Come inside before you freeze."

"See you tomorrow," I blurted, not giving Harry a second to respond before I ended the call and climbed out of the car. Mom glowered at me, our earlier conversation no doubt still running in her head, but I didn't care. She wasn't bursting my bubble. Honestly, I wasn't sure if she really could.

I had a date with Harry Russo tomorrow night—nothing would burst my bubble.

Seven

"You have a date," Margot said, expression skeptical. Her fashion sketchbook was in her lap, but she just twirled her pencil between her fingers, attention on me. "As *Stella*."

"Well, I'm definitely not going as *me*." I scoffed, pulling my legs underneath me in the lounge chair. The tapered dress pants I wore didn't want to stretch that way, but I popped open the top button, finding a position that was somewhat comfortable.

"Stella *is* you."

Yeah, yeah. More or less. "Do you mind if I get ready at your house?" I asked, leaning my head into my palm. My mind buzzed, trying to figure everything out. "Maybe I could come over once my parents get back from their lunch?"

"I guess." She grimaced down at her book. "But please wear something other than that god-awful black turtleneck."

What—it's—uh, excuse me? "It's not god-awful, it's edgy! And cute. And edgy!"

"I've got edgier things in my closet for Stella to wear."

"Who's Stella?"

Margot and I both whirled toward the railing of the upper level, finding Jamie and Nellie leaning over in a way that would've made Mom yell. Nellie looked interested in the conversation, whereas Jamie looked as if he'd rather be anywhere else.

"No one," I rushed to say, my voice a few octaves too high. Margot gave me a look. "Stella is no one."

"Oh, yeah?" Nellie narrowed her eyes at me, and I decided she was way too perceptive for a ten-year-old. "So, why does Stella, who doesn't exist, need clothes from Margot's closet?"

"Stella is a friend of Destelle's," Margot told them, nonchalance dripping from her words. Totally unbothered. Why couldn't I have sounded like that? "She's going on a date tonight and wants something pretty to wear."

"Something from *your* closet?" Jamie demanded, and even from where we sat, I could see the deep furrow to his brow.

Nellie, though, smacked him on the arm, starting down the stairs. "I'm so jealous," she said with a sigh. "Margot, when I'm big enough, can I try on clothes from your closet? Ooh, or you can design something just for me!"

Margot tapped her pencil along her sketchbook. "You like my style, kid?"

"*Love* it. Destelle, why don't you dress more like Margot?"

I took in the suit Margot wore today, a floral-printed one that curved over her figure. She had her blazer unbuttoned, and her pants stretched perfectly over her folded knees. "I don't think a suit would look good on me."

Margot looked at me thoughtfully. "Yeah, you're probably right."

My jaw dropped. "Hey!"

"Where'd you meet Stella, Destelle?" Nellie asked as she sat on the other side of Margot, fluffing her hands down her brightly colored leggings. "At school?"

"Don't be dumb, Nell." Jamie sighed, coming down the steps to stand on the other side of the couch. "They're obviously talking about Destelle. Their names are, like, only a few syllables off."

Of course I couldn't get anything past Jamie, and it made me nervous. Jamie would be the one most likely to rat me out to Mom. He'd never rat out Nellie, though.

"Syllables," Nellie announced, before saying, "S-Y-L-L-A-B-L-E-S. Syllables. Wait, so are you trying out a nickname or something?" Her expression grew perplexed, like I'd asked her to figure out a high school-level math problem. Her voice sounded distasteful. "*Stella?*"

"What's wrong with Stella?" I demanded, casting a glance at Margot, who still looked amused.

Nellie looked me over from head to toe, the mere action feeling offensive. "You don't look like a Stella is all."

Margot tried to stifle a laugh, but it slipped through.

I slumped in the armchair, staring at the picture that hung on the farthest wall above the fireplace. It was some antique, passed down through Dad's family. I had no idea why; the thing was ugly. Abstract art with a lot of oranges and puke yellows.

"Wait. So that means *you're* going on a date?" Nellie all but gasped at the realization, her eyes widening. Immediately, I felt everything in me tense. "Oh, my gosh, what's he look like? Destelle, it's been *forever* since you brought a guy over."

"Drop it, okay? I'm not going on a date," I said with an eye roll, but I looked over at my brother, whose expression was still scrunched. Great—he'd already started scheming.

"So, either you're lying or Margot's lying, because she said *Stella* was," Jamie pointed out.

"If you guys forget this conversation ever happened, I'll give you five bucks." Margot reached into her pocket. "Each."

"Margot," I hissed. "You can't bribe children."

"Sure she can," Nellie said cheerfully, gazing at Margot's bifold wallet.

Jamie raised a hand. "Twenty."

Margot's eyebrows flew up, looking torn between impressed and annoyed. "Excuse me?"

"Each." Jamie looked at me, his brown eyes still holding that same intensity. "Or else I'll tell Mom and Dad you're going on a date without their permission." His expression didn't change. "I know you've got it."

I folded my arms over my chest. "I don't need Mom and Dad's permission to go on a date."

"Right," he scoffed. "My mistake, *Stella*."

See what I mean? The kid was the king of blackmail. It wasn't fair.

I knew what would happen if I didn't hand over the money. The second Mom and Dad got home from their lunch, the twins would spill the beans. Talk all about the date and raiding Margot's closet and Stella. And, sure, it didn't sound like that big of an issue, but I knew my parents.

I couldn't risk losing Stella.

Defeat no doubt clung to my expression when I looked at Margot.

"I can't believe I'm letting a toddler blackmail me," she huffed, pulling out two twenties from her wallet and distributing them. Then she leveled her sharp gaze at me. "What happened to not bribing children?"

"It was *your* idea."

Nellie cheerfully rose to her feet with her bill in hand, and Jamie followed suit. He waved his twenty dollars in the air. "Nice doing business with you."

Margot and I both sat in silence while they climbed the stairs, one step creaking underneath their weight. After a moment, I raised my eyes to her, rubbing my hands over my knees. "I'll pay you back."

She was quiet for a moment, contemplative. I've learned not to rush her thoughts, to let her form the perfect sentence in her head. "Have you ever considered telling your parents about Stella?"

"Margot." I glanced toward the staircase, but the twins had already disappeared. "Of course not. They'd go nuclear. They'd probably throw the entire shoebox in the trash. I'm not a boat rocker like you."

"You could be. You know how to swim."

She looked at me as if she'd made some kind of point, but she didn't get it. My parents weren't like her parents, giving her ample room to be whoever she wanted to be. My parents liked everything exactly how they wanted it. Nothing out of place. That was why Mom always picked out my dresses for the country club events and why Dad always took my cell and car keys at night. They wanted to have everything done exactly how they wanted. No room for free-thinkers. No room for online colleges or wigs.

When I thought about rocking the boat, about telling Mom and Dad about Stella, a deep, suffocating sense of shame washed over me. Like I was doing something wrong. That's how they'd see it. They wouldn't understand; they wouldn't even try. Instead, they'd stuff me more firmly into the mold they carved out for me, until no trace of Stella remained.

And, when I thought about my parents finding out, I didn't want them to be disappointed in me.

With that in mind, I straightened my shoulders, almost as if I could physically brush the conversation off. "So, I can come over to get ready?"

Her hooded eyes returned to her sketchbook as she accepted defeat. "Yeah, yeah. When you come over, bring me forty bucks. I'm not paying for your demonic siblings."

Even though she gave up the conversation, it still felt as if I was the one losing, and the suffocating sensation never disappeared.

eight

$\mathcal{W}$hen I pulled up at Le Petit Bateau, I practically hummed with excitement. I'd dug around in my closet for something red to wear, and though the sweater was a little nicer than what Stella normally wore in honor of the holiday—as opposed to the usual tatters and tears—the black wig brought it to a whole new edge, one that made me feel cute.

I also made sure to deepen my blush and contour just in case Harry recognized me from Le Petit Bateau yesterday. He probably remembered the bumbling dork who spilled her water at the sight of him, and I needed to make sure he wasn't about to connect any dots.

"Hey, you," Harry greeted as he pulled the passenger's side door open, bringing in a wave of cool air. Which was a good thing because my blood suddenly warmed. He wore his usual black ripped jeans and white shirt, his red hair pushed out of his face. As he settled into the seat, I realized he had something in his hand, and he offered it to me. "Happy Valentine's Day."

A smile sprung to my lips at the small heart-shaped box of chocolates wrapped with a red ribbon. Harry had even gone to the trouble of writing *To Stella, From Harry* on it, his handwriting blocky and purposeful.

"I know it's nothing fancy," he went on, "but everyone deserves a gift on Valentine's Day."

"I didn't get you anything," I said softly, guilty. As I looked at the gift, I realized my bangs hung a little in my eyes, almost too much—a sign I'd pinned the wig on wrong. As discreetly as possible, I ghosted my palm across the top of my head, trying to edge it back ever so slightly.

"You're coming with me tonight. That's gift enough." Harry reached out and tapped one ringed finger against the heart. "Though if you offer me one of the fruit-filled ones, I wouldn't say no."

With a laugh, I opened up the chocolate box, the beautiful smell filling the air. I let him have first pick before I snatched a dark chocolate truffle, biting into half of it with a contented sigh. "Mmm, happy Valentine's Day. So, where's our first Dial and Dine stop?"

"Greenville," Harry declared as he buckled himself in, then popping his chocolate into his mouth. The dashboard glow lit his face, and for a moment I couldn't help but stare. Especially at his lips. "Have you been to Mary's Place? The diner on Main? I've got an order to pick up from there. Or should I say, *we've* got an order."

"Roger that." I put the car into gear. "So, Dial and Dine...how did you get started with it?"

"Jumping right in with the questions," he returned with a chuckle, rubbing his palms together. "I saw an ad online and thought it could be a nice way to make some extra cash. Diversifying my income and all that."

I played dumb. "What other jobs do you have?"

"Well, the gigs bring in a small amount of money, but I work full-time as a server. At Le Petit Bateau, actually." He said the last bit sheepishly. "I figured it'd be an easy place for us to meet."

"It worked for me," I told him. "I actually live in Addison, so it was a short drive over."

He leaned back into the seat, gaze on the radio. "So, what kind of music is on your playlist? If you listen to country, I think I'm going to tuck and roll."

My jaw dropped in mock outrage, even though there wasn't any country music on my playlist. "You'd jump out of a car instead of listening to country?"

"Probably. And before you ask, *no*, it's not extreme. People jump out of cars all the time. Besides, why listen to country when you can listen to the Satellite 69's?"

No way. "You listen to the Sat 69's?"

He shifted in the passenger seat, angling so his body faced mine ever so slightly. And just like that, the conversation sparked to life as we shared a smile. "What's your favorite album of theirs?"

"*Darkest Night*, hands down. That one's slower, but I really like the theme. I like how it starts out as a sweet love story with 'Isn't it Bright' and it ends with tragedy in 'Midnight.'"

He grinned at that, gesturing to my cell. "You got that on your playlist?"

"Go ahead," I said with a jerk of my chin. "I don't have a passcode on my phone."

"What kind of monster doesn't have a passcode?"

I let out a laugh. "A monster with nothing to hide."

Harry swiped up my cell, scrolling through my music list. My hands were sweating against the steering wheel, as if he was looking at some sort of personal diary. I guess in a way it *was* like a diary. I'd added all those songs because I enjoyed them, for one reason or another.

"Outside Inclusion? Nice. You don't have their latest album on here." When Harry looked over, he caught me making a face. "What, you don't like their newest? I thought most people did."

"Most *mainstream* people," I allowed, waving my hand. "They like the new stuff because it sounds like every other rock band. Their old stuff, though, has edge. Grit. I like that."

I knew I sounded like a music snob, but the words flowed out of me, absolutely carefree. Honestly, I hadn't thought this critically about my music tastes in my entire life.

Harry picked a song by the Sat 69's, one of their lesser known ones. "Have you listened to the acoustic versions of their songs? They're not on any albums, but extra versions they've posted on their website. They're good."

"I *love* acoustic versions of songs," I told him, unable to keep from imagining his fingers strumming an acoustic guitar. It wasn't often that Untapped Potential played acoustic music, but on nights when they went back to their roots, I absolutely loved the sound of it. "It gives the song a lot of soul, don't you think?"

"I definitely agree," he said, bobbing his head along with the beat.

As I braked for a red light, I glanced over at him, intending just a sneak peek, but I found him already looking at me. His eyes were so, so blue, and they focused on mine. There was such an elegance to his face that didn't quite match the rest of him, but it wasn't bad. His ripped jeans and worn sneakers screamed edgy, along with the tattoo, but he had almost a softness to his eyes, to his expression, so youthful and kind. For the longest moment, I couldn't look away.

The traffic light flicked green, illuminating his face. "You're wondering about the ink, aren't you?"

I hadn't been—I'd been too distracted by his face—but he probably wouldn't believe me if I denied it. "Just admiring."

"It's something, isn't it?"

His tone and his expression weren't overly positive. "You don't like it?"

"It...makes a statement, that's all."

I frowned a little, listening as the next song on my playlist came on. To me, Harry and the tattoo went hand in hand. It was all part of his image.

"When did you get it?" He couldn't have gotten it that long ago, could he? He wasn't *that* old. Eighteen, did Addy say? He graduated high school last year, I knew that much.

"I had been just about to turn seventeen," he replied casually. "My friend had a cousin who'd do it with no paperwork, even though I should've gotten guardian permission. Charged me way more than he should've too."

"Probably because he was illegally inking a minor." I tried to hide my shock. My parents—a lawyer and a judge—would've had a field day taking that cousin to court if they heard that. "Your first tattoo was on your *neck?* Seems...extreme."

The smile that touched his mouth then wasn't warm. "You know how people say you make dumb decisions when you're young? Back then, I was full of them."

I took another glance over at him, at the thing lines. The contrast was striking, a shadow on his skin. "Well, on the bright side, it looks really good for someone having done it illegally."

This time, Harry grinned so widely that his eyes crinkled.

"What did your parents say when you came home with it?"

"Oh, I don't have parents," he answered nonchalantly. "They passed away."

I'd been easing on the brake as he spoke, in tandem with the car in front of me, but my foot slipped, causing the car to jerk. I hadn't been expecting him to say *that.* So calmly.

"Wow, I seriously didn't mean to throw that conversation off a cliff." Harry laughed a little stiffly into his hand, rubbing it across his mouth. "Came out sounding really depressing, didn't it?"

"No, it's okay." I turned to look at him again, but he still watched the road, fingertips touching his throat, following the black lines by heart. The action almost struck me as a self-conscious one. "How old were you? Was it recent?"

Harry shook his head. "I was seven. Car accident."

My mind immediately traveled to Addy. She'd lost her father in a car accident this past November, the same accident that permanently injured Vincent's father. She'd lost her dad—Vincent had almost lost his—and Harry had lost both of his parents.

Guilt expanded in my stomach. It made my attitude about my parents so selfish.

"I'm so sorry," I murmured, and even though I wanted to reach over and squeeze his hand, I kept my fingers curved around the steering wheel. If he hadn't lived with his parents growing up, who had he lived with? I wanted to ask, but didn't want to pry.

"Tell me one fact about you," he said, flipping the conversation around, as if we hadn't talked about such a heavy thing.

But if he wanted to change the subject, I'd let him. "Hmm, one fact... Oh, I have two siblings, and they're twins. Age ten."

"Two girls?"

"One boy, one girl. Jamie and Nellie." I glanced out of the corner of my eye at him. "Your turn."

"I've always lived in Fenton County, except I grew up in Bayview. How about you?"

I shook my head. "I actually grew up in the north of the state, in Whitmore." Whitmore was rather large, with skyscrapers and fancy offices, but we'd actually lived in a suburb of the city, away from the hustle and bustle.

Harry skipped over a song that'd come on. "Why'd you move?"

Backstory. It didn't seem like it would be interesting, but I was excited to learn each detail of Harry that he revealed. My life in comparison didn't seem engaging enough to waste time on. "My mom got a great job offer, and we moved."

"What does she do?"

"She's a lawyer at one of Fenton County's biggest firms." I could hear Mom's bragging voice in my head. I'd heard her talk about it all too often.

Harry drew in a deep breath. "Oh, really? What's her name?"

"Alice Fontaine." She'd kept her maiden name when she married Dad, wanting her achievements to be under her name.

"Well, that's cool that you moved here."

I wasn't sure if "cool" was a great way to describe it. I mean, sure, Fenton County was pretty and the beaches in Bayview were nice, but ever since we moved, Addison felt like a prison. A cage keeping me trapped, my wings clipped.

"When I graduate, I want to drive across the country," I told him decisively, pretending that I'd already planned it out and gotten permission. "I want to spend next year traveling. Not skip college, but take some online classes so I can do both. I don't want to be stuck here, you know?"

He popped his elbow on the console between us, leaning closer. "You're not afraid of the unknown?"

Maybe a little, but the idea was so exhilarating, and

dressed as confident Stella, I let my thoughts wander down that "what if" path now. What would the world look like without Mom and Dad constantly telling me what to do? I could stay up as long as I wanted, go to the restaurant I wanted, order the food I wanted. Heck, I'd get a salad with *extra* dressing and croutons. I'd wear sweatpants out of the house. I'd be free.

"In the summer, you can go with me," I said before I really thought about it, glancing his way with a grin. "We can explore the country together."

"I'll bring the road trip snacks," he promised, the Caribbean waters extra blue.

I pulled into the bumpy parking lot of Mary's Place, then let the engine idle while Harry hurried inside. The music still played in his absence, a soft song filtering through the speakers. The melody was almost haunting, sweet and low, like a ballad played at a high school dance. It was the perfect song for the night, perfect for Valentine's Day.

This wasn't a song on my playlist—Harry must've searched it himself.

It took him only a few minutes to pick up the food, and then he came back to the car, a plastic bag in his grip.

"So, the address is 220 Lincoln," he told me as he settled in, quickly grabbing the seat belt. "My GPS says to take a right."

So a right I took.

We spent the rest of the night driving around the county, but stayed mostly to the west side, around Greenville and Hallow, grabbing food from a few fast-food chains and even a few sit-down restaurants. Harry ran the food to the door, my headlights illuminating his path, and I quickly decided that I would enjoy doing this as a job. Turning my music up loud, going from place to place, and dropping off food. What a fun way to make money.

"Tell me," I said, lifting my chin a little, glancing at him from the corner of my eye. "Give me the inside scoop. Why do you sing?"

"Why do I sing," he echoed, then hummed a little. "I've been obsessed with music my entire life. I've always loved how you can tell such a powerful story with lyrics. You must know what I mean—we listen to the same music."

I liked that we had that in common. My taste in music was a *me* thing, not just a Stella thing. "And your love of listening to it made you want to create it?"

"Exactly." He knocked his knuckles on his window. "For the longest time, I thought it was just one of those dreams that never comes true. That I'd just be writing music and never do anything with it."

"You were afraid your potential would be untapped," I said with a smirk, trying not to laugh at my own joke.

But Harry did, even though it might've been a pity laugh. "Spot-on, actually. But good things come to those who wait, yeah? Take the next right here."

"So is that where the name came from? *Untapped Potential?*"

He shifted in his seat before nodding. "Yeah, pretty much."

As we pulled into the driveway of the last house, Harry turned to me, shuffling the fast-food bag. "Do you want to do this last one?" he asked, almost as if he were presenting a great honor.

And it absolutely felt that way. "Really?" I couldn't help but gasp, staring at the bag as if it were a bar of gold. "I'm allowed to?"

"Don't see why not." Harry winked at me in a way that made my blood rush. "Live your delivery driver dreams."

The bag crinkled loudly as I grabbed it from him. In the process, I accidentally overlapped my fingers with his. His skin was warm against mine, and I quickly pulled back, trying to ignore my kick-started heartbeat. "I'll be right back."

"Don't trip," he called to me cheerfully, watching me climb from the car.

Whoever owned this house had scraped their driveway completely clean of snow and ice, which made my trek to the front door easy. As I got closer, I found myself almost nervous. I just had to hand the bag of food over with a smile —the customer had paid through whatever app Harry had on his phone. Easy-peasy.

When I got to the doormat, I swallowed hard before knocking three times, glancing back at Harry. The headlights were shining right at me, nearly blinding, but I could still see the outline of Harry as he gave me a thumbs-up.

"Eloise, the door!" I heard a voice call from within, sounding very masculine.

It took only a moment for the door to tug inward, revealing a tall, slender girl with dark hair. She seemed to be about my age. "You're Harry?" she asked with an arched eyebrow, looking me over with a curious expression. "No offense, but you don't *really* look like one."

"He's in the car," I said, feeling a little more than discombobulated. I hadn't expected I'd be talking beyond *here's your food.* "He let me deliver this one."

"Bummer," she said with a sigh, and then quickly added, "Not trying to be rude, but I was hoping for a cute guy."

I so didn't blame her. I'd hope for a cute guy too.

Without waiting, I held the bag out to her. "Here's your food."

The girl, presumably Eloise, took the bag from me. "Thanks."

"Have a good night," I called before she shut the door, milking this customer service thing.

Through the slat, I could hear her laugh. "You too."

Once I got back into the car, I grabbed Harry's arm, giving it a squeeze. He watched me with amusement glittering in his eyes. "That was so much fun! She was so nice!"

"They aren't always. Sometimes they're grumpy." He looked me over, laying his hand over mine. "If I'd known you were going to be this excited, I would've had you run all of them to the door."

Honestly, I had to agree. I should've asked for a turn sooner.

Even though I didn't want to, I pulled my hand out from under his, gripping the wheel to get rid of the tingling sensation. "You said you do this a few nights a week, right?"

I asked, putting the car into reverse and backing down Eloise's driveway. "Do you always bring along company?"

"Only the ones who are easy on the eyes."

I raised an eyebrow at him. "Which means you invited me along because you thought I was pretty."

"You said you thought I was cute," he pointed out casually, voice catching on a chuckle.

He had an answer for everything, and his responses never failed to make me smile. I really liked that about him. "Fine. Just two people spending time with someone they think is attractive."

"Two *single* people."

My lips pressed together. "On Valentine's Day."

"So, a date."

Date. I decided that I loved hearing it come from his mouth, especially since he was talking about *me*. "A date," I confirmed, bringing some of my hair over my shoulder, making sure it hid my grinning profile.

I pulled into Le Petit Bateau fifteen minutes before nine, which would give me barely enough time to scrub off the makeup and get home. Cutting it close, but I couldn't bring myself to care.

Even when I put the car into park, neither Harry nor I moved, the two of us looking out the windshield, listening to the radio. "I'm glad I got to spend tonight with you," he told me after a moment, resting his head along the back of the seat. "Even though you were probably bored out of your mind and wasted half a tank of gas."

"Are you kidding? Running the last meal to the door

totally made up for all of that." And it so didn't hurt that Harry Russo sat in that seat beside me.

Though I wanted to sound more teasing and nonchalant, our proximity in the warm car made my words feel much more flirty. Maybe it was because the dashboard lights highlighted all the high planes of his face and illuminated his eyes, which were so endless.

Not for the first time, he struck me speechless. After months of watching him onstage, here I was, sitting with him in a car. Alone. Not even a foot away. No Vincent, no Natasha, no Jonathan—no prying eyes.

My brain seized on a thought while the cabin grew quiet: *Is he going to kiss me?*

It'd been ages since I'd kissed someone. I never really had time for boys, not with everything Mom and Dad put on my plate. And wow, what would Harry's lips feel like? Taste like? He looked like a good kisser, and that thought alone made my breath quicken ever so slightly.

But then Harry edged back into his seat—I hadn't even realized he'd been leaning in—and reached for his seat belt. *What happened?*

"We should do something again," I rushed to say before he could pop the passenger door open and slip into the night. The Destelle part of me winced, waiting for him to turn me down. What if this outing changed his mind and made him realize he didn't want to date?

I thought about the girl with the purple eye shadow. What if he was wishing he'd gone out with her instead?

But I shouldn't have worried. "What are you doing Thursday?" Harry asked, eyes tracing my face in such a delicate way that I could almost imagine his fingertips on my skin. A shiver danced across my spine, in a way that felt *good*. "Around five-thirty-ish."

Thursday at five-thirty. I had to volunteer at the senior center, as per Mom's orders. Of course, she'd signed me up against my will, not caring if I had any plans. She'd be so upset with me if I canceled.

Tonight stirred something inside me, though. Thoughts and feelings that I'd never let creep in before—like doubt. Yes, Stella was used to this taste of freedom, but Destelle wanted more of it. This afternoon's talk with Margot about rocking the boat fluttered into my mind, and for a moment, those words were all I could hear.

I didn't want to be my parents' puppet anymore. I wanted to cut my strings.

"I'm free," I said, the words feeling monumental in the small space of the SUV. "I'll meet you here again?"

"What if we got coffee?" he offered. "We could sit and talk. Maybe at Crushed Beanz?"

Immediately, I pictured myself in a booth across from him, able to devote all my attention to him. Not the road, not the restaurants—just Harry. "That sounds great."

With that, Harry popped the door open, letting in the winter air, and I found myself on the edge of my seat, wanting to say something more but not sure what. I wanted this moment to last as long as possible.

"A chocolate for the road?" I asked before he could fully slide out, grabbing the box off the dashboard. "I'd be willing to sacrifice one more."

Harry quirked his mouth to the side in thought as he

chose his chocolate. As his fingers worked it out, his eyes met mine. "Drive safe, Stella," he murmured with his lips curving upward, slipping the chocolate into his mouth.

That might've been the hottest thing ever. *Swoon.* "You too."

He shut the door and made his way to his car. Once he settled behind the driver's seat, he flicked on the overhead light, illuminating him well enough that I could see him wave. The smoothness of Stella had worn off, and Destelle came through, grinning like a doofus as I waved back while putting the car into gear.

Meeting him Thursday would mean I had to cancel on the senior center. Ditching a volunteer opportunity—who'd ever heard of such a thing? Then again, it was *volunteer* for a reason. I wasn't *required* to go. At least, not required by the senior home. Mom definitely made it a requirement. Was ditching it and risking Mom's wrath worth it?

I glanced at the dashboard, noting the time. I'd just be getting home before curfew. A photo finish. Was it worth it?

With my skin still tingling, imagining what Harry's mouth would've felt like, I knew the answer to both: most definitely.

nine

onday morning, ten minutes before I needed to leave for school, I walked past Nellie's room, hearing Jamie's voice coming from within. "Syphilis," he said.

"Syphilis," came Nellie's reply. "S-Y-P-H-I-L-I-S. Syphilis."

Immediately, I poked my head inside and saw Jamie sitting on one of her floor pillows, flash cards in hand. Nellie sat on her bed, staring at her ceiling. They were both dressed for the day, waiting for Mom to get ready to take them to school.

I frowned. "Uh, what kind of cards are those?"

"I took big words from a book Dad has in his office," Nellie told me, and snatched the cards from Jamie. "Will you quiz me on one, Destelle?"

"Just one, okay? I have to head out." I readjusted my collar as I took the card.

Nellie's handwriting was scrawled across it, striking me as a bad way to practice. If she'd already written them down, she might've remembered the act of writing the letters. Wouldn't that be cheating?

I cleared my voice, trying to sound as professional as possible. "Exuberance."

"Exuberance," she began. "E-X-U-B-E-R-A-N-C-E. Exuberance."

Ding. "You should be a dictionary when you grow up," I told her, tossing the card back. Her brown eyes looked at me excitedly, determining that my words had been a compliment.

"Destelle, your skirt is wrinkled." Mom sighed when I came down the stairs, posted at the doorway with my keys dangling from her fingertips.

"Only a little." I made sure my voice held the air of respect. "I put it on the hanger too late, but I think it will be okay."

"The wrinkles should fall out throughout the day," Dad said to Mom as he walked into the foyer, thankfully taking my side. It wasn't often, and usually not about important things. "Are you still going to stay after school for tutoring today?" he asked me.

Mom, though, answered. "She is. I told Mrs. Flannery —the freshman science teacher—she'd be down within ten minutes of the last period."

Once again, no question of whether I *wanted* to do it. No choice.

But why was I surprised? Life had always been that way. With college, with my clothes, with my spare time. I'd always handed my parents control of those things without blinking—when had I started wanting things differently?

Since Stella, I thought, picturing my shoebox of secrets.

"What you're doing is good, Destelle," Dad said, as if he picked up on my rogue thoughts. "It'll look great for your scholarships and college applications."

"We've already turned those in," Mom informed him lightly. "And she's going to have the most impressive résumé. The colleges we've picked won't even dream of saying no."

The colleges *we* picked. The words settled bitterly on my chest. It wasn't like I didn't *want* to go to college. I just wanted to experience things first. And it wasn't like I wanted to travel the *world*—though that would've been a whole new level of epic. So many kids attended online colleges. Why wasn't I allowed to?

I'm not a boat rocker, I told myself, even though my talk with Margot trickled in. Sure, I knew how to swim, but I also knew when to avoid shark-infested waters. The idea of rocking the boat with Mom and Dad circling still terrified me beyond belief.

I was just so afraid of disappointing them. Even though I wanted to continue my education online, it wasn't something my parents wanted, and undermining them sounded insane. I couldn't comprehend it. It felt like breaking some sort of law.

Did that make me a good little soldier, perfectly molded into the person they wanted me to be?

All the talk with Harry last night about going on an adventure over summer was just talk. I could see that now. I could hope and dream all I wanted, but I knew who I was deep down. Destelle was not a girl who would go against what her parents said. At least not to that extreme.

But canceling my Thursday plans... I could break the rules once. Just once.

"This is Destelle Brighton," I said in a nasally voice Thursday afternoon, pinching my fingers tighter over my nose. Blood pounded in my ears, and I prayed my anxiety wasn't obvious. *Breathe.* "I'm not going to be able to come tonight and volunteer. I'm not feeling well."

"Oh, sweetie, that's okay," the nurse over the phone said immediately, sympathy sounding overly saccharine. "Probably best to stay away."

My guilt ebbed a bit at that statement, and I peered out the windshield. The outside of Crushed Beanz looked so different in the daylight, the teal awning and cursive letters looking rather commonplace instead of the alluring scrawl it looked like at night.

"Our seniors will miss you, though," the nurse went on. "Do you want me to put you down for another day next week?"

"I'll have to check my schedule and call back, if that's okay." A wave of nausea went through me at the idea of letting down the senior citizens. Were they really going to miss me, or was the nurse trying to play the guilt card? Did she know I was lying? *Breathe.* "H-Have a good night."

"Feel better, Destelle."

I hung up before she did, exhaling strongly. Along with the guilt of canceling, I couldn't shove down the hefty dose of paranoia. What if Mom called and found out I wasn't there? I mean, I doubted she would, but the *what ifs* still ran around in my mind.

After years of being trained to do nothing but obey, breaking from the mold had me nearly peeing my pants.

I got ready hurriedly in the back seat of the SUV, realizing Margot might've been right about needing something other than the same turtleneck. If I'd be hanging out with Harry often, I'd need a broader wardrobe. Which complicated things because it wasn't like I could fit any more clothing in my shoebox.

The door to Crushed Beanz chimed as I pulled it open, the scent of coffee heavy in the air, more so than it was at night. It made sense; people were probably buying coffee by the boatload in the afternoon.

Through the full line, I could see Jonathan moving at a fast pace, grabbing a to-go cup, starting on a coffee for a new customer. To his right, Vincent moved around as well, getting something from the pastry bar.

However, on the other side of the café where Untapped Potential normally performed, a girl stood on the stage, singing to a song that played over the speakers. Singing *terribly*, might I add.

"Well, well, fancy seeing you here," Jonathan called from the counter, not pausing in his movements of filling a coffee for a customer. His dark eyes trained on me for only a moment. "In the daylight, too. Has that happened before?"

I snorted. "Turns out I'm *not* a vampire," I teased, looking to Vincent while unbuttoning my coat. When I was

Destelle, I always wore my pink Claire-Haute peacoat. When I knew I'd be dressed as Stella, I opted for my black Fenta Vitalo trench coat. Stella wouldn't be caught dead in something like the frilly Claire-Haute. "How was the birthday, Vincent? Addy said she was planning something."

Vincent wasn't much of a smiler, but I definitely caught the barest hint of a grin. His lip ring caught in the light. "She had to change things around last minute, but we ended up having a good night."

"What'd she get you? She wouldn't spill the beans."

That grin came full force now, as if he couldn't keep it at bay. "Have you seen those *Evil Killer Baby* horror movies? Terrible excuse for filmmaking?"

I couldn't help but laugh. "Yeah." It was a bottom of the barrel, low budget movie that starred a deformed puppet as the monster. Definitely cringe-worthy.

"Adeline found a doll online of the baby from the movie. Really hideous." He shook his head, but the smile remained. "Looks terrifying on my bed, honestly."

"So, she was all secretive about a stuffed doll?"

He hesitated, glancing at Jonathan chatting with a customer. "Well, there's something else, but we—"

Vincent cut himself off when the door to Crushed Beanz chimed. I glanced over my shoulder, all thoughts of the conversation gone, and found Harry unzipping his brown jacket. His gaze immediately found mine, and I felt my heart skip a beat as if someone hooked it to jumper cables and it sparked.

"There she is," he greeted warmly, his expression immediately lighting up. "Looking beautiful as ever."

I smoothed my hair over my shoulder, the black strands silky, albeit a little staticky. "Funny. I was going to say the same about you."

Mimicking me, Harry ran a hand through his red hair, and I wondered how his felt. Silky? Soft? "I was feeling pretty beautiful today."

Jonathan gaped at me when I turned back, and the customer he'd been serving moving toward the lounge. Jonathan had my order in his hand; he knew it by heart. "I'm totally missing something."

"Our boy here's on a date," Vincent told Jonathan and set down a to-go cup on the counter. Before I could ask whose it was, Harry stepped in and swiped it up. Vincent knew Harry's order like Jonathan knew mine. "Stella, thanks for giving him a pity date."

"This would be pity date number two, actually," Harry cut in, raising the cup to his lips. Just before he took a sip, his eyes cut to mine. "I think I'm growing on her."

So. Freaking. Blue. "Sometimes you need to take one for the team."

Harry pulled a five out of his pocket before I had the chance to offer to pay, tossing it onto the counter. "Come on," he told me, gesturing toward the lounge. "Let's find a seat."

"Enjoy the show," Vincent called after us, tone slightly teasing.

The only open booth was nearest the stage, the booth that Addy and I normally occupied when Untapped Potential played. "You brought me here on karaoke night," I murmured, leaning over the table. The music wasn't as loud as when the band played, but I felt the need to lean in. "You planning on singing?"

"I wasn't," Harry said, setting his cup down. "You?"

"I wasn't." I jerked my chin at his cup. "Vincent knows your order, huh?"

Harry trailed a fingertip along the lid, drawing my attention to his arms. He wore a gray long-sleeve today, one that hugged his muscles perfectly. He wasn't overly buff, but in a way that made me imagine what his arms might've felt like wrapped around me. *Get a grip, Destelle.*

"It's just hot water."

"Hot water? No tea or anything?"

He grinned. "Is that weird?"

"Very." Underneath the table, I found his leg, nudging it with my boot. "But I like it."

Harry leaned back in his seat then, meeting my gaze with an intensity that made my heart stutter a beat. His full attention on me was a little daunting. "So, back to our random line of questioning. What's your favorite color?"

I thought about it. "Yellow, I think. Yours?"

"Definitely blue. What's your best friend's name?"

"Margot," I said, smiling a little. "I love her name."

"Stella's prettier," he pointed out, intrigued. "How did you two meet?"

"Well, we've gone to school together since our freshman year, but we didn't really talk until the start of junior year. Our parents are both a part of this fundraising committee, so we met at an event."

"An event?" Now one of his eyebrows peaked. "Like with fancy ties and everything?"

I faltered then, catching my slip-up too late. That was a Destelle fact, not a Stella one. Crap. I'd never really had this problem before—no one really cared enough to dive into the personal life of Stella too deeply. I'd have to be more careful.

But then again, what did it hurt to merge those lives a bit? I didn't want to lie to Harry about anything.

"And dresses that make it hard to breathe," I finally said with a shake of my head, remembering the last dress Mom made me wear. "Though Margot always wears her suits— that's really all she ever wears. Someone always has an excuse to throw one once a month, and then there's usually a country club dinner thrown in there too. Rich people love getting together and talking about money, did you know?"

His lips twitched, as if he were fighting a smile. "No, I was unaware. Makes sense, though. But even though it's probably more of a gossip fest than anything, that's cool that they're raising money for good causes."

I hadn't thought about it that way before. Each fundraiser that the next person hosted raised a lot of money for local charities or schools. It was easy to look at all the bad things, easy to miss what good could come from it.

"What's *your* best friend's name?" I challenged him, picking up my cup. "Not Vincent."

"I used to have a best friend named Terry."

"*Terry* and *Harry*?" I raised an eyebrow, nearly snorting. "Did you ever get teased at school for that?"

Harry shook his head. "We didn't go to the same school —he would've been a few grades older, anyway."

I waited for him to go on, but he only sipped at his

water, eyeing me like he waited for me to speak. "You mentioned your parents passed away when you were young," I said. "Who did you live with when you were younger?"

"A few relatives," he said, running his finger over the rim of his cup. His voice was low but nonchalant. "At first, with my grandma for a little while. Aunt for a few weeks. Ultimately, though, I got placed with a second cousin, and I lived with him until I didn't have to anymore."

"Oh, wow." I tried so hard to hide my surprise, but couldn't. "Bounced around a lot, huh?"

"Just for the first year. My grandma on my mom's side got custody of me first, but the social workers found out that *I* really took care of *her*." He shrugged. "My aunt on my dad's side got me until they could sort out where to send me next. Jeff volunteered to take me then—he already had two kids, so he didn't mind adding one more." A smile twisted his lips. "Until his wife became pregnant, twice over, then he stressed a little."

As Harry talked, I conjured an image of a little boy, auburn hair and freckles, packing his things up, setting up his bedroom over and over again. After having lost his parents, too. Passed around like a piece of furniture, quickly discarded from one house and onto the next.

"That was heavy," he realized almost worriedly as I stayed quiet. His fingers reached up and brushed along his throat. "I-I'm sorry. It's been a long time since I've had to tell anyone about all that. Probably not great second-date material, huh?"

"No, it's okay," I assured him honestly. "I like getting to

know more about you." To prove that fact, I asked, "So, your cousin's kids—were you close in age with the first two?"

"Not really. I was seven, and the oldest of theirs was three. I was more like the extra set of hands around the house, walked to the store to get groceries, that kind of thing. I got a taste of independence early."

"So, did you move out when you turned eighteen?"

"Uh, not right away. A few months after. When my parents passed, I got the house, and I had a few things to, uh, fix before I could move." I could understand that. I wasn't sure if the house had been empty all that time, but before I had a chance to ask, Harry went on. "So, you ever want to get up onstage and sing a song?" he asked, turning in the booth slightly to look toward the next girl who'd taken over the microphone.

She sang some classic rock song, and at least she could carry a slight tune. "I guess I've never really imagined it before. Not sure I'm wired that way. I'm not really... creative. Or outgoing."

"At all?" he asked, almost intrigued. "No art, no creative writing—nothing like that?"

"Nope. It makes sense, though. My parents are both analytical thinkers. I guess we're a family of nerds." I thought about Nellie spelling things out and Jamie with his love of reading. "I don't really have anything I'm passionate about. Not right now, at least."

"You want to travel," Harry said, taking a sip of his hot water. "That's something to be passionate about."

"Mmm, that's more of a dream," I told him, leaning my

head onto my fist as I gazed at him. "Something that could be achievable, one day. Hopefully. One day that might have to wait until after college." Saying the words aloud felt like admitting defeat, even if a part of me didn't quite believe them in their entirety.

Harry leaned across the table, his forearms resting on the top. "If it's something you want, something that your heart dreams of, don't let anyone talk you out of it."

I wish it were that easy. "You're probably right."

I took a sip of my latte, a good kind of tension filling the air—the kind that almost felt intimate. Harry looked at me so intensely, as if his eyes were diving into the deepest parts of me, trying to see what sort of secrets my soul kept.

"You've got the prettiest eyes, you know that?" he said after a beat.

Words like that made me want to pinch myself. "Look who's talking."

"They're beautiful," he murmured, picking up his cup again.

I studied him for a moment, watching for a crease in his expression, anything. "You say the flirtiest things," I told him. "I wonder how many of them you mean."

We were both leaning over the table, almost breathing the same breath. "With you, I mean every word."

A brief laugh dragged out of me. He was doing it again —the flirtatious words rolling off his tongue with ease. But he hadn't said them with a smirk or with amusement dancing in his eyes. He was serious.

Harry opened his mouth to say something when the song ended and the girl who'd been singing wandered off the stage. Harry glanced over his shoulder, and when he looked back, excitement filled his expression. "Come on."

"Come where?" I asked, not liking that he kept looking at the stage. "Whoa, wait, wait. Remember, I said I'm not sure I'm wired that way. Plus I think it'd be cheating if you went up there."

But Harry slid out of the booth, reaching for my hands, which I'd rested on the table. "It'll be great," he promised, his hands latching onto mine. His touch was soft, his grin infectious.

"I'm not a good singer."

"Then be terrible," he declared. "Sing your absolute *worst*. Pitch your voice as high as you can. I dare you. I'll sing terribly too, if it would make you feel better."

It was obvious then that he wasn't doing this because he wanted to perform—he wanted to sing because he wanted to have fun. He could purposefully sing badly, and he'd still want to do it. He was spontaneous, outgoing, and charismatic.

Everything I wanted to be.

I couldn't decide if I wanted to laugh and climb to my feet or snatch my hand back. "You're a weirdo, you know that?"

"Be a weirdo with me, Stella," he said as he leaned down, words a hum of a whisper sending a shiver down my spine.

He'd invoked a name that wasn't my name. *Stella*. Margot's words echoed in my mind. *What would Stella do?*

Stella would do something like this. She'd be outgoing,

carefree, fun. That thought alone had me rising from the booth.

Harry must've done this before because he walked over to the karaoke machine and scrolled through the songs. "There's one by Outside Inclusion," he told me. "I had Vincent add it to the playlist a few weeks back."

"At least I'll know the words," I muttered, Destelle taking over even though I had the Stella wig on. This anxiety, these nerves? Totally Destelle. She would never do something so wild.

He must've heard the tone of my voice. He looked over his shoulder, uncertainty in his eyes. "Hey, we don't have to—"

"We're doing this," I said, forcefully cutting him off. *Be Stella.* "You can't promise me you'll sing terribly and *not* follow through."

After pressing the button to cue the song, Harry passed me a microphone. "You take the first section and we'll orbit from there, okay?"

"I'll sing Patrick's lines and you'll sing DT's?"

His eyes twinkled. "Sounds fantastic."

Once we were onstage, I knew I should've taken the out when I had the chance. Crushed Beanz wasn't *that* full, granted—maybe like ten people total? But I could see straight to the back where Jonathan and Vincent were making coffees, and the former looked up with a wide grin on his face.

I wanted to give him a certain finger.

But Harry—he'd begun bobbing his head in time with each beat. Ugh, I was going to embarrass myself in front of him. If I actually tried, no way would I even come close to how Untapped Potential sounded. But if I purposefully sang poorly, I was just signing myself up for humiliation.

There was no way to win.

The pounding of my heart nearly made me miss the first verse of the song, but I drew in a breath, hoping my voice wouldn't quiver.

"Is it just me or is everyone so freaking happy?" I sang, replacing the different F-word that came along with the track. Inwardly I winced, but I kept going. *"Smiling, laughing, like the world isn't so depressing. Is it just me who's not so freaking happy, smiling, laughing, not ever really asking what's going on?"*

Was it too late to jump from the stage and cower in my booth? Or to run outside and jump in front of a car? I didn't think so.

When I turned to Harry, I nearly jolted at his expression. His eyes were wide, his lips parted. Jeez, did I sound *that* bad?

He'd been so lost in thought that he came in late to the next verse. And right when I thought he'd be serious—that my serious voice clued him in that he could sing his best too —he proved me wrong. His voice came out wavy, as if he were speaking through a fun-house filter, not a care in the world about proper pitch or tone.

"We-ee nee-eed to all just take a be-eeat, look past what the world wants us to see-ee."

I burst out laughing, right into the microphone. It was loud and probably made everyone wince. I laughed so hard that I didn't hear him finish the verse, didn't hear my cue to continue with my line. *"A-And we're all just"*—I gasped in air—*"looking around with r-rose-colored glasses on."*

Even though we were only twenty seconds into the song, this moment in time quickly became one of my favorite moments ever. If I'd kept a diary, this moment would *so* be in it. Highlighted and underlined. Every hilarious detail included. Because it wasn't just him singing silly and me laughing—we were doing it together.

While he sang, he looked straight into my eyes and wore the goofiest smile. And while I laughed through my lines, I looked right at him, all nerves gone.

With him, I felt comfortable. Again, it felt as if there was no Destelle, no Stella, no separation or division. Only a sense of *rightness*, of comfort, remained. I'd never felt that way with anyone. Not even with Margot. Not at this level. With Harry, I could be anyone I wanted to be—I could be *me*.

And with that thought in mind, I never wanted the feeling to end.

"We should've had someone record that," I said for the third time, my face hurting from smiling so much. The tears from laughing onstage had no doubt smudged my makeup, but I didn't even care. "It could've gone viral. 'Is the indie band lead singer actually terrible?'"

Harry laughed, and it ebbed into his voice. "No, no. 'He should rethink his career; it's never too late to become a mime.'"

I pressed a hand over my mouth to keep an ugly laugh from coming out.

"You have a great voice," he went on, sobering a bit, but the sunny smile still lingered. "Beautiful. You keep surprising me in the best way."

"I was a train wreck," I argued, covering my warm cheeks with my fingers. "A complete train wreck. What time is it? Humiliation o'clock?"

"Ah, close. The clock on the wall by Vincent's head says five minutes after six."

Immediately, my amusement faded, and I let out a soft sigh, dropping my hands to the tabletop. "I should get going soon. My family's expecting me for dinner."

Harry reached out and touched my fingers. "I like hanging out with you, Stella," he said softly, gaze falling to our hands. "I really like hanging out with you."

For the first time, I felt a flutter of unease. Not at his words—my insides did a happy dance at them—but at the fact that I kept Destelle a secret from him. "Listen, I—"

"'I think you're cool, but that karaoke was a total deal-breaker for me'?" he guessed.

"No." I chuckled, curling my fingers around his to pinch them. "I like hanging out with you too."

That caused a boyish smile to flit across his features, one that felt like a stab of happiness to my heart. *So cute.*

"Saturday," he said then, pulling his hands back. "I'm busy in the morning, but we could do something before the gig. Or after—maybe go to Downtown?"

"I'll let you know," I promised while pushing out of the booth, because both options definitely sounded enticing. It depended on what kind of alibi I could come up with. And if it meant spending more time with Harry, I'd definitely scour the earth for an excuse.

"I can't believe you went on three dates with him," Margot told me Friday after school, her voice slightly muffled by the dressing room door of her favorite store, Gilfman Cloth-ier. She'd been in there for a while, but it was understandable—it took time to put on a five-piece suit. "And you *still* haven't kissed him."

"Three dates?" I slouched deeper in my chair. "When was the third?"

Margot opened her door enough to stick out a bony hand, one finger raised. "Dancing at the club." Two fingers. "Dial and Dine." Three fingers. "Embarrassing karaoke. Can't you count?"

"I wouldn't have counted dancing at Downtown." I sighed, glancing around the store. Gilfman stores were typically sparse in terms of decor, and this one wasn't an exception. Every surface was a stark white—the tiled floors, the wallpaper, the white countertops. The only pops of color were the monotone suits hanging on the racks, mostly there for decoration. "It's not like we *chose* to do that together. Or, I mean, *went* there together. Whatever."

This time, Margot stuck her face around the door, eyebrows pulled together. "Why'd you sigh?"

"He said he enjoys hanging out with me, Margot. *Me.* But Stella isn't me—I'm Destelle."

With an eye roll, she disappeared back into the dressing room. "Listen, crazypants. You *are* Stella. Who's the person who puts on the wig? You're literally just Destelle in a wig."

"It's different. It feels like I'm an actress playing a character. Like, I may pretend to be her, but I'm not."

After a second, the dressing room door swung inward and Margot strutted out. The white-and-black-striped suit fit her perfectly in some areas but was too baggy in others.

Her pants were way too long and covered her toes. The vest hugged her stomach in a flattering way, but the caps of the jacket were a smidge too large.

Margot looked at herself in the mirror, angling her body to see how the fabric stretched. "It's so close. Just needs to be a little tighter." And then she turned to me. "You *are* her. You need to get over whatever kind of mind divide you have about it because it's not as crazy as you make it seem."

"It feels weird being with him when he doesn't know." Like my intention was to trick him or something. Maybe he enjoyed hanging out with Stella only because they were so similar. What if he saw Destelle and got freaked out by her Claire-Haute and designer boots?

"How about this?" Margot went back to admiring her suit. "Worry about all this *after* you kiss him. He could be a disgusting kisser, and then you'd be upset you let him in on your secret. So sit on it."

I frowned a little, wanting to point out that Harry being a disgusting kisser would be next to impossible. He even *looked* like the kind of guy who could kiss well. He definitely knew how to move his body when we danced at Downtown.

And now I was thinking of his hands on me, thinking about kissing him, and my face went up in flames.

Margot lifted her hand to signal one of the salesmen, who came over quickly. He was tall and stupidly handsome, his facial hair trimmed and cleanly cut. "Ooh," he murmured in a low voice, immediately catching the problem. "Oh, the shoulder pads are a bit too big, aren't they?

We typically hem the pants once they're on, as you know, so that's not a major concern." He withdrew a measuring tape from his interior pocket, but as he did so, he spotted me. "Oh, dear, do you need water? Your face is quite red."

"She's having an existential crisis," Margot said flippantly. "Ignore her."

Ha.

From deep within my purse, my phone chimed. I pulled it out and then froze when I saw the caller ID.

Be cool, I told myself fiercely, forcing the embarrassment down. *Be Stella.*

"Hey," I greeted once I pressed the cell to my ear, forcing my voice to be calm. "I was just thinking about you."

I said be Stella! That was so not Stella.

"What a coincidence," Harry's soft voice murmured in response. "Me too. Or, I mean—well, *I* was thinking about *you.*" He paused. "That was so smooth."

"*Totally.*" I bit down on my lower lip, any nervousness about talking to him totally disappearing. Margot admired her cuffs happily while the guy continued to measure her one last time. "What are you up to?"

"Funny thing, I was going to ask *you* the same question. I know we planned on maybe doing something tomorrow, but Addy and Vincent are going to get ice cream over in Greenville before the show tonight. Do you want to tag along? You'd save me from being the horribly awkward third wheel."

He was inviting me out with his friends. Was this technically a double date? Margot caught my gaze in the mirror, so I forced my expression to appear neutral, to *not* let my stupidly ecstatic grin show. "Ice cream in February?"

"Apparently Vincent is craving something called blue goo. Sounds gross if you ask me." He hesitated, but ultimately ended up adding, "But I'd love to see you. Do you want to meet at the café or over in Greenville?"

Greenville was less than fifteen minutes away, and I needed to put Stella on. No way on earth would I show up in my Eastview Academy uniform.

It was a stroke of luck, actually. After rushing out of Crushed Beanz yesterday to get home in time for dinner, I had to leave my Stella bag in the car. It'd make for an easy change. "I can be at the ice cream parlor in twenty, if that works."

"Sounds great. Drive safe, okay?"

I swear, each time he said that, my heart melted a little.

"So, what's happening in twenty minutes?" Margot asked as I collected my things, sliding my cell back into my purse. "Outing number four?"

"Outing number four," I confirmed happily, tucking my jacket over my arms. We'd driven to the outlet mall in our own cars, so I wasn't leaving Margot stranded, but I felt a little bad about leaving her alone. "Can we do a rain check on our shopping trip?"

She lifted her shoulder. "Fine, fine. Hang out with Harry Hotpants. But don't stress about Stella and Destelle, okay?"

I nodded, but I wasn't sure I took it to heart. "I'll text you later."

And as I walked across the store, passing a few high-end customers and well-tailored workers, Margot shouted after me, "And if you're going to ignore me and stress about it all anyway, make sure you kiss him!"

eleven

*L*ord have mercy, it was so flipping hard to change quickly in the back of a car. I'd first started becoming Stella only once or twice a week, but recently, these quick-changes were much more frequent. My body was *so* not flexible enough for this.

I'd have to come up with excuses for a pulled muscle.

"Stella!"

Harry called my name as soon as I stepped out of the car in the parking lot of Freezing Fred's Ice Cream Parlor, and he stood in the parlor's doorway. His hair blew crazily in the wind, one hand quickly trying to tamp it down.

I couldn't help but grin. "Hey. Where are Addy and Vincent?"

"Inside, probably already ordering their goo grossness."

As soon as I got close enough, Harry swiped up my hand, taking it and twirling me around much like he had that night at Downtown. The wig lifted off the back of my neck, but the clips held.

"What are you going to get?" I asked him, leaning into his chest. His very firm chest. "I'm assuming not blue goo?"

"Not sure. Guess it'll be a—"

"Are you guys coming inside or what?"

Uh, I hadn't been expecting that voice. When I looked over Harry's shoulder, my mood completely shifted from excitement to apprehension.

Natasha stood in the doorway with one hand on her hip, looking at the two of us with an expectant expression. Her maroon lips were twisted, but I couldn't figure out if it was a smile or a grimace. Her eyes were squinting against the sun, so it almost looked like she was glaring at us.

Harry dropped my hand, the distance and lack of warmth immediate. "Yeah, we're coming, Tash."

Yeah, see, I still didn't love hearing him say that. Mostly because when I looked at her, I could still remember how she'd stepped into his personal bubble a few gigs ago, her hand on his arm, fingers in his belt loops.

Harry hadn't mentioned her tagging along.

Harry let me go first, walking to Natasha while unbuttoning my coat. "We haven't met. I'm Stella."

"Natasha," she returned as I stepped into the parlor, expression not changing. "I recognize you from the gigs. Addy's friend, yeah?"

Harry stepped behind me, and I waited for him to say something—maybe mention that *he'd* been the one to invite me—but he didn't. "Yeah."

Freezing Fred's was a simple, retro ice cream parlor that gave off a warm and homey feeling. Addy and Vincent, as predicted, sat at a booth already with their ice creams. Vincent had a cup full of something suspiciously blue, and Addy had a small ice cream cone in her hand.

Once Addy saw me, she grinned. "Stella! Nice to see you someplace other than the café."

"Feels weird, huh?" I glanced toward Vincent, peering at his cup. "That the goo gunk?"

"It's *not* gunk," he said, mock-offended. He swiped up a spoonful of ice cream and showed it to me. "It's blue raspberry goodness."

It looked kind of good, with ripples of blue through the soft-serve vanilla. "Maybe I'll try it."

"Don't convert her to the dark side," Harry told him, and laid his hand on the small of my back, gently steering me toward the counter.

Natasha already stood in line, peering at the display of hard-dipped ice cream. "I'll have two scoops of birthday cake ice cream, please," she told the girl behind the counter, and added, "He'll have one scoop of chocolate and one scoop of cookie dough in the same cup."

"I can't believe you still remember that," Harry said with a chuckle.

"You order the same thing every time," Natasha returned with a smile. "It's not that hard to remember."

I kept a polite expression on my face, much like the one I wore at the country club events. Harry invited me because he didn't want to be the third wheel, but man, *I* started feeling like one.

His hand still lingered at the small of my back, gentle

against the fabric of my sweater. "What can I get you, Stella?"

"I think I need to try the blue goo," I said, but I curled my hands into fists underneath the fabric of my coat, feeling out of place. "In a cup."

The girl behind the counter went to work at making our orders, and she passed Natasha's off first. She licked the birthday cake ice cream while looking at Harry. "This was such a good idea."

He smiled at her as she walked off toward the booth, and as soon as she passed, his smile fell away. "So, I know what you're probably thinking," Harry said suddenly, voice cautious. "Natasha overheard us talking about ice cream and wanted to come."

"It's totally okay," I said as nonchalantly as I could, trying to will my words into reality. "The more the merrier."

"Trust me, I wish it was just us."

"And Addy and Vincent," I added.

But Harry's gaze softened as his shoulder brushed mine. "Just us."

A thread of pleasant heat unfurled in my stomach, fanning out everywhere. In all honesty, I wanted that too. I wanted to talk with him and laugh with him, to hear more about his past and aspirations. Harry was someone I could be comfortable around, and I wanted more.

Also, his shoulder brushing mine? I wanted more of that, too.

"Blue goo in a cup," the girl said as she sat it on the counter, then went to work on Harry's order. She'd cut into the moment effectively, but the electricity still clung to the air.

Addy and Vincent had picked out a U-shaped booth so we'd all fit. Natasha slid in first beside Vincent, and Harry sat down next to her, leaving me to climb in at the end. I fluffed my coat over my lap, meeting Addy's gaze. "So, what do you think?" she asked, jutting her chin at my cup.

I loaded my plastic spoon with ice cream and took a bite. Vincent looked at me expectantly, waiting for my decision. It was all right—the sugary goodness of the vanilla tasted delicious, but the blue was a little sour. "Not as gross as Harry said," I finally decided, mixing my spoon around until the blue blended in.

"Told you," Vincent said to his friend, eyes dancing as he popped another spoonful into his mouth. "You should try it sometime, Harry. You might like it."

"You can try a bite of mine," I said, offering the cup out to Harry, but when I looked over, I locked eyes with Natasha.

Sitting with Harry's ex was awkward, and I wished I knew the circumstances of their breakup because when she looked at me like that—her expression so hard—it felt as if I overstepped boundaries.

Harry, though, didn't notice the tension. Instead, he picked my spoon up out of the cup, scooping the tiniest bite possible. Without preamble, he stuck the spoon in his mouth, then slid it out past his lips.

His extremely soft-looking lips. Touching the spoon that'd been in my mouth seconds ago.

Harry shuddered, making a face. "Ew, what *is* that?"

"Blue raspberry," Vincent answered.

"Why would you like something so sour?" He stuck the spoon back into the ice cream and passed it back to me, fingertips brushing mine as he did so. "I'll stick with my chocolate."

From where I sat, I had a better view of Harry's tattoo from the side, the fingers more visible. The way his hair curled over his ear, the way his tattoo kissed his throat. He was so unique, and I *liked* it. I liked him.

Harry looked over at me then, the moment between us simmering.

"So, Stella," Natasha cut in, drawing my attention to her. "You've been coming to the gigs for a while, right? Are you a fan?"

I had to clear my throat. "Yeah, I am. Your music is really good."

For the first time, she smiled a little, and it looked genuine. "Thanks. It's been a long time coming—at least for Harry and me. Right, Harry?"

Harry stuffed another spoonful of his ice cream into his mouth, saving him from answering.

"He's always been super musical," Natasha told the table, gaze bouncing around to everyone before landing back at him. "Even in high school, you were into music. I'm glad *that* didn't fade over the past year."

"You and Harry made music on your own before Vincent joined, right?" Addy asked, leaning back against her seat. Vincent's arm draped over it, and she seemed to press closer to him unconsciously. "Vincent mentioned you were looking for a drummer when he joined."

"Yeah, we played songs before that," Harry replied, drumming his fingers quickly on the tabletop. "Nothing serious. Never had a place to perform before Crushed Beanz."

Natasha chuckled at that, laying her hand on his arm. "Plus, we hadn't really been doing anything for long before Vincent. Harry didn't want to sing again for months after he—"

"Moved out," Harry finished for her quickly, staring down at his cup. "Moving out and getting on my feet on my own was...difficult."

A hush fell over the table after that, leaving us all to eat our ice cream in the quiet. The hum of the ice cream machine was loud, and I watched as the girl leaned against the counter and scrolled through her phone.

I tried to imagine how different this would've been if Natasha hadn't come, guilt immediately trailing after the thought. Sure, the dynamic would've been different, but she hadn't said anything unfriendly toward me, at least not yet.

I needed to just cross this awkward bridge between us. "Natasha, so you went to school with Harry?" I asked, trying to channel my inner conversationalist. Destelle was good at small talk. I could do this.

"Since grade school." She leaned across the table toward me, acting as if Harry wasn't between us. "I have yearbook pictures that would make you about die of laughter."

"She doesn't," Harry objected immediately. "My yearbook pictures were magnificent."

Natasha raised an eyebrow. "Even in the seventh grade?"

Harry's eyes widened a bit, as if he could picture what she meant. "She doesn't have pictures. Nope, no pictures. Natasha, your ice cream's melting."

She rolled her dark eyes, still looking at me. "Imagine, like, strawberry red hair and tons of freckles. Your hair really darkened over the years, didn't it, Harry?"

He tore a hand through his auburn hair, ears pink. "Thank God for that."

"I, for one, definitely need to see awkward Harry pictures," Vincent declared to the group, smirking at his friend. "We should post them to the social media page."

Addy and I agreed at the same time, causing us to laugh. Natasha joined in, licking her ice cream cone.

There. Bridging the gap. Easier than I thought it'd be. I didn't want to be at odds with her; they were still so prominent in each other's lives. I didn't want to wipe that away. Besides, she seemed really cool—I wanted us to be friends.

Suddenly, a sharp chirp filled the table, and everyone looked up, trying to figure out where the sound came from. But I knew the ring in an instant: It was the tone I set for when parents called me.

I hurried to set my ice cream on the table, slipping from the seat. "I'll be right back," I told them, not meeting a single gaze as I shrugged my coat on and hurried outside. My phone still rang in my jacket pocket, and I fished it out with a flutter of nerves, Stella dissipating into Destelle in an instant. "Hello?"

"Where are you?" Mom demanded at once, but she

didn't sound angry. That was good. "You said you were going out shopping with Margot after school, but you should be back by now."

"We stopped to get ice cream," I told her, pulling my hair out of my face. One clasp pulled tightly against my hairline—too tight. I reached up and unclasped it, then fit it back into place. "I should be home soon."

Mom's sigh came through loudly. "I made an exception this time, Destelle, but you know how I feel about you going out of the house without finishing your homework."

"I only had one worksheet to fill out for English," I told her, curling my fingers into fists. "Besides, it's a Friday. I'll be home soon."

Mom was quiet for a moment. "I want you home in a half hour."

I gritted my teeth. It would take twenty minutes to drive from here back to my house, and I still needed to find a place to park and change out of Stella. It felt like I'd just gotten there and I already had to leave. But there was no choice here, only an order. "Yes, Mom."

She ended the call without a formal goodbye, but I still kept my cell pressed to my ear, staring out into the parking lot. Three cars lingered in the lot—mine, Harry's, and presumably the workers'. They all rode here together. Who sat in the passenger's seat? Vincent or Natasha?

"Everything okay?"

I turned to find Harry standing behind me, hands in his jeans pockets. He didn't have his coat on, auburn hair blowing in the wind. I tried to picture what my expression must've looked like, but the coldness made my cheeks feel numb. "I have to head out."

He ducked his head lower, peering straight into my eyes. "Is everything okay?"

"That was my mom." I sighed, finally slipping my cell back into my coat. "She wants me home, and I come when she calls."

I didn't want to unload on him—definitely didn't want to whine about my parents to a boy who didn't have any—but I also didn't want to lie to him, to put on a fake smile. Not for him.

Harry clasped my hand between both of his, rubbing his skin over mine, using friction to warm it up. "I'm glad I got to see you, though."

"I won't be able to make it tonight," I told him, studying the brickwork of the parlor over his shoulder. Mom wasn't going to let me back out of the house after calling me home. "Hopefully I can come tomorrow."

"Hey, it's okay." He held my gaze, as if trying to convey something without speaking it. "Really. I know we joke about the 'more important' stuff, but definitely do what you need to."

As I stared into his eyes, the sudden reality of how different we were struck me. We were in such different phases of life. He lived on his own, graduated from high school, where I still lived under the rule of my parents. I still had a curfew and homework and a mother who clocked how much time I spent out of the house. So, so different.

But our differences didn't make me like him any less. And of course it wasn't just because he was attractive, even though that helped. Harry was attentive and sweet, even down to coming out here to check on me. He was funny, goofy, flirty—I'd never met another person like him. Unique.

In a world full of gold cufflinks and diamond bracelets, he was a breath of fresh air.

Harry still held on to my hands, and when I looked closer at him, I noticed the goosebumps on his arms, dotting his skin.

"I should get going," I murmured, even though I wanted to do the very opposite. I wanted to stay with them and chat the day away. "Thank you for inviting me, even though I couldn't stay. I...I had a nice time."

And that was true, even though I'd been a little intimidated by Natasha at first.

"I'm happy I could see you. Even though you coerced me into trying that goo nastiness."

I watched him for a moment, debating on following through with what I wanted to do. Ultimately, I did.

I pulled my hands from his and wrapped them around his waist, settling into a goodbye hug. His heartbeat thumped unevenly in his chest, right underneath my ear. For a moment, we just held each other. It felt so *good* to be held like this, a simple hug goodbye feeling like so much more. I *wanted* it to be so much more.

When I pulled back, our faces were so, so close. Maybe it was what Margot had said at Gilfman, but suddenly I could only think about what it'd be like to kiss him.

His bottom lip wasn't as full as his top, but both were perfectly rosy. They matched his cheek color, redness shading them from either the cold or something else. These were the lips that brushed the microphone when he sang. The lips that stretched into every smile that made my stomach flutter. The lips that were so, so close to mine.

Of course Margot had to talk about kissing earlier. I couldn't think about anything else.

Wait, my brain ordered frantically, and more thoughts rushed in.

Even though Margot told me to, I couldn't kiss him without telling him the truth. What if he freaked out about Destelle and Stella? What if he thought it was weird and not worth the trouble and never wanted to see me again? Kissing him and then having him decide I'm not worth it would be...horrible.

Without warning, I jerked back from him so severely that my shoes tripped over an uneven patch of sidewalk, nearly sending me stumbling.

"I like you," he all but blurted out, a slight chuckle coming after that. His hand rose to touch his throat then, following the outline of his tattoo. "I think you're fun and sweet and beautiful, and I don't want to screw anything up."

Okay, my breath? Totally gone now. Totally evaporated from my lungs. *Beautiful*, he'd said, straightforward and sure. *Fun*.

Maybe kissing him was worth the risk.

But following the flood of happiness came a sweep of sadness. He wasn't calling me fun and beautiful. He was saying *Stella* was.

"Harry, I..." What would I say? *Harry, I'm actually two*

different people. Or, according to Margot, I'm one person who sometimes dresses in black. And wears a wig. It sounds like I'm crazy, but I swear I'm not. I needed to come out and tell him about it, but I couldn't. The idea terrified me almost as much as the thought of telling Mom and Dad.

Something like understanding flashed across Harry's eyes then, soft and genuine, but I couldn't figure out why. Had he been able to guess? But then he spoke, words gentle. "Stella, it's okay. Really. If you don't feel the same—"

"Your ice cream is melting." Natasha hopped out onto the sidewalk with both my and Harry's ice cream cups in her hands, unknowingly interrupting a moment. When she noted our serious expressions, she froze. "All good?"

"All's good," I said quickly, taking my cup from her grip. My face had to be a wave of red—it definitely felt like it. "I have to go. Can you tell Addy and Vincent goodbye for me?"

Natasha nodded slowly, trying to read my expression. "Yeah, sure."

Harry looked at me as if he wanted to say more, but ultimately decided against it. "Drive safe."

And it was like a door closing, effectively ending the conversation.

Margot was wrong. I couldn't carry on dating Harry without telling him the truth. Maybe he wouldn't care less about Destelle and Stella and all that, but all the what ifs made me hesitate. And besides, even if I told him everything, what would that change? He'd said before that he hadn't been looking to date.

What if he found out the truth and thought I was too much effort?

I hurried toward my car, mind racing. I needed to come clean about the whole dual personality thing before we went any further.

And before he moved on.

twelve

"I know weekends are typically free of volunteering," Mom began Saturday morning while I ate, dragging my spoon through my oatmeal. I'd added blueberries and granola on top, and I watched as it all blended together. Nellie, who sat at the breakfast table across from me, listened quietly while she ate her pancakes. Jamie hadn't come down from his room yet. "But you need to do something tonight."

My first instinct was to straighten my shoulders and be quick to obey. Like second nature, I wanted to jump and please her. So, it took an internal fight to not raise my eyes, to focus on the oats in front of me. She said *tonight*, which meant no Crushed Beanz. That alone irritated everything in me. "Like what?"

"Mrs. Conan needs someone to accompany Grace to an event tonight," Mom explained. "She mentioned it yesterday. I—well, you know why I jumped to volunteer you."

I scooped a blueberry onto my spoon, and before I put it in my mouth, I said, "Because she's your boss?"

"Because you're responsible," she corrected. "You have a level head on your shoulders. That attitude, though—"

"It wasn't attitude." My words were obviously contradictory of the situation, however. I cut her off. I obviously asked for death.

Nellie seemed to think the same thing, her fork frozen on a chunk of pancake.

"What kind of event?" I asked, deciding to plow past the moment. I took another bite of oatmeal, popping a blueberry. "Do I have to wear a dress?"

"It's some concert over in Hallow she wants to go to. So, no, probably not a dress."

My spoon clattered in against my bowl. Whoa, wait. Wait, wait, wait. A concert. In Hallow.

No way.

"It's at a coffee shop. Crushed Beanz, Mrs. Conan said. It starts at eight, so pick Grace up around seven-thirty."

I stared at Mom for a long moment, just breathing. My thoughts flew past me too rapidly for me to think anything through. "Coffee shop," I echoed. "Crushed Beanz."

"Can I go?" Nellie piped up for the first time in the entire conversation. "I've never been to a concert before."

"Maybe when you're older," Mom returned, voice firm. It kept Nellie from begging for an exception. Instead, she merely returned to cutting her pancake.

It slowly sunk in. I had to take Grace to Crushed Beanz tonight. I would listen to Untapped Potential tonight, but as *Destelle*. Curly-haired, Claire-Haute, heeled-boot-wearing Destelle.

"You know, I'm not feeling that great, Mom. Maybe I—"

"Don't do that," she ordered, her words like a slap on the wrist. "Don't lie. I've raised you better than that."

She had, of course. I should've thought through my response before blurting it out, should've waited until later in the evening to be "sick." Thinking had become difficult in my frazzled brain, and I just blurted the first thing that came to mind.

I abruptly swiped up my bowl, carrying it to the sink. "Seven-thirty," I told Mom, clearing my throat to erase the tension in my voice. "All right."

"You'll have a nice time, I'm sure," Mom said, opening the fridge and retrieving a jug of orange juice. "Maybe they'll end up being your next favorite band."

I made a little noise in acknowledgment, but it almost sounded like a whimper of fear.

I took the stairs two steps at a time, pulse pounding. At breakfast, Mom had already passed my phone back for the morning, but I needed to be in the privacy of my bedroom and call Margot. She would have advice for me. She'd talk me off my ledge.

When I got to my room, I found Jamie on the floor in front of my bed, little hands reaching underneath. "Hey!" My heart jumped in my throat at the thought of the shoebox underneath the bed, my panic ratcheting higher. "What do you think you're doing?"

Jamie jerked his hands back as if he'd been burned and turned to me, surprised. I couldn't tell if it was because I shouted or because he saw the shoebox.

"My bouncy ball rolled under your bed," he said quickly, holding a neon ball in his hand. "I was getting it."

"Ask next time, okay?" I told him, practically shoving him out of my bedroom.

Jamie stumbled over the threshold, and I shut the door in his face. My hands shook as I slumped against the wood, hands shaking. I didn't hear Jamie's footsteps retreat, but I heard Dad's voice faintly through the door, asking if everything was okay.

Lunging forward, I fell to my knees in front of my bed and reached underneath, swiping my palms along the dusty space. My fingertips brushed the box, pushed so far back that Jamie's little arms wouldn't have reached. Or at least I didn't think they would. For good measure, I pulled the box out and took off the lid, analyzing the contents.

The online college brochures were in disarray, still on top. I sifted further, finding my black turtleneck and leggings next, as well as a rolled up black T-shirt. The Stella silk bag sat underneath that, and after a quick check, I found it still in there. Just the way I'd left it. Jamie hadn't touched any of this.

My eyes roamed over the box one more time, fingertips brushing along the brochures, the several printouts I had for Ashton. The different programs were listed on the front, an enticing thought as my eyes scanned them for the millionth time.

I placed the lid back on my box of dreams and what ifs and shoved it as far back as I could, taking one long reset breath. The residual feeling of dull dread, though, didn't really subside.

. . .

I never thought I'd be walking into Crushed Beanz as Destelle, but I stared up at the teal awning in my pink peacoat and heeled boots, feeling five kinds of freaked out.

"I'm so excited!" Grace squealed from beside me, all but bouncing across the street as we crossed. "Oh, my gosh, Destelle, they're so good. A friend played me their music last week, and I just loved it. Ooh, do you remember that server from Le Petit Bateau? The hot one with the tattoo? That's the lead singer! Small world, huh?"

I was too overwhelmed to muster a good fake smile. "Small world."

Thankfully, Grace didn't know that arriving early was imperative if she wanted to get a seat in a booth near the stage, which meant we were destined to stand in the back. Out of the direct line of Harry. Small victories. And even through the glass, I could see they stood onstage, could see Harry pulling his guitar strap over his shoulder. Perfect.

I could hear Harry's voice before we pulled open the door. "We recently asked you all what your favorite song of ours was, and a lot of you said you loved our new one, 'Dance Floor.' We thought we'd open with that tonight."

Jonathan looked up when we walked in, offering us a smile. "Hey, welcome to—" He faltered then, confusion swamping his expression. "Crushed Beanz."

Jonathan had never seen me as Destelle before, but he *knew* my secret, so I wondered if that had any sway over his recognition of me. Then again, Addy hadn't known my secret and she still had seen the similarities. It made me that much more worried about Harry spotting me.

"Thank you!" Grace said to Jonathan with a wide smile, unbuttoning her coat. "I can't believe there aren't more people than this. Destelle, you're going to *love* them."

Jonathan's face cleared, confusion wiped away. *Destelle.*

Really, I thought to Grace. *Because it feels like I'm going to throw up.* "I can't wait." The lack of enthusiasm was astounding.

Grace didn't seem to notice it. "Can you hang on to my coat for me?" she asked, stuffing it into my arms without waiting for an answer. She wore a pretty gray sweater, one that made her blonde hair appear more vibrant. "I'm going to see if I can get closer." And then she hurried off, squeezing into the tight spaces between the crowd, her slight frame disappearing.

"Yeah, *Destelle*," Jonathan mused once I walked closer. "You're going to love them."

I laid her jacket down on the countertop, and my Claire-Haute was quick to follow. The band began playing their song, the one Harry claimed he wrote about me. It made my insides feel even more unsettled. Two worlds merging.

"I'm freaking out," I whispered to Jonathan, plopping down on one of the barstools and covering my face with my hands. "What if Harry recognizes me? You did. Within, like, point-five seconds."

"That's because I was waiting for *Stella* to walk in, so I was already thinking of your face. It's not like you to miss two nights in a row." Jonathan picked a coffee mug from the rack, moving toward the espresso machine, working on my unspoken order. "I'll be honest, though, it *is* kind of funny how different you look. Almost like Stella is your sister rather than your alter ego."

I nodded my head slow. That was a good thing. Addy had thought the same thing when she asked me about it, back when she'd seen *Destelle* at the gas station. She told me I had a doppelgänger.

I looked Jonathan in the eye. "Harry almost kissed me yesterday."

Jonathan set down the mug, his jaw all but dropping. "What do you mean, *almost?*"

"I pulled away."

The shock morphed into impatience. "Details, girl. Now."

He leaned in close while I told him about yesterday, down to Natasha showing up. I told him about the hug and how it almost led to a kiss, but I couldn't. How could I kiss Harry without being honest? The longer I drew out the secret, the harder it would be to come clean.

"I don't really understand," Jonathan said after a moment, a crease forming between his eyebrows. "Help me understand: Why is Stella such a big secret? Why are you nervous to tell him?"

Gosh, the million-dollar question. "It started out as an escape from my normal life," I told him, glancing around as if someone were going to overhear me. "To be someone else. What if...what if he doesn't get that? What if he thinks I'm fake for doing that? A coward?"

"A coward?" he repeated, unconvinced.

"People can judge Stella and it's no big deal. But I don't think I could take it if they judged *me*." Harry's voice cut between my words then, and Vincent's drumbeats accented it perfectly, building the tension to the notes. A shiver worked its way over my skin, slipping down my spine. "If *Harry* judged me."

"If he judges you, screw him," Jonathan said simply, and then frowned. "Figuratively."

I almost smiled. "And then there's the fact that we are so different. Harry and Stella are similar, but Harry and Destelle are...different."

Without warning, Jonathan pinched my arm, making me jump. "You are Stella."

"People keep saying that, but I'm *not*."

"You are," he insisted, leaning his forearms onto the counter. "It's not like you're conjuring an entirely different personality. How Stella acts, how she responds, that's all coming from you."

I rubbed my arm ruefully, turning to stare toward the stage. I only caught glimpses of their heads as the crowd shifted and danced. "So, you're saying I should tell him."

"I'm saying that 'different worlds' thing is bullcrap, and I think you know that. If you like him, be with him." Jonathan let out a sigh. "I'm living vicariously through you and Vindy, all right? My love life is tragic."

I couldn't help but snort. "What is *Vindy*?"

"Vincent and Addy," he said in an obvious tone, rolling his eyes. "I tried coming up with a cute name for you and

Harry, but your names are hard. You could be...Harella—
ooh, no, that one's really bad."

"Could be Stellarry."

Jonathan looked at me like I was crazy. "That's *such* a
mouthful."

The crowd shifted enough that I had a straight shot to
Natasha strumming her guitar. "She came with us
yesterday when we got ice cream. Do you think that's
weird?"

Then again, they *were* in a band together. It might've
been weird if he left her out.

"Stella." Jonathan spoke firmly enough that it had me
turning back around. I almost corrected him—that when I
looked like this, I *wasn't* Stella—but he would've tried to
prove his point again. "If he liked her, he'd be with her. But
he likes *you*. I think you should tell him," he said, and
leaned back when a customer stepped up to examine the
menu, hurrying to add, "and let the chips fall where they
may."

With all the risks involved in that, I quickly began
shaking my head. Destelle Brighton wasn't a risk-taker. The
mere idea made me feel panicked, as if I'd been dropped
into the middle of the ocean without a life vest.

You know how to swim, Margot's voice whispered in
my mind, but I didn't want to swim. I wanted to close my
eyes and pretend it wasn't happening.

Untapped Potential's music was as good as ever tonight,
but I couldn't fully dive into the beat and atmosphere. I was
too on edge. Every time the crowd shifted, giving me a

glimpse of the stage, I turned so my back was to it. No way was I going to risk Harry spotting me.

"Capture my attention
Hold it with a gun
Just a game, risk it all
Aren't we having fun?"

Once the gig ended, Untapped Potential spent a lot of time talking with their fans. Grace, who refused to leave without getting an autograph from each member, still lingered in the thick of the crowd. Some listeners had dispersed, but a lot remained, wanting to chat with the band as long as possible.

It irked Jonathan. "We're technically closed right now," he grumbled. "We can't start cleaning if they stick around."

"Maybe they'll have to host a meet and greet specifically for talking to fans," I suggested, watching as one group of people headed out into the night. "Looks like the crowd is thinning."

Thinning enough that I spotted Addy at her booth, scribbling in her bullet journal. Her blonde hair toppled over her shoulder like a waterfall, and the way she held her head up with her fist hinted she was getting tired.

If I were Stella, I would've gone over there and talked to her about tonight's set. Would've told her how great Vincent sounded. Would've apologized for leaving so suddenly last night. Instead, I swept my curly hair over my shoulder, bunching my coat tightly in my fists.

Come on, Grace, I thought at her as two more people disbanded from the group. I wanted to go before the crowd thinned any further.

As if hearing my thoughts, Grace parted from the group then, clutching her cell phone reverently. "They signed it," she murmured, staring down as if she were holding a gold bar. "They all signed my phone case. I'm never getting a new one."

"That's fantastic," I said as eagerly as I could, offering her coat out to her while hopping off the barstool. "We should get going before it gets any later."

Grace looked up at me excitedly. "They play here every weekend, isn't that amazing? We should make this a weekly thing!"

Behind me, Jonathan started coughing loudly, like he'd choked on a laugh.

"I don't know, Grace," I said, shoving my arms through my jacket as another group of people headed out.

The gap their absence created offered a glimpse of the band. They stood in a little group, mingling with the fans who'd stayed behind. Vincent and Natasha were talking to a group of girls, and behind them stood Harry, his head bent down over his own cell phone. His thumbs moved quickly, and a stab of curiosity had me wondering who he could've been texting.

"Okay, I'm ready," Grace said with a sigh, buttoning her coat. "Oh, this was such a fantastic night. My friends are going to be so jealous."

I fished my car keys out from my pocket, placing a hand

on Grace's back to steer her toward the door, just in case she decided to go back and keep talking.

Right before we got outside, though, my cell phone dinged, loudly. Loud enough that it seemed to echo in my ears. I pulled it out of my pocket, reading the text before I registered who the sender was.

Crushed Beanz missed you tonight. :)

For several reasons, a flutter spread through my body.

I looked up, my gaze magnetized back to where Harry once stood, thumbs typing on his cell. Except now those thumbs were still, and his gaze was no longer trained on his phone.

No, his eyes had risen directly to me, on the cell in my hand. A small crease indented between his eyebrows, but before he could take a step forward, I shoved Grace out of Crushed Beanz, practically fleeing into the night.

*T*n hindsight, running away probably wasn't the smartest move, but confronting Harry with Grace there was not an option.

As soon as we got out to the car, though, I shot back a quick text. **I missed Crushed Beanz right back.**

I waited all night, but Harry didn't text again, so no questions about my look-alike at Crushed Beanz.

A part of me wondered if that was my moment to come clean and I just missed my window.

"I can't believe we're already into the last week of February," Margot muttered after she put her car into park, the auto-locks popping. She'd parked in the closest spot possible to the door. "Which means the next stupid country club event is coming up. Who do you think will host it this time? My money's on Mr. Harvey."

I reached for the door handle but didn't tug it open yet, looking out at the church building looming before us. On Sunday, Mom had come home from church telling me about the volunteer opportunity for Monday after school.

Apparently, Pastor Liam decided to do some spring cleaning a bit early this year and needed helpers. Mom thought we needed the good karma, and apparently so did Margot's mom.

They didn't even let us come home and change out of our school uniform first. The tights and pleated skirts were *so* not suited for cleaning.

"On the bright side," I said, "we only have so many of these left before we go off to college."

"Speaking of..." Margot turned toward me. "You decide on where you're going?"

Everything in me tensed. I've never really talked to Margot about my college plans, not really in-depth. For the longest time, an online college was a wish I didn't want to speak aloud in fear of it going up in smoke. But talking about it with Harry felt different—like it might actually be a possibility.

Still, I didn't know how to answer. "Acceptance letters don't go out until *at least* the end of March."

"Yeah, but do you have a place you're hoping on?"

I thought of all the colleges Mom had me apply to, all the big names, ones that would impress her friends. I thought of all the college brochures and printouts underneath my bed. At this point, I should've thrown them out. "Not really."

Margot drummed her thin fingers along the leather of the steering wheel. "Our parents put so much pressure on college, but it seems silly, doesn't it? There's not one road to happiness."

"What, you don't want to major in political science like

your parents?" I asked teasingly, to which she rolled her eyes. "Could be a mayor of your own town."

"Just like *you* desperately want to be a lawyer, right?"

I almost smiled. "At least you know what you want to do," I said, smoothing my palms over my tights. "You know you're going to a fashion institute. With designs like yours, you'll get in anywhere you want. I don't know what I want to do."

Margot was quiet for a moment, clearly struggling to figure out what to say. So, instead, she tried to lighten the mood. "I know what you want to do." Margot turned back to look out the windshield, gesturing at the building. "Clean a stuffy old church."

"At least it'll go by quicker since we're together," I said, finally popping my car door open. "Besides, there's a few other cars in the lot. I'm sure he's got other people here."

"He'd better," she grumbled, but climbed out of the car.

When we got inside, I could immediately hear Pastor Liam's voice, the booming quality almost startling. "The vacuum is in the storage closet, Joan. Peter, can you show her?"

Margot let out a sigh before we turned the corner into the basement, as if she were getting it out now before she faced the pastor.

He saw us immediately, looking up from the clipboard he held in one hand. "Ladies! Oh, I'm so glad you're here. Thank you so much for volunteering to help."

"*We* didn't necessarily volunteer," Margot muttered.

I elbowed her as discreetly as possible. "We're happy to help, Pastor Liam. Where do you need us?"

"Destelle, if you could help with the painting, and then Margot, if you could go upstairs and wipe the sanctuary windows, that'd be amazing."

Margot relaxed beside me, no doubt appreciating the fact that she got stuck with the lesser of two evils. "Sounds great to me."

Pastor Liam clapped his hands once, creating a loud echo in the space. "Perfect. Destelle, the room is down at the end of the hall to the left. There should be a volunteer in there, so the paint should all be opened. I'll grab you a smock or something you can put over your clothes. Margot, I'll go find some window cleaner."

"Not fair," I told her once he was out of earshot, heading down the hall. "Why can't I wipe things down?"

"You'll be too busy getting paint in your hair," she said, almost sounding cheerful. "Hey, hopefully the room is small. If it's you and someone else working on it, it should go fast."

One could hope.

After shrugging off my jacket, I balled it up against the wall outside the room, not risking getting paint on it. "I should've brought headphones or something." I stepped into the doorway of the room. "I could've listened to—"

Harry Russo.

I flew backward into the hallway, pressing my spine against the wall.

Even though I'd stepped out of the room, I could still see the image. Harry Russo. Ripped jeans and a white shirt. Auburn hair tucked behind his ears. Paint roller in hand. Did I imagine the whole thing? Did my brain conjure the image of him? Because there was *no flipping way* he stood in the middle of my church's basement.

Margot poked her head over the threshold, and her eyebrows raised. "Holy handsome."

I'd never showed Margot a picture of Harry—I'd always been too afraid of what she'd think, what she'd say. I shouldn't have worried, apparently.

This was worse than seeing him at Le Petit Bateau with my mom, worse than seeing him Saturday night at Crushed Beanz. Those instances, I hadn't been trapped in a room with him. All afternoon.

How did this keep happening?

"Switch jobs with me," I told her, desperate.

"What? Why?"

"Just—switch me, Margot."

Margot leaned into the doorway, peering at him openly. "What, do you know him?"

"*Margot,*" I hissed, reaching to tug her back, but she lifted her hand.

"Hey," she called, offering him a closed-lipped smile. "Haven't seen you around here before. Trust me, I think I'd notice a face like yours on Sunday mornings."

She was definitely flirting with him. I was going to pass out.

"Hey," Harry greeted her, and oh, my gosh, he really stood in there. That was really his voice. Not my imagination. "I heard Pastor Liam needed help, and I thought I'd volunteer."

Aw, thoughtful and sweet. I'd grumbled because I'd been forced into helping and he did it out of the goodness of his own heart. If I wasn't on the verge of a freak-out, I might've swooned.

"What'd you say your name was again?" Margot asked him, and any thoughts of swooning disappeared. *Poofed.* Gone. Because he would say—

"Harry. Harry Russo."

And she would look at me the way she looked at me now—eyes wide, expression almost a demented sort of amused. I could see the gears clicking in her mind, every-thing falling into place. Could see the exact moment an "aha" light went off. "Interesting," she mused with a barely contained smile, and once more I fixed her with an intense stare.

Please, I tried to convey telepathically. *Don't say anything. Just don't.*

Margot enjoyed moments like this, these awkward, forced kinds of moments. That's why she came to Mrs. Holland and me at the last fundraiser. And Margot, being my best friend, knew how much I struggled with the whole Destelle/Stella mindset, how much I struggled with wanting to tell Harry.

I could easily see her saying something now. Hopefully my silent, wide-eyed begging came across.

"Destelle," Pastor Liam said from behind us, making me jump. He held a spray bottle and a rag in one hand and an ugly piece of fabric in the other. "Found a sheet you can throw over your clothes. I cut a spot at the top for your head."

A sheet with a hole cut out for my head. Glamorous. This just kept getting better and better. Pastor Liam had zero clue I was self-destructing. Like, full-on melting down.

After passing me the sheet, he handed the cleaning supplies to my friend. "You ready, Margot?"

"Ready as I'll ever be, Pastor Liam," she returned happily, grabbing the items from his grip. To me, she said, "Face the music." With a wink, she sauntered off with Pastor Liam, leaving me alone in the hallway.

Was that my heart beating that loud, or was someone banging on the floor upstairs?

I could turn around. Totally could've walked back outside. I could've even called a car to take me home. I didn't have to go inside that room. But that meant I would've left Harry painting by himself.

The longer I stood out in the hallway, the more the prospect of entering seemed daunting. Was this the time to come clean about Stella? After Friday, this moment seemed inevitable.

But come on. Did it have to be *now*?

No, I decided. It didn't have to be now. I could just walk in, pretend he wasn't there. As long as I didn't face him full-on, he wouldn't recognize me. Right? Probably not.

Hopefully not.

Swallowing hard, I pulled the sheet over my head, effectively shielding my school uniform. Even if he didn't recognize me as Stella, I couldn't help but remember the other day at Le Petit Bateau, spilling water everywhere. Would he recognize me from there?

Why was Destelle destined to be forced into awkward situations around him?

Drawing a deep breath in, I turned into the room, definitely on the brink of having a heart attack.

Harry had his back to the doorway, thank God, so he didn't notice me enter. Paint supplies littered the ground, cans opened, extra brushes at the ready. The room itself looked like it'd been primed, and even one coat of paint looked as if it had been layered over the red walls. It probably needed only one more coat. *Dear God, please let it be only one more coat.*

Without a word, I snatched up a paint roller, taking advantage of Harry's turned back, and started on the wall opposite. I held my breath, physically unable to breathe in or out until—

"Oh, hey," Harry said, surprised. "I didn't hear you come in. I'm Harry."

Yeah, I know, and I'm freaking out. "Destelle," I returned, not turning.

"Destelle. That's a pretty name."

If he'd hesitated, I didn't notice it. No recognition at all, which honestly surprised me. Stella and Destelle sounded so similar. But wait, another weird feeling worked its way through me. He said it was a pretty name—was he flirting with me? As Destelle? My Stella side felt offended.

And whoa, wait. Hadn't he said the same thing about Stella? What, is that his go-to phrase?

I tried to fight a frown, but I wasn't sure it worked. "Thanks."

"I like your sheet."

Now I definitely was full-on frowning, accompanied by burning cheeks. "Thanks."

He fell quiet for a moment, and I couldn't help but wonder what he was doing. My body wanted to turn to see his face, but I forced myself to stay still. "I'm going to turn on some music from my phone, if that's okay," he said eventually. "Any particular song you want to hear?"

I almost asked him if he had any country music on his playlist, just to see how he'd react. "No."

We lapsed into unbearable silence then, or *near* silence, as he put on a song by Outside Inclusion. One that I absolutely loved, but there'd be no humming or toe-tapping.

With the silence, the air felt ten times thicker than before. I could almost taste the paint in my mouth, and I held the roller almost limply, the sheet scratchy against my skin. *This is fine*, I told myself, drawing in soothing breaths. *This is fine.*

I kept waiting for Harry to say something, but he didn't. I looked over my shoulder, but he minded his own business, totally engrossed in swiping his roller along the wall. Or maybe just pretending to be that way.

Apart from the faint music coming from his phone and the sticky sound of a paint roller along a wall, the church basement was quiet.

I could do this. It was a little awkward, but Harry had no clue what was going on. So, as long as I kept to one wall and he stayed at the other, it'd be fine.

Except, when I turned around to reload my roller with paint, Harry turned at the same time. And we locked eyes.

I froze like a deer in headlights, watching as that crease from Saturday night returned between his eyebrows.

I practically tripped on the hem of the sheet when I

moved to load my roller up, letting my curls fall over my profile. *Bawk-bawk,* my thoughts taunted me, but I couldn't do it. Stella had been a secret for so long that coming out made me feel sick with nervousness.

"You know, you look familiar," he said, and suddenly the paint roller felt several pounds lighter. "Can't place where, though."

"Hmm." *Don't look up, don't look up.*

Pushing to my feet, I turned back toward my wall, looking at the section I'd already painted but not really seeing it. Even though I tried to hear, I couldn't tell if Harry rolled his own brush into the paint. He wasn't walking across the plastic covering the floor either. I fought the biggest urge to turn around and check, to see if he watched me. Adamantly, I told myself I didn't want to know.

Suddenly, I could hear my cell phone start to go off where I'd left it in my coat pocket. I stiffened immediately, turning toward the doorway, wondering who'd be calling me.

But when I glanced over my shoulder, I found Harry with his cell phone in his hand, and it lit up with a call being placed.

Everything in me froze.

"You gonna get that?" he asked, raising his eyebrows a bit expectantly. Recognition flared in his eyes now, blazing like a fire threatening to burn my cheeks.

Completely frozen. I didn't even think I was breathing. "T-That's not mine."

Purposefully, Harry tapped his thumb on his phone screen. Instantly, my cell stopped ringing.

"And here I thought I was losing my mind," he said with his normal teasing lilt, his expression still unreadable as he slid his phone into his pocket. "You should've seen me Saturday night. I almost couldn't place the face, but you do have the prettiest eyes."

Suddenly, it felt like a balloon popped inside me. That door I'd been shoving closed flung wide, knocking the wind right out of me. "I—I've heard that before."

"By some handsome suave, no doubt."

He'd said the words with a straight face, but a startled, nervous laugh burst out of me. "He *was* pretty cute."

His blue eyes looked deeper, and embarrassment struck, itchy and warm in my veins, as if he were analyzing every part of me. I held still, waiting for the judgment. "Destelle," Harry said, the name sounding like a delicate song on his lips. "Stella. I can see the connection."

"I—It's such a long story," I hurried to say, certain I was moments away from him pulling back, moments away from him writing me off as some weirdo. "It really started as an outlet. Like, normal me wears pink, but Stella can wear black, that kind of thing. Margot calls her my alter ego, which sounds weird. But, I guess, in a way she is? I like her, though. Stella, I mean. I like that I can be whatever I want when I'm her, you know?"

Harry blinked at me for a moment before he bent down to place his paint roller in the tray, movements slow.

"I know. It's embarrassing. I'm embarrassing."

"Not embarrassing," Harry quickly contradicted, and finally a sliver of emotion slipped through: amusement. "I wouldn't have pegged you for a nervous fast-talker, but dang. I think a few of those words clocked eighty miles an hour."

A part of me was relieved that he made a joke, but another part of me wondered if he was only trying to deflect the situation because it really freaked him out.

"So this..." he trailed off, taking a step toward me. *"This* is the real you?"

"I'm not as fascinating as Stella," I told him, gripping my roller tightly, feeling like I wanted to blend into the wall. "Not edgy and cool. I'm not someone you'd be interested in."

"I don't know. That sheet's pretty edgy and cool if you ask me." Harry took another step until he stood right in front of me, those blue eyes peering into mine. Almost as if he looked into my soul, not seeing Destelle, not seeing Stella. Just seeing me. He reached out, and with a gentle finger, he traced the collar Pastor Liam carved into the sheet. "So dressing differently makes you Stella?"

"Stella's a kind of mindset," I said, swallowing hard. "She's confident and fun. Destelle would never have gotten up onstage with you at Crushed Beanz. Destelle, she...she never would've gone up to you at Downtown. Destelle's a chicken. The clothes...well, they help me get into character, so to speak."

Okay, yeah, I guess it was super weird that I talked about myself in the third person. I didn't know how else to explain it.

His finger moved up to touch my cheekbone, drawing a soft, invisible line along my skin. I fought back a shiver. "So, does Stella want to take the summer to travel, or is that Destelle?"

"Both," I whispered. "But Stella made me want the freedom more."

He nodded a little in thought, corners of his lips twitching. "And was it Stella or Destelle who thought I was cute?"

My parted lips twitched into the tiniest of smiles. "Both."

Harry's eyes coasted over me once more, slowly taking in every part of me. "Honestly, I have to admit, the wig makes you look pretty sexy."

Sexy. He called me sexy. While I was holding a paint roller.

He called me sexy in a *church.*

"Then again," he went on, one corner of his lips lifting. He swiped his thumb along the top of my cheekbone, the touch a whisper of contact. "You look beautiful without the wig too."

Something about the way he called Stella sexy and Destelle beautiful made the butterflies in my chest take flight. I wasn't sure why the distinction felt so important, so immensely world-changing, but it did. "You don't think I'm a weirdo?"

"If you're a weirdo, I'm a weirdo," he said with a slight laugh. "So, do you want me to call you Destelle?" Not a trace of hesitancy or awkwardness clung to his voice—he just looked at me as if he genuinely wanted to know which I would prefer. "Or Stella?"

It would make sense to call me Stella only when I wore

the wig. However, something about the way he said that name—*Stella*—made my chest feel light. The feeling I had whenever I wore the wig.

And even though I wasn't wearing the wig now, that feeling still bubbled up inside me.

"Whichever rolls off the tongue, I guess."

When Harry looked at me like this, with eyes holding an infinite amount of gentleness, I felt seen. As if he saw into the depths of my soul and he liked what he found. More yet, I felt like I could see into the bottom of *his* soul, and I loved it. Yes, Harry had an edgy rock band exterior, but the kindness and gentleness inside his being creating the perfect match.

Harry swiped up his paint roller again, holding it like a sword, his smile like like a ray of sunshine. "Are you going to talk to me this time, or make me suffer in awkward silence?"

"I think I can hold a conversation," I said, shyness creeping into my voice. It was strange how different it felt to be around him. Not in a bad way, but in a way I had to get used to.

However, a weight fell off me, and I didn't realize how crushing it had been until it finally, finally rolled away.

Harry hadn't pulled back. He hadn't pushed me away. He'd embraced it—*me*—without even flinching. I could've kissed him.

We started work once more on the small room. Our conversation kept us company this time rather than the low tunes. Now that the awkward barrier had disappeared, it was fun to talk about the music. I recognized most of the songs, and I laughed every time he lunged for his phone, knowing there were curse words riddled in the lyrics and not wanting Pastor Liam to overhear.

Despite the rocky beginning, I was so, so glad Mom signed me up for this.

It took us about an hour to work through the small space, especially since Harry had a head start before I arrived. I watched as he went to apply one last coat along the baseboard.

"So, the other day," I said, slipping my paint-stained hands into my pockets without a care. "At the ice cream parlor. I didn't kiss you because you didn't know about Destelle," I said quickly, before losing nerve. "Or, know about me. Or...us?" *Cringe.* "If you'd have known, I—well, I would've kissed you back. Probably."

Harry looked up at me while his roller paused, blue eyes widening in surprise and something else. He opened his mouth to say something, but a voice cut in.

"How's it coming in here?" Pastor Liam came through the doorway and immediately folded his arms, regarding our work. "Whew. That didn't take long at all."

I snatched Harry's cell phone and halted the music. "We made pretty good time."

"It's nice to see progress come along like this, huh? Just think of how the church will look when everything's done." Pastor Liam glanced around the room. "You can leave the brushes; I'll clean those up. Thank you two for all your help today. I'll mark down the time." Pastor Liam's eyes lingered on Harry.

And Harry flashed him a smile in response, standing

and setting the paintbrush beside the others. "Thanks, Pastor L."

I shrugged off the sheet, careful not to get any paint on my school clothes. He saw me as Stella all this time; the fact that I was wearing a schoolgirl outfit and he saw me in it was a little mortifying.

Once we reached the back exit, Harry took a step forward and grabbed the handle of the door, but didn't tug it open. Instead, he turned to me, expression suddenly serious. "I want to hear everything about you. About Stella, about Destelle, and everything in between. Is there a third alter ego I should know about?"

Standing next to him in my pastel pink jacket, we couldn't have looked more different. With his ripped jeans and combat boots and tattoo, he looked edgy, hard-core. My parents would've rather died than see me with someone like him. But Jonathan had been right Saturday night when he said that the "different worlds" stuff was silly. Because I felt right standing beside him like this, as Destelle, not Stella. "Just two."

"Well, I can't wait to learn more about them."

The words were perfect. No judgment or derision, no sarcasm or irony. His words were genuine, as was the look in his eyes. It wasn't like Margot, who rolled her eyes and went along with me. It wasn't like Jonathan, who thought I was weird, but didn't poke fun.

And maybe because *he* said it, that made it five million times better.

I stepped closer, into his bubble of space, and his own

hand fell from the door handle. He leaned in, causing my eyes to flutter shut.

"Are you two seriously about to kiss in a *church?*" Margot demanded loudly, climbing the stairs with her own coat on. She looked both of us over, that devious smirk back in her eye. "Sounds like a sin if you ask me."

Harry pulled the back door open then, letting the last traces of February air into the building, immediately cooling me down. "Would've been worth it," he said, gaze catching mine as I walked past him.

"Now, see?" Margot nudged my shoulder. "Coming clean wasn't so hard, huh?"

She was wrong—it *was* hard. And terrifying. But the burst of freedom that hit me made me realize how *good* it felt to embrace Stella more instead of forcing her to be a weekends-only kind of façade. I could integrate her into Destelle.

As I looked up at Harry, with his soft freckled cheeks and relaxed expression, I knew he'd had a hand in that. His acceptance of it all was something I would never take for granted.

I held his gaze as I answered Margot's question, nearly grinning ear to ear. "It was so worth it."

fourteen

hat week, Mom went easy on my caseload for volunteering, which made it easier to go out without canceling on too many people. Wednesday, when I asked to go out, I had an excuse readily available. I'd rehearsed it several times in front of a mirror to pass the lawyer test: I wanted to go to the library to study with a few girls from school.

Dad barely batted an eye as he pulled my keys out of his desk drawer. *Passed.*

"Delivery number four is a success," I declared as Harry slid back into the driver's seat, the interior light beaming until he shut his car door. Flecks of snow clung to his hair, melting quickly in the heat of the cab. I looked at the Dial and Dine app, refreshing. "Order number five hasn't come in."

Harry turned over his shoulder to watch as he backed out of the driveway. "The night's still young."

It was. I didn't need to be home until eight, which gave us a little less than two hours.

With my free hand, I reached up and smoothed my fingertips down the Stella wig, making sure it clung firmly in place.

Harry noticed the action when he turned around. "Can you walk me through your process on Stella?" he asked, pulling out onto the main road of Bayview slowly. "I want to know more."

"It's only a wig," I said with a brief smile, setting his phone down in my lap. "I braid my hair back, put on a wig cap, and then secure the clasps in place."

"But why wear her tonight?" He glanced over at me, flipping on his blinker to turn into a half-empty strip mall lot. "Since it's only going to be you and me, I mean."

I couldn't explain the stab of amusement that struck me when he referenced the wig as *her*. Yeah, I did that, but it was funny hearing someone do the same thing. "I just like it, I guess."

And I wasn't *all* Stella tonight. I wore light-wash denim jeans, which Stella never would wear. My gray sweater could've been part of her wardrobe, but it definitely fell more into the Destelle category. Like the two personas blended together, at least for tonight.

Harry parked the car in an empty space, leaning back into his seat. "Wednesdays can be slow sometimes. I usually park and wait for a delivery to come in."

Mimicking his posture, I rested my head along the back of the seat. "I like this," I told him, staring out at the pavement. "Delivering food. It's peaceful."

"You should sign up to be a driver."

"I don't think I'd like it without you."

Harry slowly drew one finger down the curve of the steering wheel, giving me just enough time to wonder what that finger would feel like against my skin. He tilted his head back, exposing his neck a little more, giving me a glance at the tattoo. "So," he began, drawing out the word, eyes glittering. "You would've kissed me, huh? At the ice cream parlor?"

I couldn't help it—a startled laugh burst out of me. "I mean, I might've. Maybe. The odds were really fifty-fifty."

"Mmm. And what are those odds now?"

"Forty-sixty."

"Are those odds in my favor?"

"Eh."

Harry chuckled at that, returning to running his hands down the wheel, gaze set on the sky beyond us.

His car smelled so much like him, almost to an unbearable, mind-boggling degree. It was relatively clean, but in the back, his guitar case lay along the seats and sheet music littered the ground. "So you went to school with Natasha. Where'd you two go?"

"Bayview High," he answered at once. "It was okay. Easy to blend in."

"Even with that?" I asked, tipping my head at him, gaze trailing to the ink at his throat.

Harry touched the skin there, a smile moving his lips, but the light didn't flicker on behind his eyes. "You'd be surprised how many people left me alone once I got it."

Honestly, I wasn't sure I would be surprised. If a girl from my school got a tattoo like that on her neck, I might've steered clear too. "Why didn't you go to college?"

"I wanted to take time off school," he replied, and that not-so-happy smile disappeared. "I figured I could always take online classes if I wanted. Maybe in the fall."

"That's what I want to do. Online classes, I mean. The idea of tying myself down to another place for four years feels so...suffocating."

"I say you should do it. Even if you did a year online, most credits typically transfer."

I turned his phone over, trailing my fingers over a long scratch along the back of the black case. "My parents would never let me."

Harry reached over and laid his hand on my thigh, close enough to my knee to be respectable but high enough to make my heart skip a beat. "If you decide to do it anyway, I'll still pack the road trip snacks."

I looked over at him. The sun had started its descent, disappearing behind the tall buildings that loomed in Addison's city center. Still, a few rays peeked out, casting their glow across Harry's face, highlighting his freckles. In this light, even his eyelashes looked more reddish than brown.

"Seventy-thirty," I said suddenly, holding still underneath his hand and gaze.

One corner of his mouth lifted. "Really," he murmured, shifting in his seat ever so slightly. "What made it jump so high?"

"Snacks. Obviously."

The other corner raised now, and he leaned across the space between us. "I'll remember that."

My heartbeat fluttered like a frantic butterfly as he

came closer, and I tipped toward him as well, desperate for this moment.

A second before our lips met, one single freaking second, Harry's phone chirped. I jolted in surprise, his hand falling off my leg, and I focused on his LED screen, blinking several times to see clearly. "Uh—it's from Hallow. A fast-food restaurant."

"Ah, skip it. That's pretty far, and all of our orders have been on this side of the county tonight."

I tapped *decline* on the app, refreshing to a blank screen. There were no other orders.

And then we lapsed into quiet. I still couldn't calm my pulse down, the sheer closeness of his mouth to mine still fogging my senses. The moment disappeared, of course, completely obliterated.

"So, Stella," Harry began, trying to break the silence. "When did she come into being?"

"Around November." I coasted my fingers through the strands, not a single knot or snarl. I prided myself on how well I maintained the hairpiece. The lifetime of a wig could be cut in half without proper handling. There'd always be an option to get another, of course, but since this was the wig that started the entire persona of Stella, it felt senti- mental. "Margot and I were shopping, and I saw a wig store. We went in, planning to try some on for fun, but I really liked this one."

Harry shifted the wig hair back from my profile, hooking it around my ear. "I like it too."

"The clothing and the fake earrings were another staple of Stella," I went on. "Something that was so different from

Destelle. And that's really why I chose dark colors for Stella—it was something Destelle wasn't allowed to wear. But I like it."

"It suits you," he told me, the warm look in his eyes not fading. "Both sides do."

Okay, the moment was coming back.

Except another chirp broke us apart, though this time not nearly as startling. "An order from a restaurant on the other side of Bayview."

"Let's do it," Harry said, and I pressed the *accept* button. All the delivery details lit up the screen then, and I turned on the directions. Harry pulled out of the parking space. "You know, you've spoiled me. I like it when you can deliver with me. My little shotgun rider."

He moved to rest his hand between us, palm turned up. An easy invitation. He didn't even have to ask.

I slid my palm along his, curling our fingers together. "Good." And I settled back into the seat, fully basking in the beauty of this moment, never wanting it to end. "Hey, can we swing into this gas station?" I asked, pointing out the windshield. The station sat a bit back from the road, one of the lights in the canopy flickering. "I can get us some snacks for the rest of the night. You know how I feel about road trip snacks."

I expected him to laugh at that, bringing up the conversation from a few moments ago, but he didn't. Harry's hand in mine tensed ever so slightly before he extracted his fingers. "Uh, sure, yeah."

"Will it affect the delivery time?" I didn't want to put us behind schedule.

"No, the food probably wouldn't have been ready when we got to the restaurant yet anyway." But the flat tone of his voice hadn't changed.

As he pulled up to the door, I unbuckled my seat belt, turning toward him. "Want me to grab you a soda?"

His grip on the steering wheel seemed tight for the car being in park, wide gaze on the gas station door. It almost didn't look like he was breathing. "No, I'm fine."

The change in his demeanor was enough to make me pause in opening the door. I couldn't figure out what triggered it, but it had me settling back in my seat. Maybe it was the gas station itself. It *was* poorly lit, grungy looking. I realized then that I didn't know much about the Bayview area. Was this a bad part of town?

"You know what? We can keep going. I'll just get a drink to go from the restaurant."

"You sure?" Relief dripped from the two words, the tension in his expression cracking.

That's when I knew I'd made the right decision. Whatever was up with this gas station, he didn't want to be here. That was enough for me. "Yeah, definitely. I think this restaurant has cookies to go too, so I'll get one of those. I might just split it with you," I added with a smirk, hoping he'd return it.

And he did. With a slight smile, Harry wasted no time in putting the car into reverse, pulling back onto the main road. The palpable relief still remained, though, even as he reached for my hand again. As he pressed his lips against my knuckles, he murmured, "Sounds perfect to me."

"I can't believe your parents are out of town on a Friday night and you're *not* throwing a party." Margot sighed dramatically, propping her sketchbook on my bed. She wore loose pants today, her long-sleeve shirt clinging to her body. It was rare to see her outside of a suit or school clothes—rarer still to see her in *loungewear*. "Or have at least a few friends over."

"Who would I invite?" I demanded, knocking my head against the headboard. "Grace Conan?"

Margot's theatrics subsided for a moment, enough for her to frown. "Yeah, maybe not."

The house had felt so quiet in the absence of my parents, their constant white noise of a presence gone. They went out of town for the weekend and wouldn't be home until tomorrow night. Tonight would be the first time in a long time I could stay up late *and* still use my cell phone.

I could already imagine texting with Harry until the wee hours of the morning. Since I was babysitting the twins, attending the gig at Crushed Beanz wasn't an option, but maybe Harry could convince Addy to video chat so I could see them perform.

"How's it coming with Project College?" Margot asked, taking my thoughts far away from the place they wanted to be. "Did you tell your parents where you want to go."

And just like that, my mood plummeted. "Mom has her ideas."

"*Her* ideas. You need to learn how to tell them no," she

decided, and then lay down so her back was flat against my mattress, legs hanging off the king-sized edge. One of the longer strands of her hair fell into her eyes, and she batted it away. "Say, 'Screw your plan for my life; I'm going to make my own.'"

Dear God, the mere idea of saying that to my parents made me nearly break out into a sweat. "And then they'd probably cut me off."

"Who cares? You know I'll always be your sugar mama."

I rolled onto my stomach, combing my fingers through the little wisps of her hair. She made a face at the touch, but didn't pull away. "I skipped a volunteering session Mom signed me up for. To hang out with Harry. For karaoke, of all things."

"Sounds like you're off on the right foot," Margot said appreciatively. "You at least said 'screw you' to *that* plan she had for you."

"But then I showed up at the volunteering for Pastor Liam, so it's not like I'm kicking a whole new lifestyle." I watched as her silky strands sifted through my fingers, the action calming something inside me. It felt *good* ditching volunteering. I had to admit, it felt good to do something because I wanted to do it, *when* I wanted to do it. But I didn't tell Margot that—I was too afraid she'd use it to add fuel to her fire. "I don't know why I'm so afraid of telling them no."

"Girl, you have a lawyer and a judge for your parents. I'd be telling them what they wanted to hear too." Margot angled her chin so she looked directly into my eyes, holding my attention. "But it's *your* life. You can't live under them forever. And if you do, what happens when you're forty and they're telling you what to do? Still making you go to events, still picking out your clothes for you. Still making you turn off your phone at nine o'clock."

"My parents aren't like yours," I said with a sigh. "Your parents are way more lenient. Mine act like we're in the courtroom, like, all the time."

"And you let them."

I leaned my head on one hand, peering at her with an uncomfortable feeling stirring within me. "What should I do? On graduation day, just haul all my stuff out and move across the country?"

"I'll hire the movers for you."

Even though her words sounded flippant, I knew she meant them. We'd been friends for only a year, and when she made friendships, she dedicated herself to them. I trusted her more than anyone in the entire world because instead of offering polite smiles, Margot was honest. Almost to a fault. She wouldn't use flowery words and compliments —she was real.

"You know, we never really talked about Harry," I murmured, that unease still turning in my stomach. "What'd you think of him?"

"I think he *definitely* doesn't look like someone you'd be interested in. I didn't really strike you as a tattoo-loving gal."

"I'm not a tattoo-hating gal." His tattoo was a bit in-your-face, but I liked it. It made him feel *genuine*, not like the men at the country club who put on a mask to look their best. "Besides, it suits him."

"It does," she said, thinking about it. "I'll have to get to know him. He seems nice, but I'm not passing full judgment until I talk to him more. I, unlike all the other stuck-up sissies in our social circles, don't judge books by their covers."

A laugh pulled from me. "You'll like him, I promise. He's funny—I swear, he makes me laugh like no one has before. And it sounds dorky, but when I'm with him, I feel like...anything's possible."

Margot puffed out her bottom lip. "My little girl's got a big crush."

"It's a normal sized crush, thank you very much."

On the bed between us, my phone rang. Before I had a chance to grab at it, Margot snatched it up, jostling the mattress underneath us. "Oh my gosh, you have a heart next to his name?" she cooed, that slightly mocking expression deepening. "So sweet."

Harry. "It's an orange heart," I said, grabbing for her wrist. "Orange is a symbol of enthusiasm and admiration—give it!"

"*Enthusiasm,*" she echoed, shoving me back. The buzzing continued between us. "I can tell."

Right before I latched onto the cell, Margot pressed *answer* and flicked on the speakerphone. "Hello," she called, voice sounding strangled from pushing me off her. "You've reached Destelle Marie—ow! Stop trying to squish me!"

Mortified. I was mortified, and if looks could kill, Margot would be merely a dead body on my bed.

"Is this Margot?" Harry guessed into the phone, the amusement in his tone obvious.

Margot raised her eyebrows at me, flashing a grin. "I know I heard him talk on Monday, but *dang*, you're right. His voice is *hot*."

A dead, dead body. Maybe I could hire Jamie and Nellie to bury her in the backyard for twenty dollars.

"You should hear me sing," Harry replied with a laugh. "Ask Stella about our karaoke session. We were *fantastic*."

Any trace of annoyance or frustration with Margot went out the window in an instant, all because of one word. *Stella*. She seemed to notice it too, her lips twitching into an almost smile. Relenting on my attempt to pry the phone from Margot, I fell back onto the bed, gazing at the ceiling.

Harry laughed again, the sound crackly from the static in the phone. "So, what are you two lovely ladies doing today? Important things?"

I liked that he and I had this running joke, that in the course of just a few weeks we went from being strangers to having our own inside joke. "The opposite," Margot replied. "Destelle is holding me hostage at her boring house. She can't leave because she has to babysit, and apparently that means I'm stuck too. You should come stand in my place."

"Ah, like tap in for you?"

My brain translated his words: *Ah, like come to Destelle's house?*

Come to my house. Ha, that'd be a hard *no*. Absolutely

not. Harry Russo could not come over. The twins would
see him, tell my parents, and I'd be dead meat. I could
already hear Jamie ratting me out. "Destelle had a *boy* over
without your permission!"

Mom would skin me alive.

But then again...Harry coming over could be exciting.
Throwing caution to the wind. Being more like Stella...

"Exactly. I think someone else should suffer." Margot
lifted her eyes to mine. I could practically read her mind
when she looked at me like that, as if her gaze opened some
secret connection. *It's your life. It's your life. Don't let your
parents dictate it for you anymore.* "What do you think,
Stella?"

The name itself was a little arrow, slicing straight
through me. A challenge. What would Stella do? Stella was
brave and confident; she'd invite a boy over in a heartbeat.
She would take advantage of the fact that her parents were
gone.

Harry waited for my response quietly, letting me
decide. I knew he'd be content even if I said no. He'd never
push me.

Stella wouldn't let this opportunity pass her by.

"Sure." Not exactly the overly confident response I'd
been hoping to give, but I'd take it. Margot gave me a
thumbs-up.

On the other end of the line, I could hear the smile in
Harry's voice. "Tell me when and where, and I'll be there."

fifteen

$\mathscr{I}$ shivered like a chihuahua around ten o'clock, but it wasn't from the cold. No, I paced the foyer of my house, second-guessing Margot's probably horrible idea. All the "what ifs" ran through my mind. What if my parents had set up cameras in the house and never told me? What if a neighbor spotted Harry coming inside? What if one of the twins woke up? What if, what if, what if?

However, the adrenaline rush at the idea of Harry coming over kept me from chickening out. Sneaking a boy into the house after the twins were asleep and my parents were gone sounded crazy—which it was—but I couldn't deny it was also a little exciting.

A car drove down the street slowly, as if looking for a specific house. I recognized it instantly as Harry's red sedan. He parked on the opposite side of the street, right underneath the lamppost.

He's here, my brain screamed, and I stood in the

window like a creeper, watching the sedan's door pop open, watching a figure emerge. *Harry's here. Harry's at your house. Act cool, act cool.*

The idea of acting cool sounded so freaking elusive.

I pulled the door open as Harry started up the cobblestone walkway, his gaze still upturned at the house. His expression looked awestruck, in a way that made nerves tumble inside me, knotting together like string.

When Harry realized the front door opened, his eyes fell to mine, greeting me with a smile. I watched him take me in, from my pink dress shirt and fitted pants up to my curly brown hair. "This...this is a *house*. Actually, I take that back. This place is a mansion. My house is probably the size of the bathroom."

"Is that a bad thing?"

"No," he said quickly, stepping into the foyer and glancing away. I winced inwardly when his gaze settled on the antique picture hanging on the wall above the fireplace. "Just surprising, is all."

"Imagine how much it costs to heat it," I said with a chuckle, though my joke didn't sound as funny as it did in my head. I shut the door behind him, pulling my cardigan tighter around me. "The twins are asleep upstairs."

"So, no raging parties, huh?" he asked with a smile, his jokes infinitely funnier than mine, but my chuckle came out tense. I still wasn't used to being around him as Destelle. Gone was the confidence, the flirting banter. Totally gone. I stared up at him now, trying not to hyperventilate. "Where are your parents?"

"They went upstate for the weekend. They have friends there they like to visit."

Harry slipped his hands into his jeans pockets, rocking back on his heels. "That's cool."

We stood awkwardly over the threshold for a moment, and my mind spun for a topic. "Did the gig go okay?"

"Yeah. A lot more people are staying after to talk, which is fun. I had to pry myself away, but this was definitely worth it." He once more scanned the open foyer.

I smiled, but it immediately faltered when his words seemed to take a different meaning. Just hanging out with me was worth it to him? What did I even invite him over here for? Gosh, what did he *think* I invited him over here for?

I realized, so suddenly, how this looked. Me inviting a cute boy over after dark, no parents home. Nervousness and anxiety hit me so hard that I felt dizzy, and I desperately wished I could've taken this invitation back.

"Can we go look at the stars?" I all but blurted out, and then felt like a loser. The stars? Really? The last thing Harry would want to do would be to stand out in the cold, right? Not when he'd come all the way over here for...what?

Harry, though, proved my fears wrong when he nodded, taking a step toward the front door. "Sure."

"Actually, let's go out the back." I wanted to reach out and grab his hand, to trail ahead and pull him behind me, but I...couldn't. I was too chicken. "It's probably easier to see without all the streetlights."

That, or I was running less of a risk of someone seeing us.

I could just imagine Mrs. Cameron looking out her bedroom window and finding us on the sidewalk. She wouldn't be able to wait to call my mother.

Harry followed me through our house, and I hurried along, not giving him any more time to look at pictures on the walls or gawk at the expensive furniture through our living room.

As our footsteps creaked along the floors, a thrill shot through me. I was breaking the rules as me. Not Stella. Destelle was breaking the rules, and she, well.

She kind of liked it.

I flipped off the porch light, casting us even further in the dark. The cloud cover wasn't so thick that we couldn't see the stars too clearly, but they were very faint. Despite that, we both looked up at the sky, shivering in the icy air.

Harry's breath puffed in the cold air, and mine would've too if I hadn't been holding it in. "Have you ever seen a shooting star?" he asked me, his voice quiet.

The snow on the lawn shifted, creating a hushed noise. Like sand falling in an hourglass. "I don't think so. If I have, I don't remember it. Have you?"

"Once. Not this past December, but the year before. New Year's Eve."

I looked at his side profile, so sharp and beautiful against the backdrop of the night sky. "Did you make a wish?"

"Of course," he all but scoffed, but his lips quirked at the corners for a moment. "I'm not sure it came true, though."

I thought about asking him what it was, but I couldn't find my voice.

Should I reach out and grab his hand? It was right there, mere inches from mine. I could almost feel his fingers wrap around mine, a steady, warm pressure that would feel as if he hugged my entire body.

Great, I imagined what hugging him right now would feel like—amazing, probably. No, *definitely* amazing.

"I don't usually do this," I whispered to the stars instead. "Invite boys over."

"So, I'm the first? Ooh, that really boosts the ego."

A startled laugh broke out of me. "I mean, I'm not really a rule breaker."

Harry turned to me then, staring into my eyes. "That's a good thing, you know," he said gently. "Breaking the rules is overrated."

"Says the guy in a rock band. Who got a tattoo when he was sixteen. Without guardian permission."

Harry bit at his lower lip to keep a smile at bay. "Don't take after me. Being a Goody Two-shoes is hot in my opinion."

Flirty words bubbled up on my tongue. "So, me breaking the rules and inviting you over *isn't* hot?"

A small, slow smile touched his lips, my attention drawn immediately to them. He seemed to lean forward. "I didn't say *that*."

And just like that, an avalanche of feeling shifted inside me. The air charged between us in an instant, like a universe of little electrodes dancing, heating everything warmer. *This is it,* I thought, my brain snagging on every single detail, every single angle of his features. *He's going to kiss me.*

The idea filled me with so much energy that I pulled back on instinct, unable to be still. Without waiting, I started down the back porch steps.

I heard him follow behind me. "Where are you going?"

"To make a snow angel," I said decisively, and then flopped down onto the snow. My cardigan was a crude barrier against the cold, and the snow sunk its teeth into my skin. It wiped away the traces of nerves and the flash of heat, rapidly building to a pins-and-needles pain. "I haven't made one this year, and it's already March—the snow won't last forever."

"You're going to freeze," he said emphatically, sounding almost like a parent. "I have socks thicker than that jacket of yours."

"It's called a cardigan," I told him, pushing and pulling my arms and legs through the snow. "You sound like someone who's never made a snow angel before."

"Is that a challenge?"

And then Harry fell into the snow beside me. He fanned his arms too close to mine, hand bumping my fingers. "You're ruining my angel." I tried to sound sad, but amusement seeped through.

"Our angels are just holding hands."

Okay, I could get behind that.

Harry kept hitting my hand as he waved his arms in the snow, causing me to laugh harder and harder, and even though I strained to keep quiet—I definitely didn't want to wake the neighbors or the twins—my laugh echoed in the night.

I suddenly saw things differently. Two different worlds, maybe, but in a way that freed me from the realm I'd been trapped in. A world I was so desperate to get out of. Harry was bridging the gap between Destelle and Stella, if only for this moment. It gave me a taste of what freedom felt like, and I craved more of it.

After a few moments, Harry pushed to his feet, offering a hand to help me up. My fingers were numb as I gripped his, the heat in my blood tempering enough that I could feel the cold a bit more sharply. Clumps of snow stuck to my sweater, holding tight to my curls.

We both looked down at our angels. I couldn't help but frown at the ugly outline in the snow. "Does mine look lumpy to you?"

"Maybe. Why did my butt make so much of an imprint?"

I started to shiver, curling my arms around myself. "Hey, at least the hand holding looks cute."

And it did. The waves our arms made connected perfectly, as if our angels were actually holding hands. "Well, I'm glad I drove out here to make snow angels," he said with a chuckle.

"Why did you drive out here?" I was half afraid to hear his answer, afraid he'd say something and ruin this whole thing. Because it felt like a big question. A make-it-or-break-it question.

"Honestly?" Harry reached out and traced his finger down the curve of my cheek. His warm skin sliding against mine, like a flame melting a snowflake. "I had a chance to see you. Wasting it would've been absolutely idiotic."

The things he said were so stinking *perfect*. Like that. His words sifted into my brain and relaxed me, melting away any trace of a chill, melting until all of me felt his words. Until all of me warmed once more.

My gaze traced over Harry once more, the vaguely starry night a backdrop to his beautiful features. The chill of the snow made my brain slow down, almost like a brain freeze by association.

Harry lifted his hand and traced the curve of my cheek oh-so delicately, enough to cause me to shiver. "Are you cold?"

"No." All of me burned.

The snow shifted on the ground again with a quiet hiss, and I found myself really, *really* wanting to kiss him. We were close enough that leaning in would be easy enough, and the energy inside me made me feel like a star about to explode.

Harry's touch trailed from my cheek to the side of my round jawline, the moment between us charging. "What are my odds?" he murmured then, words almost a whisper in the night.

We were thinking the same thing. "Pretty good."

"Pretty good?"

Near perfect. It was time for Destelle to take a page out of Stella's handbook.

Without giving myself a moment to chicken out, I stood

on my tiptoes to cross those few inches between us, but Harry met me halfway, his gentle lips pressing against my own. His were colder than I'd been expecting, but so soft, scattering any thought in my brain in an instant. The smell of his sweet cologne tickled my nose. The sound of his little intake of breath as if he were surprised made my blood burn. His mouth on mine, a steady pressure I wanted more of, had me pressing closer.

Harry's hand glided along the dip of my waist almost hesitantly, as if he were nervous to touch me. But I moved closer, folding my hands between us, resting them on the warmth of his chest. I could feel his heartbeat pound rapidly through his shirt, almost in tandem with my own.

After one last lingering kiss, he pulled back, only an inch. His eyes were closed, but his lips turned up, a smile unable to be tamed. "I swear, I didn't come over for that." His voice sounded lower than it'd been moments before. "*Not* that I'm complaining."

"You sure?" I murmured, touching my fingertip to his bottom lip. "Because there's still time to take it back."

That was an absolute lie. From here on out, there was no going back.

"I've never been more sure in my life," Harry responded, and leaned closer, mouth closing over mine once more.

If I hadn't been facing my house, I would've missed it. A light flicked on in one of the upper-level windows.

Jamie's bedroom. And I'd looked up in time to see his curtains rustle.

I shoved Harry back toward the house, into the

shadows that Jamie wouldn't be able to see. My hand pressed flat against Harry's chest, and I could feel his pulse through the thin shirt. "My brother," I whispered, tilting my head toward the second floor. "His light just turned on."

"He can't know I'm here?" Harry guessed. I stood there in shock for the longest moment, my mind still numb from his kiss.

And then I heard it, a barely-there sound. "Destelle?" Jamie's voice, muffled through the walls, shot through me. "Destelle?"

I grabbed ahold of Harry's hand hard and tugged him after me, toward the fence's gate. The snow angels—there'd be two of them. Not to mention the footprints we were leaving in the snow, or the footprints Harry would leave toward his car. Right now, though, that was out of my hands.

And really, hiding the evidence meant nothing if Jamie had looked out his window.

Once we got to the gate, though, I grabbed Harry's jacket. "I'm having a love-hate relationship with breaking the rules," I told him, shoving to my tiptoes and kissing him once more. I almost couldn't bring myself to pull away. There would need to be more kissing, but *later*.

"Trust me, this is *so* not how I want to meet your family," he said, then he slowly eased the gate open, and thank God the hinges didn't creak. With one last heart-stopping smile, Harry shut the gate behind him.

As quickly as I could, I hurried up the porch steps, trying to slip silently back into the house. I kicked off my shoes and slid them as far away from the door as possible.

When I turned around, Jamie stood there, his pajamas a size too tight, blinking at me. He didn't look sleepy. Instead, he looked wide awake. "What were you doing?"

Okay, the words weren't immediately accusatory. They weren't "Who was that boy outside?" or "Why were you kissing him?" His question was easy to dance around. "I made a snow angel."

"You didn't wear a coat?"

"I was only out for a second."

Jamie blinked again, and in that moment he reminded me so much of Mom. Just staring, waiting to see if I'd crack under the pressure.

"Why are you up?" I asked him, quickly changing the subject.

"I need a drink," he said simply, and then moved away from me, but like a deer in headlights, I stood frozen.

I held still as I heard him move into the kitchen, heard the cupboards open and shut, and heard the faucet flip on. He hadn't seen. If he had, he would've said something. He would've held that information over me, nursed that blackmail material to the bitter end.

Jamie hadn't seen Harry. Hadn't seen me kiss him.

I just had to keep telling myself that.

When Jamie made his way back into the living room, he held a small glass of water in his hand. Before he passed me, he stopped. "Why are there two angels?"

"Uh, I—the first one looked terrible."

Jamie glanced at the back door behind me. I waited for it. Waited for him to open his little mouth and say something. Would there be any talking myself out of it? Mom and Dad would surely believe him over me. They wouldn't believe in the "innocent until proven guilty" mantra, not in this situation.

"Okay. Lock the back door, okay?" Without waiting for my response, he walked away, his footsteps near silent on the stairs.

I stood there, afraid to be relieved. Just like that?

A moment later, I could hear his bedroom door click closed. Just like that.

My mind moved at a whirlwind pace, unable to slow down. The adrenaline from almost being caught still trembled underneath my skin, and I knew sleep would be so distant in my future. I made my way up the staircase quietly, pressing my fingers to my mouth. I could almost pretend like my fingers were Harry's lips, in a way that was so pathetic.

I checked the hallway window before I went to bed, and I had a clear view of our two jacked-up snow angels, Harry's with the big butt and mine with the lopsided torso. Their arms were overlapping—two angels holding hands.

But then I noticed the two sets of footprints. Clearly two sets, since Harry's feet were larger than mine. If Jamie had noticed both angels, had he really missed the footprints?

Even though the idea of Jamie seeing us, possibly telling Mom and Dad about it, made me feel sick to my stomach, the happiness from what had happened eclipsed that. At least for tonight. I kissed Harry as *me*. He knew me and he liked me. Liked me enough to leave Crushed Beanz and come over to talk. He knew me as Stella and Destelle and liked the two of us. Both sides of me.

It was enough to make me do a little happy dance.

When I woke the next morning and peeked outside, the angels were gone, blown over by the winter wind, a beautiful memory I would keep with me forever and ever.

Sixteen

*C*rushed Beanz thrived in all its glory Saturday night, the scent of coffee not as strong as it'd been earlier in the week when I'd gone with Harry, but it still smelled like home. Jonathan was making an order for someone, so I ventured to where Addy sat in the booth at the front. The show would start soon, and I wanted my front-row seat.

"Long time, no see," Addy said in greeting, leaning her elbow onto the table as I sat across from her. Tonight, her hair was braided back from her face, a few strands coming loose. "Missed you last night."

"I had to babysit my siblings," I said with a smile, shrugging off my jacket. "You know, I never got a chance to ask you. How did Vincent's birthday extravaganza go?"

Addy let out a slight chuckle, trailing her fingers down the length of her purple tie. "Not as extravagant as I'd been hoping. I'd planned this whole thing, but Mom—well, she's having a rough time. First Valentine's Day without Dad, you know?"

Suddenly, sympathy pinched at my heart as I remembered her situation, how she'd lost her dad only a few months back. "I can't even imagine."

"I ended up giving Vincent his surprise at my house."

I felt one of my eyebrows arch, probably hidden behind my bangs. "His *surprise?*"

Addy, though, easily read my expression, and even in the dim lighting, her cheeks pinked. "Jeez, no! Not *that*. It's...well, it's kind of secret for now. At least until the date gets closer."

"'The date'? I thought you got him a stuffed toy."

She leaned forward, dropping her tone. "That was only part of it. The other part...well, it's about Untapped Potential. He wants to surprise Harry."

Even though I wanted to press for more information, I didn't want to pry too much. "Speaking of Harry," I murmured, glancing toward the stage. They hadn't come on yet, but they would any second. "We had our first kiss."

Delight swamped Addy's eyes, her jaw dropping. "I knew it, I *knew* it. You two are perfect together. And we need to plan a double date. That *so* needs to be a thing."

The idea of a double date with Addy and Vincent made me excited. I could just picture the four of us going out for ice cream, no Natasha this time. Or even going out to dinner, chatting as we waited for our meals. "For sure."

The crowd murmured and chatted excitedly, and Untapped Potential made their way through the fans. Vincent smiled at anyone who called his name, but I saw his eyes immediately seek Addy's, and for her, his lips only stretched wider. *Adorable.*

Natasha came next, dressed in a low-cut top, her dark hair falling in her face. Harry, trailing her, looked lost in thought.

Vincent immediately ducked behind his drum kit. Once onstage, Harry's gaze scanned the crowd, and when his eyes fell on me, the air vanished from my lungs.

And then he smiled, a wide grin that looked like he gazed at the sun rather than me. The lights were on him, illuminating every inch, and I couldn't look away.

It was hard to believe that I kissed him last night, hard to believe that he kissed me *back*. For so long, I'd simply been a fan in the crowd, our paths never crossing. It was like a dream.

"I bet everyone in this place is jealous of you right now," Addy said, a teasing note to her voice.

I thought about responding to her, but that would've meant looking away from the stage, looking away from him, which seemed impossible.

"How are we doing tonight?" Harry asked the crowd, to which they responded with a cheer. "It's been a little bit since we played an acoustic song, so we thought we'd start off slow tonight."

I settled deeper in my seat as I clapped with the crowd, preparing for the first note.

Harry started strumming the guitar, a few basic chords. Immediately, I recognized it—"A Chance At Forever." This was a softer song, one that they rarely played nowadays. Harry and Natasha used to play more acoustic songs before they brought Vincent into the band. I really liked both their music styles, but their acoustic songs touched a different place inside me, a place that left me wanting more.

> ***"Wrap my arms around the feeling***
> ***You ripped my safety net away***
> ***Dealing with the panic and fear***
> ***Having to go, but wanting nothing more than to***
> ***stay."***

In that moment, I could see into the possible future of Untapped Potential. I could see Harry and Vincent performing on a much bigger stage, playing for a much bigger turnout than tonight's. Natasha would be there too, I thought. But Addy would definitely be there, either in the front row or just offstage.

I swayed a little in my seat with the soft drum beats Vincent interjected, watching Harry's fingers as they strummed each string.

Harry was my singer boyfriend, and the realization was only just sinking in. His dedication to his craft showed in each strum of his guitar, in the crinkles by his eyes, in the deep and lovely tone of his voice. He was so passionate, so easy to long for.

Because here in my booth, I wanted nothing more than to travel back in time to last night, to that moment after his mouth met mine and before Jamie's bedroom light flicked on.

When that song ended, they switched back over to

their more lively music, but that lulling first melody left me feeling as light as a feather.

I hated how fast the gig seemed to pass, the songs flying by. Harry's gaze had strayed my way throughout the songs, and I mouthed the lyrics along with his singing. I couldn't quite tell, but it almost looked like he smiled.

When they started their last song of the night, I turned to Addy. "I'm going to go get a refill before Jon dumps the coffee," I said, raising my mug in case she hadn't heard me over the music.

Addy ended up nodding, watching as I pushed to my feet. The crowd parted to let me slip by, filling in immediately behind me. I lifted my wig a little away from the skin on my neck, relishing in the cool sensation that swept across my skin.

A guy sat at the counter, and as I got closer, I noticed Jonathan speaking intently with him. The stranger leaned his head against his hand, totally captivated in conversation.

Jonathan saw me lingering, though. "Stella," he greeted, welcoming me closer with a wave of his hand. "A refill?"

"Yes, please," I told him, passing my mug over, glancing at the sitting figure. The guy's eyes were a steely blue, blond stubble dotting his jaw and chin. He appeared to be in his early twenties, roughly the same age as Jonathan. "You here for the music?"

"I am," he responded, voice pleasant and soft. "Or, well, the singer."

I felt my eyebrows lift. "You're here for Harry?"

Jonathan sat the refilled mug in front of me. "They're

old friends," he told me, glancing at the customer. "Go way back."

I nearly smiled at that. So, they'd been talking about life stories, huh?

The guy flashed Jonathan a warm smile, turning back to me with an outstretched hand. "I'm Terry."

Terry. I knew that name. "Harry's mentioned you. I'm Stella." I slipped my hand into his.

"Stella is Harry's girlfriend," Jonathan added before I could say anything else.

I opened my mouth to interject, but the words fell apart on the tip of my tongue. Harry and I hadn't really talked about labels or anything like that; we'd just kissed. Though I liked to think that made us exclusive, I wasn't sure.

Terry looked at me closely, a crease between his eyebrows, expression strangely unsettling. "Oh. I didn't realize he and Tash broke up."

I wasn't sure what was worse: the fact that he'd called her "Tash" too or that he didn't know they weren't a thing anymore.

"I *am* out of the loop," he hurried on, no doubt seeing my worried expression. "That's why I'm here, actually. I haven't seen Harry in over a year—just wanted to support him."

From the counter, the stage wasn't fully visible, which meant Harry probably hadn't spotted Terry yet. I took a sip of the hot coffee, the taste bitter. Jonathan forgot to put sugar in my drink like he normally did.

"Why haven't you two spoken in so long?" I asked, reaching for a packet that sat in the middle of the tabletop.

"I was locked up," Terry responded, leaning back against the counter. "We sent letters here and there, but it's been a while since I'd seen Harry face-to-face."

Locked up—the phrase almost sounded foreign. Locked up, like prison? For the past year? I almost wanted to laugh. Terry didn't *look* like a criminal. With his straight-legged jeans and blue sweater, he looked as if he should be an accountant or something.

Even though I desperately wanted to know why a guy like him would've been to prison so young, not even Stella was forward enough to pry secrets from a stranger. "Well, I'm sure he'll be happy to see you."

Terry's smile was very young, almost nervous. It made me want to reassure him further. "I hope so. He's like a little brother to me."

Not even thirty seconds later, Vincent landed the final drum beat to Untapped Potential's last song, and I clapped along with the crowd.

"Thank you all for coming tonight!" Harry called to the audience. "Come back next weekend for some more music and awesome coffee."

Natasha chimed in, bright and happy, "And don't forget to follow us on social media!"

A few people stuck around, hoping to get a few autographs from the band. They were garnering fans who wanted something personal. Another rung on the ladder, and they were climbing their way up. Pride swelled in my chest.

"So, how long have you known Harry again?" I asked Terry as we waited for them to come to the counter.

"Since he was fifteen," he replied. "We've been through a lot together."

A heavy quality hugged his tone, and this time, I reached out and touched his wrist. His sweater scratched against my skin, but it drew his eyes to mine. "I'm serious. If you're as close as you say, he'll be thrilled to see you."

"Terrance Greybeck!"

Jonathan, Terry, and I all turned toward Harry's raised voice, finding him staring at his old friend with a shocked expression on his face. His dropped jaw morphed into a disbelieving grin, and then he moved forward, away from the straggling crowd. In a second, he had his arms around Terry.

"Hey, redcap," Terry said to him, a laugh accompanying the words.

Harry pulled away enough to look directly at Terry, shaking his head. "What are you doing here? You still had—"

"I got out a few weeks early on good behavior," he said, shoving Harry in the shoulder. "Not *that* hard to actually do what I'm told."

Harry's grin faltered, almost as if Terry's words triggered a different thought in him. I couldn't explain what might've caused the sudden change, but it flickered in a flash. "You were always a kiss up," Harry replied, but before he could say anything else, Natasha broke free from the few lingering fans.

"Look who decided to show his face," she declared, coming up with her arms folded across her chest. "You look scruffy."

Terry regarded her for a second before a grin cracked his features. "Tash, you look...the same, actually."

With a laugh, she jumped into his arms, squeezing him tight.

Their laughter echoed in my ears, and I couldn't help but feel a little excluded from the reunion since two out of three of them were practically strangers to me.

Maybe I needed to give them some space to catch up. Vincent and Addy now sat in the booth together, and even from where I stood, I could see that Vincent lifted her hand to press his lips against her knuckles. That was *so* not a moment I wanted to break in on.

Jonathan headed back into the kitchen with a tied-off trash bag, and I followed him. "So, Terry is totally hot," I said as he collected the remnants of garbage from the kitchen's bin. "Saw you chatting him up. Prison, that's...edgy."

"And sketchy," Jonathan countered, but I saw his lips twitch. "He didn't really strike me as the bad-boy type."

I wondered what Terry did to land him in prison, because with that sweater, he didn't look like trouble at all. "Did you get his number?"

Jonathan gave me a look.

"Hey, you're the one who said you'd talk about college-aged guys," I said, recalling the conversation we once had with Addy. "Terry totally looks college age."

With a hard yank, Jonathan tied the kitchen's trash shut, then carried both bags to the back door. He ducked outside, his figure momentarily blending into the shadows. "I'm not like you. I don't have game."

"Destelle didn't have game either," I pointed out. "Stella, though, has got some. Ever thought of trying on a wig?"

"You're *hilarious*," Jonathan said with a roll of his eyes, nudging me playfully as he came back inside.

"I'm serious, you could try Stella on." I patted the top of my synthetic head of hair. "Your alter ego name could be Jonny. Or Nathan—ooh, you could *so* be a Nathan."

Jonathan still wasn't amused.

When we got back out to the front, everyone still stood talking. Vincent and Addy had joined the conversation, and Vincent was even *smiling*. Harry's gaze immediately found mine, and when I stepped close enough, he picked my hand up, slipping his fingers around my own. I remembered the way those exact fingers strummed the guitar tonight, a delicate touch that elicited a beautiful sound.

"I actually joined in November," Vincent told Terry, glancing at Natasha, who even looked cheerful herself. "They came into Crushed Beanz one day looking for a place to play, and the rest is history."

"Definitely fate," Harry agreed. "Even better that you could keep a beat. When you first volunteered for the drummer position, I was afraid you were going to suck."

"He'd been so prepared for it," Natasha added. "Remember, Harry, you said that it was basically a pity audition?"

"Okay, well, actually—don't look at me like that, Vincent. How was I supposed to know you were going to be good?"

"I'm glad you actually did it," Terry said, eyes trained

on the boy beside me. "Started a band. You were always singing, ever since we met."

"Not like that's stopped." Natasha seemed to notice me then, and her eyes roamed over my figure, an assessing gaze that almost had me squirming against Harry's side. "Cute boots."

I glanced down at the combat boots Margot lent me, the ones that laced up my ankles. Her voice actually sounded sincere. "Thank you."

She turned back to Terry. "Well, I should head out. Don't be a stranger."

"I'll be around," he promised her, and I couldn't help but notice his eyes glance toward the coffee machines, as if looking for someone in particular. "When I saw your social media page blowing up, I had to see what all the fuss was about. I should bring my brother next time—I feel like he'd love this place."

Harry's lips curved. "He's the artist, right?"

"He is. So good, too. I think he'd thrive off all the inspiration this place has."

"Well, I'm no artist, but I feel inspired the second I walk in," Addy piped up, her wide smile so contagious. She was more of a planner than an artist, but I saw the markers she'd bring with her sometimes, watch her doodling in the pages. She definitely had a creative side.

"I'll bring him sometime," he promised, and then looked at Harry. "It was great to see you again. I'm glad to see you're doing better. Really."

Something about Harry's demeanor shifted then, but I

couldn't figure out what the change was. "Glad to see you, man. We should catch up soon."

Terry glanced at me. "I'd like that. You can tell me all about how you met your lovely girlfriend."

Gah! I waited for Harry to laugh, to deny the word, but instead he dropped my hand, using his free fingers to rest on my back. "For sure."

Terry tipped his head at me. "Nice to meet you. To meet you all." After a second of hesitation, he pulled out his phone. "I almost forgot...I got a new number. Got too many spam callers on my old one." He gave Harry a steady look.

One that Harry seemed to understand. "Here, let me put it in my phone."

"You can give it out to people you trust," Terry said, and once more, his gaze roamed the counter, but Jonathan still lingered in the back. I couldn't stop my grin from surfacing.

Vincent moved away to wipe down the countertop by the time Terry headed out into the night, and Addy propped up against the counter, filling the to-go sugar packet containers.

Harry's hand slid off my back, and immediately I turned to him. "Jonathan was the one to use the g-word," I said, the words practically bursting out of me. I kept my voice quiet enough, thank God, but I still felt like a dweeb saying it. "I know we haven't had that conversation yet, but I thought you should know. What Jonathan said. Because he said that. Not me."

"There's that fast-talking again." Harry's mouth ticked into a smile, a crease forming near his cheek. "We haven't had that conversation. But I guess I'll make where I stand clear—I'm not kissing anyone else."

"Me either."

"Great. So, we're mutually only kissing each other."

"Right."

"So, that *kind of* makes us exclusive."

"Kind of," I allowed, biting my lower lip to keep from smiling.

Addy glanced over her shoulder at us, smirking. "You two are cute. But a little weird."

"Very weird," Vincent agreed, folding the towel he'd been using. "Almost as weird as your horror movies, Adeline."

"Hey, you *love* them," she objected, and the two of them fell into a conversation.

Taking advantage of their distraction, Harry leaned in and pressed a quick kiss to my mouth. Even though it was short, it zapped through me all the same. "Terry," I started, looking up at him, only a tiny bit dazed. "He seems really nice. Were you two partners in crime? Because Terry and Harry *so* sound like a crime-fighting duo."

Harry smiled, but it didn't reach his eyes. "Not necessarily crime-fighting."

"He mentioned he spent time *locked up.*" I felt conflicted about saying anything, but I couldn't help but think of Jonathan. "Is he...dangerous?" The word felt way too offensive to describe Terry, but I had to ask.

"Not at all," Harry answered without a beat, but the tense look in his eyes remained. "He...it was a case of wrong place, wrong time."

"I'm glad you said that because you're going to give his number to Jonathan."

"Jonathan?"

I wrapped my arms around Harry's waist. "Uh, *yes*. That whole 'give my number out' thing? He totally meant you could give it to Jon. Which you should."

Harry grinned, skimming his hands up my arms. It elicited goosebumps everywhere, accompanied by a small shiver. "You're playing matchmaker?"

"*We* are."

Harry wrapped his arms around me, and I practically fell into his embrace, so warm and comfortable. "I'm glad you had nothing more important to do tonight."

"It's been a slow weekend."

Harry pressed his mouth to the top of the Stella wig, bringing me closer. "Lucky me."

Seventeen

*D*ating Harry was better than I ever could've imagined.

At first, I'd been afraid merging our schedules would be near impossible, but I wouldn't let my parents dictate my life. Granted, I definitely would not confront them about anything. Not yet. Instead, when Mom told me my volunteering schedule, I'd call the day of to cancel everything I could. "Sorry, I can't walk your dog, Mrs. Miller. Something came up." "Maybe next week I can run your car through the wash, Mrs. Robertson." "Is there anyone else who can deliver your dry cleaning, Mr. Talbot?"

Each time I canceled and took back my own time, the exhilarating sense of freedom spiked like an endorphin rush.

And I spent that newfound free time with Harry. Most nights we met at Le Petit Bateau and delivered for Dial and Dine. We'd alternate who would run food to the door, making a game of who got the friendlier customer. It was hard to tell who was "friendlier" in a three-second interaction, so we typically settled on a tie. But the winner got to pick where we'd have a snack to top the night off.

Everything was perfect.

Jamie never mentioned anything about seeing Harry that night in February, and after a while, the looming anxiety of him saying anything disappeared.

Time with him just flew by, and suddenly it was the last week of March. Mom started getting excited to hear about college acceptances, and the twins were eager for warmer weather so they could finally play outside again, whereas I was finally content with where I ended up.

Especially now.

"It's not much," Harry repeated for what felt like the billionth time, flipping on his blinker. The sound echoed loudly in his car. "It's *really* small. Nothing special."

I laid my hand over his, which had been resting on the gearshift. "Stop," I told him. "It's small because it's just *you*. No annoying parents, no noisy siblings."

"I guess."

Even though his words were uncertain, excitement rippled through me. I finally got to see where he lived. He had a freedom that I always longed for, a freedom so tantalizing, and I wanted to see it all. There was something intimate about seeing where Harry lived. Something personal. We'd been covering the basics in the month since we'd become exclusive—favorite colors, embarrassing memories, biggest dreams—but there were other things we hadn't talked about. Where he lived, past relationships.

Really, *past* in general.

Aside from this car, I hadn't seen anything that was

totally *him*. It was *his* house; he didn't share it with anyone else.

Harry continued to follow the road as it wound around a few hills before finally turning into a driveway. I couldn't help but gasp a little at the house that appeared in front of the windshield. "I know," he hurried to say. "Like I said, not much."

"Harry, it's so *cute!*"

And it was. The house, though small, was *beautiful*. The siding was a pristine white accented by black shutters on every visible window. The roof looked almost metal, and that, too, was black. A small porch sat in the front, stained a dark color, contrasting perfectly next to the white.

"I've been doing renovations since the end of last summer," he said, pulling the key from the ignition. He sat back in his seat, gazing at the structure. "I've still got a few things to do, like landscaping, but I'll worry about that later in the spring."

I looked at him closely. "You've been doing the renovations yourself?"

"You know, what I can. *When* I can. I just refinished the bathroom, actually." Harry shuffled the keys in his hand, jingling them loudly. He almost looked self-conscious. "Shall we go in?"

All too eagerly, I unlatched my buckle and hopped out of the car. The wind tugged my curls around, and I pushed them behind my ear. No Stella today, only Destelle.

Despite getting closer to Harry, it still felt strange being Destelle around him. Bit by bit, though, I'd been getting used to it.

And good gosh, it was *so* nice to not have to scramble to get dressed in order to hang out with him. Those tights were such a pain to rush into.

"When did you say you moved into this place?"

"August." Harry squinted at the building. "I hired someone to redo the siding. Refinished the porch myself —*that* was a task and a half, especially all by myself in the heat."

"You know, I'd never pictured you for the handy type."

"I'm the *broke* type," he said with a laugh. "Can't hire everything done."

I couldn't help but smile a little, taking the three steps onto the porch, admiring the handiwork. Harry moved in front of the black-painted door and stuck a key into the deadbolt, giving it a sharp twist.

"Remember, it's—"

"Harry, I bet it's amazing." And with that, I reached past him and twisted the doorknob, shoving it inward.

The house opened up almost immediately into the kitchen, and the first thing I noticed were the floors, a beautiful warm-toned wood that instantly felt homey. They matched the walls nicely, which were a crisp white. The space was supposed to be a dining room, but instead of a table with chairs, Harry had tools and other odds and ends littered around the floor.

"Work in progress." He sighed from behind me, following me in.

I could see the vision, though. The appliances weren't top of the line and were mismatched, but they blended in with the gray cupboards nicely, the countertops a sleek marble. That obviously had been redone recently.

"Remind me to hire you if I ever buy a house," I murmured, slipping my shoes off and nudging them along the wall.

"You'd be amazed at what the internet can teach you." He hung his coat on a hook near the door and reached for the buttons on my Claire-Haute. "Want a proper tour?"

His hands were gentle as he smoothed the fabric off my shoulders, hanging it up too. "You know I do."

He took me to the living room first, on the other side of the kitchen. "There used to be a wall here," he explained to me as we stepped into the living room, gesturing toward the space. "I'm an open-concept kind of guy, I guess. Plus a house this small felt so much littler with all the walls."

The living room had the same hardwood floors, but it also had a large sectional pushed into one corner, aimed at a decently sized TV. "So, you lived here when you were little?" I asked, remembering how he said his parents left him the house.

"Yeah, crazy, right? When I was a kid, I remember it being much bigger. That wall used to separate my bedroom." Harry kept walking through another archway that led to two separate doors. "This is the bathroom," he said, shoving the door open. It gave a loud *creak* in protest. He winced. "Yeah, that still needs fixing. But I redid the tile in here. Vincent thinks it's ugly, but I like it."

The tile *was* busy, with a white-and-black design, but I liked it too. It wasn't perfect, though. By the shower, I could see a few tiles that weren't cut to the exact measurements, but that almost made it more endearing.

"Very clean," I noted, and it was. There wasn't a single dirty towel in sight.

Harry snorted, pressing a hand against his throat, along the lines of the tattoo. "You should've seen me forty-five minutes ago. I cleaned like a madman. Don't look in any closets, okay?"

I nudged him in the side. "No promises."

We stopped by Harry's bedroom last on the very brief tour. He reached for the doorknob but hesitated, as if realizing that showing me his bedroom was a personal thing. I caught his blue eyes glance at me, only debating a fracture of a second before pushing it inward. "This one is the current work in progress at the moment," he said as he led the way inside.

The room was small, with a queen-sized bed and a simple oak dresser. He had his guitar case propped against the dresser, but there weren't any other decorations. No pictures hung on the wall, not a poster in sight.

"Why are you doing all these renovations?" I asked him, looking closely at his expression. "To make it feel more homey?"

"Each time I do a renovation, the value of the house goes up," he explained, analyzing his bedroom. "Quite a bit, actually."

"Ah, you want to sell it and turn a profit."

"Maybe one day. For now, I like how it's cleaning up the place."

I wrapped my arms around his waist, feeling the toned

muscles there. "And it's got to be nice to know that you've done most of the heavy lifting. Satisfying, in a way."

"Well, there's that."

He smelled so good, like body wash and candles. Underneath my ear, I could hear his heartbeat, listening to the steady *thu-thump* with my eyes closed.

I pulled back a bit to look up at him. Memorizing his features was something I loved doing, if only to convince myself that I wasn't dreaming. I categorized his freckles, the pattern so haphazard and beautiful. His lashes held their reddish tint in this light. They brought out the blue in his eyes, such a vibrant color that almost looked electric.

"When you look at me like that," he murmured, almost a whisper, "I feel like I can't breathe."

"Is that bad?"

Harry chuckled, a gasping sort of sound. "Who needs oxygen, anyway?"

I pressed my fingertip along the tattoo lines, and he stilled under my touch. *Now* I believed he wasn't breathing, almost like the air stalled in his throat. I couldn't stop touching him, though. As my fingers trailed high, toward the bottom of his chin, I could feel the prickle of stubble.

"I love this," I told him, eyeing the tattoo. "It's so *you*."

The blue in his eyes seemed to glow, emotion passing over like a tidal wave. "You think?"

"You wouldn't be my Harry without it."

Harry's thoughts weren't always easy to read from his expression—kind of like an open book, but written in a language I still had more to learn. I hadn't mastered it, but I practiced. His expression, though, was hard to read. His eyes were tender and filled with softness, but not a trace of a smile graced his lips.

Pulling out of his embrace, I made my way over to his bed, sitting on top of the comforter. As my gaze roamed over the room, I tried not to think about how he slept in this bed, tossed and turned underneath these covers. I tried not to imagine what he wore to bed. Sweatpants and a shirt? No shirt?

No sweatpants?

"You should play something for me," I told him impulsively, pointing at the guitar case a half a second later.

"Oh, I see how it is," Harry murmured teasingly, but swiped up the case. "You just want me for my voice."

"Hey, I'm not denying it."

He sat down on the bed, laying the guitar case between us. The locks popped easily as he slid his thumb along them, and he gently pulled the lid open, revealing a beautiful acoustic guitar beneath. He pulled it out, and sheet music had been trapped underneath.

"You're the one who writes the music?" I asked, picking up a random paper. I couldn't read sheet music, but it looked so elegant, so purposeful.

"I collaborate with Vincent on it. And the lyrics. Natasha...well, she's just there for looks, I guess."

The mention of his ex and her looks made my warm thoughts turn cold. "She is really pretty."

Harry rested the guitar against his thigh, leaning on it ever so slightly. With his thumb, he pulled on the strings, eliciting a beautiful sound. "We've never had the exes talk, you know."

"My list is pretty short."

"Mine too. I've only dated two people."

"You can go first." My heart beat fast, a strange surge of nerves shivering over me.

"My first girlfriend was during my freshman year. I think we called each other boyfriend and girlfriend because everyone else did it. We weren't that serious."

I nudged his leg with my foot. "You didn't break her heart into a million little pieces?"

"Nope. We both agreed we didn't really work together. Natasha, though..." He exhaled softly. "That was more complicated."

I knew this was a conversation we needed to have, to get everything out in the open, but I found myself hesitant to go down this road.

"We'd gone to school together our whole lives, but didn't start dating until the beginning of my senior year. I really don't know why it took so long, honestly."

Yeah, I was really wondering if I wanted to hear this story.

"At first, things were okay. Fun. And then I..." He trailed off, a crease forming between his brows as he thought about how to phrase it. "Well, we took a break for a while. When we tried again this past August, things weren't the same. *I* wasn't the same, you know?"

"Why'd you two break it off in the first place?"

"Lots of reasons," he said quickly, brushing it off. "And trying things again made me feel like I was back to that kid in high school, doing dumb things, making dumb decisions." His voice had turned very serious and very low as he kept talking. His fingers still strummed, creating a lulling background noise to his words. "I didn't like the way being with her felt anymore."

He still hadn't looked at me, but a haunted expression now festered in his eyes, as if he were no longer looking at his bedroom, but peering inward. "So, you broke things off for good or she did?"

"I did. In November, right after we started our band. I thought she'd ditch, but she loves the spotlight, and everything's worked out."

I couldn't help but make a face. "She doesn't still flirt with you?" The image of her trailing her finger along his arm burned in my brain. "You don't miss her?"

He stopped strumming. "It's not like that. I swear, nothing's happened between us since November, and nothing will." Harry held my gaze steadily, as if trying to show the sincerity in his eyes. "I don't feel anything like that toward her anymore. What I had with her is *nothing* like I have with you, Destelle. It's hard to explain why it's different, but it's like—like you see me, and when I'm with you, I feel like...like I'm good enough."

Seeing this vulnerable side of Harry turned my insides to mush. *Good enough.* It made me think of little Harry, bouncing around from home to home before settling with a distant cousin. I wanted to pull him into my arms, stroke my fingers through his hair.

Instead, I watched him quietly, watched the delicate way his fingers moved. "I feel the same way, you know. You don't see Stella or Destelle—you just see *me*."

"And I like what I see."

I rolled my eyes at him and his cheesy lines, making sure not to let on how much I liked it.

"So, how about you?" he asked, shifting on his bed, as if physically edging away from that conversation. "What's your short list look like?"

I pulled my legs up so I could cross them on his bed, leaning my elbows onto my knees. "One guy. We went on two dates. He'd bring me gifts."

"I'm slacking on the gifts front," Harry observed regretfully.

"His were manipulation presents." I leaned my cheek into my hand. "He tried to buy my feelings. For a while, it was nice, until he told me that after all those gifts, shouldn't I give him something in return?"

Harry's eyebrows rose. "He meant—"

"Yeah." I smiled, even now. "I laughed in his face, and we never saw each other after that. That's the extent of my very short list."

Harry's lips turned down ever so slightly at their corners. "Why so short?"

"What do you mean?"

"You're beautiful," he said in an obvious tone, letting his guitar sing a high note. "You're funny. When you sing, your voice gives me goosebumps. Why hasn't there been anyone else? Anyone...serious?"

"I never really had the time to date." With Mom running me ragged nearly all the time with little things she needed me to do, I'd never wanted to squeeze a dating life in the mix. Another reason rose, tickling my brain, demanding me to voice it. "That, and...well, I guess

I was always a little afraid of what my parents might think."

He made a soft humming sound. "You were afraid they'd disapprove?"

"I didn't want to give them another thing to control." The words drifted into the air before I really thought about them or the weight behind them, the truth in their depths heavy. Quickly, I shook my head, as if I could shake away the tension. "Play me something."

Instead of stopping immediately in the mindless strumming, Harry took the chords and wove them together, the seamless beginning of a song I recognized. It was one of their popular acoustic songs, one he'd sung at his most recent gig.

Immediately, I closed my eyes and basked in the tune, unable to keep from faintly smiling. Quietly, so much so that his voice had a near-raspy quality, Harry began to sing.

Every cell in my body fell quiet. A hush settled over me, and I wanted to absorb every note, each pitch, bask in the resonance. He sounded so different like this, on his own, with no Natasha to back him up. The acoustics of his bedroom were softer from those in Crushed Beanz, more intimate.

I moved my mouth to the lyrics, knowing them by heart. "Sing with me," he said softly, cutting into the chorus. When I opened my eyes, I found him looking at me. "Please?"

My first instinct was to say no, to laugh at the idea, but he'd started singing again, and I couldn't bring myself to talk over him. He nudged my calf with his foot, urging me to join in. And when he reached the bridge of the song, I did.

In the places where Natasha would usually harmonize with him, I filled in softly, pinching my fingers tightly in my lap. I wasn't nearly as nervous as I'd been the time we'd done karaoke together. This was different—there was no joking now, not a trace of purposefully bad singing, only a beautiful sort of peacefulness.

Harry's fingers moved expertly along the guitar strings, but his eyes traced my face as if he was the one memorizing me now. Something brewed in his expression, something that looked on the edge of happy and unhappy, of panicked and calm, and I couldn't figure out why. He held my gaze with an intensity that had me locked in.

I didn't sound nearly as good as Natasha, but as I sat on his bed, it felt right to hear my voice mingle with his, like this song had been written for this moment between us.

He strummed the final note, fingers gliding effortlessly to a halt. I held still, waiting for him to speak first. And it took him a while to do so, long enough for my lungs to burn. "I love listening to you sing," he murmured, but that look hadn't faded from his eyes. "Your voice is beautiful."

My hands trembled in my lap, and it was nearly impossible to force them still. "That was my line."

The shadow in his expression split apart, a radiant light peeking through.

"You need to record that somehow so you can sing me to sleep each night." I nearly snorted, effectively breaking the moment between us. "That sounded really weird, didn't it?"

"That's the dream, you know," he said, and gingerly placed the guitar back in the case. "Recording songs, albums, have magazine interviews, songs on the radio..."

"How do you get all that stuff?" It couldn't be impossible. So many bands advanced their careers.

"Maybe get a manager." He raised a shoulder as he stood, moving to place the guitar case back against the dresser. "Maybe find a studio willing to let us record a single or an EP. Maybe get lucky."

"It'll happen," I said with conviction, no other alternative possible.

Instead of sitting back beside me, Harry crouched down, placing his palms on my knees and hovering between them. "The idea of it makes me a little nervous. Like branching out is this scary thing. Part of me doesn't want to advance further than Crushed Beanz. Is that weird?"

I thought about the question he once posed to me. *You're not afraid of the unknown?* "Not weird," I decided, threading my fingers through his hair, the silkiness slipping against my skin. He leaned into the touch ever so slightly, like we were magnetized together. "Being afraid of change sounds very normal to me. Then again, as a girl who has an alter ego, how normal am I?"

"What about you?" he asked, eyes tracing mine. Even through my denim jeans, I could feel Harry's touch, like there was no fabric between us at all. "How's your dream coming along?"

"We're waiting on acceptance letters," I told him. "I

should hear soon, then the scholarships we submitted should be announced in late April."

"*We.*" Harry grabbed my hand, gently pulling it away from his cheek. "That's not your dream."

It was my turn to shrug. "I'm keeping my options open."

More like I was too chicken to tell my parents no. Then again, what would've happened if I *had* told them no? If I'd put my foot down, refused to fill out the stupid packets, refused to go to college?

They'd have filled out the papers themselves, and if they still couldn't make me go, they'd probably kick me out. If a soldier wouldn't obey orders, they were given the boot, right?

His eyebrows came together, enough to wrinkle his forehead. "Don't do that, Destelle."

My full name on his lips had me stilling. "Do what?"

"Act like what you want doesn't matter."

I let out a soft breath, a sick feeling stirring inside me. "It's not that I *don't* want to go to college. I just...don't want them to tell me what I can and can't do, you know?"

He smoothed his hand over my knee, the friction soothing. He didn't say anything, just listened.

"What I want doesn't matter to them. Not always." That was why ditching the volunteering over the past few weeks made me feel so powerful. I finally had control over my own life. "Margot says I need to stand up to them, but I don't even know how. Maybe that's why I want to travel so badly—I just want to run away."

"You want to experience life and what it has to offer you," he corrected. "That's not a bad thing."

It felt like a bad thing. Not letting my parents have control was terrifying. What would my life look like beyond them? Staring into Harry's beautiful eyes, a pit in my stomach took hold, growing wider and bigger with each passing second. Here I complained about my parents when he didn't get to live a life with his.

"Sorry for unloading all that on you," I said a little awkwardly, feeling my cheeks warm up. "I...I want to be open with you. I don't want any more secrets." Harboring the Stella secret for so long made me never want to go back to the realm of secret-keeping.

Harry looked at me for a moment before something dark passed over his gaze. It was a shadow much like the expression he'd had moments ago, like something unnerving passed through his thoughts. I wanted to stop and ask him about it, ask him what was on his mind, but he spoke first. "I'll always listen."

"Me too," I told him, touching my fingertips to the lines of his tattoo. I could feel his pulse beating underneath his skin, and suddenly I couldn't help but notice how close he was, still crouched in front of me. Even though I didn't have the Stella wig on, I had the urge to pull my hair away from my neck. "I'm always here to listen too."

Delicately, Harry reached up and wound one of my curls around his finger, studying it. "Sometimes I forget," he murmured.

"Forget what?"

"About this." He wound my hair another time, careful not to tug. "I spent nearly three weeks thinking about you. About *Stella*. Picturing the black hair, bangs—sometimes, when I think about you, I find myself—"

"Forgetting that I look like this? Pink and proper and curly?"

Before the uncertain feeling swamped through me, he coasted his palm along the surface of my curls delicately, careful not to tangle. "Curly hair or straight, you're beautiful. I love both."

The way he dropped that l word startled me, but in a way that had me leaning closer to him. *Beautiful. I love both.* The entire time I held my Stella secret, I'd been so afraid he might think it's weird—might prefer one over the other. But he thought both were beautiful. Both sides of *me* were beautiful.

He watched me for a moment longer, long enough that I thought he might dive into whatever was on his mind. Instead, he leaned forward and pressed his mouth to mine, as delicate as a spring breeze. I inhaled softly, drawing in the sweet scent of him. His palms still pressed into my knees, his torso caught halfway between them. *Closer*, my mind sang, blood pounding to agree. *More.*

Even though we'd been together for a month, our kisses had been nothing more than glancing, a few seconds at most. But this, with no prying eyes anywhere in sight, suddenly took a charged turn.

And I was *so* here for it.

Harry pushed onto his knees so that our mouths were at the same height, and then he edged me backward. I moved until my head touched his pillowcases, his scent everywhere, surrounding me. The bed made a noise as he leaned over me, never breaking the mind-melting kiss. I nudged his loose T-shirt upward, trailing my fingers along the bare skin of his side—his very muscular side.

Every time his mouth touched mine, my heart pulsed as if on the brink of exploding. As if someone had rigged it to a live wire and too many jolts of electricity were shocking it, leaving it trembling and shuddering. His hands were gentle, one threading into my hair, the other trailing the length of my body. One of my hands wrapped around his back, trailing my fingers along the line of his spine.

This didn't feel like me, like timid Destelle who gave polite smiles and idle chitchat. Stella burned in my blood now, in a way she never had before.

It was official: I *loved* that Harry lived alone. Nothing would interrupt this moment.

Except his cell phone, which started to ring, a loud buzz that cut into the air. With a groan against my mouth, he broke away. "Sorry, let me turn it off," he said, his voice rough and beautiful, and it made me want to kiss him again.

The breath I drew in sounded ragged in my ears, mind still spinning and pulse still pounding, and I accidentally glimpsed the name when he took his cell from his pocket. *Lily Santiago.* "Who's Lily?" I asked, more out of curiosity than anything else.

Harry launched from the bed as if something caught fire, springing away from me. His hair was tousled and his lips looked a little swollen. "I—I have to take this," he rushed to say, heading for his door. He hesitated on the threshold as his cell continued to vibrate. "I'm—I'll be out on the back porch. Give me two minutes, okay?"

"Okay," I said, digging my elbows into the bed to push myself up, but he was already gone.

The room fell quiet with his absence, the bed not as warm or comfortable. My heart rallied to break free from my chest, but with each passing second, the frantic beat quieted.

In all our conversations, I couldn't recall Harry ever mentioning a Lily. Lily Santiago.

After waiting a few minutes, I pushed from the bed, figuring I would do a little more snooping. I couldn't help but be curious about the kind of food he had in his cupboards, the drinks he kept in the fridge. Would he have any beer? He didn't strike me as an underage drinker, but I was nosy.

As I passed into the kitchen, I could see Harry out of one of the back windows, pacing back and forth. In the quick glimpses, I could see his hand pressed to his throat.

His fridge was clean of anything suspicious. It could've used more groceries, though, and his freezer held a plethora of frozen pizzas. Stuck to the side of the fridge with a magnet hung a monthly calendar, his boyish scrawl written in a few boxes. It was quickly clear that most of the dates were labeled with his work schedule—*LPB 11-7*—but there were a few other labels that I didn't recognize, all holding the initials *CS* and a few *LS*.

I trailed my finger along them for a moment before moving on.

I roamed through the house a bit more, but there wasn't

a lot to snoop through. One door I opened was a hallway closet, and I found a small pile of clothes stuffed inside. By the crumpled quality of them, I had an inkling that they were dirty clothes. *Don't look in any closets*, he'd said. Oh, Harry.

"Sorry about that." Harry's voice suddenly cut through the house, the back door clicking shut behind him. "I had to take—hey, where'd you go?"

"In the kitchen," I called, shutting the closet door as quietly as I could.

It only took a second for his voice to come again, though this time it sounded much closer. "Exploring, huh?" When I turned around, I saw his gaze trail to the door. "Find any dirty laundry?"

"Literally," I said with a smirk, backing away while raising my eyebrows. "How was your phone call? You've never mentioned a Lily before."

And just like that, the shadow reappeared. "Oh, I haven't? She's—she's a family friend."

"It seemed...urgent."

"I have to pick up when she calls," he said with a quick nod, jerking his thumb toward the living room. "Want to watch a movie before you have to go back home?"

Cuddle on the couch with him? Yes, please. But I wasn't sure I wanted to let go of the subject just yet. "Was Lily a friend of your parents, or does she know your cousin?"

"Cousin," he said, leading me toward the living room.

"Do you talk to him much? Or his kids?"

Harry didn't look at me as I sat on the couch, and he

walked to his DVD collection, analyzing the titles. "Once in a while. What are you in the mood to watch? I don't have much in the way of comedy, but I've got this one scary movie Addy let me borrow—"

"Nothing scary," I said at once, folding my legs underneath me. Harry swiped up a DVD case, satisfied with the new choice. "Are they someone you'd ever introduce me to?"

That seemed to grab Harry's attention and hold it. He straightened from the DVDs, a vaguely surprised tilt clinging to his lips as he faced me. "My cousins?"

"I—I don't know." My voice quivered, and a strange shyness suddenly rushed over me. "We've established I don't have a lot of experience in relationships. I don't know when people typically meet the family. It's been a month since we've been official."

"Well, when do you want me to meet *your* family?" His fingers lifted, as if he were about to touch his throat, but he forced his hand down. "Am I someone you'd introduce your parents to? You mentioned you were afraid they'd be controlling of a relationship."

Something about his expression seemed vulnerable, boyish. Uncertain. It pinched at my heart. I tried to imagine Mom and Dad meeting him. His auburn hair, long enough to curl around his ears. His ripped jeans—almost every pair he owned had the same tears in his knees. The tattoo, a loosely outlined inky hand wrapped around his throat.

With what they were normally exposed to, with all the

diamonds and silks, I had no idea how they'd react to Harry.

But a part of me wanted to introduce them if only to see their faces when they took him in—tattoo, ripped jeans, long hair, and all.

"I want you to meet them," I told Harry at last, because I knew I'd been silent for too long, but as soon as I said it, panic flooded me. Harry. Meeting my parents. *Nausea.* "Do I get to meet your family?"

Harry popped in the DVD and took his place on the couch, turning to me while the opening credits started. "My cousins and I don't have a great relationship," he said softly. "I haven't really spoken with them since I moved out."

"What happened?"

"A lot of things." He shook his head. "But if we *were* on speaking terms, I would introduce you to them in a heartbeat."

My chest ached for Harry then. Lost both of his parents and wasn't on speaking terms with the family who raised him. There was more to that story, but I didn't want to pry it out of him, not now. I didn't want that shadow to come back into his eyes. "They are missing out," I said confidently. *Missing out on being in your life.*

It caused Harry to chuckle, and he wrapped his arm around me. "They are. I'm sure they'd love you."

I fell into his embrace easily, leaning my head onto his shoulder. It wasn't as close as we'd been earlier, but this felt just as perfect. Quiet moments like this between us were rare. Whenever we hung out, we were always doing something—delivering for Dial and Dine, chatting after a gig. But this soft moment, with my head against his shoulder, I loved just as much.

After the movie started playing on the TV, long enough for me to think the topic passed, Harry spoke again. His voice was quiet, as vulnerable as his expression. "Do you think your parents will like me?"

I blinked at the screen, my brain unable to comprehend the moving picture. Would my parents like him? The thought seemed innocent enough, but I wondered the same thing about myself sometimes. Would they like me if I stopped being their dutiful little soldier? And then another thought trailed quickly behind: Did their opinion matter?

I settled more firmly against his side, and when I answered, it felt as if I answered both his question and the one lingering in my mind. "You'll have to meet them and find out."

eighteen

"*I* told Harry he could meet my parents."

Margot, who'd been powering through her French worksheet Monday morning, lifted her gaze to mine. Even her face held an expression of pure horror. "You *what?*"

"It—well, it just kind of came out," I said, distress building as I recalled the situation. "I asked him if I was ever going to meet his family, and then he asked if he could meet mine, and I said—I basically said, *Sure.* Oh, my gosh, I don't know what I was thinking."

"You want Harry Hotpants to meet Alice and David?" She enunciated each word clearly, looking at me like I'd just told her I planned on stripping naked between third and fourth period. "Are you—did you hit your head? Are you concussed?"

"I don't *want* him to!" I quickly objected. "I mean, I fully see how terrible of an idea that is. But he wanted to, and he asked... Margot, I don't know. Why would he even want to meet them in the first place? They're not anything special."

"He probably wants to meet them because he likes you. I mean, it'd make *sense* if you had normal parents. If he was a normal boyfriend *without* a neck tattoo that symbolizes him literally being strangled. But you don't have those things. Even the twins are weirdos."

I let out a low groan, burying my face against my French worksheet.

How much of a disaster would it be if Harry met my family? Jamie would probably glare at him the entire time. If Nellie didn't take Jamie's side, she'd probably make him quiz her with her flash cards the entire time.

"You know..." Margot said after a moment, her scheming voice on. "This could actually be your way of accessing more freedom. Without lying about where you are all the time. This could transition them into giving you a bit more slack."

"Or it could be what makes them lock down even more."

How would they even meet him anyway? Would I bring him home for dinner, force him to pass the peas to my mother?

As if guessing my line of thinking, Margot said, "You could always bring him Saturday."

"What's going on Saturday?"

"It's the first Saturday in April," she said, tone hinting at the obvious. "The Hestons are throwing a fundraiser at the country club, remember? I think it's for more parks around Fenton County or something like that. They're bringing out that band that plays music you can actually dance to, not mope around like you're attending a funeral."

Crap, I didn't remember about the Heston party.

"Harry plays at Crushed Beanz Saturday night."

"He can't take a night off?"

"He's the lead singer. They need him."

Besides, bringing him to that fundraiser made me feel like I would break out in hives. Harry Russo didn't belong at a fundraiser or fancy gala or anywhere near those people. Harry Russo, eating fancy finger food? Harry Russo talking with my *parents*? Harry Russo in a suit?

Okay, that last one wouldn't have been too bad.

I shook my head to clear it. "Margot, a fundraiser is the *worst* way to meet my parents."

"Not really," she said, tapping her pencil against her mouth in thought. "He wouldn't have your parents' one-on-one attention. Plus, I'd be there to be a buffer. I'm sure Ms. Nancy would help occupy his time. She's always grabby-handy with fresh meat. Especially when they're as cute as him."

I hadn't told Margot about Nancy's reaction to Harry at Le Petit Bateau, but it nearly made me snort that Margot knew how she'd act. "And my parents would have to be on their best behavior," I realized. "Their very best. They wouldn't want anyone to get the wrong impression of them."

"I say you should ask him," she said, turning back to her worksheet. "You might be surprised. He might find a way to get out of his gig."

Tiny zaps of electricity shocked through me,

unpleasant and jittery. "He wouldn't have anything to wear." Or at least I assumed—he didn't strike me as a guy who owned a suit.

"Please. The Gilfman Clothier can tailor a suit on short notice. Plus, it helps that he's average build—easy to match." The bell rang overhead, startling me from the intensity of my thoughts. Margot began packing up her worksheet, gathering her books. "He might say no, but I'm sure he'll appreciate being asked."

Would he? Or would he feel awkward, trying to find an idea how to say no? I liked to think we were past that awkward phase in our relationship, but I couldn't tell.

Although for once, it would be nice to show up to one of those events with a guy on my arm. To finally have a date to chat with instead of all of *them.* Someone who I could smile genuinely at, not having to force it.

I pushed out of my seat with a sigh, the absolute last to filter from the room.

"Destelle, I've organized your volunteer schedule for the week."

Mom didn't knock as she made her way into my bedroom. Granted, my door had been open, but she still could've announced her presence before barging on in.

I sat at my desk, math book spread wide before me, and hurried to pull on a neutral expression. "Okay."

She handed it to me without a word, and I quickly scanned the spread. Babysitting the twins tomorrow. Math tutoring on Wednesday. Senior center on Thursday. Fundraiser on Saturday.

Babysitting the twins would be impossible to get out of. Tutoring wouldn't work since Mom was friends with the science teacher. Senior center *could* be easy enough to skip, but that would be the third week in a row. Sooner or later, they'd ask my mom what was going on.

Which meant I was looking at an entire week without time for Harry.

"How are your grades?" she asked, startling me. I thought she'd just drop the paper off and leave.

"Fine." It took effort to keep my voice from sounding short. "Haven't gotten a paper below an A minus in months."

"Nellie has been asking when you're going to take her shopping again. It's been a while."

I fought a groan. Shopping trips with Nellie weren't my favorite thing in the world. Not because she liked to try on everything in the store—which she did, even the headbands —but because I'd always have to tell her no to the clothes she picked out. Mom's directive for when we went was always clear. *"Make sure she gets things that are sophisticated. I don't want to make a second trip for returns."*

Not that she made the first trip to begin with. "*You* could always take her."

I didn't look up, but Mom's voice took on a stern tone. "I'm not her big sister."

"Yeah, well, then why isn't it on the calendar?"

Mom didn't speak long enough that I looked up at her, a serious expression coating her features. "You have an attitude tonight," she murmured, an unspoken warning seeping into her voice. "Would you care to tell me why?"

Immediately, I went on the defense, her lawyer side obviously coming out to play in a way that terrified me. I hadn't realized my tone had gotten so frigid, inwardly cursing myself. With my parents, I always was on my best behavior. Always. I could think of all kinds of retorts that I wanted to say, but would never express them aloud.

Trying to defuse the situation, I hunched my shoulders forward, placing my hands in my lap. "I'm sorry, Mom. I didn't mean to talk back. I have a lot on my mind tonight."

"Like what?"

The way she asked left no room for brushing it off. "Just...stressing about the scholarships, college acceptances, volunteering..." I trailed off, looking at everything written on the weekly spread. Strangely enough, my heart started thudding faster in my chest. "When do you think we'll hear from the colleges?"

"It really depends. Could be a few more weeks."

My mind traveled to the college online, but only briefly. I only opened the proverbial box for a few moments. I never sent in an application for it, and it pinched my chest. Harry would say I'm giving up on my dream. Would he really be wrong?

I thought of the shoebox under my bed, all the brochures that were collecting dust. At this point, I should've thrown them out.

I nearly jumped out of my skin when Mom laid her hand on my shoulder, her comforting gesture startling me. "It'll be okay," she told me confidently. "Mr. Orchard is on the admissions board of Castleton, and Mr. Bradshaw knows people at Mullhound. They'll have your back."

If only I had connections at Ashton.

"It will be fine," Mom said again, taking away her hand. "Great things are in store for you, Destelle. I know it."

I pinched my fingers in my lap, focusing on the pain to keep me from speaking. *Great things*, she said. Great things, according to her. If I were Stella in this moment, I would've brought up Ashton. Heck, I would've applied without talking to my parents about it. Screw the consequences. But I wasn't Stella, and I kept my mouth shut as Mom made her way from my room, her parting words settling over in my mind. *I know it.*

They were meant to be comforting, but they felt like a vise.

I pulled my cell phone out from underneath my textbook, finding the contact and pressing the call button.

"Well, look at that," the voice greeted after two rings. "I was just thinking about you."

"Is this the part where I start stumbling like a dweeb?" I asked, thinking about one of our previous conversations.

"Hey," Harry said. "I'm not a dweeb. A dork, maybe, but never a dweeb."

I would've smiled if the weekly spread hadn't still been open in front of me, Mom's perfect handwriting glaring me in the face. "Whatcha up to?"

"Nothing exciting, unfortunately. I got home from work a little while ago. Then I showered because the seafood scent was extra strong at Le Petit Bateau tonight, and I smelled like fish. *So* not attractive."

"It *is* called The Little Boat for a reason." Listening to him talk made me feel calmer on the inside, like his words alone were a lullaby. "What kind of fish?"

"All the fish mixed together. Like a fish meatloaf." His laugh joined mine over the phone, but mine was the first to filter off. "What is the beautiful Stella doing tonight? This is usually the time when she's working on homework."

I pushed up from my desk chair to shut my bedroom door, not wanting any listening ears. "She was," I said, flopping down stomach-first on my bed. "Now she's talking to you because she's upset that her mother... I'll stop with the third person now."

"It was kind of fun." He chuckled again. "So, why are you upset with your mother?"

"Got the latest volunteer sheet. It's going to be a fun-filled week. The only time I have to do anything is on Friday." My eyes traced Saturday, the printed letters jumbling in my mind. "There's something going on Saturday. It's a fundraiser thing. It's super posh and lame and there'll be a bunch of old people. I have to go to it."

"Ah, more important things," he said teasingly. "Sounds like fun."

"Mom and Dad like to parade me around. They want me to schmooze, I think. Most of the people at the club have a scholarship of some sort available, and they want me to win it. The free food's nice, I guess."

Harry made a soft noise on the other end of the line. "I've never been to anything fancy. I've only seen those kinds of events on TV."

My window to ask him appeared suddenly, but when I

opened my mouth to speak the words, I immediately chickened out. "Believe it or not, TV gets a lot of things right."

Harry was quiet—so quiet that I checked to make sure the call was still connected. I couldn't hear anything more than static. And then, "Is that the kind of thing you get a plus one for?"

My heart skipped a beat. Or two. "Y-Yeah, there's no guest limit or anything."

"Something you can bring a date to?"

It was like he'd read my mind. "It's on Saturday. Starts at seven. You'd miss your show."

"We haven't had a night off in a while."

The idea of him backing out on his fans made me feel guilty, and I quickly shook my head even though he couldn't see me. "No, really, it's okay. I'd hate for you to cancel."

He spoke his next words without hesitation. "Do you want me to come?"

"I mean, it'd be fun if you could, and you can meet my parents, but—"

"If you want me to come, I'm coming," he said confidently, words spoken easily. "But I'll probably need a suit or something, right? I can see if maybe Vincent's dad has something I can borrow."

"Margot might be able to help with that." Or, more accurately, the Gilfman Clothier could help with that.

"Finally meet your parents." As that realization hit him, he almost sounded nervous. "I mean, what better time to make a first impression than while wearing a tux?"

"You can meet them a different time—"

"I'm coming," Harry said certainly, almost sounding as if he was trying to assure himself. "I should let you go so I can call Vincent and Tash. When should we meet for the suit?"

I pressed my fingers to my mouth, feeling such a varied arrangement of emotions tear through me. Happiness that he wanted to come. Nervousness at the thought of him meeting Mom and Dad. Heck, even him being at the fundraiser. The unknown was a little more than terrifying, and thinking about it too long left me beyond jittery. "What are you doing tomorrow?"

nineteen

It's going to be fine.
That was what I kept telling myself as we walked down Addison's high-end shopping mall strip, heading for the Gilfman Clothier. Harry had never been tailored before, and I found myself stressing. It was his first glimpse into how this life was. His first test to see whether Destelle's lifestyle freaked him out.

It's going to be fine.

Harry held my hand as we walked, keeping his head down from the wind. He had a black beanie tucked over his ears, his hair curling out of it. "I'm nervous," he told me, watching his boots and each step that he made. "Is that weird?"

"Don't be nervous," I told him, giving his hand a squeeze. "It's just trying on clothes. It'll be a piece of cake."

"I still feel terrible about this, you know," he said, repeating his mantra from the car ride over. That crease still sat between his eyebrows. "You shouldn't have to buy me clothes."

"You're coming with me to an event, the kind that normally makes me wish I was invisible. It's the least I could do."

His eyes, which were glaring and slightly red from the wind, didn't seem to agree. "Do I want to know how much this is going to cost?"

Given the fact that we were going to Gilfman, a high-end designer company where the ties normally cost one hundred dollars? "Probably not."

Harry groaned, but squeezed my hand back.

We found Margot standing outside the store when we approached, her back turned toward us. Even from here, I could see she'd changed from her school uniform into her favorite dress pants, which were a black-and-red floral-printed pair. She usually always wore a bright red matching blazer, and sure enough, when she turned, the color was striking. Thick sunglasses completely obscured her gaze, and I couldn't help but wonder what emotion glinted in her eyes. "There you are," she greeted in her level voice. "I started to think you got lost."

"I had to wait until my dad got home from work," I told her.

Harry gave her a wide smile. "Great to see you again, Margot."

Margot, with one gloved hand, lowered her sunglasses, letting her eyes peek over their rims. "Been a long time. I almost forgot how fitting of a nickname Harry Hotpants is."

"I don't call you that," I threw out the disclaimer immediately.

Harry, apparently, found it amusing, and laughed. "Well, I'm still flattered."

"So." Margot shoved her sunglasses back up, but I knew she was still looking at him. "Do you know what size jacket you wear?"

"I usually wear a large. I like them a bit roomy." He looked between Margot and me. Me, fighting a laugh, and Margot, who looked at Harry like he'd said something profane. "That's...not the right answer, is it?"

Margot turned her face to me. "He's so cute. He's like a puppy." She grabbed ahold of the store's door, drawing it open. "After you, lovebirds."

The freshness of the store hit me as we walked in, a sharp scent of clean cologne coating the air, and the well-lit shop greeted us. Harry openly gawked at the suits that lined the walls, the rich patterns and pieces catching his eye. "This is...much fancier than I imagined," he whispered to me, and for the first time, he sounded more distressed than nervous.

"All the men will wear suits exactly like this, so you won't be anything special," I said teasingly, but when he didn't smile, I quickly added, "Unless you don't want to go, in which case I totally understand."

"No," he said quickly. Almost too quickly. "No, I want to go."

"That's the spirit," Margot said from his other side, removing her gloves and sunglasses. "Excuse me?" she called to the man behind the counter. "We need a fitting for this fine gentleman."

Without wasting a second, the man hurried out from

behind the counter. "Of course," he said with a bright smile, coming closer. "Do you know what size jacket you wear?"

"As it turns out, I do not," Harry said, winking at me.

"You look to be a 36, maybe a 38-inch chest. Let's try a few on and see which fits best, shall we?"

Harry grabbed my hand almost like a lifeline, forcing me to walk with him. Margot trailed behind, and when I met her gaze, she grinned. Grinning was rare for her, and very, very contagious. "I'm proud that you asked him," she whispered to me. "I thought you'd chicken out."

"Me? Never." Except for the fact that he really asked me if he could come, so technically I did chicken out. Just a smidge.

The man, Markus, went to retrieve a few suit jackets while we stood in the dressing area. Harry shrugged off his coat and placed it gently over the back of the chair, almost as if he were afraid he'd damage the upholstery.

"I have a few options," Markus said as he returned, three suit jackets thrown over his arm. "Try this on first."

And it began the process of Markus making Harry try on jacket after jacket until the third one fit the best. Margot and Markus took turns looking him over each time, easily determining that the third jacket was the one.

Even though I had no clue about suits, every single jacket looked great on him.

"Do you have anything in blue?" Margot asked, studying Harry as if he were a bug under a microscope. He took it like a champ, only looking mildly freaked under her imposing stare. "Look at that complexion. And the hair color. What about the navy, Markus?"

"We have a navy in stock in his size," he replied happily. "I can go grab the set for you."

"Wait," I called, leaning forward. I'd been lounging once again on a chair, but now leaned my elbows onto my knees. "Why not black?"

Margot looked at me as if she'd forgotten I was there. "Because yellow and navy go perfectly together, and you're going to wear that yellow dress you like."

"Uh, says who?" That dress wasn't one Mom liked. She said it looked too baggy on me, didn't show my curves well —maybe that was precisely the reason I liked it so much. But Mom was already getting one heart attack Saturday night. She didn't need two.

"*I* just said. Don't you listen?" Margot turned back to the boys. "Navy. It'll go so well with your eyes, Harry."

He gave a dutiful nod. "You're the boss."

Before Markus went to get the navy suit jacket, though, he bent down and started taking the measurements for Harry's pants. He placed the measuring tape along the length of Harry's leg, marking down numbers on his hand as he went. Once he finished, he hurried off to a back room to find something close to Harry's size.

"It's weird," Harry said, keeping his voice hushed. "I feel like I'm in a spy movie."

Margot lifted an eyebrow. "I don't remember spy movies being so boring."

Harry smiled at that, totally unfazed by Margot's

deadpan personality. "This is the part before the bad guys break in, of course."

"Here." Markus passed Harry an assortment of clothing on hangers, coming back into the room in a flurry of movement. "Try these on. They won't fit exactly—we'll tailor it to your measurements, of course—but it should give us a general idea of the fit."

Harry looked at me, lifting the garments a little. "Wish me luck."

Once he ducked in a dressing room, Margot came and sat down on a chair beside me, laying her hands on her knees. "So. The tattoo."

"What about it?"

"It's very visible." She stared at me intently. "Everyone will see it."

Everyone, she said, but I could read between the lines. *Your parents.* "It's not like we can laser it off, Margot."

"I didn't know if you wanted to cover it up. They have high-necked shirts."

A stone settled in my stomach, heavy and hard. "Are you sure it's a good idea to bring him?" I whispered, afraid he would overhear. "You know how people are."

"Who cares if they think Harry is a hooligan and I'm *too masculine*. They're old and probably haven't had sex in thirty years. At least not with their spouses."

I tried to keep the laugh at bay, but it snuck out in a snort. "Jeez, don't hold back."

She waved a hand at me, the intensity in her voice gone. "I'm just saying. Bring Harry. Flaunt him. Be proud of the life you live, Destelle, and it'll be okay."

"But Harry—"

"Is a big boy. I get the impression that he can hold his own." And then her expression turned a bit more devious. "Maybe Saturday night, *you* could hold—"

"What do you guys think?" Harry stepped out of the changing room then, dressed in a sleek-fitting navy suit, his red hair loose and touching the collar. There were faint, darker blue lines in the suit to add dimension, and it really flattered his figure. He hadn't buttoned the jacket or the vest, but came out having his head down, red wisps in his eyes.

It was suddenly hard to breathe or think of anything else but him. The suit jacket came down perfectly to his wrists, fitting his arms, smoothing over his shoulders. The collar at his throat fit nicely, not too tightly, his tattoo in full view.

I knew one thing for sure: Harry Russo in a suit was probably the hottest thing I'd seen in my life.

Harry smiled a little as he turned to face me fully, fingers still on the buttons. "Does it look okay?"

I pushed from the chair and made my way over to him, lacing his fingers with mine. "You only button the top one," I told him, my voice coming out softly. The suit smelled clean, and that mixed with his natural scent had my head spinning. "You leave the bottom button of the jacket undone."

I felt Harry's touch before I realized he'd lifted his hand, and he smoothed my hair behind my ear. My curls made it impossible for the hair to stay there, of course, but the electric trace of his fingertips remained. "Does it look okay?" he asked again.

"Very."

"Very okay?"

I swallowed hard. "*Very* okay."

"Oh." Markus tsked when he came back into the dressing room, but when I turned to him, he had on a megawatt grin. "Oh, it's near perfect! That doesn't always happen, you know."

Harry glanced down at his feet as I stepped back. "The pants are supposed to look like this?"

"Of course not," Margot told him, like a patient parent talking to a confused child. "They'll hem them."

She walked closer though, examining every inch of him. If anyone could figure out the faults in the suit, it'd be Margot. She glanced at me before turning to Markus. "Do you have any higher-necked dress shirts?"

My fingers twitched impulsively into a fist. Despite my warring thoughts, I stayed quiet.

"No offense, Harry," she went on. "With these people, first impressions are everything."

When I looked back to Harry, I found his fingers touching the collar of the shirt he wore, picking at the stiff fabric. I knew what his answer would be. "I'll try it on," he said as Markus herded him back toward the dressing room. "Who knows, I might look sexier in it."

"Worth a shot," I responded, trying to match the same vein of humor, but it fell flat.

Margot's eyes were victorious, which almost made me feel a little worse about this whole situation. Here I was, making Harry cancel his band gig and come to a party filled with people who'd judge him for being himself. I was the worst kind of girlfriend.

To my surprise, Margot smoothed her hand over my shoulder, giving it a comforting squeeze. "It'll be okay," she assured, in a voice that oozed confidence. "You'll see."

Even though she sounded confident, I couldn't help but wonder if she truly meant it.

twenty

$\mathcal{M}$y house on country club nights was always hectic, an explosion of noise and flurry that could've hinted that the Brighton household was self-destructing. It was the only time that my parents lived in their own version of chaos instead of the perfect image they strived to achieve.

"Jamie, where's your tie?" I heard Dad call through the floorboards.

"Have you seen my pearl earrings, David?" Mom demanded back. "Nellie, did you take them again?"

"Jamie, I saw that—leave the book at home."

"Nellie! The earrings?"

The gentle hum of noise pumped my nerves up even higher, almost to where it was hard to steady my breathing. Yep, I was going to hurl all over the yellow dress that still hung in my closet. If Mom saw me in it, she'd make me change into something else, so I put it off until the last moment.

Yellow because it looked good with navy, and Harry would be wearing navy...

I was seriously going to pass out.

And that nausea was amplified by the fact that I hadn't told Mom or Dad about Harry. Not a peep. They had no clue I intended on bringing a date tonight. I'd figured that Mom and Dad finding out about Harry when we walked into the country club was the best idea. That way they couldn't force me to stay home, forbid me from bringing him.

Instead, they'd be forced to smile, a prim and proper attitude, stuffing all their flustered emotions underneath their masks.

Now, though, as the clock ticked closer and closer to the time Harry was supposed to arrive, I couldn't help but think that this was a bad, bad idea.

"Destelle!" Mom called up the stairs, voice echoing and breaking me from my thoughts. "We're leaving in five minutes!"

I swiped a little blush over my cheeks. The color was a bit too light for my skin tone, but it'd have to do.

Getting around as Destelle was vastly different from putting an outfit together as Stella. For one, Destelle accessorized with shinier pieces. I had a few bangles on one wrist and a charm bracelet on the other. The earrings I wore dangled to the middle of my neck, a waterfall of gemstones. They occasionally got tangled in my curls, but they still twinkled in the lights. The diamond choker I wore was a little loose, so it drooped toward my collarbones.

Of course, though, these were all pieces Mom had laid out for me to put on. I didn't even think to protest.

Mom's knuckles rapped on my door a second before she pushed it open. She wore suits to work, but for the events, she picked dresses that perfectly flattered her figure. The one for tonight was a little tight in the waist but flowing out by the hips, and always a color that complemented her skin tone. She'd pinned her dark hair up, a few strands loose to frame her face.

"You're not even dressed," she gasped, gaze wide. "Destelle, we're leaving in less than—"

"I was hoping I could drive separately," I said, cutting her off and immediately regretting it. Before she scolded me for it, I hurried on. "That way I'm not crammed in the back seat with the twins. I—I'll be right behind you in the SUV."

Mom examined me from head to toe, taking in the jewelry, my curls, even my house robe. "I suppose that will be all right," she finally decided. "What dress are you wearing?"

"I still have to pick," I lied. "Whatever one jumps out at me, I suppose."

Mom ventured deeper into my bedroom until she stood beside me, picking up the blush brush. "Well, I trust you'll wear something appropriate," she murmured, running the brush across my cheekbones. I held perfectly still. "Are you going to Margot's afterward?"

"Not tonight." There was no reason to "go to Margot's." Untapped Potential canceled their gig for the night. "I'll be coming straight home."

Mom set the brush down and tipped her fingers underneath my chin, lifting my face toward the light. "Better. You hadn't put enough on before."

Never enough.

"Mom?" I asked her before she stepped out of my room, my call making her pause. "Can I ask you a question?"

"A question?" she echoed, frowning a little. "Of course. Speak fast, we need to get going."

"If I were to bring a new guy into the picture," I started slowly, but hurried on, "would you give him a chance?"

Mom took a step back into the room, close enough to flip my hair over my shoulder gently. "Destelle, you are too busy for a relationship. You said yourself that there was so much to keep track of."

If only she knew I'd had a boyfriend for the past month. "Is there ever a perfect time for a relationship?"

"After college," she answered easily. "That's when I met your father."

"What if I were to meet someone now? Would you be nice to him? Accept him?"

Mom's face screwed up ever so slightly, as if she smelled something bad. This conversation wasn't one she wanted to have—that much was obvious. She no doubt wondered where this all came from. When did her Destelle get interested in boys again? Where could she have met someone? But before she had a chance to ask, Dad called up the stairs. "Come on, ladies, or we'll be late!"

"We'll talk about this later," Mom said, still holding my gaze.

Would we? Or would this conversation slip under the rug, something she didn't want to deal with?

Knowing that she'd meet Harry in less than a half hour, I figured it probably *would* come back up.

Once their car safely backed out of the driveway, I put on the yellow dress and looked down at the loose golden fabric. One wrinkle refused to budge, though, and my attention kept drawing back to it. *It's going to be fine*, I told myself, staring at my nail polish. *It's not like these are actually sharks you're feeding him to.*

Well, that wasn't overly comforting.

I still stood up in my room, in my tower, looking at the world below. Not a trace of snow stuck to the ground now, all of it melting away as spring kicked in. The April air was already so refreshing from the long winter. The nights were getting a smidge longer too. Even at nearly seven o'clock, the sun glimmered in the sky.

Since I stared out the window, I saw the exact moment Harry eased his car along the curb of my house. He didn't pull into the driveway, but he also didn't park in front of the neighbor's house like he did last time.

A weight pressed down on my chest, crushing my ribs. Before I could see Harry get out of the car, I stepped back, letting the sheer curtain fall into place.

For what felt like the millionth time, I ran my fingers over that wrinkle, trying in vain to smooth it out. This was his first time seeing me dolled up like this, a drastic change from Stella. Oh, my gosh, what if he didn't like me like this? I mean, it wasn't like I normally dressed like a slob around him, but I was wearing a diamond necklace. What if that freaked him out?

The doorbell chimed throughout the house, a melodic sound announcing Harry's heart-stopping arrival.

Jeez, why was I so nervous about this? Margot had said that they hired the musicians who actually played decent music, so at least Harry and I could dance together. But definitely not like how we'd danced at Downtown. I tried to imagine what everyone's faces would've looked like if they'd seen us dancing like that, with roaming hands and shared breaths. It made me shiver just thinking about it.

The doorbell chimed again, hinting that I'd been imagining that moment longer than I intended to. I grabbed my shawl and hurried down the stairs, already anticipating opening the door.

Harry Russo stood on the other side, straight out of a men's fashion magazine.

He wore the navy suit we'd picked out at Gilfman on Tuesday, and it fit him like a glove, tight in all the right places. He wore his lightly patterned collared shirt buttoned to his neck, where a matching navy tie wrapped perfectly. It completely obscured any trace of a tattoo.

He'd swept his red hair out of his face, and his blue eyes glittered as they landed on me. And seemed to trace up and down along my body in a slow perusal, one that made all the air in my lungs evaporate.

Harry opened his mouth and quickly closed it, blinking fast. "Wow," he finally managed.

"Does it look okay?" I asked, raising my shawl and clutch a bit, glancing down at my body.

"Very." Harry's voice sounded low.

My lips curved as déjà vu washed over me. "Very okay?"

His eyes held a certain intensity when he replied, "*Very* okay."

I shivered, though I tried to play it as caused by the outside air. I held my sparkly clutch out to him, trying to keep my hand steady. "Can you hold this for a second?"

He took it with ease while I shrugged my shawl on, the furry fabric brushing against my skin. It made me feel fancier than necessary, but the pink Claire-Haute wouldn't look cute with this yellow dress. "My parents will be mingling when we get there," I told him, trying to force my thoughts back on track. "So, I'll just introduce you to whoever is closest to the door first."

Looking back to Harry, I found he still stared at me like he couldn't believe what he was seeing. Pleasure and self-consciousness battled for top spot, with embarrassment being close behind. "G-Got it."

"And then we can get a drink. They usually serve champagne and don't care when we take a flute."

"Got it."

"You said that already."

"Yeah, see, I'm trying *really* hard not to kiss you right now. It's taking ninety percent of my attention."

The step I took toward him clattered as my heel clicked on the floor, and I wrapped my arms around his neck, leaning against his chest. "Only ninety percent?"

"A little more now," he murmured, eyes angling down to mine. "Ninety-five."

Warmth shot through my bloodstream as I brought my lips oh-so-close to his. "Ninety-five?"

"Maybe ninety-nine now—"

I pressed my mouth to his, silencing the last of his words. His hands rose to my waist, kissing me deeply, fully. No room for air or thought. I swear, I could've done this for the rest of my life. The way he felt and tasted was nothing short of bliss, and I leaned closer against him, craving more of this heat.

And then he broke away with a small laugh, not straying too far. "What a way to start the night," he whispered, then swallowed hard.

I traced my fingertips along his smooth cheekbone like he'd done to me so many times, bedazzled by his beauty. Someone shouldn't be so handsome, with reddish, thick lashes that framed his Caribbean blue eyes like a work of art. I could stare at them all day, wondering what story he had hidden in their depths. "You know, it's not too late. We could still ditch this thing."

"And do what?" he murmured in a way that let me know he was merely humoring me.

"We could go to Downtown," I said, walking my fingertips up his tie. "I haven't been since that night."

I watched the blue of his eyes dance as he recalled the memory of that night, and despite the cool air of spring, I felt warm.

"Sorry." Harry slipped his arm around my waist, pressing a kiss against my temple before. "But Margot is expecting us, and I'm not letting her hard work with this suit go to waste. And I need to meet your parents," he added, almost as a nervous afterthought.

"It's going to be fine," I said, echoing the mantra I'd been repeating all day. *Going to be fine, going to be fine.*

"Hey, maybe this should be my own alter ego," he told me, still holding me close. He put on an announcer's voice, smiling. "Harrison Russo, suit-wearing stud."

"Careful, I might have to kiss you again." And I followed through on that, pressing one last chaste kiss against his mouth. After grabbing the house keys, I pulled back from him, offering my hand for him to take. "Shall we?"

*H*arry, it turned out, had never used a valet before.

"Seriously?" he'd asked when we pulled up to the doors and a valet boy rounded toward the driver's side. "They actually do this? This isn't just in movies?"

I couldn't help but laugh. "It's a real thing."

And Harry was also surprised when I left my shawl at the coat check, receiving my ticket from the girl and tucking it into my clutch. "Wow," Harry said, shaking his head at where the girl disappeared. "Why not throw the jackets over the chairs?"

"So uncivilized," I said dramatically, leaning into his chest. Underneath my fingers, I could feel his heart beat steadily, unlike mine.

There weren't too many people in the foyer of the country club; they must've already gone into the banquet hall, where everyone mingled until dinner would be served in the main dining area. Mom and Dad were probably in there now waiting for me to show.

Harry seemed to catch a hint of my hesitation. "After you," he murmured, holding his arm out like a gentleman in a movie would.

With a small, shaky grin, I took it. "If we've got no other choice."

Harry patted my hand. "It can't be that bad."

"I feel like you're jinxing it."

He laughed beside me, the sound barely there.

Before getting into the main hall, we had to pass the collection of kids in the corridor. When Nellie spotted us, her eyes widened bigger than I'd ever seen them. Behind her, Jamie slowly pushed to his feet. "Uh, who is *he*?"

My date offered a hand out to Nellie, smiling. "I'm Harry."

Jamie came closer, gaze almost distrustful as he looked at Harry. Wary, at the very least. "Is this the guy you went on a date with and kept it from Mom and Dad?"

Harry blinked as I inwardly winced. *Off to a fabulous start.* "I—I wanted to introduce him to Mom and Dad." I wound my arm around Harry tighter, feeling his body press against the side of mine. "And introduce him to you too."

"I think they'll like him," Nellie said cheerfully. "I can tell. Harry, I'm really into words. Give me one to spell."

Harry glanced at me, quirking his mouth to the side. "Hmm. Cashier."

Nellie hunched her shoulders as she smiled, a burst of excitement working through her. "That's too easy," she told him, and then cleared her throat. "C-A-S-H-I-E-R. Cashier."

"That was great," he said with a grin, holding his fist out to her.

Nellie slammed hers into it. "Thanks."

"Well, we should head in," I said, addressing no one in particular. Maybe I was waiting for Jamie to say something, to step forward and be friendly as well, but he didn't. "We'll see you guys later."

"Nice meeting you two," Harry told them warmly as I pulled him away, toward the main hall's archway. "They're sweet."

"They're terrors. But they have their moments."

At least seventy people were stuffed into the banquet space, all dressed to their best, mingling and laughing. I pretended I was taking in the scene for the first time, putting myself in Harry's shoes.

Much of the ceiling was made of glass, which gave the entire room a light and open feel. The entire space had been decorated to its usual grandeur, with the sparkling champagne and the elegant tables dressed along the sides of the room. Plenty of space for the dance floor, of course, and couples mingled around it like little social butterflies.

Margot had been right—they had hired the band everyone enjoyed dancing to, and they played a carefree song.

I glanced at Harry, taking in his startled expression. Thankfully, it wasn't a *What did I get myself into* expression. "What are you thinking?"

"I—I'm thinking you were right. There are a lot of suits."

I wondered if he was calculating how much money was

in this room right now. Sometimes I did that. How much money did renting the country club out for the night cost, how much money did Mrs. Meyer's dress cost—add it all together, and how much did we have?

"I'm also thinking it's really beautiful in here," he went on before my thoughts had the chance to wander too far. His expression still looked a little awestruck. "I'm thinking I like the glass ceiling and the marble flooring. Makes me wish I'd added a skylight to my house. It's pretty."

Pretty. That it was.

But what else was pretty? *Him.* I could've looked at him all night. The way the chandelier lights graced his face looked magical. Maybe it was the warm glow that reflected against his eyelashes, or the way it streaked through his hair, bringing out hints of gold.

So freaking handsome. I wanted to kiss him.

"There you are," Margot said to my right, and I found her easing away from the wall a few feet from us. "You two seem to have the habit of being late to things. Do you make out in the car?"

Harry laughed easily at that, as if we were standing in Crushed Beanz rather than the country club. "Not in the car."

"Well, you're here now." Margot gestured toward the dance floor, where all the gossips were watching us. I caught Ms. Jennings's eye, her gaze roaming over Harry like a hungry wolf. "Go mingle."

Harry straightened, looking expectantly to me. "Who should I meet first?"

By that moment, Ms. Jennings had crossed the dance

floor to us, her mauve-painted lips spreading into a glorious smile. "I recognize you," she declared. "You're the guy from Le Petit Bateau. You served our table."

"That's me," he said with an easy grin, extending his hand. "Harrison."

He'd been serious about the whole alter ego thing. It made me fight a smile.

Ms. Jennings laid her hand in his, almost as if she expected him to kiss it or something. "Call me Ally."

Ew.

Harry took her hand and simply shook it. "Nice to meet you."

Her gaze roamed over him, much like mine had earlier when I found him at the foot of the staircase. Even though Ms. Jennings was easily twenty years older than me, I found jealousy percolating underneath my skin, simmering on high. Harry, though, didn't move his hand from my waist, a pressure that left me feeling somewhat victorious in this situation.

"Have you seen my mother?" I asked her, trying to see over the crowd of people.

"Bah, you don't want to spend the evening with your mother, do you?" She waved her hand in the air, her diamond bracelet jingling. "Let's go mingle! You know, Marty has been dying to talk to you about your scholarship application, Destelle. His wife told me about it the other day at tea. They *loved* your essay. I think I saw him over by the band—"

I grabbed Harry by the arm. "Actually, I think we're

going to find someone first," I told her, cutting her off unkindly. "We'll catch up with you later."

Ms. Jennings's eyes roamed over Harry once more. "You'd better."

Harry let me drag him through the crowd of people, going in the opposite direction of the band.

"She seems kind." Harry swept my curls off my shoulder, his finger lingering at the bare skin near my collarbone. The dress was a little more low-cut than I normally wore, but nothing of scandalous proportions. However, just that touch of his fingertip sent a shiver through me, raising goosebumps.

"These people have mastered the art of the fake smile," I told him in a hushed whisper, glancing around. No one paid us any attention, though, too caught up in their conversations. "You never know what they're thinking."

Harry's hand curved around my waist, easing over the fabric of my dress. "What are *you* thinking?"

I slid one hand up Harry's chest, feeling the stiff material of the tie and vest. *So many things.* "I'm thinking I would rather be at Crushed Beanz right now."

"I'm happy right here," he said, a smile twitching at his lips.

"Or Downtown," I murmured, wondering if his thoughts were trailing in the same direction as mine. His hands on my waist, mine around his neck, barely an inch of space between us.

A ghost of a smile touched Harry's lips as he picked up my hand from his chest. "Dance with me?"

"Uh, hate to break it to you, but if we dance like that here, we'd probably give someone a heart attack."

That ghostly smile expanded into a real one, so wide that it crinkled his eyes. "I promise I'll behave."

Harry was the one who guided me to the dance floor, moving with a confidence that it was nearly impossible for me to master, even as Stella. Even though he was the odd one out here, a stranger among the masses, he was perfectly content to just be himself. I envied that.

"I'll be honest," he said as he settled one hand at my waist, the other holding my hand beside our shoulders. "I have no idea how to dance like this."

I nearly snorted at his serious tone, peering up into his eyes. "No one's going to judge."

"Really?"

"Well, they'll probably judge, but who cares?"

Harry ducked his head closer at that, a whisper of a laugh tickling my ear.

Even though this dance was drastically different from our first dance at Downtown, I found my eyes fluttering shut as I basked in the moment. Harry's hand was light at my waist, holding me closer. As if I'd stray far.

I could almost pretend like it was just us on this dance floor, like no one else in the entire country club existed. Just him and me underneath the golden chandelier lights, dressed our best, in a fairytale of a moment.

Harry turned me in a slow circle, moving in time with the beat of the song. "How come Margot doesn't—what was the word she used—mingle?"

"She doesn't really like these things. Everyone treats

her differently, just because she doesn't fit in. At least, *they* say she doesn't fit in." It wasn't something I noticed until we met in our junior year. All the attendees treated her differently from me; they weren't nearly as welcoming, as conversational. It was almost as if they saw me as an easier mark or something. "I wish people left *me* alone in the corner."

His velvety gaze lingered on my mouth. "You don't belong in a corner."

"You say things like that." I shook my head, feeling my cheeks flush. "It makes me want to kiss you."

"Your parents are around here somewhere," he murmured, voice low enough to send a shiver across my skin. "Might want to keep things G-rated."

That was the only thing that held me back. And barely, at that.

"Destelle! There you are." I turned to find Mr. Marty Ricker, graying hair cut cleanly, and wearing a pinstripe suit, coming up behind Harry. "Your parents weren't sure you were here yet. I've been meaning to—oh. I didn't realize you were with someone."

Mr. Ricker had faltered when Harry stepped closer to me, and the former's eyes looked distrustfully at the unknown party. "Mr. Ricker, it's lovely to see you. This is my boyfriend."

"Harrison," Harry responded, giving the elder a firm handshake. "Great to meet you."

Mr. Ricker didn't respond right away, as if he were trying to gauge whether, in fact, it *was* great to meet him. Ultimately, he turned to me, animating immediately.

"Destelle, I've been wanting to talk to you about your scholarship application. The future plans category, in fact. You should've told me you planned on becoming a lawyer—all the grand conversations we could've had."

I felt Harry shift at my side, but I didn't glance over. "It only seems natural, given the role models I have. Having a father and mother both involved in the judicial system— well, it only makes sense to follow in their footsteps."

It had been the speech that Mom gave to me as she suggested her answer for that scholarship question. I'd written it down, if only to appease her in that moment. But now, with Harry over my shoulder, I felt like the world's biggest hypocrite.

"Of course, of course," Mr. Ricker murmured, and then his gaze trailed off to my side. "So, Harrison—what's your dream career path?"

"Music," he answered, and I couldn't help but hear how formal his voice sounded now.

"Harrison's in the industry, in fact," I told Mr. Ricker, pressing a hand along my boyfriend's chest. The suit underneath was stiff. "He's got a bright future ahead of him."

"Ah, music. How lovely." Mr. Ricker's face didn't seem to agree with his words, though, from the pinched lines near his eyes. "Well, Destelle, perhaps we can meet for lunch one day and discuss your application at length. I shouldn't say this, but you're at the top for our choosing."

No, I wanted to say. *Take me off your list. I don't want it.* "I'll look at my upcoming schedule and we'll plan it, Mr. Ricker."

With one last chuckle, he ventured away from us, off to

find someone else to mingle with. Distantly, I wondered if he gave anyone else that same speech. *You're at the top for our choosing.* It wouldn't have surprised me.

"Look at you, you're a natural." When I turned to Harry, I found his eyes trailing after Mr. Ricker, something like that dang shadow from before lingering in his gaze now. "Everything okay?"

"Yeah." He glanced down at me, eyes holding a good amount of uncertainty. "Everything's okay."

"Well, lookie here."

I turned to find Nancy making her way up to us. She dressed her best tonight, red hat perched delicately on her head. She'd put on lipstick for the occasion, a bright red that made her skin seem pale. "Ms. Nancy," I greeted, raising my voice a little in case she couldn't hear over the music. "Looking lovely as ever."

Nancy's eyes lifted to me before immediately shifting to Harry. Her eyes narrowed as she looked at him closely, almost scrutinizing. Harry, though, didn't let it faze him, and he offered a hand out. "I'm Harrison, ma'am."

"*Ma'am,*" she spat, but fire danced in her eyes. "How old do I look to you?"

"An age that demands respect," he returned easily, his hand not wavering.

Nancy's eyes narrowed even further at that, as though she tried to fight a smile. "That's a good answer," she allowed, and let him shake her hand. "Almost *too* good."

"He's good with words," I told her.

"I recognize you." Her gaze roamed him up and down

before snagging at his neck. "From the restaurant. Where's your tattoo? Was it those washable kinds?"

Harry laughed. "Tucked out of sight for the night," he said, tugging at the collar of his shirt.

"Shouldn't hide it," she decided. "Makes you look sexy."

The noise that came out of my mouth was *so* not lady-like. "Ms. Nancy—"

"Let me cut in, Destelle," Nancy said as she grabbed his hands once more. "Show me your moves, handsome."

Harry looked at me a little wide-eyed, but he at least looked a little amused, the shadowy expression gone. "I'll be right back," he promised me, as Nancy quickly drew away, further out onto the dance floor, the little old lady holding onto the handsome young man like a lifeline.

Ms. Nancy stole my date. Figured. Margot practically called it.

The height difference was almost laughable since he stood almost an entire foot taller. It forced him to lean down to hear her better as she spoke. She'd captured one of his hands in hers, his other hand rested at her hip, and his grin was easy as he listened. It made my heart feel warm.

"Who in God's name is that?"

My body locked up, the fight-or-flight reaction kicking in strong. I almost didn't want to turn around, to just flee into the crowd of people. That might've worked, but I could *definitely* see her following me. So, I faced the music.

And when I turned, I found Mother and Father, two fire-breathing dragons. Well, Mom looked more like she could breathe fire. Dad looked confused, as if he couldn't imagine his little girl with a boy without knowing anything about it.

"That's Harry," I said with way more confidence than I felt, turning back to look at him and Nancy.

"Harry?" Mom sputtered. "That's all you have to say?"

"I answered your question."

A thrill raced through my veins, knowing that she was melting down on the inside but couldn't let it show. For once, I almost felt more powerful than her.

"We need you to give us more information, Destelle," Dad said, his voice much calmer.

"Where did you meet him? How old is he?" Mom added with a hiss, "Because he looks too old for you."

I curled my hands into fists behind my back. "He's eighteen—only a year older. We met at a coffee shop." What was something else I could say to pacify them? Although I gloated a little on the inside about their shocked expressions, I still wanted them to like Harry. "He volunteers, too. We volunteered at the church a few weeks back."

Mom and Dad exchanged a look, probably using their telepathy to decide if I was lying. "Is that what your whole 'boy speech' was about earlier tonight?" Mom demanded.

"I wouldn't call it a speech—"

"You should've asked us for permission." Mom glanced around the space, as if someone were secretly listening in. "This isn't the place to introduce someone."

Or maybe Margot was right and this was the perfect place.

Dad turned back to Harry and Nancy, his expression still confused. Thank goodness their dance hadn't ended yet—I needed to soften my parents up some more. "What did you say his name was again?"

"Harry Russo. And, trust me, he's a great guy."

The perplexity in Dad's expression cleared the second Mom's seemed to grow angrier, especially the longer she studied Harry's face. She pursed her lips but then quickly rid herself of that expression, as if she knew it wasn't flattering. "Wait a second. Is that the boy from Le Petit Bateau? The one with the tattoo?"

Of course she recognized him. "Yes."

"Well, then, I can definitely see why you'd bring him *here*," she said in an even voice, but I knew she was anything but pleased. If we weren't around so many people, I'm sure she would've made it known. "You can dress him up as much as you want, but he still looks like he's trouble, Destelle."

Harry, trouble? Yeah, he had a neck tattoo, but he was also the gentlest person I'd met.

"You don't know him," I told her, and the resentment finally, finally snapped inside my voice. Gone was the flinching cowardice, yielding to every one of Mom's glares. It was my turn to deal it out. "He's kind, Mom. And if you'd stop being so judgmental, like all these other people in here, you'd see that. You'd see *him*, not some tattoo."

Mom raised her eyebrows in a dangerous sort of surprise. "You want to talk to me like that?" she demanded. "Really? Now?"

I hated when she did that. She'd lace an unspoken threat in her words, hoping that the fear of the unknown would get me to fall back in line. If she were judging *me*, I

might've stayed in my lane. But judging Harry? It wasn't
going to fly. "You know I'm right."

"Let's both calm down," Dad interjected, ever the
peacemaker. He laid his hand on Mom's arm. "Alice, why
don't we—"

Dad cut himself off suddenly, and only a second later, I
felt a hand brush against my elbow. I turned and found
Harry looking at me. Inwardly, I winced, wishing the song
could've lasted a few moments longer. "Harry," I said,
catching his hand with mine. "This is my mom and dad."

And suddenly the entire mood between the four of us
shifted. Mom found a smile somewhere in her cabinet of
emotions and put it on, and if I hadn't heard her tone a
moment ago, I wouldn't have known it wasn't genuine.
Dad, too, looked welcoming, stepping forward to extend a
hand. "You can call me David, though I know it's probably
strange. But Mr. Brighton seems a bit formal, right? Don't
you teenagers go on a first-name basis?"

I cringed. "Dad. Dial it back, okay?"

After I got the words out, I realized Harry hadn't taken
Dad's hand, which Dad still extended, almost a little
awkwardly.

When I looked at the boy beside me, I found his face
pale, not a trace of color in his cheeks. Whatever enthusiasm that had glittered in his eyes before had disappeared
now, and not even the shadow lingered. No, this emotion
was pure alarm.

Then he broke from his stupor, grasping Dad's hand
slowly. "H-Harry."

"Good to meet you, Harry," Dad said in a kind voice,

acting as if Harry hadn't hesitated. Mom, though, didn't offer her hand to him. "How are you enjoying the night so far?

Harry's hand stiffened in mine. "It's...something."

"A different atmosphere than you're used to, I'm sure," Mom said, wrapping her arm around Dad's.

"Mother." My voice was sharp enough that it drew the attention of people passing nearby the punch table. "He's used to larger crowds, actually. He's in a band—the singer," I told them, giving Harry an encouraging smile, but he didn't glance over. He was laser-focused on his shoes. "And they're really good. They're wanting to expand to new places soon. They're playing at a coffee shop in Hallow for right now."

Dad made a noise of approval, nodding his head. "Well, isn't that something? Alice, which of the Preston brothers is into music? Was it Sam or Trent?"

"Trent. He owns a recording studio." Mom's eyes lingered on Harry. "Have you had the chance to record any songs? You and your band?"

"Not yet," Harry said, the words forced out. "Maybe one day."

"*For sure* one day," I corrected him. "You never know who you might run into."

Harry's lips tried to smile, but didn't quite manage it.

Okay, maybe this was the perfect moment to whisk Harry away before they said anything else. I didn't trust Mom to not sneak in one more snarky comment. But right before I could interject a departure, Dad spoke up. "You know, Harry, I could mention something to Trent—he's always looking for new music, or at least he says. I'm sure he'd love a band that's local. Maybe he could swing by sometime to hear how you sound."

I blinked, totally taken back by his offer. That wasn't something I'd expected. Condescension, maybe, but not something that would help Harry move his music career along. I was utterly stupefied. Harry was too, obviously, because he looked at my dad with wide eyes.

"I wouldn't want to make you uncomfortable," Dad went on when Harry didn't respond. "And I can't guarantee his response, but it could be worth a shot."

"They play every Friday and Saturday," I told Dad when Harry still didn't respond. I squeezed Harry's hand, but he didn't squeeze back.

"Well, if it isn't the Brightons," Mr. Holland greeted as he made his way over, grinning at all of us. His suit jacket was loose on his frame, wrinkles lining his eyes. "Nice to see you, as always."

Even though I was freaking out on the inside, I forced my expression to calm. "Mr. Holland," I said with the air of someone who was thoroughly pleased. "Love the bowtie you're wearing. Is that Gilfman?"

"Oh, why yes." He chuckled while he adjusted the material, loosening around his collar. "Got an eye for fashion, do you?"

That, or Margot has the same tie.

Mr. Holland turned toward my father and took him by the arm, giving him a shake. "How have you been, David? We need to start our poker nights back up again—anything to get out of the house once in a while, you know what I mean?"

His words effectively captured the attention of my parents, who turned to Mr. Holland with their brilliant smiles. When I glanced at Harry again, though, I saw something I definitely wasn't expecting. *Panic.* Pure, electric panic. "What's wrong?" I asked immediately, confusion and worry bubbling up.

Harry looked down at me, but his mind was elsewhere. "I—I'm going to get some air," he all but choked out, quickly untangling his fingers from my own. I hadn't realized how tightly I'd been holding his hand; my grip had been the only reason our hands stuck together. "I'll be back."

"I'll come with you—"

"No," he said sharply, sucking in a breath. "I just—I need a minute."

I opened my mouth to say something more, but Harry strode away, near sprinting back toward the entrance of the country club. Dad watched him leave while Mom and Mr. Holland were talking, then Dad glanced at me. Even though the contact was a split second, I could fully read his thoughts: *Is he okay?*

I had no idea.

And then, ever so slightly, Dad tipped his head toward the door. *Go check on him.*

Margot caught my eye as I passed her through the doorway. "Where's the fire?" she asked, but I just shook my head.

My heels clacked in quick succession, and I moved

with such purpose that no one bothered stopping me this time. No one even thought about trying to call my attention away.

I found Harry striding down the long corridor that led to the front entrance, moving past the kids lingering in the hall. Nellie acted as if she wanted to speak with him, but he hurried past her, all of his focus on getting outside.

I skipped grabbing my coat as I followed Harry. He stopped outside the entrance, hands in fists at his sides. My heart hammered fast in my chest, almost making me feel jittery, like I'd drank one too many cups of coffee.

"Are you okay?" I asked him. "What just happened?"

Harry pressed a hand against the collar of his shirt— where he'd usually be able to touch his tattoo. "I thought you said your last name was Fontaine."

"What?" I definitely hadn't been expecting him to say *that*. "No, my mom's last name is Fontaine. She kept her maiden name. Brighton is my dad's last name."

Wait, this entire time, he thought my name was Fontaine? That was...a very weird thought. We'd been hanging out for almost two months and he had my last name wrong in his head. I guess the topic hadn't really ever come up, mostly because it never occurred to me. Harry didn't have a personal social media account, and my account only went by Destelle Marie. I just assumed he knew it.

But was mistaking a last name really worth his panicked expression?

I wrapped my arms around myself, pinching my fingers into my skin. One second, he was fine, and the next... "Did you hear what my parents said?" I guessed, shoulders slumping. "Harry, they're just stupid and judgmental. Who cares what they think?"

"You," he whispered, voice slowly gaining strength. "You care. That's why you didn't tell them about me before now. Why you filled out applications saying you wanted to be a lawyer." His body shivered, almost as if he were cold. "That's why you made Stella, right? You care about what they think."

"I do those things because they don't understand me," I said, my chest tingling. It felt like we were going down a road that wouldn't lead to a good place. "They don't want to understand me. It's easier to go along with what they want."

He swallowed hard, looking more devastated than anything else. "This isn't me," he said, clenching his jaw so tightly that I could see the muscles tense. "Suits and champagne flutes and fake smiles—that's not me."

"It doesn't have to be you—"

"But it's *you*." His voice came out emphatic, almost desperate. "It's Destelle. There's no—no separating that. There's no pretending that side doesn't exist. I almost didn't recognize you in there."

The wind burned my eyes. For the first time, when he said my full name, it didn't make me feel warm and fuzzy. "What is that supposed to mean?"

"Is this you?" He splayed his hand toward the country club and then glanced up and down at me. "Because the girl I'd gotten to know wasn't anywhere in that room."

"Harry, it's how these things are—" I cut myself off

when he jerked back from my touch, freezing with my hand outstretched as hurt covered me.

"You don't know," he whispered, more to himself. He looked at me almost as if he were staring at a stranger, and the panic in his gaze numbed down a bit. Gosh, if I could see inside his mind right then, I would've given anything for it. "We're from two totally different worlds, Destelle. Too different."

Again, *Destelle*. Not Stella. It seemed significant.

"Who cares?" I demanded, recalling my conversation once upon a time with Jonathan. "No one is saying we can't be together."

"Your parents will." A smile glanced over his lips, but it wasn't a kind one. "Trust me. Your dad definitely won't let you see me anymore."

"Why not? Besides, this entire time, we've made it work," I argued. "The volunteering—"

"If they haven't figured out that you were skipping volunteering already, they will." Harry's fingers picked at the button on his collar furiously until it popped undone, and he slid open another, exposing his throat, his tattoo. The action seemed to give him a semblance of peace. "When else would we have had time to meet each other?"

I wasn't an idiot. Harry looked handsome in a suit, and I may have looked pretty with the wig on, but that didn't change the fact that we were different. But we overcame that. I couldn't figure out why he was suddenly so upset about it, why meeting my parents threw him into a freak-out.

"So, you're saying that because my parents will *forbid*

me to—" I spoke the last three words with hard emphasis, "—that, what, our relationship is doomed? Really? You were completely fine when you knew me as Stella. You didn't care at all when I was just her."

"That's the thing—you *were* Stella. I could understand Stella, I was more alike with Stella—"

"You wouldn't have danced with Destelle if she asked you that night?" I demanded, the situation I'd always feared coming to pass. "If I'd come up to you with my Claire-Haute and diamond necklace, would you have danced with me?"

Harry clenched his jaw, eyes bright. "No."

I literally took a step back, as if I could fully step away from his answer. *No.* If I'd gone up to him as me, not as Stella, he would've told me no. It had been something I was afraid of way back in the beginning, back before he knew the truth. That he wouldn't have given Destelle, *me*, the time of day.

I thought about what he'd told me back in February, before we'd even gone on our first date. *I'm not really looking to date right now.*

He wouldn't have made that exception for Destelle, not like he did for Stella.

"I can't even explain it," he said as he dragged his hands across his face, settling down at his throat. "It's just too different."

"We're the same person!" I all but shouted, speaking the words for the first time aloud. "I'm Stella and I'm Destelle—nothing's changed."

"Nothing?" he echoed. "Are you going to meet that

man about the scholarship application? And then what? Are you going to accept? Are you going to swallow your hopes and dreams and be what everyone else wants you to be?"

"I—I don't know!"

He shook his head ever so slightly. "Stella wouldn't."

I hated that he was right, because he *was*. Stella would declare her own path, forge her own future. And in theory, I wanted that, but in practice? "I'm not like those people in there," I told him, willing myself to believe my own words. "I'm not."

"So, you don't give fake smiles? No telling people what they want to hear?"

The vise around my chest squeezed hard, knocking all the air. It was as if someone held a mirror to me, but instead of my own reflection I saw someone else's. My mother's.

"There's so much," he whispered, with eyes as bright as the stars. Harry simply breathed for what felt like an eternity, not speaking. "There's a chasm between you and me and you don't even see it."

"What chasm?" I demanded. "Because I'm a part of this country club? Because of money?"

His frown deepened, expression so sad. "I wish it were that simple." Harry reached into his pocket, pulling out the valet ticket with a shaking hand. "A chasm, Destelle, and we're both destined to fall in."

Sometimes the poetic way he said things was so striking. When he said things melodically, I could almost picture the song being written. I wished I had a way with words like him. Now, though, the poetic tone of his words only hurt, especially when my gaze locked on his hand holding his valet ticket. "What are you doing?"

"I—I need to go." He closed his eyes, shielding me from the Caribbean blue, and he drew in a deep breath. His body shook, even down to his fingers trembling. "I'm sorry I wasted your time."

I opened my mouth to say something, something to get him to stay longer and talk this out with me, but Harry had already turned and strode away, hurrying toward the valet booth.

For the longest time, I stood there, even after the valet brought Harry's sedan around and he climbed inside. I stood there even after his car pulled out of the parking lot. Despite wishing it to the universe, he didn't put the car into reverse, didn't turn around.

Deep down, I knew this would happen. Even in the beginning before he knew about Stella and Destelle, I'd been afraid that the truth would freak him out. His words brought that fear to life, left me feeling chilled to the bone.

I'm sorry I wasted your time.

"Destelle?" Jamie's voice seemed loud in my ear, but I didn't turn, not until Harry's car had disappeared entirely. "What happened?"

"Harry had to go home," I told him, my voice flat in my ears. I could feel the tears in the back of my throat, but none fell from my eyes. They weren't allowed to. "He wasn't feeling well."

When I turned, I found both Jamie and Nellie there. Neither of them had their coats on, but they wore twin expressions of concern. "But we didn't get to really talk to him."

"Maybe next time." Every inch of me felt numb. "Have they served dinner?"

Jamie shifted his weight. "They're making the announcement."

I lifted my chin, moving toward the doors that led inside. "I'm starving," I told them in the same low voice.

As soon as I stepped inside the country club, that was when I began to tremble, knowing that Harry wasn't there to follow me in.

twenty-two

*I*t was weird to be in a sort of limbo, not knowing whether I still had a boyfriend or not. Harry hadn't called, hadn't texted—then again, I hadn't either. We were giving each other radio silence.

On Sunday night, after a full twenty-four hours without speaking to him, I turned my phone into Mom an hour before curfew. The temptation to sit by my cell and stare obsessively was too hard to fight.

Granted, Mom was all too eager about that. When we'd gotten home from the country club Saturday night, my parents had gone on the offense.

"I mean, *really*, Destelle." Mom had scoffed, unbuttoning her jacket with flourish once we stepped over the threshold. "He has a tattoo! On his *neck*! You don't see any of the other men at the country clubs with neck tattoos, do you? Of course not. They're not professional."

"I don't love that you kept him a secret from us," Dad had added. "Why would you do that?"

"Because she wants a taste of the dark side," Mom had

told him. "What's next, you're going to dye your hair and start wearing ripped jeans too?"

If she only knew.

And then, of course, she had to add, "I get it, Destelle. Bad boys seem interesting. But your father and I have seen enough of them to know they're nothing but trouble."

"Just because he's in a band doesn't make him a bad boy," I'd said, reaching my boiling point.

Jamie had helpfully added, "No, the tattoos help."

We'd all turned to my brother, who looked at us with bored eyes. Nellie had already hurried upstairs to her room by that point, too chicken to be around any sort of conflict. I didn't blame her.

I'd never have talked back to my parents before, but Stella had given me as much freedom as she could. When it was time to take the wig off, I'd never thought twice about trying to push the envelope with Mom and Dad. Lately, though, Stella and Destelle seemed to merge, their thoughts jumbling together more often than not. It made me feel that maybe, just maybe, I could be both Stella and Destelle at the same time.

At least, I felt that way *before* Harry said what he did.

I should've messaged first. I thought about it to an almost obsessive level—thinking about *him*. What had gone wrong? What set him off? Was it the appearance of my parents? Did seeing them in all their elegant glory freak him out?

I should've messaged first or called him, but I chickened out. I'd rather wait in this limbo than have any concrete decisions.

Just as obsessively, I stalked Untapped Potential's social media page, but they reposted old content or simply lyrics to their songs. No hidden depth or meaning. Nothing to give me any insight.

So when Monday afternoon rolled around and I still had zero messages, I started to worry.

"Destelle!" Nellie called, her shrill voice snapping me from the spiral of self-pity. She stood in front of the changing room at one of her favorite clothing stores. She had on a pair of stretchy floral leggings and a plaid top, one with ruffles down her chest. "What do you think?"

I tried to keep my expression neutral as I eyed the crazy combination. "Are you sure those prints go together?"

"Of course they don't," she said with an eye roll, coming closer. "I figured I'd kill two birds with one stone instead of trying them on separately. S-E-P-E-R-A-T-E-L-Y. What do you think of them on their own?"

"I think they look cute," I said, and then paused. "You spelled that wrong."

The look of horror that washed over my little sister's face was almost laughable. "What?"

"You spelled it with an e, but it's an a. S-E-P-*A*-R-A-T-E-L-Y."

Nellie came closer, a tiny crease taking space between her eyebrows. This time, it was almost impossible to hold back a chuckle. "Don't tell Mom."

Okay, *that* wiped away my humor. "Why not?"

"I don't want her knowing I messed up." Nellie looked down at her floral pants, running a finger along the faux front pocket. "I don't want her disappointed in me."

I never thought about Jamie and Nellie facing the same insecurities as me. But here she was, worrying about what our parents thought. Just like I did. "Do you *like* spelling things out, Nellie?"

"Of course I do," she answered easily, as if the question were stupid. "I only want Mom to think I'm good at it. I'm getting better, too. I practice all the time so I don't mess up." Her eyelashes fluttered as she made a face. "I knew separately had two a's."

They were playing some kid station over the radio, and a high-pitched pop song filled the silence between us for a moment. Far cry from the stuff Harry and I used to listen to. *Sigh.*

"Listen," I started, shifting to the front of my seat. "Be yourself, okay? Always. Messing up is okay. If Mom seriously thinks any less of you for it, she can—" I broke off at Nellie's wide eyes, letting out a sharp sigh.

"Are you afraid Mom's thinking less of you?" she asked, voice quiet. "Because of Harry?"

"I know she does." I smiled, but it held no humor. "But it doesn't matter. I think we might be over."

"Over," Nellie echoed. "Like broken up?"

Ugh, the words settled like a rock in my stomach, but they were a serious possibility. If neither one of us messaged first, if I never went to Crushed Beanz again...

"I don't think you should," my sister went on. "Break up, I mean. I think you should be with him."

Her supportive words made me smile a bit, and I reached out to trace a finger on the shirt's ruffle. "You don't even know him."

"No...but I know you've been happier these past few weeks than you have been in a long time." Nellie tucked her long hair out of her face, fingers catching on a knotted strand. "I think you deserve to be happy. Especially if it's with a guy as cute as him."

"Go change into the next outfit," I told her with a chuckle. "Let me see the next atrocious combination."

"Atrocious," she said happily, "A-T-R-O-C-I-O-U-S."

I held my palm up, and she smacked hers into it.

Once she ducked into the dressing room, I eased my cell out from my coat pocket, looking at the blank screen with a little dip of disappointment in my chest. *No,* I told myself firmly, unlocking the phone. *You're going to message him first. Be a big girl and call your freaking boyfriend.*

Since the last app I used was my social media, I found Untapped Potential's latest update glaring back at me. All caps.

Untapped Potential Status Update:

THIS SATURDAY NIGHT – UNTAPPED POTENTIAL WILL OPEN UP AT DOWNTOWN IN BAYVIEW

Underneath the update, it went on to say the time and how they were opening for a band. Whoever posted the update also mentioned that they were playing their normal gig at Crushed Beanz Friday night.

I stared at the post for the longest moment, having an internal crisis in the middle of a kid's clothing store. This was game-changing for Untapped Potential. Their first gig outside of Crushed Beanz. Their first *real* gig, opening up for a band.

And Harry didn't tell me.

The wind fell from my sails, leaving me slouching against the cushiony chair. The kid's song still bopped through the speakers, but the cheerful tune couldn't lift my spirits. Pressure built in my throat, as if someone had their hand wrapped around it.

Without liking the post or even opening my text messages, I slid my phone back into my pocket, preparing to plaster on a happy smile for Nellie once she emerged.

"I don't think it's a good idea for me to go tonight, Margot," I said sadly, staring at my glum reflection in her vanity mirror.

And it seriously was glum. The week had passed at a slow and depressing rate. Day after day went by, no texts. The updates from Untapped Potential on their social media page got more and more energetic as the days went on. They were all *so stinking super excited* to play at Downtown.

I still couldn't believe that Harry hadn't texted me once even to mention it.

"I'm telling you," Margot said, fishing around in her makeup drawer for a brush. "It's probably just miscommunication. You two were all gaga for each other Saturday night. I thought I was going to have to intervene."

"Until we weren't. He came over to my parents, and after that, everything completely shifted."

Margot motioned for me to shut my eyes, and I quickly complied. "Maybe he got overwhelmed. I mean, he *did* dance with Ms. Nancy. Who knows what sweet nothings that crazy old lady whispered in his ear."

The pressure on my lid lifted, and I blinked my eyes open, looking in the mirror at the perfectly swiped liner across my lid. "I don't know, Margot. He was going on about how we were from two different worlds. He's never talked like that before."

Margot swiped up my tube of mascara, twisting the wand out. "Does he have a bad relationship with his parents? Maybe he's projecting onto yours."

A sudden, piercing ache swirled through my chest, the realization hitting me hard. "His parents passed away when he was little. He doesn't have a great relationship with the rest of his family." More like nonexistent, he'd said.

"*Sheesh.* Talk about baggage." She swiped the mascara along my lashes. "That's probably what was wrong, though. How long have they been gone? Maybe seeing your parents reminded him about his."

I hadn't even thought about how strange it might've been for him to meet my parents. Maybe it wasn't something he expected either, and he'd just been so caught off guard by the emotion. "That could've been it."

And if it was the issue, it made me want to wrap my arms around him. But even if it was him feeling strange about attending the fundraiser and meeting my parents, why hadn't he called me since? That swirl of unease expanded into a wave, and I couldn't shake the feeling that I missed something.

The Stella wig looked like silk in my lap, the color so rich and soft. I ghosted my fingers through the strands. For the first time, I found myself wondering if I should put it on. I contemplated the idea of going out just like this. Black sweater, maroon leggings, sneakers. Black choker, fake nose ring. No wig.

I'd be taking everything that was *Stella* and just leaving out one thing...the wig.

"Need help?" Margot asked, gesturing to the hair in my lap. I let her pick it up, let her move to place the wig on my head.

I watched her actions in the mirror, watched her fasten the clips into place. She positioned it perfectly, bangs falling just right on my forehead, locks draping delicately down my back. "Thanks," I told her, summoning a smile. My reflection looked like me, but not. Stella, not Destelle. "It looks perfect."

While the crowd cleared out that night, I sat at a different booth than my usual one with Addy, watching Harry sign autograph after autograph for each fan. His red hair stuck to the skin of his temples, his white shirt clinging ever so slightly to his chest.

They'd performed their heart out tonight, probably with the excitement of tomorrow. Their first gig that wasn't at Crushed Beanz. When I got my initial drink of the night, Jonathan said that Vincent's dad thought that after the

Downtown gig, they'd be pulling in numbers too big to fit Crushed Beanz.

Which meant the future of Untapped Potential was a bit unknown for now.

A large crowd had stuck around this time and chatted Untapped Potential's ears off. Vincent looked a little out of his element as he talked, introverted at heart, but Natasha and Harry seemed to thrive on mingling with everyone.

At one point, a girl even asked Harry to sign the skin of her throat. They were garnering *those* kinds of fans.

It was probably well over a half hour after the show ended before Harry finally walked up to the booth. His steps were slow and hesitant, his expression even more so. I'd never seen him so guarded. "Hey."

I fixed him with a stare way steadier than my insides felt. "Hey."

After spending all week thinking about him, and finally seeing him now, I was torn between feeling relieved and a little angry.

Harry slid into the seat across from me, his electric blue eyes trained on mine. "You're here."

I *so* wasn't having any of this back-and-forth nonsense, not after going nearly a week with no contact. "I told my parents I was babysitting the kid down the street tonight." An easy lie, one they quickly bought. "You should've told me."

Harry drew in a sharp breath as if I'd punched him, shifting uneasily. "I know—"

"How do you get a gig at Downtown and *not* tell me? I

mean, I don't know if you think we're fighting, but who cares? I would've been excited with you."

"W-What?"

"That's huge," I said, folding my arms over my chest. "That's huge for the band, and I would've celebrated with you. But I had to find out through social media?"

I kept my voice lowered in case Vincent or Jonathan could overhear, but all the emotions from the past week were filtering out.

"I—" Harry stopped, shook his head a bit. "I found out Sunday. Vincent, he—well, I would've told you, I just—" His gaze dropped to the tabletop where my fingers still traced the surface. "I didn't think you'd want to hear from me."

"Because of Saturday? I'm still more confused than anything else."

Gosh, I wished he'd say what ran through that brain of his instead of looking at me as if he'd just seen a ghost. "Your dad didn't say anything?"

"My dad?" I frowned. "He was worried about you randomly leaving the fundraiser. In fact, right after you went home, he found Mr. Preston. He said he'd try to show at a gig and listen to your sound. If you'd told me about Downtown, maybe he could've shown up there."

I expected Harry to smile at that, for excitement to flood his expression and reanimate him, but whatever was going on had dulled all those emotions. His chest rose and fell slowly. "Tell your dad thanks for me."

"Harry." I wanted so badly to reach out and grab his hand, to shake his shoulder, *something*. Make some sort of physical contact, but he remained out of reach. "Tell me what you're thinking."

"Terry went to prison."

"*Again?*"

A little huff came from him, torn between a laugh and a sigh. "No, before."

"I know. He mentioned it to Jonathan and me. You said it was the wrong place, wrong time."

Harry ran a hand through his hair, tucking the ends behind his ear. The coffee counter behind me apparently demanded his attention, and when I looked, only Vincent worked on cleaning the machines. "He was involved in something stupid. Says it was the worst thing he's ever done."

I leaned my head on my hand, trying to connect the dots he laid out. "What'd he do?"

Harry still watched Vincent, not me. And jeez, I swear that my heart started to beat faster because he held on to the suspense as long as possible. "He robbed a gas station," he murmured. "Two, actually."

"Robbed," I echoed, straightening. "Like, with a gun?"

"They weren't real guns. Just toys. His sentencing should've been longer—should've been *a lot* longer—but he had a great lawyer and struck a deal." He rubbed his hand along his tattoo. "You remember the gas station you wanted to stop at when we delivered for Dial and Dine? That was...that was one of the gas stations."

So *that* was why Harry reacted that way when we pulled into the parking lot. I thought about how sometimes Mom defended people who'd actually done crappy things.

Still, though. The image in my head of Terry walking into a gas station with a weapon was insane.

It made my stomach turn. "He seemed like such a good guy."

Harry's gaze finally, finally turned to mine. "He is."

"I mean, I'm sure he's *nice*, but how good can you be if you rob a gas station? Or *two*?" I shook my head. "When was this? A year ago?"

"A little over."

Dang, must've been a fantastic lawyer and a fantastic deal if he got a little over a year's sentence for a robbery.

Harry swallowed hard, leaning over the table and dropping his voice. "I'm bringing it up because I...well, I—"

"Hey." We both turned at the sound of Jonathan's voice, finding him with a rag and spray bottle, shaking it at us. "Lovebirds. Stop canoodling. I've got to wipe down this table."

I grabbed my jacket from the seat beside me and shoved to my feet. Harry was slower to react, but followed suit. "Are you excited for tomorrow?" Jonathan asked me. "It's going to be epic."

Tomorrow, Untapped Potential's first gig outside of Crushed Beanz. I forced a smile. "You got the night off?"

"We're closing down Crushed Beanz so he and my dad can go," Vincent told me. "My dad says he's going to make his own Untapped Potential T-shirt."

I couldn't hold in a gasp. "Tell him I *definitely* want one."

Harry trailed behind me, quiet. Vincent lifted his hand to us once we were at the door. "See you tomorrow, you guys. Stella, Addy told me to tell you she'll finally dance with you tomorrow."

Of course they'd assume I'd go, probably assumed Harry had already asked me. Which he hadn't. "I can't wait."

The weather had started to warm up beautifully for the beginning of April. A light jacket was all I really needed for the night air, and I drew in a deep, refreshing breath of it.

Since spring break started next week, it'd be the perfect weather to head to Bayview with Margot. The water might be a little cold, but the sun would be warm on our skin.

There wasn't anyone on the sidewalks since it was so late, but Harry and I waited for a few cars to pass before crossing the street. The parking lot still had a few vehicles parked in it, but I focused on mine.

"I—I should've told you about the gig," Harry said finally, uncertainty clinging to his words. "I'm sorry."

Tension seeped out of me at that. *Sorry.* It disarmed me. I didn't *want* to fight with him. I just wanted to understand. I wanted us to go back to the way we were before Saturday night. "I didn't mean to sound judgmental of Terry."

"There was a lot involved with it," he said, his voice barely above a murmur, almost swept away with the wind. "He wasn't acting alone. H-His friends put him up to it. Made him drive the getaway car."

"What sucky friends," I scoffed. "'Hey, you want to go rob a gas station for fun?' Who even does that?" And then I winced because, crap, I did it again. Being judgy. "Were you friends with those same guys or only Terry?"

Harry's gaze focused on the side of my SUV. The closer

we got, the more I could see our wavy, blurry reflections in the paint. "I was friends with them too."

"You don't talk to them anymore, right?"

I felt his gaze on me as I popped open the back seat door. "No."

I reached for the Stella bag, bringing it close to me. "Well, good," I said to Harry, grabbing the hem of my sweater and then pulling it off, leaving me in nothing but a tank top. I reached up for the clasp of my wig. "Listen, we need—"

"I care about you," he blurted, and when I whirled around to face him, he looked at me with such intensity that it almost made my knees weak. Suddenly, I froze, lowering my hands from the wig. "So much. This past week was horrible because I couldn't stop thinking about you, and all I wanted was to hear your voice."

"Then why did you say all those things?" I demanded, a tremble working its way across my skin, and it wasn't from the cold. "'Sorry for wasting your time'?"

"Because I'm a coward," he said simply, but the dismal expression still covered his features. "All those things I said about you and me being from different worlds, I—I just didn't want to lose you."

Lose me? With a slight shake of my head, I took a step toward him, not reaching out, not yet. "What set you off? Ms. Nancy?"

The joke didn't make him smile, not even a little. "I'm just afraid...afraid you'll realize you deserve so much more than me."

Without giving him a second to react, I grabbed the

hand that hung limply at his side and pressed his palm against my cheek, against the spot he always coasted his thumb over. His fingers were cold and a little rough, but I leaned in to the touch. "I want *you*. No more, no less."

I gazed deep into his eyes, waiting for a response that wouldn't come. His gaze looked stormy against the night sky, the light blue almost gray and cloudy. They weren't the happy ones I'd grown so accustomed to. No Caribbean waters in sight.

With a whisper, I told him, "You make my heart happy."

Pain cracked through those stormy eyes, and he let out a soft sigh, one sounding something like defeat. "And you make mine sing."

Every thought emptied from my mind like a bowl of water dumping out. The words themselves felt as if they were etched onto the surface of my heart, a little doodle of *Harry Russo*. And though his expression wasn't excited or beaming when he said it, warmth still spread through me, taking away any trace of a chill.

Still holding his hand to my cheek, I leaned forward and kissed him softly, lingering in the gentleness of this moment. At first, he didn't respond, his body stiff and mouth unmoving.

I pulled away with an inward sigh, the warmth scattering.

Before I moved too far back, he pushed forward, pressing his mouth firmly against mine, his hand becoming a more prominent pressure against my skin. His other hand curved around the dip of my waist, holding me close to him.

I tugged him against me until I could feel only the SUV and his body.

I wanted him to know that I was here for the long haul. The 'different worlds' mentality didn't scare me, not anymore. How could it when we worked so well together? I cared about him more than some stupid 'different worlds' thing.

My heart hammered hard as the kiss deepened, especially when his hand cupped the back of my neck, and I could feel each and every point of contact. His scent filled my senses, disorienting me to where I could barely remember my name.

I pressed against his chest enough to separate us, gasping in a breath. "You can't do that again," I told him, and later I'd be embarrassed of how winded I sounded, but I didn't care in the moment. "You can't go a week without talking to me."

"I was afraid," he said, features pinched.

The words didn't make any sense, but I only pulled him closer. "Don't be." And I kissed him again.

I combed my fingers through his hair, wanting to be just a smidge closer. A bright light swept over my closed lids, probably a car passing by, but I didn't care to look. Didn't care about anything but him.

Even though I technically still had the wig on, I felt like *me*. Not Stella and not Destelle—not one or the other. I wasn't kissing Harry because I was Stella, bold and confident, and I wasn't kissing him because I was Destelle, wanting to taste the wild side. I kissed him because I wanted to, because I needed to, and I never wanted the moment to end.

"Destelle Marie Brighton."

The sound, the name, the volume of it all had me jerking back as if electrocuted, every muscle in my body jolting and locking up. Harry's hands dropped and he flinched away from me, the moment splintering apart like shattered glass.

As Harry stepped aside, he gave me a full view of a black sedan parked directly behind him, the headlights illuminating us like two spotlights. So bright that at first I couldn't see who stood between the lights, couldn't see the angry mask that was something straight from a horror movie.

But when my eyes adjusted, everything in me dropped.

Mom stood in front of the car, and I could see Dad sitting behind the steering wheel. Both staring at me.

In a disheveled tank top.

With heavy makeup.

Wearing the black Stella wig.

The boy I'd been making out with standing beside me.

I couldn't stop the words before they tumbled from my mouth in a horrified whisper. "Oh, crap."

twenty-three

I'd never been more scared in my life.

This moment was one that I'd never really let myself imagine, the one where Mom and Dad finally found out about Stella. I mean, sure, I'd thought about it, but I could never get very far down that road. Imagining their reactions scared me way, way too much.

But here I was, staring one of my biggest fears in the face.

And that face was *furious*.

Mom was silent, clearly fighting to find an ounce of patience to give me. Dad probably glared daggers at Harry from where he sat behind the wheel, but I couldn't look away from Mom.

At first, I wondered how she might've recognized me—I was still wearing the Stella wig—but she would've spotted my SUV.

"Get in the car," she said, voice dangerously low and barely level.

Yeah, I would've agreed to be anywhere else *but* that car.

"Destelle." Her two syllables were enunciated in a warning. "Get in. Now."

I could appreciate the fact that she at least tried to keep it civil in front of Harry. "I—I'll drive the SUV home."

"No, you'll get in *our* car." Mom finally looked to my side, turning the evil eye onto the boy beside me. "Harry, move away from my daughter."

There goes the civility. Harry, though, took a healthy step away from me, obeying without question. I shivered from the new distance. "Mom—"

"What is this?" she demanded, gesturing a hand at my body almost chaotically. "W-What's all this *black*? What's on your *head*? Destelle Marie, is that a *nose ring*?"

I tugged off the Stella wig, wincing as the clasps caught in my real hair. "Can you calm down?" I asked her while I tore the fake nose ring off, and once the words were out, I immediately regretted them.

"Calm down," Mom echoed, placing her hands on her hips. "Okay, Destelle. Let's all calm down. Why don't you tell me—calmly—exactly what you're doing with him?" She spoke as if she knew she made a valid point, and I realized then that I was on trial. "Tell me exactly how this is *babysitting*."

I could see everything come crashing down now, like little buildings made of sticks being knocked over by the wind. Mom knew that I'd lied about babysitting tonight—it wouldn't take her any time at all to find out all the lies in the past.

Maybe it was that realization, or that I saw my life flash before my eyes, that made me say, "I lied to you."

"Yeah, I kind of figured that out for myself."

"I've *been* lying to you. I didn't go babysitting tonight. I haven't been to any of the volunteer opportunities you've set up since the middle of February."

From the corner of my eye, I saw Harry's head tip toward me, and he probably gave me wide, panicked eyes, thinking I'd lost my mind.

Mom took a step closer to me, but when she spoke, her voice was neutral. If someone listened to the words, they'd have no idea she was angry. "Harry, I think you should head home. I'll take care of Destelle."

Take care of. I almost snorted. *What is she going to do, murder me?*

"T-This is my fault," Harry said, and took a step forward. "I asked Destelle to come tonight—"

"Oh, I already know how much of a bad influence you are."

Harry full-on winced, as if Mom had shoved him. "Mom, stop it!" My rage had reached its boiling point, and if I didn't think she'd grab me and try to shove me into the car, I would've taken a step forward. "Don't talk to him like that! He hasn't done anything to you!"

Harry ducked his head, as if he couldn't look either of us in the eye, and in that moment, I hated my mother for making him feel so low.

Before Harry took another step away, I grabbed his wrist with a free hand. "I'll see you tomorrow at the gig. Nine o'clock sharp."

I watched his eyes go from me to my mom, and when he looked back, he had returned to how he was before—panicked, sad, weary. Mom didn't object; in fact, it was almost as if she wasn't listening to us.

"Drive safe," Harry said instead of acknowledging my words. And then he walked off toward the employee lot of Crushed Beanz, where he'd parked his car.

"It's him, isn't it?" she asked once he left, her eyes scanning my body. "He's making you be this way, making you dress this way. You're in a tank top, for crying out loud!"

"He's not making me be *any* way!" Of course she'd try to blame this all on him. "He makes me feel alive, Mom, more than I have—"

"Alive." Her voice sounded unrecognizable, caught on a scoff. "You're seventeen, Destelle. Dating a guy with tattoos and mystery may seem fun now, but what plans does he have for the future, hmm? Does he even have *any*?"

"Don't act like you know him. He wants to advance with his music career—"

"Music career." Disdain dripped from her voice. "He doesn't have one, Destelle. No records, no albums. That's not a career."

I recoiled from her tone, from her heartless words. "When did you get so judgmental? When did you turn into *them*?"

To me, "them" was obvious. All of those people at the country club and the fundraisers who cared more about image and prestige than actual human decency. They'd put on fake smiles, give phony compliments, but there wasn't anything genuine behind their mask.

The sedan's door popped open, and Dad stood up. Interesting that he got out only now, once Harry left. "Get in the car, you two. We can talk about this tomorrow."

Mom pretended that she couldn't hear him, fixing me with an intimidating stare. "He's taking you down a path that you can't reverse off of."

"No," I said, emotion gripping my throat. "*I'm* taking myself down a path, one that *I'm* choosing. Not him. Not you. A path that you can't control anymore."

"Destelle, give your mother your cell phone and get in your car," Dad said, voice forceful, in a way that was much scarier than Mom's. "Now, before you say anything more that you'll regret later."

He was wrong. I wasn't going to regret any of it later.

After slamming my cell into Mom's outstretched palm, I settled behind the steering wheel, the coldness of the surrounding air finally settling over my skin. Even so, I could barely think of it in that moment. I could barely think around the rapid beating of my heart, the way it pulsed like a roaring wave in my ears. Everything crashed down around me. Something was going on with Harry, and my parents found out the truth about the double life I'd been living since November.

Things were changing, and I wasn't sure I was ready to face it.

I put the car into gear and drove home, and Dad's headlights stayed in the rearview the entire time.

.   .   .

Dad determined that everyone needed to sleep off their anger before we got into the Harry conversation, so he pushed off the verbal chew-out until Saturday morning. I couldn't really sleep my anger off, though. I'd been tossing and turning all night. No matter how I tried to lie in bed, I couldn't get comfortable.

Now I sat in a chair in Dad's study, slumping back against it. The chair was usually a formality, a piece of furniture in the space to take up the room, but whenever one of us kids got in trouble, we were doomed to sit in it while Dad doled out a punishment.

My eyes were on my father, who looked at me evenly. It was only Dad and me having this conversation, but I had no doubts Mom would come in later. "Destelle," he began, voice deceitfully calm. "Why don't you tell me what went on last night?"

Let the trial begin. "I went to Crushed Beanz to listen to a band play."

"Instead of babysitting, like you explicitly told us you were going to do."

"Yes."

Dad made a show of shifting in his seat, never taking his eyes off me. "Your mother called Mrs. Heston a little before ten. Asked what time you'd left her house." He raised an eyebrow. "Mrs. Heston promptly replied that you were not, nor had you been, at her house."

Of course *that's* what ruined it all—Mom checking in on me. I'd always been afraid of that happening, Mom calling the place I was supposed to be volunteering at, and she finally did.

"So, we tracked your cell," Dad went on, walking me through their process. "Found your phone in downtown Hallow. Found *you*, half-dressed, wearing a wig, kissing a boy against your car."

Half-dressed. It wasn't like I had no shirt on at all. "He was my boyfriend. I'm allowed to kiss him."

Dad caught the word. "Was?"

Some wind dropped out of my sails, shoulders slumping as I remembered Harry's expression even before my parents showed. "After the way Mom talked to him last night, why would he want to be with me?"

"Your mother thinks I should ground you," he said with a sigh, rubbing his forehead. With the action, I found my gaze latching onto his wedding ring, the gold catching in the morning light that peeked through the window. "You deserve it, you know. We've raised you better than to lie. And you've been lying this entire time about your volunteering services." Dad lowered his hand, gaze intense. "Think about it, Destelle. Think about who I am, who your mother is. We can't have a child going off the rails."

"Yes, because you and Mom are God's gift to the judicial system," I muttered, slumping even lower in my seat. I wished he'd get on with it. "You two are just mad that I'm acting out."

Dad snorted, but it sounded more amused than angry. "Well, yes, we are—"

"That I'm not being the perfect daughter you've forced me to be."

Dad, though, didn't mind clinging to this moment, and let his silence linger in the air. Maybe he was mulling over my words and the venom I'd laced in them. Maybe he was trying to come up with an apt punishment. Maybe he was thinking he forgot to put deodorant on—I had no clue. "We want you to have a good life."

"There's not one road to a good life," I pointed out, feeling hopelessness rise in me. "College doesn't equal a good life. Fundraisers and parties and money don't equal a good life. That's what *you* want. But what about me? What do *I* want?"

He watched me, obviously taken aback by my words. Probably surprised by how firm my voice was. I was almost positive I'd never spoken to him that way before. I would've died at the thought.

I wondered if he even knew what I truly wanted.

The longer the silence hung in the air, the more helpless I felt. There was no changing his mind, no getting either parent to listen to me. To actually *hear* me. It was like pounding my fists on a door when no one was even home.

"How long have you been parading around like this?" he asked. "How long have you been lying about where you're going? How long have you been—" He fumbled for the words. "—dressing up like a character?"

A character. Of course, he couldn't even fathom how important that *character* was to me. He hadn't even asked. "Awhile."

"Destelle," Dad began, and then let out a sigh. Now that the trial was over, it was time for the sentencing. I knew the verdict before he opened his mouth. "You're grounded. You're only to go here, school, and any volunteer opportunities your mother sets up. Nowhere else. No seeing Margot, no seeing Harry. Not until we decide when, and I—I wouldn't expect it to be soon."

"Harry's gig is tonight. He's playing for the first time at a place outside of Hallow." My hands instinctively clenched, and I imagined forcing my hand through a wall. "Downtown, it's a place in Bayview—"

"If this had been a one-time occurrence, Destelle, we could've waited until tomorrow to ground you." Dad rubbed his hand over his forehead again, as if *he* were the one in pain with this punishment. "But you've been lying to us for weeks. Possibly longer. We can't condone it."

"Harry's gig is tonight," I repeated, that freaking quiver in my voice making me angry. A bomb started ticking in my chest, a timer running out until I finally exploded.

"I know." Dad's lips turned down in a frown. "And you're not allowed to go."

Boom.

My heart pounded like a drumbeat in my ears, the rushing of blood loud. It was like an Untapped Potential song in my body. A shot of heat rippling across my chest, a lyric of pain in my jaw, a strum of resentment taking root. My father sat across the desk, his own expression stoic, neutral, and it only made me more furious.

"I'm not a doll," I told him, trying to control my voice, but the emotional quality of it snuck through. "I'm not a doll in a dollhouse you can prance around."

"I know that, Destelle."

I took a step away from him, wanting to get as far as possible. "No. You don't."

When I hauled open his study door, nearly letting it crash into the wall, I found Mom standing on the other side. She'd obviously been listening. Her eyes met mine, and where I thought I'd find a triumphant expression, I only found blankness. Emptiness. She hid her thoughts from me, but I couldn't have cared less.

"One day," I said to her darkly, voice shaking with the threat of tears that took residence in my eyes, "when I don't come home for holidays and never call you on your birthday, think of this moment."

And then I barreled past her. When I pushed farther into the hallway, I saw Nellie and Jamie standing in the doorway of the living room, both of them looking at me. I didn't even give them a second glance.

Without another word, I took the stairs two at a time, stupid tears already tracking down my cheeks.

twenty-four

J was going to the Untapped Potential gig tonight, but I couldn't figure out *how*.

My bedroom was on the second floor, so there was definitely no chance of me sneaking out the window. I had no cell phone, so I couldn't call Margot to pick me up. No doubt Mom and Dad hid my car keys somewhere. Dad probably kept an eye on the back door while Mom watched the front.

I was under house arrest, and no matter how I tried to work it in my mind, I couldn't find a way to escape.

Morning passed into afternoon quickly, and the hours seemed to tick by faster and faster.

Instead of pacing the room or staring at my ceiling, I picked out my outfit for the gig because I *was* going. I decided on a pair of dark-wash jeans and a black semi-see-through top. Using them as fuel for my determination, I laid them out on my bed, strengthening my resolve.

But even though I set my clothes out, there was no way

I could grab the wig. I'd left Stella in the car last night, and I wouldn't be able to get to her.

As the day went on, no one came and interrupted my plotting.

The only viable option played around in my head. There was a gas station about five minutes away, and if I managed to get out of the house, I could walk there and borrow the phone. Call Margot or even call a car service, I wasn't sure. But it was really my only chance of escaping.

If I could even make it out the door.

It was freaking ridiculous that it came to this.

By the time eight o'clock rolled around, I knew that making a break for it was my best option. No other idea came to me. Quickly, I changed into my gig attire, grabbed my fake ID from my nightstand, and headed to my door.

When I opened it, though, I found Jamie standing on the other side, fist poised to knock.

"What are you doing?" I hissed, afraid Mom or Dad would hear my voice.

Jamie pressed a finger to his lips and then grabbed my wrist, drawing me across the hall into his bedroom. Nellie was already in there, sitting on his bed near his window. Once Jamie shut the door, she beamed at me. "We're breaking you out."

"Breaking me—what?" I glanced between the two, and their expressions were almost identical. Excited, wide-eyed. "How on earth do you plan to do that?"

"Well, I called Margot from the home phone," Nellie said. "She's parked and waiting down the street in front of Mr. and Mrs. Lee's house."

Jamie hopped on his bed, right next to his window. "I'm going to go downstairs and ask Dad to make popcorn so Nellie and me can watch a movie. Nellie will ask Mom to help her study her flash cards in the living room. In that little window while they're both distracted, you can leave through the front door."

I watched him for a moment, imagining the scenario in my head.

"If you leave, you'll probably get into a ton of trouble," Nellie said, her excitement dimming a bit.

"We have no idea how we'd keep them from checking on you," Jamie added. "And they probably will. Soon. They know the gig starts at nine, so they'll want to make sure you're still in your room."

Got it. Once I was out, I was on my own. My opening of time to get out of the house decreased by the second. "Why are you two helping me?"

Nellie grinned. "Because we believe in true love."

Jamie, however, had different sentiments. "We don't like it when you're unhappy."

Then they looked at each other. "And...well, we want you to come home for the holidays and call us on our birthday."

My heart pinched. They'd heard what I'd said to Mom. "You guys." I moved closer and wrapped my arms around them. They both fit perfectly in my grasp. "I'll always call on your birthday. Always."

Nellie spoke against my chest, voice muffled. "And bring presents on Christmas?"

I pinched her, making her laugh. "Only the best."

"Okay," Jamie muttered after a moment, growing uncomfortable. "We'll go downstairs now and start. Listen for the sound of the microwave and then come down. Dad shouldn't be able to see you then. Good luck...Stella."

Though my mood had been dismal all day, an easy smile broke free.

So it was settled. Like a little football team huddle, we broke apart, Jamie and Nellie branching off to their respective jobs. I stood on the upper steps of the staircase, listening close as the scene unfolded, waiting to spring into action.

"Mom," Nellie called. "I added a few new flash cards. Can you help quiz me?"

"Sure," Mom replied, and her voice had a strange note to it. Soft, almost sad. For all I knew, though, she could've been reading something on her phone. "What's the first word?"

"Hey, Dad?" Jamie spoke over them. "Can you help me pop some popcorn?"

"You're getting old enough to do it yourself, bud," he said, and the normal tone of his voice grated on my nerves. Of course he sounded okay and nonchalant, as if he hadn't taken my life away from me.

Jamie hesitated, probably trying to find a counterresponse. "Well, can you show me which buttons to press? I want to make sure I do it right."

I waited and waited, straining my ears for the noise. And then—there it was. The microwave beeped as someone pressed a button, and then, as quietly as possible, I sprinted down the stairs.

Opening the door was the tricky part. The giant door had a tendency to make a loud *click* when the locks pulled back, and there was no time to take it slow. At any moment, Mom could look up from the living room, or Dad could pass through the kitchen archway and spot me.

I pulled it open quietly, with only a muffled sound coming out.

When I shut it, though, my grip slipped, and the door let out a loud *click*.

I didn't waste any time. Turning on my heel, I sprinted down the cobblestone walkway to the sidewalk, running toward the Lees' house. My sneakers slapped the cement, the wind pulling my curls back.

Margot's car was in sight, and even through her tinted windows, I could see the outline of her behind the wheel. I stuffed myself into the passenger's seat as quickly as I could, gasping for breath.

"Drive," I told her, fumbling to buckle my seat belt. "Drive, drive, drive."

"Jeez, okay, hotshot," she grumbled, pulling away from the curb. As she did so, her eyes scanned me, lingering on my hair. "What about Stella?"

"She's been abducted. My parents found out. About everything."

Shock fluttered along Margot's face as we pulled off my street, safely leaving my house behind. "I wondered why Nellie called me about the prison break."

"I guess this is me telling them 'Screw you,' huh?"

"I'm proud of you, kid."

I smiled back at her, noticing for the first time that she

didn't have a suit on. She wasn't wearing lounge pants either. She had on *jeans*. "What are you wearing?"

Margot glanced down at herself, shifting in her seat. "Well, I figured a suit might stick out at a club, right?"

"Oh, my gosh, you're coming inside?" I didn't hide the excitement in my voice. I hadn't thought Margot would want to come into a place like Downtown, but then again, I hadn't thought Margot owned a pair of jeans. "Seriously?"

"Seriously. I'm eighteen, so I'm allowed in. Besides, I've never heard Harry Hotpants perform—now's my chance to see the band in all its glory."

"You are going to *love* them," I declared with absolute certainty. "This is going to be so fun."

Margot took her hand off the wheel to wave it in the air. "Yeah, yeah, so much fun. I hope it's worth it. But tell me— on a scale of one to ten, how badly did David and Alice freak?"

I gave a humorless laugh. "An eleven."

We arrived at the club ten minutes before Untapped Potential was set to go on, and a long line had already formed at the door. My name had been on the list, though— Untapped Potential was able to tell them certain people who could get inside in case there was a wait—and Margot and I waltzed right in.

"Wow," she murmured, looking around at the wide room of people. And there were *so many*. The anticipation made me antsy, bouncing on the balls of my feet as my pulse quickened. "We can try to get to the front near the stage."

I'd wanted to see Harry beforehand, but I didn't have time. No doubt he'd be getting ready to go on, and since I didn't have my phone, I couldn't even text him. It made my heart hurt, knowing that I couldn't wish him luck, but he didn't need it. They were going to be rock stars.

A healthy crowd waited for the DJ music to switch over, waited for the band to come on. This was *way* bigger than the normal turnout at the coffeehouse. Energy pulsed through me, coupled with a sweet excitement.

"Oh, my gosh, I *knew* it!"

When I turned to the voice, I found Addy making her way through the crowd, gaze locked on me. She didn't have her signature tie on, but a baggy graphic T-shirt that she'd tied off at her waist. By the way it fit her, a part of me couldn't help but wonder if that was Vincent's shirt.

With her ripped dark jeans, she looked like an edgier version of herself. Adeline to her Addy.

"I *so* knew it!" she declared again, a triumphant grin crossing her delicate features. "Well, sort of. I thought I recognized you that day at the gas station, but you convinced me it wasn't you."

Addy was talking about the time she saw me as *me*, Destelle, no wig and no makeup. Margot and I had stopped for gas, and when I walked out of the store, I came face-to-face with Addy. It was the first time the lives of Stella and Destelle had ever come close to crossing.

If only I knew that in just a few months, things would be so different.

Addy reached out and nudged me in the shoulder. "You could've said something. I wouldn't have shared your secret."

"I should've come out and said, 'I have an alter ego and it's totally normal'?" I asked teasingly, happy that she was so accepting of me. That'd always been a big fear of mine—whether someone would understand or would judge.

"Uh, yes! You would've saved me from questioning my sanity." Addy turned to Margot. "And you gave me the watercolor Gilfman tie. Thank you so much again, by the way—it's one of my favorites."

Margot flashed a rare smile, probably remembering how she parted ways with that necktie. "I'm happy you liked it."

"I'll tell you all about it some other time, okay?" I told Addy, reaching up and touching my curls. "It's a long story."

"I'll hold you to that," she promised, and then glanced back toward the stage, waiting for our group to come on. "I'm freaking out for them. I mean, I know they're going to be great, but I just can't wait. Vincent was so excited this afternoon. This is a big moment. You would know—you've been attending their gigs longer than I have."

"It's been a long time coming." I reached out and gave her fingers a squeeze, noticing her fidgeting. "How did it happen? How did they get a gig here?"

"Oh!" Addy smacked a hand to her forehead. "*This* was Vincent's extravaganza gift I gave him! I talked the owner here—who thinks he's tougher than he is, honestly—into booking them a spot. Vincent held off on telling Harry until the last minute so Harry couldn't stress too much about it."

I thought about the times Harry said he was afraid of branching out. "You are seriously the best girlfriend ever," I told her happily. "Hey, have you seen Jonathan?"

"He's closer to the stage with that guy Harry knew. Terry, I think."

Ooh, so they were hanging out tonight together. Knowing what I did about Terry, I felt conflicted. On one hand, I definitely wanted to root for him and Jonathan, but on the other, the idea of Jonathan being with someone with such a sketchy past was...well, sketchy.

"Mr. Castello is backstage," Addy went on, standing on her tiptoes to see the stage. "He was so excited, wanted to be up close and personal."

"I'm excited to finally hear them play," Margot said, folding her arms across her chest. "From how Destelle talks about them, they'd better be epic."

Again, I was struck with my two worlds colliding. Addy called me Stella, Margot called me Destelle. Granted, I didn't have the wig on, so it made sense. But still, it made me pause. Though Harry sometimes used my real name, he mostly called me Stella.

This was the first time that the names truly felt interchangeable. Like I truly felt like Stella *and* Destelle, wig or no wig.

Like we were one person.

When Harry and I argued outside of the country club, I'd claimed that Destelle and Stella were one person, that it was just *me,* but it was another thing to finally *feel* that way.

"Does this place have any places to get a drink or something?" Margot asked, glancing around. "I'm dying of thirst."

"There's a bar in the back. I'll show you." I tucked a curl behind my ear as the stage caught my eye. "We'll catch you in a bit, okay, Addy? I definitely want to dance."

Addy grinned. "Sounds great."

Before I turned my back on the stage, I could see the stagehands back away from the spotlight, finishing setting up for the band. Untapped Potential would be on any second. Anticipation shot through me, humming under my skin.

"Addy seems really nice," Margot said as we walked away. "She's got great taste in fashion, that's for sure."

Nellie would've agreed. "She does."

As we started pushing through the crowd, it erupted with noise and excitement, and the strobe lights overhead flashed. For a moment, I was thrown back to the memory of Harry and me on this very dance floor. Practically strangers. Even back then, we'd been so in sync. And now, standing here for his band, it felt like everything came full circle.

I stopped in the middle of the floor, pivoting to face the stage. Several bodies tried to eclipse my view, but I could still see him.

"How is everyone doing tonight?" Harry called into the microphone, and every inch of my body shivered, goosebumps rising on my skin. *This is the moment he's been waiting for.* I swallowed hard past the pressure in my throat. "We're Untapped Potential."

After tonight, that potential might just be tapped.

"Destelle," Margot said, tugging on my arm. "Is that Mr. Preston?"

Her words startled me. Mr. Preston, as in Mr. Preston who owned the recording studio? Uh, *what?*

I whirled around, following her gaze. A man in a fitted suit leaned against the bar. No one else stood with him, his attention focused on the stage and the beat that came from it, the lyrics lulling from the microphone. *Good sign.*

"Dad must've mentioned the gig to him," I said, dumbfounded. But when would he have had the chance? I hadn't told Dad about it until this morning. "Oh, my gosh, Margot, this—this is crazy." I turned to her, my jaw practically unhinged. "Mr. Preston could change everything for them."

Margot looked at me for only a moment before a sly grin passed over her face. Without another word, she slipped through the crowd and strutted toward him with ease, leaving me stumbling in her wake. "Mr. Preston!" she greeted with a voice dripping so much sweetness that I almost didn't realize it was her speaking. "Fancy seeing you here."

When his eyes landed on her, Mr. Preston's face tensed. It almost reminded me of how Mrs. Holland looked when Margot approached her at that event back in January. Almost like he was afraid of her. "M-Margot." Then his eyes slid to mine. "And Destelle. Great to see you two here."

"Wouldn't miss this for the world," I said, fully

knowing that this was probably my last time out of the house until I turned forty-five. "What are you doing here?"

"I'm here to listen to Untapped Potential. That's your boyfriend's band, right?"

I did an internal happy dance. "How did you know they'd be playing tonight?"

"When your dad told me about them last Saturday, I looked up their social pages. They're growing fast, huh?"

Ah, so Dad *hadn't* told him about tonight. My resentment returned in full force.

But then Mr. Preston tipped his head to the side. "Well, and your father called me this afternoon to tell me. He really wanted me to come down and hear them."

And then that resentment evaporated. Even after everything, Dad still reached out to Mr. Preston about tonight? Even after seeing Harry kissing me last night, even after my lying? I wasn't sure what to make of that. I also couldn't help but wonder what Mom thought about that. "Thank you so, so much for coming. It means the world to the band."

"They're very good," he called as the music picked up its tempo. Harry's voice mingled with Natasha's, a perfect blend. "I can see why they're growing as fast as they are."

"They're definitely going places," I agreed, trying not to grin like an idiot. "I'm waiting to see what label snatches them up first."

Margot laid her hand on Mr. Preston's suit coat, as if they were long friends. I watched as he stiffened. "What's your label been doing nowadays, Trent? Looking for new talent?"

He seemed to squirm under her touch, but didn't back away. "Actually, we are."

"Fantastic. You know, I've got a feeling that this band is exactly what you're looking for." Margot gave him a squeeze before pulling back, looping her arm uncharacteristically with mine. "Well, we're going to go enjoy the show. Have a great night, Mr. P." And without another word, she dragged me toward the other end of the bar.

My gaze locked on Harry smiling through his song, moving with energy around the stage. It was certainly much bigger than Crushed Beanz. I caught him grinning at fans, could see the dancing bodies moving rhythmically to Vincent's drum beats. They were loving it, having the time of their lives. Natasha seemed into the moment too, the focus on her face artful.

"Margot," I whispered to her as quietly as I could as she leaned alongside the bar, waiting for the server to come over. "What was all that?"

"What, chatting it up with Mr. Preston?" she asked innocently, ordering a water and passing over a couple bucks. "Remember when I said I caught Mrs. Holland with someone who *wasn't* her husband?" She raised her eyebrows at my shocked expression, looking pleased with herself. "I didn't think you'd appreciate my blackmail."

Despite it all, I grinned. "I'll accept it this once."

We went farther into the crowd, and I kept my eyes peeled for Addy as Untapped Potential started their next song. I found her with Jonathan and Terry. It was so strange to see Jonathan without his apron on—I couldn't remember a time where we'd seen each other outside of

Crushed Beanz. Ever. The tight shirt he wore complemented his muscles well, and his black hair was all tousled.

"Good to see you, *Stella*," Jonathan greeted with a wink, reaching out and tugging on a curl of mine.

"They're so good!" Addy called over the music once, grinning ear to ear. Her cheeks were a bit red from the heat. "I don't know what it is, but they sound so much better here!"

"The acoustics, probably," I said with a laugh, looking at Terry. He wore another sweater tonight, a gray one that looked white under the lights. "Glad you could make it."

Terry smiled, leaning forward while pointing to his head. "I like your hair."

Right, because my curls were out in full force tonight. Gone was the silkiness of the black Stella wig. Still, I grinned back, adding with a chuckle, "Thanks."

The band switched songs, starting to play their newest. "Dance Floor"—the one that Harry had written about me. I felt my lips curve into a stupidly wide smile, and I latched on to Addy's wrist while glancing at everyone else. "Come on, let's dance."

I expected Margot to object, but she simply sighed, letting me grab her arm. "All right, *fine*." And we all made our way farther up toward the stage.

I thought it would be different dancing as Destelle and not Stella, but I felt perfect. I felt like *me*. Margot was on one side, Addy on another, my two worlds colliding. Jonathan and Terry danced in front of us, creating a little circle of personal Untapped Potential fans.

And in the speakers, blaring loud, sang Harry's voice, a rope tying it all together.

The strobe lights flickered and flashed in my eyes, and whoever was on light duty did an amazing job. Each beat and clash of a drum, each tear and snag on the guitar, and Harry's beautiful, silky voice made this moment even more surreal. They sounded fantastic, and I almost found myself wishing I could record this show, play it on a constant loop.

With a quick glance around the crowd, I saw that they enjoyed the music too. The infectious energy that moved through the bodies only doubled with each beat and lyric and strum of the guitar.

I grabbed Addy's upper arms. "You're amazing for this, you know that? Seriously, the best girlfriend ever."

"Trust me," she said with a laugh, glancing at the stage. "Vincent made that *very* clear."

When the people in front of us parted, I saw *him* again, and I swear, all the air vanished from my lungs. Poof. Evaporated. Gone. Because he looked like a god standing on that stage, the spotlight on him lighting him up in all the right places, on the planes of his cheeks, catching in the red of his hair. He wore one of his signature white T-shirts, black suspenders loose over his shoulders. The tattoo on his neck stuck out vividly, his throat contracting as he sang.

Hypnotized. I was totally and utterly hypnotized by Harry Russo.

Energy had been injected into him tonight, and maybe it was because he finally understood how beautiful it could feel to branch out. With each thump of the beat, Harry moved around the stage, smiling and singing out to the crowd. It was the liveliest I'd ever seen him at a gig and I almost couldn't handle it.

We all danced until Untapped Potential ran out of their designated time slot. The band they'd opened for took the stage for the rest of the night. Sweat dripped down the center of my back, my heart racing as I finally, finally stopped dancing. Addy was all smiles, bouncing on her feet. "We have to go congratulate them!"

Terry glanced at Jonathan, a grin on his features. "I'm down."

Jonathan tore a hand through his hair, his eyes very, very bright and happy.

We all started following Addy, as she knew where to go, but I stopped when Margot hesitated. "Are you coming?"

"You all go. I'm going to see if I can find Mr. Preston, see where his thoughts are."

Margot's tank must've been running on empty, I knew. She was introverted and tended to stick to herself. I didn't want to push her outside her comfort zone—anymore than she already was by coming here tonight—but I wanted her to know she was always welcome with me. "You can come, you know."

She shook her head, her expression content. "You go kiss your hotties. I'll work my magic."

"I'll call a car to get home," I told her, finally letting Addy drag me back a step. "If you don't hear from me after spring break, my parents have probably killed me and buried me in the yard."

"If they have, I'll see you in the next life," Margot called after me with a wink before turning away. "Oh, and Stella?"

I looked back, finding Margot giving me a rare, genuine smile.

"You were right," she said. "I really did love Untapped Potential."

twenty-five

*A*ddy picked a seemingly random door and shoved it open, revealing a long room with two couches along the wall and a mini fridge in the back corner. I saw Natasha first, packing her guitar into its case, the biggest smile on her face. Behind her, on one of the couches, sat Vincent, staring at his hands with a blissed-out expression. And then I spotted Harry.

Even though Jonathan, Terry, and Addy all pushed into the room, and Natasha and Vincent were there as well, everyone else simply fell away.

Harry's eyes immediately lifted to mine, showing me the electricity that crackled in his gaze. An awestruck grin stretched across his lips. He looked at me for a millisecond before moving.

And then he stood before me, arms sweeping around my waist, pulling me right off my feet. A startled laugh burst from me. He was sweaty, but I couldn't have cared less. In fact, it almost made me burrow closer, drawing in his scent. "*Ohmygodohmygod,*" he kept saying over and over, his low voice in my ear. He trembled, coming off a high only the stage could provide.

Harry pulled away and quickly pressed his mouth to mine in a deep kiss, causing a shockwave of heat to scatter across my body. And just like that, the memory of how he'd acted last night fell away. His panic from last Saturday became nothing but a distant thought. I curled my fingers into his hair, savoring the taste. One of his hands slid down my spine to press against the small of my back, bringing us flat against each other.

This moment? This one made it *totally worth* sneaking out and my possible demise tonight. Totally worth it.

"Okay, lovebirds." Someone sighed, but my brain couldn't comprehend who it was. "Single people over here feeling very awkward."

But Harry didn't lean back, not for another moment. Not that I was complaining.

When he did, he pressed his forehead to mine, sliding a hand down my hair, fingers twining in the curls. "I didn't think your parents would let you come." He pulled back enough to swallow hard, and a shadow of last night swept across his features, threatening that blissful happiness. "How did you—"

"No," I cut him off, lifting my chin. "Don't worry about that. Don't let it ruin this moment."

He didn't say anything else, but his expression didn't immediately clear. When we both pulled away to face the rest of the room, Addy was elbowing Vincent in the ribs, pointing at me. "That's Stella."

Vincent snorted. "I mean, given the way they just made out, I hoped it was."

"I *told* you I thought I saw someone who looked like Stella."

"And I believed you," he insisted, wrapping his arm around her.

"I figured you were you by the way Harry's face lit up when he saw you," Natasha told me, expression holding what looked like respect. "He only smiles like that for you."

By way of agreement, Harry's lips brushed my temple.

Natasha sat down on the couch with a loud exhale, a faint smile on her lips. "I can't believe we did that. I mean, we *finally* played someplace other than Crushed Beanz." She glanced over to Addy and Vincent, who cuddled on the other couch beside Jonathan. Terry leaned against the wall beside Jonathan, his hand against the back of the sofa. "No offense, V."

"None taken. I'm as excited as you are." Vincent nudged his knee against Addy's. "Thank you for setting this up, Adeline. I mean it. You should've seen Dad's face—he was so excited."

"I'm the best, I know." She flipped her blonde hair over her shoulder. "Where'd your dad go?"

"He wanted to sit and watch the other band play. He'll be back once we load the equipment up."

Harry wrapped an arm around my waist. "Addy, thank you. You got us to a place a lot of bands only dream about."

"What he said," Natasha added with a grin, glancing between Harry and Terry. "This time last year, things were so, so different, huh?"

"*So* different," Terry agreed.

Natasha shook her head a little. "Dreams really come true, I guess. I mean, I barely got by in school and, Harry, you were stuck in—"

"Tash."

Harry's voice was terse, almost as if the word had been dragged out of him. Around my waist, his arm stiffened, mood changing on a dime. When I looked over, his gaze locked on Natasha, his expression almost looked oddly intense.

I opened my mouth to ask him what was wrong, but Natasha carried on. "Well, things were just different last year is all. You and I weren't even playing music yet, Harry."

"Crazy how far you can come in such a short time," Vincent added.

Addy gave a small smile, but it wasn't at full volume. "So much can change in a year."

Vincent laid his hand on her knee, giving it an affectionate squeeze.

The moment passed, but Harry's arm still tensed around my waist, the line of his body stiff and firm. I tried to think about what this time last year would've looked like for him, and then realized that I didn't know.

I looked up at Harry, at the line of his jaw, at the scripting quality of the tattoo at his neck. Sometimes I forgot that the lines actually formed a hand because I was so enamored with how it looked against his skin. Sometimes I forgot that Harry—this sweet, innocent Harry that I knew

—once got a neck tattoo at sixteen without permission. In a friend's garage.

They seemed like two different people.

Everyone decided to go out and celebrate, and Natasha and Vincent loaded their equipment, ready to take it out to their vehicles. "Stay here and enjoy the free drinks in the mini fridge," Harry told us with a grin, grabbing his own guitar case. "I'll be right back."

"I should head out," I murmured to him, quietly enough so the others couldn't overhear. They were talking to one another anyway, most likely weren't listening. "My parents probably know where I am, but sooner or later they'll send out a task force after me."

Harry reached out and drew his thumb down my cheekbone. "I'll take you home."

I didn't want to agree, but I also didn't want to say no. Staring at him now made me think of the future. I had no idea when my parents would let me see him again. "I'm not sure what will happen after tonight," I told him in a quiet voice, not looking at his expression. "I snuck out to come, and I can't imagine that'll go over well."

"You shouldn't have—"

"You thought I'd miss tonight?" I asked, keeping my voice light. "As if. Even if I wasn't dating you, I'm still Untapped Potential's biggest fan."

"You shouldn't have snuck out," he finished anyway. "Things were already tense."

"I wasn't going to miss this," I insisted, making my tone as serious as possible. "This is huge for you."

He watched me for a long moment. That buzz of

excitement had dulled down now, my words probably not helping the mood. "Give me five minutes to load this all up and I'll drive you home."

Before he had a chance to back away, I pressed a firm kiss against his mouth. His lips immediately responded, savoring the moment before parting. "Five minutes," I echoed, letting him go.

Once Harry hurried out into the hallway, I turned back to the three who still remained. Jonathan and Terry were bent over Addy's phone, and suddenly music filtered out. "Ugh, you can hear my horrible voice singing," she said with a groan, glancing up. "Stella, come look."

"I think that's *my* voice," I teased, plopping down in the seat beside her. She'd recorded the stage for a little bit during our dancing, holding the camera high above the heads in the crowd. "You have to send that to me."

"Just think, one day they'll have it all recorded on an album," Terry said, slipping his hands into his pockets. "That quality is going to be amazing."

Addy let out a soft, happy sigh. "I hope it doesn't take too long."

I thought of Mr. Preston out there and wondered what else Margot could've said to him. Whatever it was, I hoped it was convincing.

"Excuse me?"

We all turned toward the doorway at the voice, finding a woman standing over the threshold. She was tall, almost taking up the entire archway with her cropped blonde hair tucked behind her ears. She looked at all of us. "Is Harry back here?"

"He ran some stuff to his car," I told her, flattening my palms over my knees. "He'll be back in a minute."

She nodded, but didn't move out of the doorway. Instead, she scanned us once more and then began looking at the space, not saying anything else.

I caught Jonathan's eye and saw the way he tilted his head ever so slightly toward her. *Go.* So, with a sharp breath in, I pushed to my feet. "I'm Stella," I told her, coming closer to extend my hand.

"Lily," she returned, and took it.

"Lily," I echoed, looking at her in a new light. "Santiago?"

She tilted her chin at her full name. "Do I know you?"

"I'm Harry's girlfriend," I told her, glancing back at everyone. They all had expressions of confusion, except for Addy. She looked at the woman closely. "You came to listen to him play?"

Lily nodded, folding her hands in front of her. "He mentioned he was playing here tonight at our meeting on Thursday. Thought I'd come support him."

Meeting? Before I had a chance to ask, Addy spoke up. "How do you know Harry?"

I turned back around to tell her that Lily was a family friend, went way back, just as the woman said, "I was assigned to him when he got out last summer."

So many of the words didn't make sense. *Assigned. Got out. Last summer.* Lily's expression was calm and collected, which made what she said even more confusing.

"Wait, you're not—you're not a friend of his family?"

"No," Lily said. "I'm his probation officer."

twenty-six

"*I*—I'm sorry. His *what?*"

The shocked words didn't come from me, but from Jonathan, and dully, I realized he'd stepped to my side. I could see his dark hair from the corner of my eye, but the details hit my awareness and then disappeared, hitting me and then bouncing away. Mostly because my full attention was on Lily, her words echoing and bouncing in my brain like a song itself.

I'm his probation officer.

Assigned to him when he got out.

Got out of...

Probation officer.

Distantly, I noticed discomfort cross Lily's features. "I should head out. Can you give Harry my best?"

"Of course," Terry interjected, and he stepped beside Jonathan. His voice sounded normal. Like what she said didn't surprise him in the least. "Have a nice evening."

Lily looked at me for a beat longer before turning out of

the doorway, leaving all four of us quiet behind her. Addy had turned off the music from tonight, leaving us in silence.

A beat passed and none of us spoke. We didn't even move.

My body pivoted toward Terry as if on its own accord. "What did she mean, *got out?*"

Terry ran a hand along his jaw, skin scraping the stubble there. The action was jerky, almost nervous. Ultimately, he didn't answer.

Logical thought seemed to shrink to the back of my brain. "Got out..." I whispered. "Of *prison?*"

"No!" Terry rushed to say, and then came up short, like he didn't want to continue. "It was juvie. Lily's his juvenile probation officer."

Juvie. A juvenile detention center. Probation. They were all words I knew easily from both Mom and Dad. A lawyer and a judge. But they made no sense in connection with Harry.

"Why?" I found myself asking, still feeling detached from the moment.

"I can't tell you," Terry said. "He should be the one."

"*Why?*" I demanded again, but his answer wasn't any different.

"You'll have to ask him."

I was making Terry so uncomfortable. In the back of my mind, I knew that. I knew he probably wished Harry would hurry, wished Lily hadn't shown, wished someone else would say something. Maybe he wished I'd back off. But the longer I stared at Terry, the more I thought about *him.* Where he came from. Where he was this time last year...and why.

It was stupid, absolutely ridiculous, positively insane to even comprehend. But it was a thought that, once it'd taken root, I couldn't weed it out. Not without him clearing the air. "What you went to prison for," I said, and my voice came out quiet, muffled. "Harry wasn't...involved in that, right?"

Terry flinched, firm expression dissolving into something like a mask of acute pain. He reached out, almost like he was going to touch my arm, but he dropped his hand at the last second. "You need to talk to him."

The implication was easy to hear, to know, to see. There was no denial, just deflection. I knew what it meant. *Yes.*

All at once, everything stopped. The trampling of thoughts, the buzzing in my ears. Terry and I looked at each other, neither of us saying anything. Addy and Jonathan were somewhere in the room, and I wondered, distantly, if they were as horrified as I felt.

Because I felt absolutely horrified.

"Stella." Addy's voice filtered through my thoughts, cutting through my dazed attention.

I turned to her, watching as she wrung her hands, lips parted in shock. "Did you know?"

"What? No! I mean, I'd seen that woman with him at Crushed Beanz before, but I had no idea who she was." Addy turned to Jonathan. "Did you?"

"Of course not," he answered immediately, taking a step toward me. "I had no idea."

The room whirled around then, like someone took the scene and jerked it sharply to the side. It took me a second to realize that it was because I turned on my heel, and without another word, I escaped out into the hallway.

And ran straight into Harry. "Whoa, where's the fire?" he asked, his voice so light and happy, and it made everything in me shrivel up. I saw the tattoo then, and instead of seeing it as elegant lines, I saw it as rebellion—a sixteen-year-old breaking the rules. No, not just rule breaking. Doing something *illegal*.

As he watched me, looked into my eyes, his expression fell. "What's wrong?"

"Don't touch me." I tried to keep my voice firm, but it came out gasping, a whisper that could've been lost over the roaring of blood in my ears. And my world turned once more as I pushed away from him, heading down the hallway toward the way we all entered.

"Stella!" he called, and a second later he stood in front of me, blue eyes wide. "Wait, wait, what happened? What's going on?"

"Did you go to juvie?" The words were loud, ugly. That gasping whisper turned into something stronger, but it also wavered more. "Do you have a probation officer?"

Harry froze. Every part of him. "W-Who said that?"

It didn't feel like I was breathing.

"Did you rob a gas station?" I recoiled from him, and I could feel my face screw up. "*Two?*"

Harry's chest rose and fell rapidly as he stared at me, lips parted, a deep crease between his brows. Gone was the euphoric expression he had while onstage, as if it had never been there to begin with.

I clenched both hands into fists at my sides. Everything pinched in me, my chest, my stomach, my throat. "Tell me you didn't."

Please, I wanted to add, and my thoughts were desperate. *Please say you didn't. That you could never. You would never do anything so horrible. My mother wasn't right about you. Just tell me you're a good person.*

His voice came out rough when he responded, unwittingly replying to my thoughts too. "I can't."

I stared at him, but it wasn't him. The red hair, the white shirt, the freckles along his cheekbones, the tattoo—it was all the same, but it wasn't. I stood in the hallway with a stranger. He looked a lot like Harry, but wasn't.

Feeling sick to my stomach, I shoved past him, not caring that my shoulder jarred into him. I needed to get outside, to take in a breath of fresh air before I suffocated.

"I can explain," he told me, voice growing in frantic fervor as he caught up with me. "There's—there was *so much* that went into it, and I—"

"You lied." My voice sounded angrier than I felt. Instead, there was merely an expanding balloon in my chest. Some sort of dark emotion filled it, but it hadn't burst yet, hadn't swallowed me whole. "You lied to me."

"I didn't," he insisted, the desperation clear and enough to cause the balloon to swell wider. I shoved out of the VIP hallway, nearly stumbling into the guard standing post. "Stella, please, I—"

Whatever Harry said next got swallowed by the bass

dropping from the track the band played, and for a moment the pulsing lights blinded me. *Get outside,* I told myself, forcing my footsteps straight. *Breathe.*

And there it was, the rectangle beacon that I aimed for. I shoved outside, into the coolness of the night air. It wasn't enough. It didn't freeze the searing tension that gripped my insides.

"Wait," Harry pleaded. "Please, okay—let me explain—"

"Explain? Harry, you had a *gun!*" My voice echoed in the night, and I backed away from him, almost afraid to stand too close. People around us stopped to stare at the spectacle we were creating—*I* was creating—but I was beyond caring.

Harry, a gun in his hand. Harry, bandana over his face. Harry, tattoo of a hand clutching his neck. The image made my stomach turn and my head feel light, like I was on the verge of passing out.

Harry looked like a deer caught in headlights, too afraid to move. "It...it wasn't a real one."

Last night at Crushed Beanz, he'd said the same thing. *They weren't real guns. Just toys.* He'd been talking about Terry. When I asked him what was weighing on his mind, he told me about Terry. It was easy now to see what he was really trying to say.

"I was stupid then," he said, taking a step closer to me, holding out a shaking hand as if to say *Please, hear me out.* "I—I didn't know—"

"It was a year ago, Harry!" A year ago, a year ago. Three hundred and sixty-five flipping days. "A person can't change that much in one year."

My words still echoed in my ears from last night. *How good can you be if you rob a gas station?* How could he do something like that? It changed the entire way I looked at him. It changed *everything*.

"Destelle." Harry took another step closer, causing me to take a large jump back, maintaining the distance.

"Don't...don't touch me."

His expression faltered as he looked at me, no doubt reading the fear on my face. "You know me. I'd never hurt you."

But did I know him? I thought I did. This whole time, after nearly two months of being together, I thought I knew him pretty well. Did he really go to Bayview? He said he wasn't on speaking terms with his family—was this why? I even thought of him being in the church basement. Was he really volunteering, or was he there for community service? Oh, gosh, the thought made me sick.

If Harry was capable of something like robbing a gas station with a gun... He wasn't the person I had thought he was. Not even close. After the whole speech about Destelle and Stella, and he had a secret like *this*?

"I *can't*—" My voice choked. "Harry, I can't even *look* at you."

If I hadn't known any better, I would've thought he had tears in his eyes. The desperation on his face made everything in me *hurt*. Each breath in caused a searing pain, and each breath out felt worse. "Please, just let me tell you everything. Let's go somewhere and talk, because I swear to you—I can explain it."

"Oh, my gosh, you were the guy onstage!"

We both turned at the sudden screech and found a group of five people making their way outside the club. They were no doubt coming out for fresh air, their cheeks pink and their hair sticking to their skin, but their eyes latched on to Harry immediately, completely ignoring me.

"You were so great up there," one blonde girl told him.

"And so hot," another interjected, causing her friends to laugh.

For the first time since I'd known him, Harry didn't conjure a smile for the fans. He didn't rush to say anything to them, didn't even look at them. His eyes never left mine, gaze pleading. For what, I had no idea.

I looked at my boyfriend of nearly two months, but could barely recognize him.

The intensity between us fissured as soon as the blonde girl stepped unintentionally in front of us, severing the connection. At that moment, the balloon burst. Like an elastic band snapping, the ball of emotion exploded through my body, starting in my chest until the pain worked its way to my stomach, my throat, burning behind my eyes.

This was worse than him leaving me at the country club. So much worse. Now I knew what he'd been so upset about.

He'd been right. We were from two completely different worlds.

I turned around on the sidewalk, ignoring the looks from those who lingered in front of the club, and practically bolted in the other direction. Harry called after me, calling for Destelle or Stella, but neither one listened. Instead, I ran and didn't look back.

Not even when my tears began to cloud my vision. Not even when they started to fall.

twenty-Seven

I didn't leave my room.

If I'd had my cell phone or Jamie's tablet, I would've been reading all the articles I could find about the gas station robberies last year, scouring them for one specific name.

My brain literally couldn't compute the image of Harry walking into a store of any kind, raising a toy gun, demanding money. Harry Russo, with the dimpled smile and infectious laugh. Harry Russo, with the kind eyes and flirty personality. Harry Russo, the boy I'd been thinking nonstop about for months now.

A criminal.

And he confessed to it. *Tell me you didn't do it.*

I can't.

I thought of all the times Harry dodged questions about his past. All the times he'd phrased things vaguely. The time he broke into my car without batting an eye. His past had always been there, smoldering under the surface.

When I thought about Harry, a physical, near-crippling

pain tugged behind my chest. It went in tandem with a stinging behind my eyes. So much had happened in the past two months, and it felt as if it had all just been thrown away.

For almost the entirety of spring break, I stayed in my room. My parents didn't bother me, too furious that I snuck out. When I sauntered back into the house after getting dropped off by a taxi, they were on the verge of screaming. And they might've too, if it hadn't been for the makeup streaming down my cheeks.

When they left for work, only then did I venture downstairs to grab something for breakfast, stashing away food to get me through the night. Even Jamie and Nellie didn't press. They knew whatever had happened at the gig hadn't been good.

Everyone left me alone.

Until Wednesday night, when a knock came at my door.

"What?" I demanded, annoyance clear in my tone, angry at whoever crossed the unspoken rule of leaving me alone.

Jamie poked his head in first, eyes darting all over before finding me on my bed. He had his pajamas on, still too small for him. He was finally getting his growth spurt. "Can I come in?" he asked.

I answered by jerking my chin, pushing to sit up. My hair felt several kinds of tangled, my pajamas like a second skin by now. "What's up?"

Jamie hesitantly sat down on the edge of my bed, his eyes trained on the bedroom door. He looked uncomfortable to be in here, which wasn't surprising—he rarely ever came into my room. "Nellie is brushing her teeth."

I nodded slowly, not really following.

"Mom and Dad were talking," he said softly, kicking his feet against the edge of my bed frame. "About your boyfriend."

I tried to ignore the pang that went through me, almost like he'd shoved his little fists into my chest. "What were they saying?"

"I couldn't hear anything else, only his name." Jamie turned his chin toward me, but didn't look. "What happened?"

His voice came out so small, almost as if he waited for backlash for asking. But I wasn't going to yell. Instead, I picked at the hem of my pajama pants, staring at my chipped nail polish. "Nothing."

"You've been crying." He got the words out quickly, before thinking about it. "Almost every night. I can hear you even with my door shut. Nellie can too."

Once more, it felt as if he punched me in the chest, all the air forced out of me in a harsh gasp. "I didn't mean for you to hear."

He still kicked the bed frame, but instead of staring at the door, he finally turned to me. His eyes were an exact copy of Dad's, warm and protective. "What happened?"

"He...he lied to me. About who he was."

Jamie stopped kicking. "Like how you lied about Stella?"

My fingers stopped picking at my pajamas. "It's different."

"Is it? Even with the wig?"

I opened my mouth to tell him yes, our lies were much different, when what he'd said really settled in. "How did you know about the wig?"

Jamie knocked his foot twice, harder, against the bed frame. "I saw you put that shoebox under your bed. You're really bad at keeping things secret, Destelle."

"Hey, *you* aren't supposed to be snooping," I told him while rocking against his side, feeling more animated than I had in days. I could still imagine his little figure crouched at my bedside, hands searching for his "bouncy ball" underneath. "What were you even looking for?"

"I heard you telling Mom you had a brochure for a college you wanted to go to. I wanted to find it."

"Why?"

Jamie shrugged his little shoulders, resuming his kicking. The steady *thump-thump* of his feet almost became lulling, and I let the conversation go, a thread blowing away in a wind. "Why is it different?" he asked after a moment, going back to our previous conversation.

"He did something bad," I said, the words almost acidic on my tongue. I didn't want to say them. Confessing them to my little brother felt like a disservice to Harry. I didn't want Jamie to think poorly of Harry, but there was no dodging the truth.

Jamie thought about that for a moment. "Is he sorry?"

"What?"

"Is he sorry?" he repeated, shifting his weight on the bed.

Was he sorry? My first instinct was to laugh. "It's not that simple, Jamie."

His body slumped forward before he pushed to his feet. "Well, I guess I kept your secret about making out with him in the backyard for nothing."

"Whoa, wait! You saw that?" My eyes grew wide, practically bugging out of my head. "You didn't say anything."

His mouth quirked to the side, almost sadly. "You didn't either. You lied." Jamie paused at my bedroom door, hand gripping the handle. "Is that different too?"

Jamie shut the door before I had a chance to respond, leaving me staring at the knob with an ever-growing pit in my stomach. After a moment of silence, his final words hanging in the air, I fell back onto my bed. The ceiling hadn't changed since I'd last looked at it, and the swollen feeling in my chest hadn't either. *Is that different too?*

It was all varying shades of different. Lying about a kiss wasn't as bad as lying about an alter ego, but that wasn't as bad as lying about a crime. Then again, he hadn't lied—he just never told me. That was the worst.

I'd gotten my cell phone back Friday morning, which would've surprised me if I'd cared more. When I came out of the bathroom from my morning shower to find it on my bed, I barely had a twinge of emotion.

Except maybe apprehension, for a few different reasons. Why had they given it back to me? After everything that happened, I thought they'd have taken it back to the store or something by now.

And then the other reason for the apprehension, of course.

Had Harry texted?

I'd tried to tell myself that it didn't matter, but that was stupid. I couldn't lie to myself anymore. So, with all the determination I had left, I'd moved toward the bed and lifted the screen. I powered it on and waited for any notifications to come in.

It took me ten minutes to accept that all the notifications had come in and Harry hadn't texted.

Addy had, though. She'd sent me the video from the concert, and a few texts after that. Margot, too, had sent a message, completely oblivious to the whole situation. Instead, she merely asked:

So did your parents bury you in your yard?

A part of me wished.

I had no energy left to text back either of them. So, setting my cell on the nightstand, I went back to staring vacantly at nothing, all my thoughts circling like a Harry Russo-themed merry-go-round.

And that was how Mom found me hours later when she got home from work. She poked her head into my bedroom, face all business, like always. "You've got some letters. From colleges and a few scholarship boards."

It was one of the *last* things I wanted to talk about. Possibly ever. I rolled onto my back and glared at the ceiling, wishing I'd locked my door. "What do they say?"

"How would I know?" she asked, and strangely enough, her voice almost sounded gentle.

"We both know you already opened them."

"I didn't, actually." Mom's voice came closer, and her face edged into my peripheral. She held the envelopes to me, seals unbroken. "They're yours to open."

There were three of them between her fingers, one logo visible. *Castleton.* Despite my grim mood, I took the envelopes anyway.

But they weighed heavily in my hand. They probably weren't that heavy in reality, but simply touching the stupid things made me feel weak. Harry's voice, so determined and firm, echoed in my ear, recalling a conversation once upon a time. *If it's something you want, don't let anyone talk you out of it.*

"You can open them," I told Mom, holding them back to her, not even shuffling through them. Whatever their contents possessed in no way enticed me. "You're more excited to find out than I am."

Mom didn't immediately break into the envelopes like I expected her to, though. Instead, she merely looked at them, tracing her finger along the edges. In my head, I chanted over and over *Walk away, walk away,* hoping she'd be able to hear me. I wasn't in the mood for an argument. I really wasn't in the mood for anything.

I could hear her lips part, and it was another second before she spoke. "You are my doll, you know."

That got me looking at her uneasily. "Uh, what?"

"What you said to your father. That you weren't a doll." She didn't lift her eyes from the college envelopes. "Well, I used to think of you as my little doll, did you know that? When you were young. For the longest time, it was just you. Took us so long to get pregnant again after you—we thought it would be just you. When you were a baby, I could dress you how I wanted to, style your hair how I wanted. You always had so much hair." She smiled a bit at that, recalling a memory. "I always thought of you as my little doll."

I could remember Mom always styling my hair, always laying out an outfit. When I was younger, I didn't mind. I used to like it. When had I gone from enjoying the attention to wishing she'd just give me space?

"There comes a point when every teenager needs room to breathe," she went on. "And I wasn't ready to give you yours."

"You would never be ready," I said, feeling the stubborn anger bubble up, like a toddler stomping their feet. Instead, I turned my gaze away, staring at the wall. "You would pick out the names of my children if I let you."

Mom sat down on my bed then, and I heard her slide something along the floor. She was quiet for a while, long enough to make me feel uncomfortable in her presence. "If you love something, you're supposed to let it be free, right?" She shook her head. "I didn't get that. Not until you made me realize I held you too tight."

She leaned down to grab something from the floor. There was a rustling sound, and she brought it to rest on the bed without a word.

The Stella bag. I stared at the black Stella bag, Mom's hand still wrapped around the straps, the zipper half undone. Even from here, I could see where I'd hastily stuffed the wig into it Friday night.

I stiffened before I quickly forced my body to relax, trying to look as nonchalant as possible. "What's that?"

"Let's skip that part, shall we?" Her old stern expression flitted across her face before she reached for the zipper, opening it all the way. Her fingers slipped in, and she gently pulled out the black wig, careful not to let the strands catch on the zipper's teeth. She held it almost reverently, as if this weren't the same wig I'd worn when she nearly breathed fire last weekend. "Why do you wear this?"

"I like being someone else." I watched Mom stroke her fingers through the strands. "I like being who I want."

There seemed to be something else she wanted to say; I could see it in her eyes. I could see the gears in her brain whirring, her analytical mind working it out. Ultimately, the intensity passed, and she held the wig to me. "Can you put it on?"

Put it on. Me. In front of her. This whole moment felt so wrong. Maybe I'd fallen asleep and dreamed Mom coming into my room because this didn't feel like real life. I couldn't even figure out where this new version of her came from. Maybe it was the idea of her losing me, the idea of me pushing her away completely, that scared her.

Whatever the reason, I didn't deny her request.

Slowly, I took the wig from her, my fingers slightly unsteady. I didn't bother pulling out the wig cap or braiding my hair back. Instead, I quickly grabbed the tie off my wrist and put my hair back into a tight, low bun, then layered Stella over top. The wig fit awkwardly, of course, and probably looked horrible since I didn't have a mirror to style it, but Mom's eyes immediately widened at the sight.

She reached out and gently adjusted the wig so that my bangs sat correctly on my forehead, smoothing everything down. It reminded me of all the times Margot helped me get ready for a night out, all the times she smoothed my hair, coated mascara on my lashes. It was a gentle touch that oozed tenderness.

"Destelle," she said, but the word was low.

"Stella," I corrected her, and then tensed, because correcting Mom wasn't a thing I did. She didn't yell, though. She just blinked. "When...I wear the wig...I go by Stella."

Dad stepped into the doorway then, slipping his hands into his dress pants pockets, crossbody case resting at his hip. "I'm home," he told us gently, and I watched as his eyes roamed warily over me. They fell to the wig, of course, lingering there. "You look good with bangs, Destelle."

"It's Stella," Mom corrected him, and even though she sounded a bit mocking, it still felt nice to hear her say it. Like a crushing weight had been rolled away.

"Stella." Dad ventured into the room, his one hand falling to his bag. "I got an email today."

I was sure Dad got a lot of emails today, but I couldn't figure out which one would have to do with me.

Dad exchanged a look with Mom, one I couldn't read. He pulled a piece of paper from his bag, a trifolded sheet, and offered it out to me. "I think you'll like this one."

I stared at the paper before accepting it. What on earth could possibly be on an email to *him* that *I* would like? With a frown, I brushed the Stella hair back over my shoulder as I unfolded the edges.

And froze. Solid. Like a block of ice. I recognized the insignia in the top corner first, the name scripted in a scrawl I'd memorized. *Ashton College.*

Ashton. Yes, it was an online college, but it also was so much more. The name I'd associated with endless freedom, endless opportunities.

And I couldn't look past the logo. I really couldn't.

"Your little brother came to me one day with the college name," Dad told me, but my blood pounded loudly in my ears, almost drowning him out. "I put in the application. You'd be surprised at how easy it is to apply to an online college."

"What...why..." I opened my mouth and closed it, staring at that logo with a spinning mind. "What changed your mind?"

"The point of raising a child is to let them grow into who they want to be," Dad said, and Mom nodded ever so slightly, even if it looked a little strained. "Not who *we* want you to be."

"You deserve the right to make your own choices...even if we may disagree with them."

Dad squeezed her shoulder.

"We want you around for Christmases and birthdays," she added, and for the first time ever, I saw Mom's eyes fill. I'd *never* seen Mom cry. "We love you too much to lose you."

Dad pressed against her side. "It was easy to get caught up in the glamor of it all, in the reputation and everything. But none of that is worth ruining our relationship with our kids. With *you*."

They were the words I'd always wanted my parents to say, to *believe*, and right in that moment, they were giving me what I always dreamed of. A chance of freedom—a *choice*. I could've wept at that.

But I looked back down to the letter. Mom's and Dad's eyes were on me, and I knew there was probably an intensity there, but I couldn't look. Nerves would finally swallow me whole if I looked. Instead, I'd pretend my parents weren't there. With a deep breath in, I glanced down.

At first, the words were gibberish. They all blended together, the sentences turning into one incoherent blob of ink and mush. Indecipherable. I almost asked Mom to read it, to take it from my shaking fingers, when three words stood out. *Pleased to accept.*

No way. No way, no way. I almost couldn't feel totally excited because this moment didn't feel real. It felt like I'd been trapped in a dream, becoming self-aware but still unable to wake up. Even so, I didn't want anyone to pinch me.

When I looked up, I found Dad grinning. And Mom—well, she wasn't smiling, but her face also wasn't pinched. "I should've listened to you," she said slowly. "Should've thought about what you wanted more. And I'm sorry I didn't give you the freedom you wanted."

"We," Dad corrected, stepping close enough to place his hand on her shoulder. "That *we* didn't give you the freedom you wanted."

"I just want to explore," I told them, turning back to the paper, rereading those words again. "The country, the world. Myself. I...I don't think I really know who I am." I didn't know who I was without my parents' direction, but one thing was for sure. "I'm excited to find out."

"Well, we'll be here to find out with you." Mom straightened her posture. "The best part is that the credits transfer if you change your mind."

A startled snort came from me. "I can't believe I got in."

"It's an online college," she said, a line forming between her brows. "Doesn't everyone get in?"

"Alice," Dad murmured, and I watched his fingers squeeze her shoulder again. "Destelle, there's something else downstairs I want to show you. It's in my study."

Nellie stepped into the doorway, her eyes immediately locking on my head. I forgot all about the wig until she said, "That's so pretty! Can I try it on?"

"How about later?" I asked, reaching up and easing it off.

Mom got to her feet, holding her hand out to my little sister. "Nellie, why don't you help me with dinner?"

"I get to help you?" Nellie's eyebrows rose with a happy sort of surprise. "Can Jamie help too?"

"Don't burn dinner," I told her, standing as well. "Or I'll be furious."

"Furious," she said automatically. "F-U-R-I-O-U-S. Furious. And don't worry, I won't. It's Jamie you have to worry about."

Dad led me into his office, but I lingered in the doorway as he made his way around the oak. His movements were swift as he opened the drawer beside his desk, the one he normally kept my cell phone caged in. "It took me some time to find this," he told me. "I couldn't remember if I kept it in the office or here. Turned out, I'd placed it in my glove box. So I'd always have it with me, I suppose."

It didn't take him more than a second to fish out something—an envelope with a crease on one corner. Without a word, Dad offered it out to me.

I narrowed my eyes at him, wondering what kind of game he played at. Another envelope? What, another college acceptance letter?

I took it from him and eased the broken seal apart, finding a letter inside. It'd been written on a piece of notebook paper, folded and creased. The black ink looked rushed, written across it—*handwritten*. Once I pulled it completely out, I saw the name.

Harrison Russo.

I immediately looked up. "Why do you have this?"

Dad sat down in his desk chair. "He didn't tell you that part?"

Apprehension weighed on me like a second skin as I looked at him, barely breathing. "What part?"

"I was the judge on his case," Dad said, returning my gaze evenly. Everything about him was neutral, calm. "When he was tried in juvenile court, I was the judge on the case."

At first, his words made no sense. They were words I knew, but the order he'd placed them in turned the sentences into gibberish. Last year, Dad was the judge on Harry's case? Dad *knew* Harry before all of this?

Understanding hit me like a punch in the chest.

I practically fell back into the chair opposite from Dad,

the air all but shoving from my lungs. "Am I—I mean, am I allowed to read this?"

"He sent it to me months after the case closed. Of his own volition. You can read it."

Even though Harry had printed the front of the envelope clearly, the way he wrote in the body of the letter was messy, nervous, almost hard to read. After a moment of debating, curiosity weighed heavier than the guilt of invading his privacy.

August 9

Dear Judge Brighton,

I'm not sure if you remember me or not, but my name's Harrison Russo. I appeared in your courtroom earlier this year for a robbery. You probably remember me—I was the kid who practically peed his pants when I was escorted into the room. I also have a neck tattoo that totally doesn't fit my personality, if that clears things up.

I've been wanting to write a letter for a while now, but I'm really bad at organizing my thoughts. I got released from the detention center last month, and I know what you're thinking—I was supposed to get out in June, when I turned eighteen. I'll be honest with you. Juvie sucked wasn't fun. It wasn't supposed to be fun, though, right? Anyway, I had a hard time, had a bad attitude, but I remembered something you told me. I had this one chance—one last chance—to turn things around.

You took a chance on me. Some days I still ask myself why, because I'm nothing special. I'm just a kid who followed the wrong crowd, did things he wasn't proud of. You said you saw some good in me. Said I was a victim of circumstances. Honestly, I remember thinking that was a load. No offense. It just felt like I didn't deserve a second chance. I'm not sure if I can see the same that you see, but I want to try. I want to be the person you think I can be. I can't change what I did, but I can do better.

I guess this was kind of a selfish letter, huh? I'm talking all about myself. I wanted to thank you for saying the right thing when I needed to hear it. Thank you for taking a chance on me. Thank you for not throwing away my case—throwing me away. Things would've been so different.

I've got a feeling good things are ahead, and I'm forever grateful you gave me a second chance. Thanks for giving me a second chance, and seeing—what did you call it?—my untapped potential.

Sincerely,

Harrison Russo

I traced my finger along the two unmistakable words. *Untapped potential.* "What did you do?" I asked Dad, not looking up, not yet. In my mind's eye, I could see Harry slouched over a table, pencil frantically at work. "How did you take a chance on him?"

Dad's chair squeaked as he leaned back. "I could've charged him as an adult. Could've ruined the beginning of his adult life. But the prosecutors and I worked it out that he would be tried in juvenile court instead, since he was still seventeen."

"Why?" I asked, mouth dry. "Why take a chance on him?"

"Everyone should have someone who takes a chance on them," he said, leaning his head on his hand. He had such an even expression, no emotion displayed: his work face. "You know a bit about his life, correct? He hung out with people older than him. Pressuring him to do things. After being bounced around from family member to family member after his parents died, he lived with distant family members, practically invisible. No good influence, no support system."

When he phrased it like that, that tightness in my chest reappeared, picturing a young Harry with freckles and tousled hair. I looked away from Dad, back down to Harry's messy scrawl. *A victim of circumstance.* "Did you ever send a letter back?"

"I did not." Dad smiled a little; I could hear it in his voice. "It's not often I get thank-you letters. I didn't write back because he didn't need me to. He needed to figure out his way back to himself."

"You met him. At the country club. Did he seem... different? Like he'd found his way back to himself?"

"You know him," he returned evenly. In that moment, I had the strangest feeling that he embodied the nagging voice in my head. Smooth, even, turning questions back on me. "You know him more than I do. Do *you* think he's found his way? Could you see the Harry you knew doing such a thing? From what I remember you telling me, you said he was a good man."

Gently, I folded the letter and stuck it back in the envelope, then offered it to Dad. As soon as he took it, I fell back, slouching against the leather upholstery. "He should've told me."

"Yes, he should've. But do you think things would've

ended any differently if he'd told you sooner?" Dad put the letter away. His eyes lingered on the drawer, and he spoke to it. "Destelle, for the past few years, you've done everything your mother and I told you to without question. Why?"

Was that a trick question? I tried to dig, to really come up with an honest answer, about what I felt deep down. "It was all I knew," is what I came to at last, brushing my fingertips over my knuckles. "I wanted to make you happy. Make you proud of me. I didn't want you to be upset with me."

"You wanted to make us proud, and it was all you knew. Now, tell me. What would you have done if we told you to help us rob a gas station?"

"I wouldn't—"

"No?" He cut me off gently. "What if we'd never been good influences?"

I knew he was right, of course. Without good influences, it would've been easy to not know wrong from right. Everything in me still hesitated, though, uncertainty and apprehension mixing inside me, weighing down like cement.

"I think you should listen to his side of things," Dad went on, and opened the drawer back up. "Just listen. You don't have to see him again after that, but if you care about him like I think you do, you should hear him out. You might find that his story...it's not what you're thinking. Not quite. He deserves that much."

Dad offered my car keys out to me by the ring, and the

fob swung back and forth like a pendulum, a ticking metronome, waiting for me to decide.

Only when the fob stopped swinging did I grab the keys, closing my hand around them. "You like him," I said.

"I do," he agreed. "He's a good kid who got lost down a dark road."

I looked at the car keys in my hand, my taste of freedom, the promise of unknown. Listen to Harry's side of the story. In the days that had passed since I found out about his past, I'd been almost desperate for the truth. *All* of the truth. Why did he do it? Did he regret it? Was he sorry?

And right here, cradled in my hand, I had a way of finding out. Jostling the keys once, I let out a breath. "Thanks, Dad."

Dad watched as I rose and made my way to the door. His eyes were light on me, expression content. "No problem, Stella."

twenty-eight

Being out of the house for the first time in almost a week was weird. My entire spring break had come and gone, and I barely ventured out of my bedroom. The last time I'd been sitting behind the wheel of my car, things had been so different.

I wasn't wearing Stella tonight, not to the full extent. No wig, no nose ring, but I did wear the black turtleneck. The heeled boots, though, were definitely Destelle.

Like the best of both worlds.

My heart hammered as I made the last turn, taking the route I knew by heart. Day or night, I'd never forget this path. Hallow was an easy village to navigate. It wasn't as big as Addison or Bayview, but so many memories lived in Hallow, ones that would be near impossible to forget.

As soon as I made my final turn, my stomach dropped. I'd turned onto the main road in Hallow, the one that held my favorite coffee shop, and the road was practically empty. No cars lining the streets. No cars in the lot. As I drove past the café, I caught a glimpse inside the windows: no excited crowd.

It was Friday night, and Untapped Potential wasn't playing at Crushed Beanz.

The SUV's tires squealed as I shoved it into park, fumbling my phone from my pocket. After a frantic check, I found Untapped Potential's latest post from last night.

Untapped Potential Status Update:

We have to cancel our Friday gig—our poor singer has come down with the flu. Hopefully we can perform for you Saturday night! In the meantime, what's one Untapped Potential song that always cheers you up?

I put the car back into gear before I realized it, then merged onto the roadway. This was a route a little less known, a little less memorized, but I tried as hard as I could. So much pent-up energy danced inside me, no way I'd swallow it and go home.

And even though I could've called him, this definitely wasn't a conversation to be had over the phone.

Harry's house was easy to picture in my mind, but it took me nearly an hour to find, especially in the dim light of the sky. I'd turned down the wrong road three times, and even then I drove past his house, too busy looking at the other side of the street. I didn't know the exact address, so I couldn't plug it into the GPS. But when I spotted the siding and the porch with a red car parked out front, I slammed on the brakes.

He was inside. This was it.

For the longest moment, I sat in the driveway. Did I even want to know? Did I want to learn all the secrets he kept? Everything that happened?

Ugh, as soon as I thought the questions, I knew the obvious answer. Of course I wanted to know. After four days with nothing but my raging thoughts to keep me company, I needed to know. All of it.

Just because I missed him didn't erase what happened. What he did. I wasn't sure I'd ever understand.

But I'd never understand if I never asked.

I popped open the car door, stepping out into the breeze. Finally, my warmer weather arrived. Gone was the cold of winter; the briskness of spring came as a nice reprieve from all the snow, but all of me still felt chilled.

My chunky-heeled boots carried me on the cobblestones that led to the porch, a click-clacking accompanying my racing heart. It reminded me of the drumbeats in the newest Untapped Potential song, the one Harry had written about me.

The porch creaked under my weight, and I stopped right in front of the door, heart hammering a mile a minute.

I really could throw up. Ugh, maybe this had been a bad idea. I checked my posture, standing up straight, even though everything in me fluttered nervously. Was it too late to run? I hadn't knocked yet. He didn't know I stood on his porch. I could just turn around and—

Right as I thought that, the front door swung inward, and Harry stood on the other side.

He looked terrible. Completely terrible. His auburn

hair was all rucked up, his skin pale. His eyes were wide as they settled on me, and the first emotion I caught was disbelief. "Destelle."

"Harry," I returned, glad my voice sounded slightly steady. Only slightly. "Hi."

"Hi." His hand still clung to the doorknob, tension keeping his body ramrod straight. Caution flashed across his expression, like he was afraid to hear me speak.

I curled my hands behind my back to hide their quivering. "So, do you really have the flu, or is this something more important to do?"

Our old joke, but he didn't react to it, not this time. He seemed to be holding his breath.

"Can we..." I cleared my throat, clearing the emotion. "Can we talk?"

Harry took a jerking step back out of the doorway, making room for me to pass through. "Y-Yeah, for sure. Um, come on in."

I tried to look at the situation as if I were Margot, the Queen of Assessment. I thought about how she always looked at her suits with a keen eye, spotting the problems, making decisions. So, that's what I needed to do. Harry wasn't truthful with his past—he hadn't lied, but it was definitely something he should've told me. It was a huge secret he kept. It was a *criminal* secret he kept.

But then again, if the situation were reversed, how would I want everything to play out?

My eyes darted all over as I ventured inside. It wasn't particularly untidy, but it wasn't nearly as clean as when I'd been there last. A pizza box sat on one countertop, lid closed. I saw a few half-empty water bottles, and the collection of tools by the door remained.

The mess seemed to make Harry nervous, because I watched as he glanced around the space, probably wishing he'd had a second to hide it all. "We can sit on the couch," he offered, swiping his palms against his thighs. The gray sweatpants he wore were loose—and I realized it was the first time I'd seen him in something other than ripped jeans. "Or we can stand. W-Wherever you want."

"The couch works," I said.

Gosh, this was so awkward—I had no idea how to act around him, how to feel. What to say. So many unknowns, so much uncertainty. And I hated it.

His actions were stiff as he led us to his living room, and he held himself rigid, tension running through his veins. Despite the strained atmosphere, his eyes were wide and open, so much emotion in their depths that it almost caught me off-guard.

"My dad showed me the letter," I told him once we both settled, my hands folded formally over my knees. I fully dived into this conversation. No turning back. "He wouldn't tell me anything else, but he showed me the letter. Your letter."

"Okay." Harry touched the skin of his neck, tracing his tattoo. "What did you think?"

"That your handwriting needs some work."

A small smile flitted across his mouth.

"I want you to tell me everything from the beginning." The couch creaked as I leaned back against it, torn between looking at him and looking away. "I want to understand."

His nod was jerky, and his whole body shifted, all rigid lines positioned so his hands folded over his knees, moving like a puppet on strings. A more severe dose of anxiety flashed across his features, a static glare in his gaze.

"Um, so, it was New Year's Eve. Last year. I was home alone—Jeff, my cousin, had taken his family to some party his work threw—and one of my friends texted me. Leo. He asked if I wanted to go driving with them."

"Driving?" I echoed, feeling my brow furrow.

"We did that. We'd just drive around, listening to music. I didn't want to be home alone on New Year's Eve and figured we'd end up at a party somewhere. Leo always knew someone who was throwing a party. When they got to the house, I immediately thought something felt...different." Harry stopped looking at me then, eyes darting on anything *but* me, almost as if he were seeing the scene unfold instead of the room in front of him. "I got into the back seat, and Terry looked at me in the rearview mirror— he was driving. He said that I needed to stay home."

As he spoke, voice a soft sort of nervous, I tried to picture the scene in my head—the car, the friends, the voices. "He knew," I guessed.

"Yeah, he knew. I didn't. I laughed at him and put my seat belt on—as if I'd stay home on New Year's." Harry swallowed hard. I wondered how often he'd told this story before. At least in this depth. "We drove around for a little while before Gage said he wanted to stop at a gas station. Terry pulled into the closest one, and I started to get out of the car. I figured I'd get a pop or something while we were there, you know? Why not?"

My body clenched, guessing what came next. Did I want to hear it? Did I want to know? By how nauseated I felt, I wasn't sure that I did. And by the pale look of Harry's cheeks, it seemed he didn't want to say it.

I'd already dived into the deep end. No turning back.

"Terry turned around and grabbed my arm. I remember it hurt, so much that I thought he was trying to break my wrist. He told me I needed to stay in the car but didn't say why." Harry's fingers moved to bracelet his wrist now, tracing the echo of the memory. "Leo grabbed my other arm and pulled me from the car, though. Said that my pop would be on him. That it was a late Christmas present. I remember laughing—only Leo would consider a pop a Christmas present."

Leo sounded a lot like Margot.

Harry curled his fingers into fists before relaxing them, trying to stop the quivering. "I was picking out a drink when Leo and Gage pulled out the face masks, the kind that curl around your ears. Leo grabbed my face and put one on me before I even knew what they were doing. Gave me a plastic gun. Everything happened so fast. I remember looking at it, thinking he was joking."

Harry in a face mask, Harry holding a gun.

"God, I..." Harry sighed harshly, eyes brightening as he looked at me, the blue electric, almost as if they were high-lighted by a sheen of tears. "I just followed them to the front, holding the stupid thing. Looking at it like I couldn't figure out what it was. It was like I couldn't even move my body. Like there was some disconnect from what was happening. Destelle, I *swear*, I never lifted it, never did *anything*."

The pain in his eyes was clear, pinching at his face. It knocked the air from my lungs. "Harry—"

"They had to drag me out once they realized I wasn't moving," he said, rushing on, not letting me speak. His words started coming faster, like a faucet flowing, unable to stop. "Even on the video footage from the station, you could see them dragging me out. I left the pop on the counter. And Leo and Gage couldn't stop laughing while they were counting the money, like—like they were crazed. I mean, they'd broken into cars before—maybe stole a package or two off someone's porch—but *never* anything like this. I tried so hard to keep from crying. I remember being so afraid when Terry looked in the rearview, afraid he'd see and tell them."

"Did he?" I asked, wondering if Harry then looked like Harry now. Electric eyes, a watery sheen to them.

He shook his head. "They stopped at another gas station, but I stayed in the car that time with Terry. Terry was the one who called the police, actually. He was offered a deal for his cooperation—that's why he was out so soon. He told me to get out and get away from them while I could, but there was no way. I—I was there for it. I deserved the punishment as much as anyone else."

Harry had a clear opportunity to run away and didn't take it. *I deserved the punishment.* In all honesty, he probably could've gotten away with leaving. Only three guys robbed the first one—they could've assumed the third was

Terry. It could've been a done deal. But Harry had stayed behind. Faced the music.

Out of everything he'd said since we'd sat down, that sounded the most like the boy I knew.

"I remember thinking my parents would be so ashamed of me, and that was—" His voice cut off then, and he let out a sharp sigh, placing his hand over the tattoo on his throat, fingers perfectly aligning with the ink, and he squeezed ever so slightly. When he spoke again, his words were thick. "That was one of the worst parts, I think."

"What happened then?" I asked.

"The cops came before Leo and Gage even got out of the store—they'd been searching for us. We were all arrested, all processed. I was so freaking terrified they'd try me as an adult—they should've. I was turning eighteen in almost seven months. But your dad..." Harry blew out a breath and leveled his gaze with mine, lips pressing together. When he spoke again, reverence coated his voice, expression a little disbelieving. "He fought for me, Destelle. When I told him I didn't know what was happening, told him the truth of all of it, he—he *believed* me. I...I still can't believe he did that. He could've washed his hands of me, assumed I was lying. He gave me a second chance."

Harry's letter floated up in my mind, his gratitude showing through the scribbled words.

"How long were you in juvie for?" It was nearly impossible to picture him being in a place like that.

"I was supposed to be there until June, when I turned eighteen, but I—well, I had a hard time adjusting. Had a bad attitude. Nothing serious, but that bad attitude added a month. They assigned me Lily as a probation officer, making sure I'd stay on the straight and narrow." He gave a soft scoff. "As if I'd do *anything* like that ever again. I don't even drive over the speed limit anymore."

I swallowed hard, thinking about my conversation with Dad earlier. "At the fundraiser—that's why you were so upset. You recognized Dad."

I could still picture Harry's expression from that day in my mind's eye, how he stared at Dad's hand for several moments before finally taking it. How different would things have been if he'd known who my dad was all along? If Harry had known my actual last name.

Once more, a small smile flitted across Harry's face, only lingering for a second as he traced his tattoo. "When I saw your dad, it was like all my fears came true. You were too good for me. And when I just knew you as Stella, I figured that secret wasn't that big of a deal. It sounds stupid now."

"You said you and Stella were more alike," I said, recalling that conversation, and little puzzle pieces suddenly connected. "You thought she'd understand what happened. You didn't think Destelle would."

"I should've given *you* more credit."

Honestly, though, I *had* freaked out. But I would have, whether I'd been dressed as Stella or not. "That's why you wouldn't have danced with me if I looked like *me*, not Stella. Because you would've been afraid of telling me the truth."

Harry let his hand fall from his throat, and my gaze caught on the ink, the elegant way it curved over his skin. "I hate myself for what I did, for doing *any* of it. That's why Jeff doesn't talk to me anymore, because of everything that happened. I don't blame him—I was a terrible influence for his kids. Even down to getting a stupid tattoo when I was sixteen." He looked up at me. "For the longest time, I thought I could pretend it didn't happen. Pretend that was a side of me that didn't exist, a past that had been wiped away. You made Stella because you wanted to feel free. When I was with you, I felt like I could be free too. Free of my past, free of the shame and embarrassment and guilt. It wasn't like I felt like a different person, but everything that weighed me down just wasn't there. But then *not* telling you became so...horrible."

He'd taken the words from my brain and spoke them in a much more beautiful way. He'd described exactly what Stella was to me. A way to break free of everything that tied me down. As time went on, I realized I wasn't a different person when I was Stella—she was still me and I was still her, just *freer.* He'd literally read my mind.

"As soon as I saw your dad at the party, I panicked. It was like fate wanted me to come clean, but I knew it might mean you'd never want to see me again. You wouldn't see me the same. Which I get." Harry's forehead wrinkled. "But I realized your dad would probably tell you for me, and he'd tell you to stay away from me, and that would be that. No matter how kind he was to me then, he wouldn't have wanted you around me now."

I couldn't imagine being in Harry's shoes, spotting Dad, the judge who showed him kindness when he needed it most, finding out he was my father.

"I was going to tell you," Harry insisted, weaving his fingers together as if to keep from reaching out. "After the show at Downtown. When you came to me at Crushed Beanz and your dad hadn't told you, I was going to come clean after the show. I know that sounds convenient, but I didn't want to hide that part of me anymore. Not with you because you—you're so important to me."

My brain didn't miss the fact that he'd used the present tense, sending my insides into a flurry of emotion.

"When I thought about where I wanted to be in a few months, I always saw you," he went on, chest starting to rise and fall faster. "And I never wanted to risk it."

Goosebumps skittered along my skin, an involuntary shiver slipping down my spine. "You saw me in your future?"

"Front row at every gig. My Dial and Dine delivery driver. The girl I could sing to, sing *with*. I could be myself with you." Harry reached up once more and traced his tattoo. "And I'd be there for you when you wanted to explore the world, riding shotgun, snacks in hand. Writing more songs about you, because I've an endless supply of inspiration. Dancing with you without a care in the world. I thought I was doing the right thing, but I—I ruined it, anyway."

I opened my mouth to say something, but nothing came out. Maybe it was because emotions flooded me: apprehension, caution, happiness, nervousness. He'd really struck me speechless, and I gaped at him, overwhelmed.

"It was the worst mistake of my life. The biggest regret. I just surrounded myself with people who were bad influences. It's easy to see that now, now that I've finally got good people in my life." He took a deep breath in and then let it out slowly, as if to reset his thoughts. "I should've told you the truth, Destelle. You deserved to know the truth from the very beginning. I can't apologize enough, but I'm so, so sorry."

The words were a signature on a letter, a period on a sentence, the end of his explanation. It all finished with *I'm so, so sorry*. After everything, my body felt tight and heavy, as if I'd been walking for hours and someone finally offered the chance to sit down. The house had blended into the background while Harry spoke, and even now, when he finished and looked at me, I still couldn't focus on any detail.

It was the biggest mistake of his life. His biggest regret. He'd been in a bad situation with bad people. Been in the wrong place at the wrong time. Mom and Dad had seen so many cases of that exact situation. Victim of circumstance.

My brain, for several moments, was at war, divided cleanly down the middle.

Harry participated in a crime—there was no denying that. But he hadn't *knowingly* done it. He hadn't walked into that gas station with a gun in his hand. He hadn't pointed it at the clerk. He hadn't even taken the soda.

Harry *was* arrested, but only because he opted to stick around and face the consequences.

For a split second, his past was a whole separate entity between us, like a clear wall. I could see him through it, but was unsure about jumping over it. Unsure about him.

My eyes fell to his tattoo, to the black lines. He was a

boy with a kind smile, a beautiful voice. He was a boy with messy handwriting who texted in perfect grammar and prided himself on doing things the right way. The boy who hadn't batted an eye when I revealed the truth about Stella.

"My dad put in an application to Ashton for me," I said, my words sounding random. "That was the online college I had my eye on. The only one, really."

Harry, though, took it in stride, knowing I had a point somewhere along the way. "He did? That—that was your dream."

He knows me. He knows exactly how I tick. "Mom said that the credits would transfer if I changed my mind, but I don't think I will." I held his gaze and cataloged every single minute expression. The firm line of his jaw, the loose purse of his lips, the arch to his brows. I took it all in, putting it to memory. "You still interested in riding shotgun?"

I memorized the expression on his face before so I could forever remember the way it morphed after. His eyebrows flew up as his eyes widened, and the loose purse of his lips disappeared when his firm jaw dropped. The hands on his knees spasmed, body jerking once more like a puppet on strings.

When he spoke, it came out as a whisper. "Really?"

"I knew Untapped Potential was always going to go places, but I never thought our paths would cross," I told him, emotion starting to clog my throat, like a hand wrapping around my neck. "I didn't know you before, but I know you *now*. I trust you *now*. I never saw myself in your future, but now that I have, I can't imagine anything different."

And the truth in my words nearly struck me speechless. Before Harry, the idea of being on my own was so arbitrary. Who would be my shotgun rider on road trips and adventures? Margot sometimes, but she'd go off to college in the fall. Who would stick by me then?

Once Harry came into the picture, there was no other person I could imagine in that passenger seat. No other person I *wanted* to imagine taking that journey with me.

His eyes rapidly scanned my face, looking for any hint of falseness, of uncertainty, expecting it. But there was none—I meant it. I couldn't imagine experiencing life with anyone other than him.

Maybe we were from two different worlds, but I didn't care.

"What are my odds?" Harry asked suddenly, looking almost afraid to hope.

A startled laugh burst from me, mostly at the desperation on his face. "Why don't you find out?"

In one swift movement, Harry leaned closer until his leg pressed against the side of mine, and he was everywhere. Tilting toward me, eyes scanning mine several times, waiting for me to pull back.

Without wasting another second, I closed the gap between us.

The second that our lips met, that balloon-like feeling burst in my chest, but this time the explosion of feeling was as if a million butterflies had lifted into the air. All the weight pressing me down disappeared, replaced by the feel of Harry's mouth on mine. I laid my hand against his throat, touching the tattoo, and he slid the pad of his thumb along my cheekbone the way he always did.

This feeling was the same. I realized now that this was the Harry Russo I knew. The one who was gentle and tender and such a good kisser. Hands so soft and careful and lips like fire.

There was forgiveness in this kiss, honesty, trust. We were both finding ourselves, and we were finding ourselves together.

I didn't know who he was this time last year, but I knew him now. And I trusted him now. I would've trusted him with my life.

"Thank you," Harry gasped against my mouth, pulling away to meet my gaze. "Thank you for coming and talking to me. I'm glad you had nothing more important to do."

I settled deeper in his arms. "Nothing is more important than this."

Harry traced his fingertip down my cheek, touch as delicate as a summer breeze as he murmured, "I feel the same way."

This time, he kissed me softer, sweeter, but it still made my toes curl in my boots. Harry accepted me for me, and I accepted him for him. There was a Harry Before and a Harry After, and there was a Destelle and a Stella.

Two different sides of each of us, both equally loved.

epilogue

"*Y*ou got your phone charger?"

"Of course I do."

"What about your Stella wig?"

I laid the last dark shirt into my suitcase, rolling my eyes. "Yes."

"Extra underwear?"

I looked up sharply, locking eyes. "Nellie."

My sister raised her palms from where she sat at my desk chair, immediately on defense. "Just asking, sheesh."

"Hey, a girl needs her panties," Margot said helpfully, sitting elegantly on the side of my bed. She'd unbuttoned her suit jacket and let it hang open, exposing her silk shirt underneath. The picture of elegance among the chaos of my messy, tornado-ravaged bedroom. Packing for a trip constituted as a natural disaster when I was in charge of it, apparently. Every piece of clothing I touched wasn't good enough for the first ever trip by myself. Nothing was good enough.

Destelle was breaking out into the world for the first time—I needed something *different*.

That was probably why I ended up packing most of my Stella clothes.

Even though everyone knew about Stella at that point, I still enjoyed wearing the wig and the dark clothes. It was different now. I didn't dress as her as an escape anymore. We were one and the same.

"Do you think I'll fit in that suitcase?" Margot went on, tapping her finger along her chin. "I want to go on a vacation too."

"It's not quite a vacation," I reminded her, flipping the flap of my case over. "Most of it's work."

"We need to plan a trip for you and me. Bayview's cute and all, but I want to go to a coast outside this county. Where there's a beautiful beach, beautiful *boys*..."

"Ew," Nellie commented.

"When I get home, we'll plan it," I promised, brain already whirring on locations.

Jamie chose then to walk into my bedroom, his eyes darting between all of us. "Mom's freaking out downstairs."

"Is she not going to let Destelle go?" Nellie asked, her voice almost sounding excited. I couldn't help but give her another look.

"No, she will. I think. She's—well, I don't really know what she's doing. Besides freaking out."

I tugged the zipper on the rectangular suitcase and hauled it off my bed, extending the arm with a sharp *click*. "Well, let's go check on her. Nellie, can you grab my carry-on?"

She hopped out of my desk chair and snatched the bag from where it sat by my closet, hefting it over her shoulder with a groan.

"Hey." Margot caught my arm to hold me back, waiting for my sister to leave the room. "I'm really proud of you, Destelle. I'm happy for you."

"Margot," I said plaintively, wrapping my arms around her slender frame and squeezing. In our time of friendship, we definitely weren't huggers, but that didn't stop her from squeezing me back. "You always rooted for me. I'm in your corner, you know. You've got big things ahead of you too."

"That fashion institute won't know what hit 'em," she teased, and pulled back to peer down into my face. Her rare bout of affection nearly made me emotional, but it made me realize the seriousness of this moment. Of the evolution of Stella and Destelle, merging their futures into one. "Great things are in store for you, kid. Seriously. Don't forget to text me road trip pictures."

"Destelle!" Nellie's voice shouted up the stairs. "Come *on!*"

"Go, before they change their minds," Margot said with a laugh, shooing me out of my bedroom, following me with my red suitcase trailing after her.

Once we got downstairs, I knew exactly what Jamie meant by "freaking out." I could hear it clearly: Mom was crying.

"That's my cue," Margot said, passing over the handle to my suitcase. "I'll head outside until the waterworks subside."

I propped the suitcase up to follow the sound of Mom,

and as I got closer, I could hear Dad trying to shush her. "It's only three days, Alice. Three days. She'll be up in Grisham Falls—that's not far at all."

"I—I just feel so out of control," she told him.

"I think that's the point," Dad responded gently.

"It is." I stopped in the doorway of the kitchen to find Mom slumped at the breakfast bar, Dad standing behind her and rubbing her shoulders. "The complete point."

Mom hurried to wipe her tears away. "Three days," she echoed, straightening her spine. "I can handle three days."

"I'll call, I'll text, and you can even watch the livestream on Untapped Potential's social media page, like I showed you, remember? I'll be streaming it the whole time."

"Stella!" Nellie called from the front of the house. "His car pulled up!"

A shot of happiness and excitement rippled through me, and without giving any of them a second thought, I turned to hurry out of the kitchen.

Dad's voice trailed after me. "Come on, let's see her off, yeah?"

Margot and the twins were already outside when I got to the front door, the latter two flagging down Harry. The sight of his car had my heart skipping a beat, the future I'd been dreaming of just moments away from becoming a reality.

Harry parked in the driveway, a red beacon of freedom, and when he emerged, he had a gigantic grin on his gorgeous face. "You ready to do this thing?"

"Beyond ready," I told him, stepping close enough to

wrap my arms around his neck. He smelled like sunshine and happiness and independence. "Are the others on the road?"

"Yep." He trailed his fingertip along my cheekbone. Despite the heat of the day, his touch was cool, a refreshing touch. "Natasha texted me that she left an hour ago."

"Your first gig outside of Fenton County," Dad called, stepping out of the house with Mom trailing him. They stopped beside Margot. "Moving on up in the world."

"And the first recording session after being signed to Preston Records," Harry returned happily, an easy smile on his lips. "I swear, I'll be like a kid in a candy store. It'll probably be embarrassing."

It turned out that Margot's intimidation technique—or *persuasive conversation,* as she called it—on Mr. Preston had worked wonders. The Saturday after their gig at Downtown, Mr. Preston had come into Crushed Beanz with an offer they'd been dreaming of: a chance of recording their first single at his studio in Grisham Falls.

And once they wholeheartedly accepted, Mr. Preston pulled some strings to get them a slot to perform at a club up there. Expanding their horizons.

"I'll livestream every second of it for the social media page," I said, wrapping an arm around his waist. Natasha showed me how to stream to the page a few weeks ago, and I got to upload one of their gigs. The idea of seeing Harry's reaction alone made me excited, anxious, and I wished we were in Grisham Falls already. "Just think—this time tomorrow, you'll have begun the process of recording your first single."

After Mr. Preston offered them a contract to record their first song, Untapped Potential had an easy time picking which one to debut with. Ever since they released it, it'd been their most requested at gigs. Their fans loved the beat and loved the lyrics.

And, ever so fitting, it was the song Harry wrote for me. "Dance Floor."

"Text me when you get there," Dad said, and his hand landed hard on Harry's shoulder. He looked directly into Harry's blue eyes. "And stay in your own hotel room, son. I booked two for a reason."

Harry's cheeks turned pink then, his hand dropping from around my waist. "Of course, sir."

"Harry. It's been months." Dad gave Harry's shoulder one last, more affectionate, squeeze before letting go. "Call me David."

It *had* been months. Months since Harry and I accepted each other for who we were, months since we'd found each other again. And in those months, so much had happened. Endless Dial and Dine trips, coffee dates galore, and even the occasional movie night over at the Brighton household. Nellie loved forcing Harry to quiz her with her flash cards—to which he happily complied—and Jamie loved talking about the movies with Harry, especially when they were action flicks.

We'd all fallen into a steady rhythm, and it was just...perfect.

I tipped my head toward Mom, standing near the house, squinting against the sun. "I'll see you in three days," I told her with a smile.

Nellie hugged us goodbye after we loaded my luggage into the trunk—hugged Harry longer than her own sister—before she let us get into the car. Dad patted me on the back, much like he had with Mom, and Mom...she didn't move from where she stood beside Margot. Her eyes, though, were very shiny. "Love you," she said to me, the words faint but there.

So much had changed in the past few months. The transition into her giving me more space was hard—especially when it came to turning down volunteer opportunities—but we started to find our new normal. I was allowed to keep my cell phone at night as long as I turned it off by eleven, which felt like a monumental step. She'd let me go out as much as I wanted with Harry, as long as I kept my grades up to her standards and was home by curfew.

And "love you" had been a part of that, on rare occasions.

"So," Harry said as he backed down the driveway, and I waved at everyone, watching the five of them wave back. "How's your first adventure as a high school graduate feel?"

Right. I'd officially graduated from Eastview Academy two weeks ago. Online classes didn't start until the fall, which gave me the entire summer of freedom. As per our agreement, my parents were to be hands-off for the first semester. Or, well, as hands-off as they could force themselves to be.

When Untapped Potential began touring, they'd have to fully let me go. And though I was excited, I couldn't deny that I was happy they still cared.

"It feels great," I told Harry, sinking deeper into the seat. "Especially since I've got you at my side."

Harry only drove a little ways down the road before he eased the car to the side, tires crunching over the gravel. "Very romantic," he mused, putting the car into park. He reached over to run his fingers through my hair then, winding around my curls. "I figured I'd wait to kiss you until your family couldn't see."

Gosh, I'd never get used to the way he looked at me, the simmering Caribbean waters full of amusement and happiness, like a serious ray of sunshine on Earth. His auburn hair looked so vibrant in the light, so beautiful against his skin. So freaking beautiful.

So freaking mine.

"Let's go achieve our dreams," he murmured, leaning close enough that we shared the same breath.

I pressed my mouth against his, lingering, drawn in by his taste and scent and touch. All of him, all the time. Achieving my dreams? Facing the future? Finding freedom? I gripped him tighter, knowing I'd dive into all of that headfirst.

Against his mouth, I murmured, "Together."

Before You Go!

Reviews are so important for authors, especially for indie authors. If you enjoyed this book, please head over to Amazon and leave a review!

Sarah Sutton

WHAT ARE FRIENDS FOR?

What Are Friends For?

Who said falling for your best friend was a good thing?

OUT OF MY LEAGUE

Out of My League

Fake dating the captain of the baseball team is all fun and games until someone catches feelings.

IF THE BROOM FITS

If the Broom Fits

How do you move on from someone you never fell out of love with?

CAN'T CATCH MY BREATH

Can't Catch My Breath

Can she break free of the past and find true love?

ACKNOWLEDGMENTS

This book had such an army of people helping me turn it from a lanky little caterpillar into a beautiful butterfly. Seriously, an army.

Thank YOU, readers!

Thank you to Brook, Melanie, Kate, Tessy, and Arceli for being part of this book's infancy (AKA beta phase) and for helping me find ways to improve. Ariel, I'm so thankful for our friendship and having you to bounce things off of. You were one of the final eyes on this piece and you gave me nothing but fantastic advice. big hugs!

A massive thank you to my editor, Amy, for polishing this bad boy up. Who knew I used "breathe" so many times. ;)

Thank you to those in the writing community for always being constant cheerleaders. Without any of you, I have no idea where I'd be.

My parents need a big thank you as well, because they always get the brunt of my pre-publishing anxiety. Every.

Step. Of. The. Way. Your talks interject nothing but peace and confidence in me, and I don't know what I'd do without you.

And finally, thank you to Him for His never-ending love. Thank You for the gift and talents You have graced me with, and for the doors of opportunity You open. Your hand guides me along this journey, and I am eagerly and lovingly stepping forward.

CPSIA information can be obtained
at www.ICGtesting.com
Printed in the USA
JSHW021005290521
14958JS00001BA/1